SILVER STRANDS

By

Eileen Bennett

PUBLICATIONS
www.FiresidePubs.com

Cover illustration by Krishna Mathias

Fireside Publications II
5144 Harbour Drive
Oxford, Florida 34484

www.firesidepubs.com

ISBN: 978-1-935517-24-5

First Edition: September 2013

For additional copies of *Silver Strands,* please visit:

www.amazon.com
http://kadinbooks.com
or contact the author at:
ebchristianna@gmail.com

The universe is a complete unique entity. Everything and everyone is bound together with some invisible strings. Do not break anyone's heart; do not look down on one weaker than you. One's sorrow at the other side of the world can make the entire world suffer; one's happiness can make the entire world smile.

~Shams Tabrizi

CONTENTS

For Chrissy

Dedication

I would like to dedicate this book to my lovely mother, Marie
Tedesco, who imbued in me the precious essence of life: We are all
connected to each other in one way or another. My mother's
philosophy is simple:
"We may never know how far-reaching our actions – good or bad
– may be."

Acknowledgements

A special thank you goes to my dear "writing buddy," fellow journalist Nelson Trout, who was my cheerleader and source of constant support as I wrote this book.

Most of all, a very special thank you to the love of my life, my husband, Chick, who is the inspiration for everything I do.

Prologue

When Mary Martucci Miller was young, life seemed simple and endless, stretching out before her in an arrow-straight line, a never-ending ribbon of birthdays, southern New Jersey summers, Dreamsicle sunsets and mellow Septembers. No more. Now, at age forty-five, Mary views her life in fragments. Images, which were once clear, defined, finite, now seem like a puzzle missing a solitary piece.

What is that word?

Holograph!

That's it, *holograph*. Those pictures that make you slant them this way and that way; then you see objects differently, depending on the angle from which you view them. And in this holographic version of her life, a piece of the puzzle is distinctly missing.

Mary is stuck in one of those road-rage-inducing traffic jams. After two hours sitting in the same spot, she puts her car in park and closes her eyes, shielding them from the sunlight of the bright autumn day. She suddenly feels bone-weary, in both body and soul. Yielding to temptation, she leans against the headrest, falling into a sleep-like trance.

"I want to go back," she whispers, to nobody in particular. "I need to see the Silver Strands again." During the ensuing reverie Mary's thoughts become separated from the echo in her mind, so she doesn't even hear the words as they emerge from her mouth.

Time for another visit to Dr. Lee.

Mary glances in the rear view mirror of her 2000 Sable and reads the words:

Objects may be closer than they appear.

She chuckles, emitting a sound more like a guffaw than anything even remotely light-hearted.

Objects may be closer than they appear.

Objects may be closer than they appear.

Objects may be closer than they appear; she repeats the phrase over and over again in her mind.

Oh yes, and objects may be much more evil than they appear, Mary thinks sourly, pursing her lips almost imperceptibly.

A thin salty streak oozes from her eye and streams down the curving crevice forming her cheek. She doesn't wipe it away as she hardly perceives its presence. The red-and-green Christmas decorations in Stanley's Dollar Store cause her face to distort in disgust at this, her very worst, irritant; *Halloween is barely over and already they're pushing Christmas.*

"Christmas Creep," she mumbles. "They even have a name for it now."

All she knows is that somehow she is stuck in this damn traffic snafu. And every driver's nerves are frayed to the breaking point.

Good will toward man, my ass, Mary thinks.

A shrill horn shrieks behind her, and her reverie snaps back to the present. She has no recollection of the words she had just whispered in the "trance." Neither does she recall bemoaning the fact that she no longer can see the "Silver Strands."

She guides her vehicle to Commerce Street, hoping to find Luna Park empty. She desperately needs solitude now – right now – to sort out all the revelations she has uncovered with Dr. Lee's help last week.

A quest which had ostensibly started out as a search for a news story, now ends up as the unearthing of something very, very dark in the world; something that simmers just below the surface of friendly pleasantries, of polite greetings, of lifelong friendships and sacred family bonds. There is a positive side to all things. Mary forces herself to remember:

Love never dies.

And that thought alone tips the scales in her favor. She smiles.

The shadows of Mary's mind begin to drift, wandering back to a destiny-changing autumn day in 2002. It was a day much like today. Now, when she looks back on it, she views it as *that day* in her mind's eye. She thinks of *that day* often. As hard as she tries to push it out of her mind, the more it returns with a vengeance, almost as if it has a mind of its own. Another souvenir from *that day* is the throbbing pain forever present in her hip.

That day was September 12, 2002. Mary had the day off from her job as a copy editor at *The Beacon*, the town's small daily newspaper. The day before, the paper did a one-year-anniversary retrospective piece on the 9-11 World Trade Towers tragedy in New York, and she had put in a double shift. In exchange for the extra work, she had *that day* off.

That day was a cloudless autumn day, as she recalls, with the maple and oak trees lining Main Street aglow in prisms of red and orange and green, and a slight cool breeze officially waving goodbye to summer. It was a *Halloween kind of day*. Orange-and-black decorations festooned the small shops on Main Street, and the leaves, which had already met their demise, crinkled under her feet.

Mary smiles as she remembers how confident she felt *that day*. Her usually uncooperative long dark hair had responded to the lack of humidity in the air by being shiny and straight, undulating in the cool breeze. Her makeup looked especially natural, a trace of eyeliner accentuating her large dark Italian eyes. She had just dropped a few pounds, and her True Religion jeans hugged the curves of her petite body perfectly. The magenta color of her simple pullover top made the rosy hue in her cheeks fairly pop. One of her guilty pleasures was to grab a matinee and sit in the darkened theater with similar-likened strangers. Desperate for a diversion from reading such grim news copy, Mary deftly steered her Sable into one of the many vacant parking spots at the Regal Theater.

What the hell, I have the rest of the day off, so I can do as I damn well please.

That day the Regal was featuring one part of the movie theater's black-and-white homage to Halloween series; today's choice was the 1922 silent classic *Nosferatu*. Mary had seen it dozens of times, but it never failed to scare the wits out of her. She loved it.

When the movie ended, she stepped outside the theater to the blinding sunlight and fumbled in her purse for her sunglasses. Before her pupils could adjust themselves to the change of light, she stepped off the curb and directly into the path of a New Jersey Transit bus.

That day was the first time Mary died.

One

September 4, 2013; 8:32 a.m.

"Gotta run," David says, as he heads for the door.

"Whoa, love of my life, how 'bout a kiss first?" Mary is getting used to David's mad rush out the back door, and it is this very comfort level with his absence that is starting to bother her.

"Oh, sorry, babe," he says, leaning over to give her the traditional peck on the cheek.

The door slams, leaving Mary alone in the house with her thoughts. She feels blessed to have the love and support of her devoted husband, father of their three adorable girls. After the accident, doctors initially had cautioned her that she might never be able to bear children. But she and David proved them wrong in a big way. Marlee had turned seven already while Kandee, just one year older, was developing into a precocious eight-year-old. And Cecee, their oldest daughter at ten, constantly made her parents proud by mentoring and caring for her younger sisters. Mary shook her head in disbelief as she wondered how the years had gone by so fast.

The girls, still nursing a summer hangover from sleeping in, and long days at the beach, caught the school bus earlier. Labor Day had come and gone. Mary had already accumulated too much vacation time and was *ordered* to take some days off from work; so no work for her today. Oddly, she is not pleased. She enjoys having her mind diverted on words and grammar. Bending down to collect the girls' bowls of half-eaten cereal from the table, she groans, as an unexpected sting of pain runs down her back.

After the 2002 accident, Mary endured months of grueling physical therapy. She pushed through the pain and performed the exercises religiously. Results were amazing, astounding the doctors. One of the many injuries she sustained, a fractured pelvis, prompted a surgeon to caution her that she might never walk again without a cane. But again, she beat the odds.

Other than an unobtrusive limp, and the occasional throbbing in her legs when the weather settles just right, Mary's physical condition has remained good. Mentally, however, her death-dance with the bus scarred her psyche, leaving her at the mercy of severe panic attacks. The unexpected terror floods her being, amidst flashes of dread and doom.

She becomes paralyzed with fear – but there is nothing tangible to the fear. Breaking out in a cold sweat, she is certain her thumping heart will pop out of her chest. The several minutes it takes to subside feel like an eternity to the suffering woman. Often the attacks come out of nowhere with no detectable trigger. Like today, Mary is starting to feel the first pangs of loneliness, and an alarm bell suddenly goes off inside her.

Oh, no, not the panic attacks again. Please, not the panic attacks again, she prays.

These attacks, Mary believes, are the worst remnants of her accident. The throbbing pain in her hip is nothing compared to the paralyzing fear of the panic attacks – the complete and total belief that she is going mad.

Mary's first experience with this strange phenomenon was the worst, because she had no idea what was happening to her. She believed she had indeed gone mad, that maybe the bus accident had caused some kind of neurological damage to her brain that the doctors missed. She remembers the autumn day was sunny, a day much like today, and she was still engaged to her longtime boyfriend, David Miller, still trying to return to her pre-accident life.

While heading to the town library, Mary unexpectedly broke out in a cold sweat; her skin felt wet and clammy as the beating of her heart pounded against the walls of her chest. Although the library loomed straight ahead, it seemed to fade into the distance, turning what should have been a short walk into an endless trudge, sapping all her fortitude, every ounce of strength in her spirit. She felt unable to force her feet to walk, while the screaming of her internal voice deafened her.

Walk somewhere, anywhere... people are staring... don't just stand there... people will think you're crazy... Jesus Christ, just put one foot in front of the other!

Unable to remember walking to the library, the last thing Mary recalled was huddling in a corner of the library's first floor, quivering with fear.

What is happening to me?

She trembled.

The assault on her psyche was like being confronted with an angry Tyrannosaurus Rex that only she could see. People gathered around her in a murky, slow-motion style. Mrs. Marriott, the librarian, hovered over her, her wrinkled face a mask of confusion and concern.

"Are you okay, dear? Are you okay?" Mrs. Marriott kept asking, her voice Ping-Ponging between panic and concern.

The ever-efficient head librarian, Mrs. Marriott obviously had never seen anything like this before, and did *not* want this happening on *her* watch. Observing Mary struggle but being unable to find her voice, Mrs. Marriott, with a shaking hand, offered her a lukewarm cup of water in a paper cup.

Mary looked at it incredulously, wanting to say, *"How the fuck is water supposed to help me?"* But she said nothing, and robotically grabbed the cup and took a sip.

The rest was a blur of campus security, ambulance sirens and medical technicians. When the campus doctor finally examined her and grilled her with questions, he disappeared into another room. Mere minutes passed before he returned declaring, somewhat glibly, in a clipped, very professional and icy tone, "Ms. Martucci, you've just been stressed out – a little panic attack. It's your body's way of saying you're working too hard. It's nothing to be alarmed at. I've prescribed some Xanax for you. You've got to cut back on stress. These things happen, especially after the trauma you've been through. I'm sure you'll be just fine. You've got to learn to relax." His eyes never left the prescription pad as he spoke, and he quickly left the room after handing her the slip of paper.

7

But Mary wasn't fine. The panic attacks increased, each one worse than the last. The Xanax made her sleepy, and she took them only as a last resort. For a month, she struggled with anticipatory anxiety – constantly being on guard that another panic might descend on her. Eventually, she embarked on a journey of counselors, therapists and psychologists, all of whom pointed to "stress," which Mary suspected is what one says when at a loss for an answer. Only one psychologist even mentioned the term, "panic attack."

But rather than dealing with the problem, he uttered an ominous warning: "People who suffer from panic attacks in their youth are more likely to suffer them again later in life."

Gee, thanks loads, Mary thought.

Fortunately, just as suddenly as the panic attacks had engulfed her, they dissipated. Gone. *Pssst.* She even forgot the ominous warning words of the therapist about their probable return.

A year later, Mary married David and is still happy with family life and her job as copy editor/fact checker at the *The Beacon*. As the years float by, the family grows, soon including their three little girls. Mary and David and the girls become one with the routine of everyday life – the kind of peaceful existence on which one does not dwell or even question or acknowledge. One merely accepts it as their right.

September 4, 2013, 10:10 a.m.

Mary is trying to decide what to do with her rare day off from work. David and the girls have already left this morning, which started so routinely. Mary is looking forward to a relaxing day that starts out fine but suddenly takes a turn south. Like a freak comet smacking the Earth, a panic attack invades her soul, sending her body quivering with inexplicable fear and dread, a feeling of unrelenting doom covering her like a cloak of maggots. She desperately tries to calm herself to throw off the maggot-shroud, but the more she fights, the more mired she becomes in the inexplicable panic.

She sits for hours in her bedroom, shaking, waiting desperately for the girls or David to come home. The wait seems infinite. One can only describe it as an unrelenting migraine that will leave only when it's good and ready and not one damn minute before.

Finally! David opens the front door with a giant thud and a cheery cry.

"I'm home!"

Mary runs into his arms, latching onto him as if she is dangling from the precipice of a giant cliff. Stunned and baffled, David holds her tight.

"What babe? What is it?" is all he can say.

Mary says nothing but heaves deep sobs – sobs of fear, fear of the unknown, of falling down the rabbit hole.

David holds Mary close to him and lets her cry herself dry. He is alarmed, but tries to keep a calm façade for her sake. She had told him about the panic attacks years ago, but since they had never returned, he had forgotten all about them – until now.

When she is able to compose herself to speak, only wails of fear emerge.

"They're back," she whispers at last. "They're back."

And David immediately remembers the story she had told him of her first panic attack and the episode at the library.

9

He pulls her back, holding her shoulders firmly, and looks deep into her eyes.

"We're going to get through this. Okay? We're going to do whatever we have to do to get through this – doctors, counselors, whatever you need, babe. We're together on this." He embraces her tight again.

She feels her soul calm a bit – just in time, as the girls come prancing off the school bus and barge into the house arguing – quite loudly – about whose turn it is to load the dishwasher. Mary wipes her eyes, mumbles something about her "darned allergies," and the girls never realize anything is wrong.

But Mary knows she must start to face reality. The panic attacks have returned with a vengeance. Mary, who has always so prided herself on being fearless, is now consumed with fear; wet-your-pants, flop-sweat, feel-like-fainting fear and panic.

Family and friends – the people who most want to help you – listen, helplessly, as if you're speaking in some kind of ancient Aramaic language. You try to explain you're locked in a jail with invisible bars. You can't explain the fear, the panic – because there's nothing to fear except your own mind. People start to think you're a regular Disneyland of mental illness. If you think it's hard to tell your loved ones about your strange malady, try telling it to a stranger – even a trained professional.

For the next few weeks, Mary endures a flurry of appointments with counselors, therapists, psychologists and psychiatrists.

They all yield a diagnosis of "panic disorder."

Great, she thought, *At least whatever the fuck this is, it has a name.*

And, most of them profess, it is easily treatable with something called "behavioral cognitive therapy." Mary researches the term on the internet like a miner scouring for gold. The closest definition she can find in a rational term is:

"Cognitive-behavioral therapy is based on the idea that our thoughts cause our feelings and behaviors, not external things, like people, situations, and events. The benefit of this

10

fact is that we can change the way we think to feel/act better even if the situation does not change."

Well, Mary thinks, *it sounds plausible.*

The next step is to play "pick the therapist." Oh, the internet can easily divulge what a therapist claims his/her specialties are, but you don't know for several sessions whether or not you'll click with that person.

September 9, 2013, 4:01 pm.

Dr. Regan

Mary's initial time out of the gate in her quest for a therapist is a beaut. The first shrink is a disaster. Dr. Regan is a Ph.D., who immediately begins – benignly – berating Mary for not appreciating the things she is given in life; decent looks, above-average intelligence, a loving family and friends.

Mary can feel her heart sink deeper and deeper in despair as this portly, pompous, immaculately-groomed elderly man drones on, articulating each syllable as if he is addressing a college class. His office isn't very large, but it is dark, save for the sunlight from the singular transom window. It reeks of mahogany and Lemon Pledge and is crammed with cold, no-frills furniture. Medical and psychology books fill the wall-high bookcase. It all looks very professional to Mary.

She is waiting for the "cognitive behavioral therapy" to begin. It doesn't. Instead, Dr. Regan announces he is going to try hypnotherapy first. Mary tries to hide her disappointment, thinking, *Oh, what the hell have I got to lose?*

"Okay, now, Mary, we're going to begin," Dr. Regan says in a deep, husky voice. "Close your eyes and relax... relax as you've never relaxed before. All you will hear is the sound of my voice and you will do everything I tell you to do."

Mary gets comfortable in the faux-leather armchair but is hardly relaxed.

I'll give it a whirl, she thinks, still skeptical. *What the hell.*

Dr. Regan speaks in a monotone, throaty near-whisper.

"You are in a beautiful garden. Roses and lilies and lilacs surround you. You're deep, deep in the woods. You can see glints of sunlight through the umbrella of trees. No harm can reach you because I won't let it. You are safe – utterly at peace. There is no danger – not in this world, where you are."

Dr. Regan drones on for several more minutes about the peaceful garden, a soothing waterfall, the cooing of tiny birds

12

in the trees and the flitting visits from butterflies and dragonflies.

Hey – I am starting to relax, Mary thinks, in pleasant surprise.

And that's when Dr. Regan drops the Big Reveal.

"I want you to open your eyes now, Mary," Dr. Regan says in his throaty monotone voice. "And when you do, there will be no furniture in this room. The room will be entirely empty, except for you and me and the chairs on which we are sitting."

Mary opens her eyes – what she expected to see she can't say – but there is every stick of furniture exactly where it had been when she closed her eyes moments ago.

"Do you see any furniture?" Dr. Regan asks, his smug tone louder now.

"Yes, I do. I don't see anything different," Mary says, a hint of anger and disappointment in her voice.

Dr. Regan stammers and stutters and finally ekes out, "Are you sure?"

Am I sure? Yes, I'm sure. I'm as sure as I can see the top of your bulbous stomach sticking out above that huge mahogany desk, you fucking idiot! Mary wants to say.

"I'm sure," she answers tersely instead.

"Well, I don't think you're giving this exercise the proper attention it deserves," Dr. Regan says sternly. "You have to commit to therapy if you want to get well, Mary."

She can't believe what she is hearing. This pompous ass wants to blame her for his party-game approach to therapy.

"I think we should set aside three times a week for you, Mary," Dr. Regan says, a twinge of annoyance and dismay in his voice. "Make a series of appointments with Denise, my receptionist. And, as we discussed before, panic disorder is a lifelong battle. But I must emphasize, this is going to take some serious work and commitment on your part."

"No, it's not, Dr. Regan," Mary responds calmly, "because you're full of shit. And I'll be goddamned if I'm going to waste my money on parlor tricks. It's been a real pleasure to meet you." She shakes his hand, pretending not to

13

notice his wide-open jaw, and strides out of his office, past Denise-the-receptionist and the other waiting patients. She wants to scream out to them, *"Run! Don't waste your money!"* But she says nothing. Instead, she feels, for the first time in a long time, a slight grin cross her face as she thinks of the stunned look on Dr. Regan's face.

Mary walks from the deep recesses of the dimly-lit doctor's office into the screaming-yellow sunshine and for a second, it blinds her. She isn't about to repeat the same mistake twice: She fumbles in her pocketbook and reaches for her sunglasses. She waits several minutes until her eyes adjust to the glaring sunshine. Much better, she thinks, as her pupils refocus to the bright light. At long last, she feels liberated. She asserts herself and feels an adrenaline rush of victory consume her. The panic attacks that had been barking at her this past week are quashed, at least for now. Mary barks back, and they vanish.

Two

September 23, 2013, 4:32 p.m.

Mary loves this time of year in South Jersey. The heat of the summer is starting to fizzle out, but it is still warm enough not to have to worry about coats for the girls, who, blessedly, are back in school. Mary allows herself one trip to Mr. Booth's farm market at least once a week. In the summer, you can be sure Mr. Booth, or "Mr. B," as everyone knows him, will always have the freshest, juiciest melons. This time of year, Mr. B's stand will feature the first of the pumpkins' harvest – large, fat ones, and hundreds of miniature ones, grouped together like a tiny orange brigade outside his garden gate. Indian corn and sunflowers, those last nods to summer's bounty, are always a bonus. Truth be known, visiting old Mr. Booth's vegetable stand is a treat in itself. Mary likes to think of it as a well-deserved gift that she can give herself at the end of an especially stressful workweek at *The Beacon*.

Mary didn't really need all those melons she bought in July and August. Some weeks, even with the girls home from school, she ended up heaving one or two in the compost pile. But her new therapist – her *wonderful* new therapist – Dr. Jill – has Mary routinely perform "exercises" in cognitive behavioral therapy. That means even though you'd rather crawl up in a ball than face the possibility of a panic attack in public, you force yourself to go out and interact with people.

Jill is working wonders with Mary.

"Get out there!" is Dr. Jill's mantra. "The more you avoid a situation, the more power you give it."

She prescribes a small dose of Xanax for any severe panic attacks, but Mary does not feel she needs the pills. Still, she never leaves the house without double-checking that they are in her purse. She goes to work every day, performs her job at the newspaper efficiently, then comes home and makes dinner. She has settled into a comfortable routine. So today, even though she doesn't need any more produce or flowers, she treks back to Mr. B, more for the kindly chatter than the produce.

It isn't quite time yet for Indian corn or sunflowers, but Mary loves chatting with Mr. B. His easy-going, down-home charm calms her. She likens his soft voice to the cadence of the ocean. She isn't sure how old he is. If she had to guess, she'd say mid-80s. But that is just a guess. He could be in his 70s, or even his 90s.

Mary only knows that she feels completely at ease with this gentle old man. He surveys his customers from an old iron yard chair, the kind that allows the sitter to lean back and then swing forward if so inclined – and Mr. B often seems to be so inclined. He is perpetually dressed in tattered overalls that must have seen a thousand harvests. Mr. B always sports an immaculately white T-shirt underneath the overalls, and a well-worn Phillies cap low on his head. His face is crinkled and sunburned, but his blue eyes are bright and clear. Mary secretly marvels at the fact that he never wears glasses. Vanity, she wonders? Nah, not Mr. B, who seems more concerned with the amount of rainfall for his crops than the ketchup stains dotting his overalls. *Some people spend their whole lives without needing glasses*, Mary thinks fleetingly. She often sees him gracefully weaving his tractor up and down his fields without ever seeming to be squinting.

Time appears to take a back seat at Mr. B's place. The last of the shore traffic is still whizzing by, but one need only park their car at the side of the road and walk a couple of steps downhill to his farm market and the traffic noise fades into a drowsy lull. Today, Mr. B is leaning back in his chair, reading *The Beacon*'s sports page.

"Phils don't seem to be straining themselves these days, do they, Mary?" Mary rarely follows the Phils – or any sports team, for that matter – but since she works at *The Beacon*, Mr. B. just assumes that she knows everything about everything that appears in the paper. Mary gladly plays her part in the charade. After all, it makes for pleasant, distractive chatter.

16

"Doesn't seem that way, does it, Mr. B? You're not making any bets on the World Series, now are you?"

"Sweetie, the year the Phils make it to the Series, there'll be ice castles in Arizona!" Part of Mr. B's charm is the unexpected sayings and off-the-wall analogies that are certain to make you grin even if you are in the dumps.

"No, no, I didn't mean the Phils, in the Series," Mary fumbles, laughing. "Two different things, I meant... I mean, I meant... "

"Take it easy, Mary. I know what you meant," Mr. B, says, cackling out loud now, the laughter of a soul that has appreciated a million jokes in its lifetime. "I'm just tickling with you. So how are things in the hard-hitting world of news?"

"Well, I can't say much for the hard-hitting news part, but as far as *The Beacon* goes, we're on kind of shaky ground. Advertising hit a new low this month, and they're saying if it doesn't pick up by the holidays, we may be facing some downsizing."

"Downsizing? You mean 'firings.' Right? It's amazing how they can find fancy words to sugarcoat and soften even the most awful things, huh? In my day, they called things what they were, and trust me, everyone was a whole lot better off. They knew where they stood right from the get-go."

"I hear you, Mr. B. It was a different era, wasn't it?"

"You betcha it was, Mary. People did things up front back then. More honest and up front, you know. People had just come out of the Depression, and there was no place for phoniness. We had integrity – dignity. An ace was an ace and a spade was a spade – not a lot of whining about whatya got and whatya don't. Young folk nowadays, they don't got a cell phone, they think they're deprived."

Mr. B peeks at Mary from under his cap realizing he is rattling on.

"But enough of that. You don't need to hear an old fogy like me goin' on about the ol' days. What can I do for you today, hon?"

17

"Just for the record, I love your stories about the ol' days, Mr. B," Mary says, flashing a genuine smile. "I think I'll just grab a couple of the smaller pumpkins for my front porch. I've got to have at least three, or the girls will be at each other's throats."

Mary and David have learned to always, always, always, buy things for the girls in threes – three of the *very same* thing. To deviate even a tad – size, color or weight – would almost ensure a verbal melee. Mary carefully picks out three miniature pumpkins, trying to make sure they are nearly identical in size. Still, despite her most noble efforts, she is sure one of the girls will find another's pumpkin is "better" than hers. Well, so be it, Mary thinks with a sigh, cuddling three of the tiny orange gourds to her breast.

"I guess this is it for today," Mary says with a smile. "I'll probably be picking more up next Friday for carving."

"Sounds good to me, Mary," Mr. B says, collecting her money without counting it. "See ya then. And say a prayer for the Phils, will ya, please? Don't know if it'll do any damn good, but it sure as hell can't hurt."

"Sure enough, Mr. B," Mary says smiling. She heads home, the smile still lingering on her face.

The smile on Mary's face melts as soon as she walks through her front door.

"Mary, where'd you put the goddamn Hellman's?" David is in a particularly cranky mood today. He rarely swears, and never in front of the girls. His choice of words puts Mary on alert. It is a cue that things are not going David's way at work.

Ten-year-old Cecee isn't just the oldest of the three girls; she is the most intuitive and can smell disharmony in the air. She tries to distract her younger sisters, Kandee and Marlee, who just turned seven, with their Barbie Dream House on the kitchen table.

"Oh," David says, sheepishly, realizing Cecee is staring at him, startled. But that doesn't stop him from still being annoyed.

18

"Top shelf in the door. Right here," Mary says, gently pushing David aside while plucking the mayonnaise out of the refrigerator and placing it on the kitchen table.

"What's up?" Mary asks, touching his tanned and weathered, muscular arm.

"Oh, hell, they're putting the screws to me down at the plant. They still expect me to do a 60-hour-job in a 40-hour-workweek, and no overtime. I have just enough time to make this damn sandwich and swing by the plant to see what's cooking. I'm sure one of the new guys have screwed something up by now. Don't wait up for me."

Monday is David's usual day off, and Mary is disappointed. She had hoped David would be home for family movie night. But instead of showing her dismay, she nods, knowingly. The South Jersey Sands mining plant had steadily been losing money the past few years. The company had hired a blowhard corporate boss, Nelson Bitterman, from headquarters to take over the plant, and announced his appointment with all the pomp and solemnity one would offer a visiting dignity. Bitterman is known in the corporate world for his ruthlessness, his determination to stay the course of profit, profit, profit, even if it means severe downsizing – or, as Mr. B would say, firings.

Yes, Nelson Bitterman had come in with guns blazing, determined to prove to the powers-that-be that he is going to yank the sand plant out of the red and put it back into the black. He wasted no time calling a meeting of the foremen, announcing that, "by gosh, things are going to be different now. Overtime" he'd said, "is a thing of the past, and that word no longer will be a part of South Jersey Sand's vocabulary. If you can't get your job done in the allotted work week, then I will find someone who can."

And he makes sure every last employee knows that he means what he says.

As one of South Jersey Sand's senior foremen, David Miller is feeling the heat. David, now in his mid-40s, has always been somewhat of a health nut, watching what he eats and faithfully jogging two miles at least three times a week.

19

But since Bitterman came to town, David finds himself eating more bologna and mayo sandwiches for supper than sit-down dinners with the family. His jogs are becoming a distant memory.

Mary watches David slap his sandwich together, throw it in a paper bag and rush out the door, without closing it. She doesn't realize she is shaking her head in dismay, with the girls, especially Cecee, watching her. It is the first time she actually feels anger toward a complete stranger.

I'll bet this Bitterman guy never worked overtime in his life, she thinks sourly. *And I'm guessing he has no clue what it's like to care about a real family.* She had heard through the grapevine that this Bitterman fellow is divorced and has no children. *One of those assholes who is married to his job I'll bet,* Mary guesses.

This shouldn't be happening now, she thinks, *just as the family routine is starting to hum like a finely-tuned motor.* Marlee, their youngest, is just getting comfortable with school. The girls are all at that pleasant middle ground: No more day care, and the terror of adolescence is still a couple of years away for Kandee and Cecee.

No, not fair, Mary thinks.

This is the time of our lives when we should be showing everyone, "Look, we made it. They said we wouldn't last, we couldn't be a lasting family, but we are."

Mary's family has never been pleased with her choice of husbands. It's not that they disliked David. Quite the contrary, Mary's parents, Kathy and Sam Martucci, are very impressed by David's intelligence, sensitivity and work ethic. He finished community college in a little over a year. He could have pursued his studies, but he chose to take a job in the sand plant, knowing it was steady work, with good pay and an excellent health plan.

But there was no getting around the major sticking point: David Miller is Jewish. For the devoutly-Catholic Martuccis, this made David absolutely unacceptable as a spouse for their daughter. And then there is that other thing – a double

20

whammy against David, if you will. He is divorced. Although David considers his first marriage a short-lived mistake – he and his wife divorced amicably after realizing their error less than two years into their marriage – the Martuccis simply cannot accept a divorced man as their son-in-law. With Catholics, marriage vows last beyond death and divorce is a non-negotiable deal-breaker for a prospective suitor.

Mary didn't care. With all the proverbial abandon of a young woman deeply in love, she married David in a Presbyterian church. Kathy and Sam Martucci didn't attend the wedding. They had made sure their daughter received a full twelve-year Catholic education, and they certainly weren't going to see her throw it all away just to marry a Jew. Dear Lord, David doesn't believe in Jesus Christ! And he is a *divorced* Jew at that. A double damnation in the eyes of the Catholic Church. Her parents' absence at one of the most important days of her life made Mary simultaneously seethe in anger and wax broken-heartedly. Her older brother Sammy – with whom Mary was extremely close – was the only family member on Mary's side to attend the ceremony.

Mary still has never had second thoughts about David. Nothing she has ever done in her life has ever felt so right. David is a good, decent man. Of this she is certain. She had recited her wedding vows slowly, deliberately:

"I, Mary Martucci, take thee, David Miller, to be my wedded husband, and I do promise and covenant, before God and these witnesses, to be thy loving and faithful wife; in plenty and in want, in joy and in sorrow, in sickness and in health as long as we both shall live." Silently, she added, *Take that, Mom and Dad.*

To outsiders, Mary and David are an improbable couple, even putting their religious backgrounds aside. Mary is short and petite, with jet-black hair and solemn, lark-dark eyes. David is tall and gawky, with sandy blond hair and effervescent blue eyes.

Mary tends to be introspective, and somewhat self-conscious. She doesn't make friends easily, because, she feels, the bridge toward a true friendship must be built with lots of small talk and confessions about one's self, something she finds extremely painful to do. Whether it is due to her strict Catholic upbringing, her traditional Italian background, or something else, she doesn't quite know. She only knows that meeting new people makes her feel very self-conscious and she always feels as though she is being interviewed by a prospective employer.

Mary's parents taught her that first impressions are everything. Mary's mother, Kathy, constantly picked away at her every etiquette infraction.

"Sit up straight. Take your hands away from your mouth. Use a tissue when you sneeze!"

It seemed like a never-ending parade of do's and don'ts. Oftentimes, when they were visiting company, Mary would sit stiffly in a chair. She was careful to quash the temptation of wiping her dripping nose with her sleeve. It is that always-on-guard behavior drilled into her that makes her uncomfortable around people, even to this day.

David, on the other hand, always seems completely at ease, even with strangers. He is not only annoyingly adept at small talk, but actually seems to enjoy it. Strangers tend to sense that, and gravitate toward him. David isn't particularly religious, although his paternal grandparents, about whom he remembers little, were Holocaust survivors. He never knew his father's parents, who died in the camps. David's maternal parents, Mark and Esther Miller, were what Esther unabashedly called "Curtain Jews."

That meant on Yom Kippur, the most important holiday of the Jewish year, when other Jews were fasting and atoning for their sins, David's parents would come home from temple, pull the curtains together on the windows of their modest brownstone apartment in Rockaway, and feast on a roast chicken and vegetables. David's mother was a pragmatist. Esther decided that "starving" her children, David and Becky, wasn't teaching them anything. Rather, she chose to emphasize "good" and "bad" to her kids. She put little emphasis on the religious trappings. She wanted to name her son "Sean," (she thought it sounded regal) but deferred to her parents, who wanted a more traditional Jewish name. Secretly, Esther always wanted to name her daughter "Kellie," or "Jennifer," but she had already forfeited that name fight over David, and she had resigned herself to her parents' wishes. But she insisted everyone call her daughter "Becky." A small victory.

The Millers successfully hid their "curtain" religion for several years, until one December, when David was five and Rebecca was three. Esther had seen the way their eyes lit up at the Christmas display in the downtown stores. They were fixated by the lights, the music, the sheer splendor and ethereal magic of the holiday season. There and then Esther decided they would get a Christmas tree, something she never had.

She marched David and Becky down to the Christmas tree stand and picked out the largest blue spruce she could find. She paid the salesman extra to tie it to the top of her old Chrysler. Esther's neighbor, Mrs. Horwitz, was sweeping the front steps outside her large brownstone, when Esther and the kids pulled up to the curb. Mrs. Horwitz looked at the tree wrapped with twine atop the car roof, and stopped, aghast, in mid-sweep.

"Afternoon, Mrs. Horwitz," Esther said nonchalantly. "We're having a Christmas tree this year," she said bluntly.

Even though he was just a child at the time, years later David swore he could still remember the stunned look on Mrs. Horwitz's face. He recalls she muttered something in what he could only guess was a prayer in Yiddish. In any case, that was the end of the Millers' "Jewish Charade." The jig, as they say, was up. Mark Miller had learned long ago that trying to cross his wife was a formidable task indeed, and he found it easier to just go along for the ride.

Esther was a monument to contradiction. She shopped for clothes at the local Save-A-Lot-Mart. She adored color – the flashier the better. On their few "nights out," Mark would hold his breath – fearful of what Esther would be wearing – until she emerged from the bedroom. She adored the color purple for some reason or another, believing it was innately regal and always in style, even if the garments hailed from the Save-A-Lot-Mart.

Mark – an ultra-conservative dresser who thought even pin stripes were garish – was both embarrassed and proud of his wife's fashion sense. She wore her purple outfits with a wild flair, either not noticing or not caring (or both) what people whispered about her. Ironically, as frugal and garish as she was in fashion, when it came to perfume, she splurged. It was the one luxury she allowed herself. She adored the French perfume Shalimar, a heavenly mix of sweet scents – but the base note – and most pronounced – is vanilla. Esther loved that she could leave a room with the sweet scent still lingering in the air, a subtle reminder of her presence. Shalimar, made in Paris, was extremely pricey for the Millers' budget. Esther only wore it on special occasions. She squirreled it away in her top dresser drawer for fear that Becky might get her little hands on it, as all curious little girls are known to do.

Esther wanted to instill her down-to-Earth standards in her children. Much to her parents' chagrin, she downplayed the role of religion in her kids' lives. Instead, she chose to emphasize morality; that every living thing on this planet is to be respected and honored, be it person, beast or plant. If her children treated everyone, and everything, with respect, she reasoned then there would be no sins for which they would have to atone at Yom Kippur.

It all made perfect sense to her, but her parents, Jacob and Rebecca, saw it as a slight to their heritage, their religion and the suffering the Jews had endured in the concentration camps.

Esther's parents knew their daughter and her family weren't abiding religious doctrine, but the openly defiant act of a Christmas tree – well, that too much. It was like a slap in the face. It drove a chasm between Esther and her parents that would never be bridged. Esther's parents saw certain *kareit*, or divine punishment, for their daughter and her two children. They believed that Esther would lose not only her own spiritual connection with God, but would doom her children to the same tragic fate. Esther and her family would never know God's loving presence, they believed, and her parents never missed a chance to warn them about their bleak fate.

As a result, David and Becky had a strained relationship with their maternal grandparents.

The two children never knew their paternal grandparents, Beatrice and Arthur, since they lost their lives during the horrors of living in the concentration camps. That, Esther thought, was a blessing in disguise. She was sure Mark's parents would have taken the same stance as her own – seeing them all as poor heathens, doomed to an eternity without God's love. And truthfully, she couldn't blame them, knowing the awful terror they had endured in the camps.

When Jacob and Rebecca died, only months apart, Esther and Mark dutifully followed all the Jewish rituals, sitting shiva and covering the mirrors in their parents' living room with plush cloths and tearing a piece of their clothing. In reality, Esther had long ago shunned her parents' theological traditions. She had instead embraced an unshakable confidence that she was raising her children with a definitive moral code, a good compass by which they could live their lives. Right was right, wrong was wrong. It followed that there would be no sins "to atone for."

The end result for the next generation was fairly predictable. Neither David nor Becky was particularly religious, but like their parents, they turned out to be innately good people. In her elder years, Esther remained a no-nonsense person. *Right was right, wrong was wrong.* Aging was nothing to be feared; that goes for people as well as for wine. If you needed a strict set of guidelines to tell you right from wrong, well, maybe you're just missing some vital mechanism in your soul.

By the time David met and fell in love with Mary, Esther was tethered to a walker and was steadily heading for a wheelchair. She lived alone after Mark died, still in the same cozy brownstone in Rockaway. Esther adored Mary, and the feeling was mutual. Unlike her mother, Mary's Catholic religion was not an issue. Mary grew to love Esther like a second mother, confiding in her on many occasions when a talk with her own mother might prove awkward. Esther often called her, "*Mary, my lovely*," which tickled Mary immensely.

As luck would have it, both sets of parents turned their children off to their diverse religions in distinctly different ways.

Mary followed Esther's lead when it came to religion. The whole faith issue had become the sticking point between Mary and her own parents, Sam and Kathy Martucci, just as it had become a barrier between Esther and her parents. Sam and Kathy, ultra-devout Catholics, could not reconcile themselves to the fact that their daughter wanted to marry not only a non-Christian, but a divorced man at that.

Kathy's parents, Joe and Abigail, strict Catholics themselves, ironically proved to be more flexible on the issue than their daughter. Abigail urged Sam and Kathy to acquiesce to Mary's choice.

"David's a good man," Joe whispered to his daughter when they were alone. "Mary loves him... surely you remember what love was like. What if Sam hadn't been Catholic? Would you have given him his walking papers? I think not. Give those kids a chance, Kathy. Lord only knows, marriage is hard enough without having your in-laws against you, too."

All Joe's cajoling did no good. Sam and Kathy Martucci refused to attend their daughter's wedding. Joe and Abigail wanted to be there, but they were well into their 90s and were homebound. David and Mary were married in a non-denominational church ceremony, with Mary's side of the church nearly empty.

Kathy's parents struggled even to acknowledge that their daughter was married. The bitter alienation between daughter and parents lasted almost two years after the wedding. Since Mary was an only child, the rift was especially stinging.

After Cecee was born, Mary's parents realized their boycott was costing them too high a price. They grudgingly made amends with their daughter and her husband. They settled into a comfortable relationship with Mary and David only after David had agreed to bring the children up in the Catholic faith.

David had never been particularly religious, and since the faith issue was such a big stumbling block with Mary's parents, he acquiesced on the religion issue. Truth was – he couldn't care less. Mary, however, was adamant on one thing – no Catholic school. Catechism classes, fine. But no Catholic school for her kids. She had been subjected to twelve years of Catholic schooling, and often referred to herself as a "recovering Catholic."

Growing up, the endless Catholic rituals had exhausted her. The Sunday Masses, the Holy Days of Obligation, the mortal sins, the venial sins, and all the in-between sins. Just too damn regimented and complicated. And the guilt. Dear Lord (no pun intended) – the guilt! She didn't think God – if there was one – would want his (or her) children performing like soldiers under the threat of eternal damnation and burning in a sea of fire. Instead, Mary chose Esther's decidedly simple rule of life.

Do unto others as you would have them do unto you. It doesn't get any clearer or more succinct than that, Mary thought.

As an adult, Mary's faith had been tested – and lost – when she was a young bride. Her beloved Grandma Abigail had died of pancreatic cancer. Mary was devastated. She watched her grandmother agonize through a slow, lingering, pain-ridden death. She had prayed, but it seemed like empty whispers into the wind. When even the highest doses of morphine did not assuage her suffering in the least, Mary's prayers had disintegrated into bargaining sessions with God.

Please God, just let her die in peace. Just stop the pain. Please God, just stop the pain. Take her now.

But Grandma Abigail lingered for months, drifting in and out of consciousness, waking up only to find her tiny body wracked in agony and begging for death. When she finally died, Mary's first emotion was relief. It took several hours for true grief to set in. Grandfather Joe was devastated. He died

27

only months later – technically of a brain aneurysm, but Mary always believed it was truly from the loss of his lovely bride.

In retrospect, it was the last time Mary could remember actually praying, the last time she truly felt that she was talking directly to God. There was, of course, the rote prayers she had said in school and at Sunday Mass, but after her grandmother's death, there was no further personal dialect with God. In time, the idea of a loving God faded for Mary. She may have had her doubts about God, but she had no doubts about karma. As she got older, her faith, like Esther's, had morphed into the Golden Rule: *"Do unto others...."*

And it had worked – at least up until now.

Just as the Miller family had settled into some kind of normal routine, a sense of comfort and stability, this Nelson Bitterman had pranced into their lives, throwing their happy family regiment into turmoil. According to Mary's perspective, it simply wasn't fair.

David was a hard worker, a devoted employee, and now this Bitterman jerk was making his life hell – so much for the Golden Rule. She felt a twinge of anger, and yes, hatred, toward this stranger, this interloper who threatened to rob her family of its security.

September 23, 2013, 5:30 p.m.
Kate McGee

"Where's Daddy, Mommy?" Marlee asks as she pops a chicken nugget into her mouth.

David's official days off are Sundays and Mondays, but these days there doesn't seem to be any room for "days off." The sight of David at home is rapidly becoming a rarity.

"He's got to work today, Bunny. Eat your nuggets."

"Father Neeley says it's a sin to work on Sunday."

Mary looks at Marlee, speechless for a moment.

"Well, I don't think that's exactly what he means, Bunny. I think Father Neeley means God created the Earth and then rested on Sunday. I think he means that Sunday should be a day of rest for most people, except for people like your daddy, who have to do important jobs to help other people."

"No," Marlee says, shaking her small blond head adamantly. "Father Neeley says it's a sin to work on Sunday. No one is supposed to work on Sunday. That's God's day, he said."

Mary considers a few choice words for Father Neeley, but instead finds herself smiling at her young daughter's face, so uncharacteristically serious.

"Just eat your nuggets, Bunny."

Mary jumps, as the shrill sound of the kitchen phone ringing breaks the momentary silence making them both laugh, before she turns to pick up the receiver.

"Hi Mar. Ya busy? It's Kate McGee."

Kate is a fellow copy editor at *The Beacon*, and lives just down the road from Mary and David. Kate isn't exactly a gossip – at least not the mean-spirited kind. She does, however, take particular relish in passing on the latest "unsubstantiated rumor." A faithful church-going woman, Kate fancies herself a person who does not spread gossip – just "community news." It might be the rumor of a PTA board coup in the making, or a planned vote by the local Zoning Board to allow a Wal-Mart.

Kate is a garrulous and friendly person who always seems to be the first to know the latest town doings. Kate never gossips – just ask her and she'll tell you. When it comes to offering her opinion, however, she never minces words. The Eversons, a young, well-to-do couple, is her latest target.

"Never see either of them at any community functions," Kate says with a sniff. "Guess they're too good for that. We're not in their social circle, I guess."

Kate can be pushy at times, although Mary knows she has a good heart and sweet spirit underneath all her bluster.

Mary likes Kate, despite her aggressiveness. However, she can barely tolerate Kate's husband Ralph, who has just squeezed in enough election votes to win a seat on the City Council. Mary finds him pompous and egotistical. Rarely can you get a word in on a conversation with him, before he shifts the subject back to himself. Even normally good-natured David finds Ralph's egocentricity insufferable. On the few double dates Mary and David share with Kate and Ralph, the topic of discussion rarely veers off course – Ralph's latest city ordinance, Ralph's campaign coffers, Ralph's snobby remarks about the way his political enemies dress. The fact that he always wears a bow tie is the topping on the cake for David.

"What a pompous ass," David whispers to Mary following one of their rare double dinner dates.

As Mary tries to juggle the phone receiver, Kate continues talking, obliviously, on the other end.

"No, not too busy. I'm just feeding the girls," Mary is able to squeeze in just before Kate bombards her with a rambling narrative.

Kate rarely listens. She talks. And if you try to get a word in, she'll talk right over you without missing a beat.

"Good," Kate says. "Listen, a group of us are getting together to throw Mr. B a surprise party. He'll be 85-years-old next month. I'm in charge of the food, and I was hoping I could get you to bake the cake. We're trying to do this pretty much on a shoestring here, and we want to make as much of the food as possible. We're taking a collection up too, and we want all the money to go for a nice gift."

"Kate, slow down, for God's sake," Mary shouts into the phone, hoping Kate will come up for air so she can speak.

"First of all, no problem, I'll take care of the cake. Count me in on the collection. Not a problem. He's a dear. It's about time people did something nice for the old guy. He's such a sweetheart – such a gentleman. Eighty-five, huh? I would have guessed older, actually."

"Well no one would even have known about it if it wasn't for that nice young census-taker poking around here. They're doing an update for the next census, and it turns out they have a special category for people over eighty. Mary Moore down at the post office heard the census-taker talking about Mr. B. I guess you can imagine he made quite an impression on the young man."

Mary laughs.

"Oh, I can just imagine. Mr. B probably talked the poor guy's head off, and if he was a Phillies fan, I'm guessing he had a hard time leaving."

"He does love his Phillies, doesn't he?" Kate says. "Okay, Mar, gotta go. I've got a million more calls to make. I knew I could count on you. Thanks, darling."

"No problem. Talk to you later."

Mary leans against the wall, shaking her head and smiling as she hangs up the receiver, sure that Kate has already hung up and is well on to her way to the next phone call.

31

Three

September 24, 2013. 9:06 a.m.
Gary Elliott

As Mary walks through the parking lot of *The Beacon*, she smiles, letting her imagination recreate the expected greeting she will receive upon entering the newsroom:
"How are you today, Mary, my love?"
The voice in her head is so real she turns, expecting to see her charming boss, Gary Elliott. Instead, her smile disappears under the force of a nervous shudder as she notices Tom, the newspaper's handyman/janitor. His name actually is Tom Thomas. She often wonders what must have been going through his parents' mind to anoint him with such an unimaginative name.

He is short, missing teeth and has questionable hygiene. She can't determine whether he is thirty-years-old or maybe even sixty. He keeps a filthy baseball cap pulled low over his forehead, tilted just enough for him to see. He gives Mary the creeps, always looking at her sideways, as if studying her but doesn't want her to notice. She finds him repulsive. He reminds her of the stereotypical child molester.

Mary assures herself that the newspaper must have done a background check before hiring him. Still, she hurriedly walks past Tom to the back door, swipes her key card, and yanks the door shut behind her even though it would have closed eventually on its own. She hurries down the hallway to the newsroom.

The newsroom at *The Beacon* is buzzing even more than usual this morning. The welcoming aroma of coffee fills the air as Mary strides past the reporters, some wearing earphones, and deeply engrossed in telephone interviews, or holding their heads, staring at their computers, desperately hoping the right words will flow through their fingertips. Nobody notices Mary as she makes her way to the copy desk, or "horseshoe" in the middle of the newsroom.

Mary loves the rhythmic hum of the newsroom. It is comforting. It just feels *right*. In control – like all is right with the world. She wraps her burgundy blazer around the back of her chair, flips on her computer and makes room on her desk, pushing the shabby Merriam Webster Dictionary aside. She doesn't need the dictionary any more – Lord knows you can find the definition or spelling of anything on the internet. Besides, the old dictionary doesn't have the latest technical terminology the reporters throw at her. Still, Mary finds it impossible to part with the old MW, which was a college gift from her parents.

"How are you today, Mary, my love?"

The voice startles her; then she smiles and turns to find Gary Elliott, *The Beacon*'s city editor, standing behind her, a chipped coffee mug with faded painted cherries on it, declaring "Number 1 Dad" in his hand and a huge smile on his face. He is wearing his usual beige Dockers, a rumpled shirt and tie that can only have come from Wal-mart. He jokingly calls it "the metrolook for desperate single men." Well into his 50s now, Gary sports silver hair and a matching beard and mustache – all of which almost always need a good trim. Still, he is handsome in a Marlboro Man sort of way.

Mary adores Gary. He hired her as fact-checker/copy editor years ago, fresh out of college. Unlike the other bureaucratic editors at *The Beacon*, Gary doesn't care a whit about political correctness. He perennially calls Mary, and the other female copy editors, "love," or "m'dear," or "princess," making the senior editors and the papers' lawyers wince, visions of sexual harassment lawsuits dancing in their heads. But not one woman saw Gary's endearments as anything more than sweet talk. Mary thought of Gary as a true newsman in the old tradition.

Unlike the other editors, Gary is not a college graduate. He hails from some tiny town in Idaho, of all places. He is what old-timers refer to as a "bulldog" reporter. Once he gets the scent of a juicy tale, he never lets go until he gets the story. He has the chops to stand up to powerful politicians and mobsters alike. There have been a couple of close calls in his career – like the time the found a crudely made bomb under his 1998 Honda. It left him unfazed. He is divorced; and his kids are grown and live out of state, so he has no worries except for himself. And getting the story was – and still is – more important to Gary than his life.

"I don't have all that fancy book learnin'," Gary often jokes in a mock-Southern accent. But he has an absolutely fascinating, uncanny talent of smelling a good story and ferreting it out, despite incredible odds. He has garnered several national news awards at much larger papers owned by Worldwide Media. He calls his job at *The Beacon*, a small daily, his "retirement job," after moving back to southern New Jersey so he can be near his elderly parents." The huge conglomerate, Worldwide Media, is *The Beacon*'s parent company, and Gary has worked at several of the chain's larger papers in the past.

Mary loves Gary's sense of himself. His ego is not inflated, but he has an unfaltering sense of confidence, particularly when it comes to news. The reporters, particularly the younger ones, idolize Gary. He has that rare leadership gift of guiding his troops without being condescending or boastful. He clearly remembers being a cub reporter on the small daily newspaper back in Emmett, Idaho. It can be very daunting to a newbie. He is never arrogant or patronizing to the young journalists he takes under his wing.

He is absolutely comfortable in his skin. With his sterling record of accomplishments, he has carte blanche at *The Beacon*. It drives the senior editors crazy with jealousy; yet they dare not challenge him.

Gary is charmingly self-deprecating, which at first made the higher-ups underestimate him, but not for long. They can wince all they want at Gary's utterances of "sweeties," and "dolls" at the female staffers, but Gary is considered a legend in news circles. He also has an uncanny knack of spotting news reporting talent in others.

He has seen something in Mary – a fire, a drive, a need – all the makings of a good reporter. *She no more belongs on the copy desk than I do,* he thinks. He has made it his private mission to make a reporter out of Mary. Somehow, he picked up on her secret wish to break out of the copy desk and land a job in the field.

She never dared confide her dream to anyone for fear she'd be laughed out of the building. She majored in French Literature in college, for God's sake. She not only does not have a journalism degree, she doesn't have any degree – political science or English – that could be conducive to a reporting job in this Internet Age.

About a year ago, Mary hinted to Gary, in a wistful tone, that she wondered what it would be like to cover a real news story – "with a real byline." But she quickly dismissed the idea. "I've got too many skeletons in my closet," Mary said, half-chuckling, thinking of her episodes of panic attacks and what people would think of her if they knew.

"You make me laugh, doll," Gary said. "You should hear the bones rattling around in my closet. They dance to the rhythm of the night. Lighten up, dammit. You're too damn hard on yourself. And trust me, half the people don't know about your 'skeletons' and the other half don't care."

Gary now is sitting on the edge of Mary's desk.

"I've got a project for you, princess," Gary says, taking a sip from his coffee cup.

"I'm all ears," Mary says, smiling and looking up from her computer monitor.

"Well, actually, I'm hoping for more than your stunning stock-in-trade of the English language and your brilliant talent in finding the real lede in those pieces the reporters hand over to you," Gary says, with a sly smile.

"Enough, enough flattery already! How 'bout just telling me what you want?" Mary says, holding her hands up in defeat, still smiling in spite of herself.

"OK, here goes." Gary rolls out a chair for himself.

Mary is intrigued. Rarely does one of Gary's "projects" require a sit-down. He's always on the go and it's a rarity to see him actually sit and chat.

"You know Meg O'Reilly over in Features? She's doing a kind of religious story for Worldwide's news service. It's a big deal, hon. The head honchos are all over this one. They're determined to make a name for themselves – or at least to impress the stockholders." Every now and then, the big-wigs at Worldwide deign to communicate with some of their smaller newspapers or radio stations.)

"Think you can elaborate on that? What kind of "religious story" are we talking about?" Mary is wide-eyed and can barely contain her excitement.

"Well, that's just it, sweetie. We're not quite sure where all this is going just yet. We're kind of speaking in broad terms. Spit-balling. Worldwide is looking for a story that can be syndicated out to its other papers – the "big" ones. But they want a hometown touch. That's why they came to *The Beacon*.

I don't think you get any more "hometown" than we are.

They're really on this one, Mary. I know, because they're willing to spend money. That's always a good sign. They're looking for a story that can be a contender for a Pulitzer. That's tough enough, but the gods-that-be have decided it's got to be a 'spiritual' story."

"Okay, I'm listening," Mary says slowly, nodding her head. She puts down her coffee cup and leans forward, genuinely interested now. "Hmmmm... spiritual, huh?" Her voice fairly drips with skepticism. Her initial enthusiasm is beginning to dim.

Gary detects the doubt and quickly adds, "Yeah. The Marketing Department, apparently they conducted a survey among readers. It shows that, especially after 9/11, the public wants to know more about... well, about that *other realm*." He rolls his eyes slightly, an obvious clue that he too isn't altogether buying this idea himself, but is willing to give it a whirl. You don't dangle a Pulitzer Prize in front of Gary without him pouncing, no matter how ethereal the subject matter may be.

"Gary, where on God's green Earth is all this going?" Mary asks, trying not to sound too anxious. She is excited about the idea of breaking out of the copy desk, but has reservations about the subject matter. It is, after all, so *vague*.

"Well, we're still in meetings, but in a nutshell, it looks like Meg's going to focus on how different religions view the afterlife. Is it heaven? Is it hell? Is it a bowling alley?" he adds with a slight snicker. Gary isn't looking Mary in the eyes. He is staring into his coffee cup. Mary suspects that is deliberate.

"You mean... like good and bad? Angels and demons?" she prods.

"Yeah... ya know, good and evil. Dr. Jekyll and Mr. Hyde. God and Satan. Angels and devils. Letterman and Leno. You can figure that last one out for yourself," Gary says matter-of-factly.

"Gary. I've never done any reporting. I'm no reporter."

"Exactly. Trust me on this one, love. I've got to have a top-notch reporter, and there's none better around here than Meg. But I also want a layperson – you know, a Joe Blow who thinks like the average guy. Not like a 'reporter' but still able to sniff out a real story. Meg's great – don't get me wrong. She's a pro. I just think this assignment calls for a different kind of reporting team. There has to be room for – well, *fantasy* for lack of a better word.

"Jesus," Gary says, shaking his head at his own words, "I never thought I'd say something like that." He puts his coffee cup down, almost in disgust. "Look, what I'm saying is anyone can write first-person accounts of near-death experiences. Sure, I want hard facts. But I also need someone with a very open mind – someone who's... well, *open* to new experiences."

"And why would you think that should be *me*?" Mary asks, looking him straight in the eyes.

"Well, I know about your accident some years back," Gary says, avoiding her stare. "I'm not going to lie to you because I respect you too much, Mary. But I've heard the stories of you dying on the operating table several times before they brought you back. That kind of experience can be very useful in this type of piece."

"Whoa," Mary says, standing up abruptly, her arms in the air. "Gary, you heard wrong. Yes, they said I technically 'died' on the table a couple of times. But I hardly remember a damn thing about it. I saw no white light, and the last time I saw my dead relatives was at their funerals."

"I've got a hunch about this, honey," Gary says, putting his hand on her arm. I know it sounds a little squirrelly right now, but just think on it. Okay, princess?"

"I don't know, Gary," Mary says cautiously.

"Look at this way: Meg will be doing the legwork – the heavy lifting, if you get my drift. It means you'll be doing nothing for the next year or so except double-checking her background notes. No night shifts, either, Mary. You and Meg can set your own schedules. And – I can't believe I'm saying this, considering the cutthroat cost-cutting climate around here right now – but if you guys run into legitimate overtime, you can put in for it. Think on it, and let me know if you're game. Okay?"

Mary doesn't hesitate. The idea of not having to copyedit those endless boring city council and sewage rate stories is too tempting to resist. Besides, the project, even in its infancy, may sound a bit nebulous, but it also sounds very intriguing. Lord knows she could use the overtime, especially with David's company's belt-tightening. And the idea of working normal hours clinched the deal.

"I'm game. Sign up me up. Now."

Gary smiled a victory smile. "Well, my dear, you got yourself a deal. I'll tell Meg to touch base with you when they've nailed down the story outline. I think you'll enjoy this, princess."

"Me too," Mary says, smiling.

As Gary strides away, chatting with reporters en route to his office, she wonders if he had a life outside *The Beacon*. He never spoke of any. She only found out about his divorce through office rumor. And the only hint that he has any children was that coffee mug.

Mary sits back in her chair and stares at her computer monitor, not really seeing its cursor blinking. She is stunned that so many people know her experience surrounding that accident years ago. She barely remembers anything. The paramedics who responded to the scene told Mary's parents that after she had been struck by the bus, it propelled her clear into the air and down on the roof of a passing car. She was airlifted to the nearest trauma unit. It wasn't until a year later – after her mother took her to a particularly excruciating rehabilitation session that she heard the rest. Her mother Kathy had been so moved watching her daughter heal that once she had burst out crying.

Alarmed, Mary stopped her exercises and limped over to her mother.

"Mom, what's the matter? What is it?"

"I don't know what we would have done if we lost you Mary. We did, you know. At least two times on the operating table. Thank the Lord they were able to bring you back. They almost weren't going to try one last time, thinking you couldn't be revived."

Mary stumbled back and found the nearest chair. She didn't remember any of this. Not one damn thing. And she still doesn't.

Four

September 26, 2013. 4:01 p.m.
"They Found. . . A Growth"

Mary's heartbeat quickened with anticipation and relief when she spotted David's Explorer parked in the driveway that evening... She had been chewing over Gary's offer all week, not saying a word to David, waiting for tonight. Eating dinner alone with the girls on Friday nights had become routine lately; then after they go to bed, she waits up as late as she can until he gets home. Usually exhausted and cranky, he is in no mood for talking. But tonight appears to be different. It is a rare Friday night off for David, and Mary is pleased to see there are no last-minute setbacks that would keep him at the office. She decides to take a gamble and broach the subject of her work situation to him.

"Hey, I'm home!" Mary shouts as she opens the front door.

"Call your mom, babe," David says, peering around the corner from the kitchen. "I think it's important. She wouldn't tell me what's going on. Just said she wanted to talk to you as soon as you got home. I didn't push it."

Mary detects a hint of annoyance in his voice, but she doesn't question it either. She can just imagine her mother's demeanor – polite and pleasant enough, but chilly. Her mom has the uncanny talent of making David feel like an intruder in his own home, even on the phone.

"Was she upset? I mean, did she sound upset?"

"Couldn't tell," David says, licking the mustard off his fingers. The girls are eating already. Gave 'em hot dogs. Go 'head and call your mom. We're covered in here."

It isn't unusual for her mother to carry an air of the dramatic, so Mary doesn't become overly concerned that she'd told David it was "important." The last time she left an "urgent" message it was to say that the veterinarian diagnosed their elderly cat, Edgar, with cancer and he had to be put down. Still, the impact of imagining her mother's words floating out in the air sent Mary heading straight for the phone. David, out of disinterest more than respect, she suspects, leaves the room.

My parents have put a wedge in this family with their damn religious hang-ups, Mary thinks. *If they would only see David for the good man he is; if they just gave him a real chance... But there's little chance of that – not till hell freezes over.*

By the time Kathy Martucci picks up the phone receiver in the kitchen, Mary has talked herself into a snit. There is no hiding it in her voice.

"Yeah, Mom, it's me. What's so important?" Mary fairly snaps.

Silence.

"Mom?"

She hears her mother sniffling on the other end. Mary feels the annoyance drain from her body, replaced by a wave of anxiety.

"Mom? Mom!"

"Mary, it's your dad. He's sick."

"Sick? What do you mean 'sick'? You mean his achalasia?"

Kathy tells her mother to hold on as she takes the phone into her bedroom. She doesn't want the girls to hear this conversation.

For years, Sam Martucci has suffered from a sometimes severe case of achalasia, a disease of the muscle of the esophagus. The ring of muscles in his throat cannot relax, resulting in a difficulty in swallowing. At its worst, Sam had gone weeks without eating solid food, resulting in bouts of dangerous weight loss. But he has always bounced back. Sam has been prodded and poked and endured dozens of endoscopies with dilation procedures, where physicians tried to open up, or expand, the esophageal muscles. He has been to nearly a half dozen specialists, and they all come up with the

41

same diagnosis: There is no cure for achalasia, just treatment for its uncomfortable, and sometimes embarrassing, symptoms.

Sometimes when the disease was in full swing, Sam would struggle to swallow, resulting in a gag reflex. He and Kathy stopped going out to restaurants because Sam becomes so uncomfortable from the stares of nearby diners. There have been dramatic breakthroughs in acid reflux medications in recent years. This leads to better medications in treating the more serious disease of achalasia. The new medications on the market are a godsend. Even after a bad bout with achalasia, Sam has always rapidly regained the weight he had lost. It's a disconcerting see-saw health pattern, but Sam always seems to weather the storms well and bounce back.

"Well, partly, yes, it's his achalasia," Kathy says, her sniffling starting to fade. But it's something worse, dear. "They found a growth."

The word "growth," makes Mary momentarily freeze. Finally, after several seconds, she asks, already knowing the answer, "Where, Mom?"

Kathy hesitates a second before answering.

"In his throat."

Mary knows immediately that this is serious. The doctors all along have said they wanted to monitor Sam's condition to make sure it didn't turn cancerous. They had always hinted that he has a better-than-average chance of developing esophageal cancer because of the achalasia, but never said it outright. They just emphasized that he has to be vigilant in his checkups.

"Are they going to take a biopsy?" Even to Mary, her voice sounds like a squeak.

"They already did, Mary. They did it today. They found the growth today, and Dr. Bill wanted to do the biopsy immediately."

Dr. Bill has been the family physician for years, and he is the first line of defense for Sam's health, even before the throat specialists had their chance at him. Dr. Bill is ruthless with HMOs. There is even a rumor that he had come to fisticuffs with a HMO pencil pusher who denied a referral for one of his patient's tests.

"When will we know?" Mary asks her mother impatiently.

"Dr. Bill said he should have the results within a few days. He'll call."

"Where's Daddy?" She was surprised to hear herself call her father "Daddy." Usually it was "Dad." Suddenly she feels like a little girl again, remembering her father as a strapping, protective giant of a man.

"He was watching the game. I think he might have fallen asleep. Mary?"

"Yes, Mom?" Mary says, stifling the choke beginning in her voice.

"I'm scared."

"I know, Mom. So am I. But we'll get through this together. Okay?"

"Mary?"

"Yeah, Mom?"

"Say a prayer for you father, would you?"

"Sure, Mom."

Screw the prayer, Mary thought, after hanging up. Instead, she does what any fact-checker worth his or her salt does – she heads straight to her computer to find a reputable online medical site, which gives her the facts about her father's illness. She checks out several different sites, and they all concur on one thing: If the growth in her father's esophagus turns out to be malignant, his chances of survival depend entirely on the cancer's stage. If indeed, the growth is malignant, then his chances of survival depend directly on whether, and how far, the cancer has spread. The site WebMD states:

"As with many cancers, esophageal cancer treatment has a greater chance of success if the cancer is caught early. Unfortunately, by the time esophageal cancer is diagnosed for many people, it is often already in an advanced state (has spread throughout the esophagus and beyond)."

Mary's world swirls around her. Her stomach begins to churn and nausea is on the horizon. She tries not to panic, but she can't shake the distinct feeling of dread as she stares at the words on the computer screen.

"What was so important?" a voice behind her says.

"Huh?" Startled, Mary doesn't see David walk into the room.

"Your mom. What was so darn important?" David asks again as he bites noisily into an apple.

"It's my dad. He's got a growth in his throat." Mary hates hearing the words that are coming out of her mouth.

David stops in mid-bite.

"A growth? That doesn't sound too good."

"I know that, David," Mary snaps. "Of course that's not good."

"Take it easy, doll. I mean... well, did they take a biopsy or something yet?"

"Yeah, but we won't know anything certain for a couple of days."

"Oh, damn, hon. How's your dad taking it?" David isn't close to Sam Martucci by any stretch of the imagination, but he has lost enough friends and family members to cancer to know how devastating the disease is.

"He's doing okay, I guess. You know my dad, nothing bothers him. Mom's not doing too well, though." Mary surprises herself when she bursts into tears. She has a distinctly bad feeling about this whole thing, and mouthing the words out loud makes it sound all the more chilling.

"Oh, babe, I'm so sorry, sweetie," David says, closing the door so the girls, eating their hot dogs in the other room, won't hear. "I'm so sorry, babe," he says again, holding Mary close now. She feels her tears and snot dampen David's cotton shirt. The rest of the night is a blur. She and David give the girls their baths and get them ready for bed. Mary spends the night staring at the ceiling trying to imagine her life without her father. Salty tears drip down her face and into her mouth. She hears David snoring, and tries not to wake him.

Five

October 3, 2013
MR. B.

For the first time in a long time, Mary finds herself wanting desperately to have a personal conversation with God. She feels like a hypocrite but doesn't care. Although she barely slept during the night, she isn't tired. When the alarm clock begins to beep unmercifully at 5 a.m., she clicks it off without looking at the time or even caring about it.

David is on the afternoon shift, so he doesn't stir. He will have the morning all to himself until he goes to the office around two o'clock, even though he doesn't have to be at work until three. Arriving early allows him to get a jump start on his work load. So, he continues to snore softly.

Dazed, Mary eventually drags herself out of bed and gets dressed. During her drive to work, her body is in the car but her mind travels elsewhere, in a trance. She parks her car, looks around trying to get her bearings then heads for the door, grateful that creepy Tom isn't anywhere nearby.

"Hi princess! What's shakin'?" Gary Elliott, making his daily rounds at *The Beacon* newsroom wearing his Dockers-and-rumbled-shirt uniform, comes up behind Mary before she sees him.

She looks up, staring blankly at him. "Oh, hey, Gary," she replies robotically as she sits down at her desk.

Gary takes one look at Mary's red, swollen eyes, and knows something is amiss. He rolls up a chair next to her.

"Spill," he orders. "What's wrong?"

Mary seldom shares personal information easily with people. Other than Kate McGee, no one knows that Mary's father has health problems. The previous night, the dreaded call came from her mother: The biopsy is positive. Even worse, the

45

cancer is at an impossible stage for surgery. Brutal chemotherapy and radiation treatments are in Sam Martucci's future, and even then, doctors cannot guarantee a desirable outcome. No one says the word "terminal" yet, but the diagnosis is certainly out there, hanging in the air. It will take only one doctor to deflate the word, send it bouncing down into reality, destroying any hope. It is a tenuous state at best she thinks, delicately balanced on doctors' compassion. No doctor wants to be the one to dash all hope for a family's loved ones.

"It's my dad, Gary," Mary fairly croaks out.

"What about your dad? Is he okay?" Gary whispers, leaning close in now.

"No. He has cancer."

"Oh, damn, Mary, I'm so sorry. Is he undergoing treatment?"

"He starts chemo and radiation next week."

"How does it look?"

"Not good." Mary feels her voice choke up again.

"May I ask... did he get a second opinion?" Gary asks softly.

"Oh yeah," Mary says, near to tears now. We've got second and even third opinions. They're all the same. Pretty grim." She lowers her head so if the tears start flowing, Gary won't see them.

"Anything I can do, Mary?"

"No, but thanks, Gary. Thanks for asking."

"I'm here if you need to talk, okay? If you need time off, let me know. Okay? We can work something out. Listen," he hesitated a moment, "I hate to bring this up now, but are you going to be up to that religious piece with Meg? I mean, I don't want to lay more stress on you than you can handle right now, kiddo. Just give me the word if you think you need to focus on your family. We want you on this project, but not if you feel you're needed with your dad. You think on it. Let me know."

"Thanks, Gary. I appreciate it."

The truth is, Mary has barely thought about the project with Meg O'Reilly. In fact, she had forgotten about it in all the hoopla of meeting with doctors and oncologists and health insurance agents. But she is thinking about it now, and actually, it seems like a blessing in disguise. Gary had said they could set their own hours, and Meg seems like an easy-going type, so unlike some of those other intense, driven reporters who easily work an 80-hour work week and expect everyone else around them to do the same.

No, I'll take this project, Mary thinks, nodding. *Besides, it's best not to have an idle mind, even for a moment.*

Mary is physically and emotionally exhausted. Between work, the girls, and visiting her father, she is stressed to the breaking point. She feels tinges of panic, and briefly worries that the panic attacks from last month will return. She'll be damned if she allows herself to fall into that mine-pit again. No, this time she is going to take time out to share her feelings. She is not going to keep her worries and concerns all bottled up again.

There is, of course, a major problem. Mary can't go to her mother. They've never been close, and their relationship has been especially strained since she married David.

David, meanwhile, is working major overtime at South Jersey Sands, and when he comes home he is cranky and just wants to be left alone.

That bastard Nelson Bitterman has hijacked my usually good-natured husband, Mary thinks sourly.

Mary has lots of acquaintances but no close friends – at least none that she trusts enough with her innermost worries. She briefly thinks of confiding in Father Neeley, but quickly brushes that idea away. Father Neeley would probably just rattle off some Catholic doctrine he knows by rote, and Mary is way past that. She wants real, down-to-Earth answers, not some vague religious "It's-just-in-God's-plan" speech. Mary is still ruminating about her dilemma as she drives home from work. On her way, she stops at Mr. B's farm market for some fresh corn.

"How's my favorite fact-checker?" Mr. B is leaning back in his iron chair, perusing the latest edition of *The Beacon*. Mary hears him before she sees him and flinches slightly.

"Oh, you scared me. I didn't see you there, Mr. B."

"Well, I'm where I'm always at... don't move from this spot too much anymore. Besides, you were lookin' like you were on a different planet for a minute, there, Mary. How you doin'? How's your dad doin' these days?" Mr. B knew Sam Martucci was battling an especially nasty, aggressive form of cancer, but he didn't think it was his place to inquire about the details.

"Not too good, Mr. B." Mary is leaning over the corn, her back to Mr. B, when a cry suddenly erupts in her throat. She puts her hand over her mouth.

Mr. B listens to the stifled sob soberly a moment before finally commenting.

"Mary, Mary, Mary. That's too bad, sweetie. I'm so sorry," He stands up, fixing his overalls and pushes his Phillies cap back on his head. "How bad is it? I mean, if you don't mind me askin,' that is."

"Oh, Mr. B, he's in real bad shape. He can't even swallow. He's got a growth – a tumor, in his throat. He can't eat anymore. He can't even swallow his own saliva. I hate this. I hate seeing him like this." Mary is unable to stop the words from spilling out. It seems she barely takes time to think before they come marching out of her mouth like a faulty gumball machine.

"He's so scared, Mr. B. He knows he's dying. I know he does. He's always been so full of stamina, so full of faith. He was so strong physically and spiritually... so certain about things. And now he's just like a scared little boy. I'm not a lot of help to him. Damn, I don't know if I even believe in God. And I don't think that's what he wants to hear right now, anyway. I don't know how to make him feel better."

Mr. B. stands in front of her with his arms folded, nodding his head, as if all her ramblings make perfect sense to him. Considering the long life he's lived, maybe they do.

"That's perfectly understandable, Mary," he says, putting his arm on her shoulder.

"We all have to face death in our own way. It's rarely easy, sweetie. Your father is going through the death process.

48

He's beginning to deal with his own mortality. Sure, we all know we're goin' to die some day, but the only way we can really deal with it is in the abstract.

I saw my dear Maureen go through the same thing. She was a good woman, too. A woman of faith. Never hurt another living creature – a real angel, I swear to you. But when she knew she was dying – and she *did* know she was dying – all the things she believed in, heaven, hell, good, evil – all that melted into a fear I just couldn't ease." He stops for several seconds to collect his thoughts and emotions.

It is obvious to Mary that even though many years have passed since his wife's death, his heart still lies in shattered pieces.

Finally, he speaks again. "She was young when the good Lord took her. Left me with a thirteen-year-old girl, Mollie, to raise. Everyone has to accept their death in their own time. For my Maureen, it came at the end. The very end. I knew it, because just before she closed her eyes for the last time, she smiled. A real peaceful smile. And I knew then, that she didn't fear anything no more. She was at peace."

For a few seconds Mary is able to forget her own problems as she listens to Mr. B talk about his wife. She had never heard him mention her by name, or at all for that matter, and to hear him talk so intimately about her now takes Mary by surprise.

"Your dad will be at peace, I'm sure of it," Mr. B says. "The only thing you can do now is to be there to listen. Listen to everything he has to say, even if it's difficult. That's what he really needs right now. You are his sounding board. Let him bounce his fears and regrets off of you, Mary. Heck, we all got 'em. Now he needs you more than ever. He needs you to be his emotional accountant. You mark my words, Mary, that's the best thing you can do for your dad right now. Give him a chance to voice his triumphs and regrets and he'll die in peace too – just like my Maureen." With tears flowing freely now, Mary hugs Mr. B. He smiles and hugs her back.

Thank you Dear Lord, for giving me this one person in whom I could truly confide.

Six

The Vigil

Mary spends every spare moment she can muster at her parents' home. Kathy Martucci is very sensitive to her dying husband's physical needs. He can no longer swallow solid foods. The tumor growing in his throat has seen to that. The doctors inserted a feeding tube into his stomach to assist his meager intake of nourishment provided by the "Ensure" food supplement being fed to him – the sticky-sweet protein concoction is poured into an IV bag, and pumped through the tube into his stomach.

The disease is taking a tighter grip on Sam Martucci with each passing day, becoming even more evil and unrelenting. Swallowing his saliva had grown to be impossible, so a kidney-shaped vomit cup is always nearby. Kathy handles the difficult scene with grace, her face never showing the concern and worry; and yes, if one is to be perfectly honest, the disgust she feels.

She is the picture of efficiency and compassion, constantly checking on the IV bag, making sure her husband is as comfortable as he can be under the circumstances, and quietly flicking off the lamp when he dozes off into a blessed respite. But Kathy is simply not equipped to handle the emotional needs of the dying. Certainly not for this man, with whom she has spent more than half her life. She is in deep denial, emotionally tending her husband as if he has the flu instead of terminal cancer. She can't bear to say the words that need to be said out loud.

Sam wants to confide his fears to his wife, but each time he tries, he looks at her face and sees a flash of dread wash over her. He knows it will be too painful to lay his fears at her doorstep right now. Kathy has too much on her plate just taking care of his minute-to-minute needs.

The ill-fated man remains silent about his fear of death – no longer a hazy image somewhere in the future, but a door, which, for him, is right around the corner. Sam has always believed in heaven – at least in a Catholic heaven. And he had done all the "right" Catholic things to get there. He's never cheated on his wife and never missed Mass. He also has attended confession regularly, which is stipulated to wash away all those "mini" sins like lying to his boss about a sick day which he occasionally took to play golf. Yes, when one looks at his spiritual scorecard, he comes out way ahead of the game.

But Sam is still human, and the specter of losing his physical being is shaking him to his core. Everything leading up to this point – the love of a good woman, a good, dutiful daughter, doting grandchildren, a great job, a wonderful home – everything now seems to have just been ploys to distract him from his inevitable mortality. He reflects on the hundreds of funerals he has attended over the years including those of his parents, his brother, good friends and business acquaintances – all gone now. He had prayed solemnly and sincerely along with all the other mourners for that person whose turn it had been to lay in somber repose. He is keenly aware that now his time to be mourned is nearing.

There are moments – usually in the early hours of the morning, when it is so dark and so silent one could almost hear the house breathe – that Sam finds himself staring at the street lights outside the window, literally frozen with terror. That is probably a good thing because he fears if he dares to move a muscle, he will literally scream in hysteria. That would not do; he must remain strong, even as death approaches, and not transfer his own anxiety to his faithful wife.

He and Kathy no longer share a bed since he has finally succumbed to the notion of using a hospital bed. Still she sleeps in the same room with him on a nearby sofa. He can see Kathy's sweet face in the glow of moonlight peeking through the window, and while she is slightly snoring, Sam marvels at

51

that familiar face. She has grown old and time has made its mark on her, but the essence of femininity and compassion softens her still-lovely features. He would like to say he hopes that Kathy will find someone else – a companion – with whom she could grow old after he dies, but that is a lie. He has to admit that he wants her all to himself, even after death.

When friends visit, Sam always tries to be cheery, fluffing off concerns about his health, as if he himself could care less. He can't help but notice the fleetingly shocked look on their faces as they notice him wasting away. He is merely a shadow of the strapping man he once was. No one ever stays more than an hour. After they leave, and Kathy is in the kitchen preparing his nourishment, Sam is once again left alone to deal with the fears bouncing around his mind.

Mary stops by her parents' house on her way home from work more often these days, as if she senses the time clock is winding down on her father's life. She feels a need to spend every spare moment she can with him, fearing that later she will regret any time she has squandered.

One evening, quite by accident, Mary hears her mother talking on the phone with her best friend, Mary's "Aunt Suzanne." Suzanne isn't really an aunt. She's just one of those people who are so close to the family they can easily wear the moniker. She must be more than eighty years old by now.

Kathy, oblivious to Mary in back of her, is whispering and crying into the phone.

"No, Suzanne, I can't do that. I know he's suffering – Lord knows I wish I had it in me to do it. But I can't. I'm not judging you. You did the right thing with Warren. But this is different. Sam is still coherent; I can't give up on him yet."

Mary makes a slight noise, and Kathy jumps a bit. She raises her voice and composes herself.

"I have to go, Suzanne. I have to check on Sam."

She hangs up without waiting for a reply.

"What was that all about?" Mary asks, truly curious.

"Oh, nothing," Kathy says, with a wave of her hand. "Your Aunt Suzanne was just making some suggestions to make your father more comfortable. She means well."

After going to bed that evening, Sam sleeps very little and has an especially restless night. The next morning Mary notices the dark circles under his normally large brown eyes are more pronounced than ever, and a flush of worry rushes through her.

"Dad, how are you sleeping these days?" Mary asks, trying to sound nonchalant. She pulls the large easy chair up to the sofa, next to where Sam is hooked to the IV.

"Can't complain," Sam squeaks, without looking at her. "I guess any day... I wake up... and I'm still here... is a good day," he adds, with a feeble attempt at mirth.

Kathy wanders into the room.

"I say that all the time," she says, offering a weak chuckle. Although Mary knows her mother is trying to lighten the mood of impending death in the room, she thinks it's not only futile but is downright silly.

"Mom, do you have some coffee out there?" Mary has just finished a cup of coffee, but needs an excuse to talk to her dad alone.

"Oh, sure I do. But, let me make you a fresh pot. That will taste a lot better."

"Dad, what's wrong?" Mary whispers, leaning in close to her father, as soon as Kathy leaves the room.

That's all it takes for Sam to start crying, quietly. He turns his head away from his daughter, embarrassed by his tears.

"What, Dad? Talk to me."

Sam angrily wiped the tears away. "I don't want to worry your mother."

"Never mind Mom. She'll be fine. You're the one I'm worried about." Mary can hear the clatter of coffee cups in the kitchen. Her mother is making the coffee.

"Look at me, Dad," Mary says, leaning a bit closer to her father.

He looks up at her, curious now about the sound of a conspiracy in her voice.

"I'm going to get Mom out of here for a while later this week. That way, you and I can talk in private, Okay? Besides, Mom can use the time off. She could go see a movie with one of her friends. That sounds good, doesn't it?"

Mary saw a flash of relief, mixed with appreciation wash over her father's face.

"Yeah, baby, that sounds great."

"Here you go, hon," Kathy returns carrying a huge mug of coffee, still steaming. "I brought you some cookies too."

Mary is relieved that Kathy hasn't heard a word of their conversation. "Mom, can you give me and Dad a moment?" she asks bluntly.

Kathy, though taken aback, composes herself quickly.

"Of course, dear," she says, closing the door quietly as she leaves.

Mary feels herself becoming irrationally angry that her father's faith hadn't properly prepared him for death. Wasn't the whole point of Catholicism to live a good life and then be promised an eternal *happy* life? She feels he has been cheated, but she isn't prepared for what her beloved father is about to say.

"You've got to get that marriage annulled, Mary," Sam says in a husky whisper. "I don't want to die knowing you're going to hell." Stunned, Mary at first thinks she didn't hear him correctly. His throat cancer has made his voice sound like sandpaper scraping against glass, and it makes some of his words unintelligible. She often mistakes them for something entirely different than what he is trying to say.

"Dad, what did you just say?" Mary asks, leaning even closer to her father's mouth now.

"Do it," Sam ekes out. "You can't get into heaven if you're married... to...," his voice trails off for a minute before he gets his second wind, "a Jew, and a divorced man at that."

His words are husky with pain, but he spits them out with determination. It seems that after taking that spiritual inventory, he now is obsessed with the one thing in his life that he deems a "failure."

Certain of what she heard this time, Mary bolts to a rigid, upright position.

"Dad are you fucking *kidding* me?" She is so shocked at the nature of his request she uses the "F" word to her father for the first time in her life – and on his death bed to boot.

"I'm not annulling anything, Dad. I love David; we've been married for years and we have three little girls. Or maybe we should just pretend they don't exist, huh?"

Mary is shouting at her dying father. Knowing it and unable to help it, she takes a deep breath and tries to regain a sense of calm. She lowers her voice.

"Dad, it's the painkillers talking. Surely you don't mean you want me to divorce my husband. I mean divorce is wrong, even in *your* book. Right?" Mary is desperately trying to make sense out of her father's request.

"No divorce," Sam squeaks out. "Annulment." There is a twinge of desperation in his voice.

"Okay, Dad, that's not going to happen, okay? I love David. We have a family – a happy life. Don't you want me to be happy?" She is trying a different tact, but it isn't working. Sam obviously has given this a lot of thought in the dark solitary hours of night.

He is a pragmatic man. He has spent his entire life devoted to his wife and family and his faith. Out the door in his trim black suit and gray tie by 6:30 a.m., back at 5:30 p.m., day-in-and day-out, sitting behind a desk, faithfully – mind-numbingly – doing the accounting of books for companies at which he couldn't even afford to buy a decent suit. But it was all worth it, because that's what the Catholic Church professed. You go to work. You protect and care for your family and neighbors. And you go to Mass every Sunday. And you always, always, marry in your faith. To question anything that is even remotely non-Catholic was heresy – and sure-fire damnation.

The fact that Mary married a man who did not believe in Jesus Christ had wounded him profoundly. He kept his silence over the years for the sake of the grandchildren, but now he is running out of time. For some reason – it might be his impending death or the effect of the pain-killers, Sam has fixated on Mary's marriage, believing his last mission on Earth is to see Mary's union to David annulled.

"God... takes care... of children," Sam whispers, almost croaking now. "You don't have to worry about the girls. But you have sinned. Don't let me die knowing you won't be with me in Heaven. I couldn't bear that my beautiful Mary. Promise me."

Mary looks at the bedroom doorway to see if her mother is near. She isn't. If Kathy had put Sam up to this, surely she would be hovering to see what Mary's reaction would be. No, this is entirely Sam's thinking. And it is obvious to Mary that he has been ruminating over it for quite a while.

Mary turns away from her father. She is shaking.

What the hell. Why not make my daddy die happy? What he doesn't know won't hurt him.

She has absolutely no intention of really annulling her marriage, but – and this was a difficult thought – he won't be around much longer. She turns back to her father.

"Well, Daddy, if it's that important to you – if you think that's what I have to do to be with you in Heaven, then I'll do it. It won't be easy, you know. David is going to be very hurt."

Hey, she thought. *I guess I have to make it believable.*

"I know, pumpkin," Sam croaks. "But there are more important things than our happiness. We must obey God. He loves us."

"I know, Daddy. You're right, Daddy."

She watched her father smile slightly then doze off, apparently relieved he no longer had to carry the burden of his daughter's sin.

It's a cool, crisp, sunny day when Sam Martucci takes his last breath. One could still feel the change of seasons click even before the autumnal equinox had officially kicked in. Something is in the air. After so many pain-soaked, sleepless nights, Sam experiences an unusually tranquil night, peaceful and free of agitation.

Kathy is asleep on the sofa near the hospital bed that has replaced their king-sized canopied bed. A bright sliver of sunlight pierces the lace curtains and lands directly on her eyes, as she awakes with a distinct feeling that something is different. Something – or someone – is missing. She looks straight away at her beloved Sam, his once-spry, energetic body is reduced to a skeletal mass. The few strands of gray hair he has left look wildly tossed, like they have been through a cotton-candy machine.

An immense feeling of *knowing* consumes her being. She knows he is gone.

"Sam. Sam! Oh my God! My dearest Sam." she screams from the depths of her soul, screams devoid of sound, screams that refuse to surface beyond the inner sanctum of her mind. Kathy embraces the love of her life, her soul mate, feeling his bones and thin flesh, still warm, through his thick flannel pajamas. She rises and stands erect for a long moment, slowly adjusting to the feel of the room about her.

Kathy quiets the screaming in her head. She doesn't cry. She has long ago been dried of tears.

Truthfully – although she would never say it out loud – Sam's passing is, in a strange way, a relief. Not because of the bedpans or the constant changing of sheets or begging him to ingest, *"Just a little more, just a little more"* of that God-awful sweetly-sick-smelling Ensure.

No, the relief is seeing her Sam truly at peace after so much suffering. His eyes are closed and his face wears a blank look, but that is just fine with her. It is so much better than seeing the contortions his face made when the tides of his pain rushed to shore. Worse still, Sam was building immunity to the morphine drip and the Xanax. Kathy had dreaded the time when the effect of the painkillers would be like dropping a dime in the ocean. Even in her grief, there is an underlying layer of relief. Sam is no longer suffering.

Kathy covers Sam with a blanket up to his neck and kisses him gently on the lips. She heads for the hallway to phone Mary and other relatives and friends, and the funeral home. The formal grieving process is about to begin.

Of course there will be a full Catholic Funeral Mass, and the Knights of Columbus, to which Sam belonged, will provide an honor guard adorned in their feathered hats and grand regalia. Sam had served in the Army during the Vietnam War, but he rarely spoke of his time "in country" and made it clear to his wife he wanted no military funeral.

The day of Sam's funeral is damp and gloomy. The sky is offering up a heaping serving of cumulous clouds that looks like mashed potatoes on a ceiling. Father Neeley performs the Mass and graveside services. There had never been any question of that. Father Neeley is a de-facto member of the Martucci family. He has been present for nearly every family birth and death in the Martucci clan. The fact that he did not marry Mary and David is still a sore spot all the way around.

Mary likes Father Neeley, and regrets that he did not preside over her wedding; under Catholic doctrine, a divorced person cannot marry in the Catholic faith.

Kathy and Sam − faithful Catholics both − were against the union. David was Jewish − a person who does not believe in Jesus Christ − and divorced. That's a double-whammy in the Catholic Church.

But that was not going to stop Mary from marrying David. Mary merely got another Christian minister − Rev. John Everett, a Presbyterian − and along with David's rabbi, Stanley Kornbluh, co-celebrated their union "until death do you part."

As she looks back now, she knows it was the right thing to do. She and David and the girls are a happy family.

The graveside services for Sam are short, thankfully, after an hour-long Mass, and the girls are getting antsy. Cecee asks the question which is on all three girls' minds: "Where's Grandpa now?" she whispers to her mother.

"Sweetie, Grandpa's not coming back. You have your memories of him now. Right? Remember when he took you girls to Atlantic City for the beach? You had fun. Right? Try to remember that day and you'll remember Grandpa."

Father Neeley, a ruggedly handsome man, sports thick straight silver hair, speaks softly and confidently, particularly when it comes to faith, and walks with a smooth, almost regal gait. He baptizes babies, marries the young adults and buries the old. He is a fixture in the community, never missing an opportunity to involve himself in charitable events. In the winter, he opens his church, St. Lucy's, to any vagrants, meth fiends or worse. It forces him to sit up most of the night to make sure the religious statues, bronze fixtures or anything not nailed down isn't stolen. He sneaks a nap every so often on the hard wooden pew at the back of the church, but is always on guard. Opening the church at night is against diocese policy, but Father Neeley respectfully and quietly ignores the policy. Although the church board – as well as most people in the neighborhood – knows about his "indiscretion" no one ever reports him to the diocese.

Mary likes Father Neeley but finds his unshakable faith and adherence to strict Catholic dogma annoying. Still, on occasion, she enjoys chatting with him. His soft voice calms her frantic soul. Two weeks after her father's burial, Mary is on a park bench, lost in her thoughts, when Father Neeley wanders by.

"Mind if I join you, Mary?" he asks politely.

"Not a bit," she replies, sliding over.

"Please sit down.

They talk for nearly an hour about the change of seasons – the trees exchanging their costumes from pastel to flaming hues. She notices for the first time the color of his eyes matches the clear October sky – a kind of cornflower blue, with specks of white around the pupils. They exchange small talk. Mary guesses, correctly, that Father Neeley is checking on her state of mind after her father's death. Satisfied that Mary is coping well, Father Neeley slaps his hands on his knees and stands up.

"Remember the good times with your dad, Mary," he suggests. Your father was – is – a good man.

Mary has the oddest feeling, one completely foreign to her. Even though the conversation is so superficial, when he stands up to leave, bidding her, "Have a great day," she finds herself oddly disappointed. She must admit she is sexually strangely attracted to him – a big no-no in the Catholic Church.

Secretly, she wonders why such a handsome man chose celibacy and the priesthood over a family or even bachelorhood. Is he gay? It's doubtful. The vibes Father Neeley gives off are distinctly heterosexual. Mary knows little of his past. She had heard that he was a local high school football hero years ago. But he left town to attend Princeton, and didn't return for several years – and when he did, he was a priest, a shocker for most locals, who expected him to be the CEO of a major company by now.

Later that day, Mary is just getting the girls settled down for dinner when the kitchen phone rings.

"That's probably Daddy, saying he's got to work late," Mary says to no one in particular. "Hello," Mary says into the receiver, while pouring milk for Kandee.

"Mom... Mom! That's too much." Kandee says, trying to put her hand over her glass.

Kate McGee is on the phone. Always one who feeds on drama, Kate sounds like she is positively salivating at the thought of dispensing a juicy gem of gossip to someone.

"Mar! It's Kate. Did you hear the news?" she squeals into the phone, her voice a mixed fusion of disappointment and excitement.

"Hold on a minute, Kate," Mary replies calmly as she puts the milk down. She untangles the phone cord and leans against the wall, readying herself for a long conversation.

"Go ahead, Kate," she sighs. "What's so urgent?"

"They found Mr. B dead this morning."

A dazed feeling overwhelms Mary as her body stiffens against the wall. Her mouth is moving but no words come out.

"You know he's always out at his market stand at the crack of dawn," Kate goes on. "Well, this morning, a couple of his regulars got worried when they didn't see him. They knocked on the door and didn't get any answer. They called the cops then waited while they broke in the house.

"Mr. B. was found sitting in his armchair in front of the TV. Probably died watching *The Price is Right*, don't ya' think? You know how he loved that show."

Mary grabs her stomach, feeling like someone has just punched her. *First my dad and now Mr. B.*, she thinks, trying to hold back the tears.

"Mr. B is dead?" Mary tries but can't absorb the words coming out of her mouth.

"Yeah, isn't that sad?" Kate responds, the excitement in her words finally giving way to dismay. "And they can't even locate his daughter. But you know, he *was* kinda up there in years. No real surprise, I guess. Still, I can't imagine going by that farm market without seeing him out there in his chair. He was kind of like, you know, the unofficial mayor of that street. I don't suppose there's many people around here who he didn't know by name."

"Yeah," Mary says, still absorbing the news. "You know, Kate, I've known that man for I don't know how many years. But I don't think I ever really knew him at all. You know, a lot of people – including me – don't even know his first name. We just always called him "Mr. B.""

"Yeah, me too, Mar. I mean, people have always said he was some kind of war hero or something – won a medal during WWII or something. They said he saved another soldier."

"Does he have any family? I know he was widowed at a young age, but he only mentioned the one daughter – Mollie." Reacting from a mounting surge of guilt, Mary feels an urgent need to know everything about Mr. B's life. She remembers that he had a wife, Maureen, who had died many years ago, but knows little more than that.

"Well, I don't know for sure, but years ago people told me about that daughter of his. From what I hear, she was a real disappointment. The word is her father booted her out of the house soon after his wife died. The daughter had become a real druggie. The hard stuff, too. Heroin. Meth. That sort of stuff."

"Really?" Mary is genuinely surprised. "I don't think I've heard him talk about his daughter that much at all. Wow. How sad. He was such a nice gentleman."

"I hear ya, Mar. I really don't know of anyone who has an unkind word to say about him. He was just such a dear old thing, wasn't he?"

Detecting that Kate is eager to continue their long talk about Mr. B., Mary asks, "Do you think there'll be an obituary in tomorrow's paper?"

"Can't tell. If it's true about the daughter being estranged and all, I don't know of any other family member that's going to step in and make arrangements," Kate says, almost off-handedly.

Mary suddenly can't stand the idea of Mr. B's arrangements being left to strangers. She realizes that Mr. B was as much of a dad to her as her own father had been. She'd traveled that road by the farm market for years, and Mr. B had quietly, gently, become a very important part of her life.

"I'm calling the paper to see if anyone's contacted them about an obit," Mary says. "If not, I'm going to see what we can do. It's just not right that that poor man's final arrangements are left to strangers."

"Really?" Kate sounds genuinely surprised.

"Yeah, really. I gotta go, Kate."

"Sure, okay. Let me know how you make out."

"Sure enough."

"What's going on, Mommy?" Kandee asks. Mary suddenly realizes that the girls had heard enough of her conversation to glean that something sad had happened.

"It's Mr. B, Bunny. He died last night." Mary and David don't believe in pulling any punches when it comes to the girls.

People *die*. They don't *pass away*; *go home to be with the Lord*, or *go to sing with the angels*. They *die*.

"Does that mean he's not going to be out at his market anymore?" Marlee asks, her brown eyes large and questioning.

"Of course, stupid. How's he going to be at his market if he's dead?" Cecee can be very impatient with her younger sisters.

"That's enough, Cecee," Mary says, stepping in before a full-blown argument can begin.

"Well, Father Neeley says that good people go to heaven. Is Mr. B going to heaven, Mom?" Again, Marlee's brown eyes are big and searching. Heaven was a touchy subject.

Mary wasn't too sure if she believed in a heaven or a hell, but right now Marlee is young enough to still believe in a heaven.

"I don't know," Mary answers. "That's between God and Mr. B. I would have to say, though, that Mr. B was a good man, so the chances are quite excellent he'll be happy." Marlee is satisfied with the reply. She begins to dig into her mac-and-cheese with gusto.

"Is Daddy eating with us tonight?" Mary places a piece of chicken on her plate.

"No, Bunny, he's not. He's got to work late."

"*Agaaaaaaaaaaain?*" Kandee exclaims, more as a moan than a question. "Yes, Bunny, I'm sorry." Mary suddenly feels an irrational pang of guilt for David's absence.

"So what else is Father Neeley teaching you in catechism?" Mary asks the girls, hoping to change the subject.

Mary couldn't care less what Father Neeley is teaching the girls, but she is hoping small talk will take their minds off David's empty seat at the table.

That bastard Bitterman. Mary is inwardly fuming. *He's making all those poor people work overtime just so he can impress corporate and get that in-ground pool at his mansion. Jerkoff.*

Seven

A Painful Souvenir

Mary decides to walk to work the next day. She still suffers a slight limp from her devastating accident on *that day* back in 2002. Still, she considers herself lucky. How many people survive getting hit by a bus? It's like a bad joke. If she had to survive with just a bum hip, Mary considers herself blessed. She remembers little about *that day* but is told that she is lucky that the bus had been slowly pulling up to the curb when she walked directly into its path.

Mary knows full-well that if the bus had been traveling at its regular speed and she'd walked in front of it, she would not have survived. She suffers a severely-broken pelvis and two shattered legs. The pain is so intense that doctors place her in a self-induced coma. There aren't enough pain-killers in the world to quell the throbbing ebb and flow of pain which invades her body. The coma lasts well over two weeks.

She remembers climbing clumsily, laboriously, out of the coma. Her eyes are beginning to focus on the stark hospital room. It has straight-back chairs and light sea-foam-green painted walls which, she suspects, have seen better days, judging from the chips of lacquer. She looks down at her hand and sees the plastic body temperature gadget on her index finger. She closes her eyes for another long minute.

When she reopens them, first one sluggish eye then the other, she glances back down at her hand, looking in hazy amazement at what she sees. A group of shiny silver ropes – strings-like strands – are wound around her wrist and flow gently down the side of her bed, wending themselves deftly through the small slit at the bottom of the closed door.

They shine – no, they *glow* and throb – with the intensity of a thousand midnight stars on a clear July night. Mary blinks.

They are still there. She brushes it off as a figment produced by the combination of pain, the morphine drip and finally emerging from the abyss of the weeks-long coma.

I'm dreaming, she thinks. *No.... this is no dream,* she realizes. *I am awake. I can hear the nurses down the hall. I can smell coffee.*

It feels as if time is standing still. As if she merely took a vacation from life and inexplicably she is back again, with no memories of her trip. When she looks down at her wrist again, the glowing strands are gone. She doesn't have time to dwell on them. Her surgeon, Dr. Levin, bursts through the door. Mary looks down at her hand wondering where the silver ropes have gone.

Dr. Levin, a kindly old soul, has gray hair and a gray beard that matches his gray satin tie and impeccable Italian-tailored suit peeking out from his white hospital jacket. One of the nurses must have alerted him that his patient had finally regained consciousness as she was being weaned off the morphine-drip and Oxycodone. She is now able to speak in distinct – if only short – sentences. Dr. Levin pulls up a chair near her bedside.

"You were very lucky, my dear," Dr. Levin says softly. He then launches into a routine he had, no doubt, recited hundreds, if not thousands of times before:

"Your pelvis and legs were shattered in the accident. The surgery actually went better than I expected. I believe you will walk again. The worst case scenario is that you'll need a cane. We're going to start you on physical therapy just as soon as we think you're able. Our goal is to get you up and on your feet. And, no pun intended, my dear, we'll take it one step at a time after that. But you have to be prepared to work very hard at physical therapy. I won't lie to you. It will be long and probably a bit painful. So I need to know that you're committed to getting well."

Mary, still groggy, tries to pepper him with questions, but gets only vague answers, no matter how hard she pushes. She surrenders to Dr. Levin's obscure answers because she is becoming so tired, so sleepy.

"Did I have wires on my wrist?" she mutters.

Dr. Levin looks puzzled at first, and then chuckles. "Oh, yes, dear, you had tubes all over your body. You were in pretty bad shape."

"No," Mary whispers, "I'm talking about the ones that were glowing. They were silver. *Silver Strands.*"

Dr. Levin cocks his head and, much to her annoyance, again chuckles. "I don't know about any *glowing* tubes," he says. "It was probably just the light reflecting on something." Then, the doctor abruptly changes the subject.

"There's one thing you really should know, my dear," he relates as he stands and pushes his chair back behind him. "This happens sometimes. I find it is important to tell my patients. I believe they have a right to know." The doctor hesitates a moment as if deciding what to say next.

Mary's eyes flutter opens a bit wider. "What is it, Doctor? Is something else wrong?"

"We lost you – just for a short while, now mind you; but you were gone," he at last stammered. "You gave us quite a scare."

As excruciatingly tired as she is, Mary forces herself to listen. Dr. Levin's words are soft and calming, and that doesn't help. Mary starts to doze off to the hypnotizing drone of his voice.

"You had to be revived twice with a defibrillator, Mary," he says solemnly. "Your heart stopped for nearly two minutes. Nothing for you to be concerned about now, I promise you, although, as I said, you gave us quite the scare. Nothing you have to be concerned about, but I personally believe my patients should be aware when something like that happens."

Mary nods – and drifts blissfully off to sleep. The conversation about the "silver strands" barely registers in her conscious mind, and if it did, it immediately takes a back seat to her unconscious.

Today, years later, as Mary limps slightly down Commerce Street, she hardly remembers the conversation she had with Dr. Levin. In fact, she barely recalls him – other than his being the surgeon who put her broken and battered body together again. She is thinking about Mr. B now – sweet Mr. B, and how she will never see his kindly, wrinkled, smiling face again. She feels as if she has lost her father all over again.

Robbie Renwood

"Hi there, Golden Boy!" Mary chirps merrily to Robbie, the local mailman. Mary delights in teasing him about his golden, just-scrubbed good looks. He has thick blond hair with sapphire eyes shimmering underneath long wheat-colored lashes, and the kind of body that only a man under thirty can claim. Taut muscles peek out from razor sharp creases in his uniform. Twenty-four-year-old Robbie Renwood is lucky enough to have landed the job of postman for Mary's suburban neighborhood. Shy, but friendly, Robbie accepts Mary's gentle joking with a smile and a wave.

"Hi there, Mrs. Miller!" Robbie is sorting packages from his canvas bag, the one with the handle and wheels. "How are you today?"

Mary never tires of gently teasing him because she senses a shy, sensitive spirit beneath all those good looks. If Robbie knows he is exceptionally handsome, he never lets it show. His shyness borders on painful. It is several weeks before he can introduce himself to all the people on his mail route. Even then, he keeps his beautiful sapphire eyes averted, talking only to their shoes. He seems to have relaxed over time, finally settling into a neighborhood routine and even managing to squeak out small talk with some of his "people," as he likes to call them. Mary watches him as he walks down the street, a slight spring in his step. Robbie is an enigma all right. He never speaks about himself. The gossip mill reports that he'd tried college, but that didn't work out, and Mary never hears him speak of family or friends.

Still waters run deep, Mary thinks. *He's going to make some girl very happy.*

"I'm just fine, thank you," Mary answers with a smile. "My hip is bothering me a bit today, but I'm not complaining. *Besides,* Mary thinks, *what 24-year-old guy wants to hear about a middle-aged woman's aches and pains?*

68

"Good to hear," Mrs. Miller," Robbie says with a polite grin. Their eyes lock for a minute and Mary finds herself actually gasping at the purity of his ice-blue gaze. Robbie doesn't seem to notice, and for that, she is glad.

Yep, some lucky girl, Mary thinks, a slight smile breezing across her face. Mary starts walking in the opposite direction toward *The Beacon*, but she can't help but briefly turn to watch Robbie practically skip down the sidewalk. He's in a good mood today, for sure, she reasons.

Good for him. The kid deserves it. Maybe he's in love.

By the time Mary walks into *The Beacon*, her hip is throbbing. She leans against the front counter for a second to keep the pain lion from growling so fiercely. She has learned to live with the pain – indeed, there are times she even embraces it as a memento that she is still alive and strong enough to bitch about it.

"Mary, are you okay?" Carol Warren, the receptionist and switchboard operator for *The Beacon* calls out.

Her perpetually smiling face is the first to greet *Beacon* customers when they walk through the front door. Carol is petite, a little pixie powerhouse of energy. Her fiery red hair gives a hint that she is not someone that shies away from an impolite or nasty customer.

"I'm fine, Carol," Mary lies. "Just have to get my second wind here."

Mary's near-death accident is no secret to *The Beacon* staff. No one talks about it, at least not to her, but the periodic limp she has is a constant reminder to everyone that she has been through hell and back. Carol looks at Mary with concern now, her big dark eyes taking in the image of a frazzled woman propped up against the counter, her breathing labored and a slight eruption of sweat beads crossing her forehead.

"Can I get you some water?" Carol asks.

Mary suddenly realizes what a pathetic image she is projecting – something she abhors.

"No, no, Carol, I'm fine, just a little winded." Forcing a smile on her anxious face, Mary inquires, "How about you? How you doin' today, dearie?"

69

Carol's facial muscles relax.

"Doin' well, Mary. Phones haven't stopped ringing, but you know me – I like it busy. Makes the day go faster."

Carol is like a demure, welcoming sentinel that guards *The Beacon* staff from the outside world. She is efficient – that much is clear to Mary. Anyone who has to answer the cascade of phone calls that pours into *The Beacon* every day has to be perpetually on her toes. Carol's job also includes keeping track of which reporter is on assignment and who is in the office. It is a never-ending merry-go-round of chaos, but she seems to juggle it all with the aplomb of a seasoned, executive personal assistant.

When Carol first started working there last year, she was a jangle of nerves, and the unrelenting onslaught of phone calls and visits from customers had seemed overwhelming. Several times Mary thought she spotted a tear of frustration and desperation in her eye. Mary gave her a month before she expected her to go screaming out the front door, looking for some sort of less stressful job.

But Carol had surprised her by turning out to be quite the trooper. And now the switchboard has become *her* playground – her domain. You dare not invade *her* territory without *her* permission. Yet she always manages to conduct the General Patton-like demeanor with a perky smile and a voice brimming with cheeriness. She has developed a confidence and mastery of efficiency that Mary secretly envies.

Mary, as well as many others, is quite sure Carol is well-compensated for her work, but no one begrudges her the compensation. The woman keeps the office humming like a well-oiled machine. There is a rumor that she had to take a family leave one time and company profits actually took a noticeable dip. No one is sure if the two incidents are connected, but it has now turned into a bona fide office legend.

Now, how many "switchboard operators" can lay claim to that?

Carol wears only designer clothes – Jimmy Choo shoes are her favorite. Her outfits hail straight from the pages of

Vogue, and accentuate her graceful little figure. Her red hair is always stylish and her nails are always manicured.

Rumor has it that Carol's husband Bob is rather well off, although no one seems quite sure what he does for a living. Carol refers to him as an "entrepreneur" when she speaks of him. But Mary has it on good authority that much of the money the couple enjoys is from an inheritance. Carol took the job at *The Beacon* not for the money, but to fill her empty days and to socialize. Carol simply is not a woman who can be content with shopping, attending fund-raisers and lunching with the other well-to-do ladies every day. That is one reason Mary likes her.

Mary and Carol have become friendly over the past year, sharing anecdotes about their husbands and their kids. Carol periodically gushes over her husband Bob.

"Someday, Mary, someday he's going to make us all *really* rich. He's a genius. He has all these ideas – I mean he's brilliant. It's just a matter of getting things patented now. And then our ship will come in."

How much more do you need? Mary wants to ask her, but keeps her thoughts to herself. *Not my business.*

Mary can't help but wonder why Carol – the social butterfly that she is – never entertains at her home. Mary has been to Carol and Bob's three-tiered Victorian home several times, always on business, usually to drop off work papers. It is furnished with velvet and brocade armchairs and leather sofas and peppered with gorgeous antiques that make any professional collector salivate.

The exterior of the huge home – Mary stops short of calling it a "mansion" – appears as if it belongs on the cover of "Architectural Digest." The elegance of the interior is stunning. The design of the edifice, with its cathedral ceilings, screams out for evening cocktails or grand holiday parties. Bob's oak-paneled den features a huge fireplace and a grand mahogany desk. It has matching leather chairs which carry an aroma that seems to scream "money!"

Carol and Mary had gone to high school together, but they could not have been more different. Mary was shy and disappeared into the background of English nerds and math and science clubs. Carol had been stunningly gorgeous in high school with a figure that turned all the guys' heads, especially when she wore her cheerleader's outfit.

Even as Carol ages, she retains her lovely red hair, probably with the help of a certain concoction of chemicals, her peaches-and-cream, spotless complexion, and stunning figure. Mary entertains doubts about Bob's entrepreneurship ability, but she keeps them to herself. Carol prattles on and on about Bob's skills as an inventor and salesman while Mary nods, keeping a semi-smile frozen on her face.

Hey, he makes her happy. That's all that counts, Mary thinks. *So what if this guy is an eccentric loser? They're happy.* He holds down the fort, bill-wise, and he stays at home spending long afternoons in his den, making overseas phone calls. Mary guesses it all evens out anyway. If nothing else, Bob is a glorified "Mr. Mom" who tends to the house and their two adolescent girls while Carol works.

When she finishes exchanging greetings with Carol, Mary makes a bee-line to her work station.

"Oh my God, this chair feels so good!" Mary exclaims to no one in particular as she plops down in the old revolving chair at her desk. The pain in her hip and leg is starting to subside. Like an ebb tide, the pain visits her on a regular basis. She no longer gives it the power to control her life. That was long ago.

The reason she walked the three blocks to work earlier today was to tell the pain just that.

"Fuck you, Pain! You can't hold me down any longer."

And she always feels better after giving the pain the finger.

Eight

Meg and Will

"Mornin!"

Hearing the unexpected greeting, Mary nearly jumps off of her comfortably worn seat when Meg plops down in the rustic wooden chair next to her desk.

"You ready to start, cupcake? We're working together. So let's get this shit on."

For a feature writer who often deals with religious issues, Meg O'Reilly has a mouth on her that could put a war-weary Marine to shame. She is often crude, can be rude and is always a magnet for men.

By the age of thirty-three, she has won some of the top prizes in journalism, starting out as a crime reporter at twenty-two, straight out of college. She maintains her long blond hair in a perpetual Farrah Fawcett-style, never changing it over the years, because, as she explains matter-of-factly, "That's what guys like. And if the guys like it, it's easier to get the story from them."

She became fast friends with the police and firefighters on her beat – mostly men. Charming the guys and talking trash with the few women in the group, she disarmed them into thinking she was unaware of her good looks. Her language was positively unfiltered, and would make some of the cops blush. Little did she care. Meg was tough as nails and could hold her own liquor against any guy.

Before she became a writer for Features, Meg worked the police and crime beat. She had found it ridiculously easy to distance herself from the sometimes-grisly crime stories then go home and enjoy a glass of cheap merlot. She loved to watch "CSI" reruns and enjoyed pointing out all the errors in police procedure on the show.

Cost-cutting had combined the Features Department with the Religion Department; so it was not unusual for Meg to think of the department as "fluff" – something she herself eschewed as "bogus hocus-pocus." If anyone had ever told her she'd end up in the Features Department, she would have busted a gut. She called it "the place where the headline-grabbing stories are about old ladies who collect antique buttons."

Yes, Meg had covered her fair share of murders, rapes and every violent crime known to man. And she was damn proud of it. She had chalked up enough favors with emergency personnel that she would get the story no other reporter could – and she was well compensated for it. At thirty-two, though, Meg had covered the one story that sucker-punched her on a visceral level – the one story that would put her out to pasture – or at least relegate her to the dreaded Features Department.

The story that changed her career was the tale of a tragedy that pierced her journalistic armor and clawed its way into her soul. It happened on a lovely day, one of those magical spring days where you actually smell the Earth awakening from its long winter's hibernation. It was early April, but the temperature had tip-toed its way from the mid-40s to a string of delightful mid-60s days. The crocuses outside Meg's apartment were arriving early that year. Still, today Meg recalls the day in vivid detail as she relives it often:

She had walked into *The Beacon* office that morning to find Gary Elliott blocking her way from entering the newsroom.

"Don't take your jacket off," he says. "Second and Commerce streets, downtown. Now! Chop-chop! They just found the body of a little girl washed up in Luna Park. I already sent two photographers. I want this for first deadline."

Without missing a beat, Gary walks to reporter Will Wheaton's desk where Will is sitting with his feet propped up on his desk, sipping a cup of coffee and waiting impatiently for his source to call back.

"Main and Poplar – fatal pedestrian hit-and-run. Just came over the scanner. Go get it," Gary says without stopping for an answer. Today promises to be anything but dull for *The Beacon*'s staff.

"Aw shit, man." Will puts his coffee mug down. "It never fails. Every time I'm waiting for a call this happens. Main and Poplar? Nice part of town," he says sarcastically to anyone who is in earshot. "Probably just a homeless guy or a hooker."

Will fancies himself an investigative reporter, although truth-be-told, the tips he gets from his sources (addicts, hookers and disgruntled or fired City Hall workers) seldom pan out. A not-so-happy Will grabs his jacket from the back of a chair and heads out the door.

Tammy Brenner

Meg pulls her candy-apple red 1965 vintage Mustang into an empty space next to the police cars, ambulances and other emergency vehicles. An inheritance from her late uncle, the car is her pride and joy. The Mustang looks new and doesn't have so much as a tiny ding from a renegade shopping cart on it. And Meg intends to keep it that way.

She ambles along her way through the soft earthy path into the woods leading to Luna Park. She had long ago forfeited high-heels in favor of fashionable pumps. When your next assignment might be on the beach or on a high-rise scaffolding – with little or no notice – you learn quickly that fashion takes a back seat to safety. Still, the small kitten heels of her black pumps begin sinking into the ground covered with the past year's harvest of pine needles. Inching her way to the yellow garland warning, *POLICE LINE DO NOT CROSS* she immediately spots Rich Shaw, the Chief of Police.

Meg and Rich enjoyed a brief affair years ago when she first came on the paper. The chemistry was explosive between the young, ruggedly handsome newly-named police captain and Meg, a fresh-faced, Christiane Amanpour wannabe. Unfortunately – or, as Meg would later say, fortunately – Rich was a newlywed. Their brief affair, which Meg judiciously kept secret, ended amicably. Meg and Rich remained close friends, a rarity for young lovers who grow apart. They both rose through the ranks in their respective careers.

When she finally reaches him, Meg asks cavalierly, "Chief?" careful not to call him by his Christian name in public, "can you give me any idea what we have here? I'm told we have a body wash."

Rich looks up at Meg, startled at her voice. It is obvious he is in deep reverie, or concentration, something bordering a trance. Rich always maintains such a calm demeanor and is so matter-of-fact at violent crimes scenes that he has a calming influence on others. Although now, as chief, his presence is not required, he usually does attend. The look on his face this time is so – "devastated," the only word Meg can think of.

"Rich?" she repeats when he fails to answer her.

"Some goddamned prick killed a little girl. Stay back, Meg. We're trying to preserve this entire area."

His terse tone of voice takes her by surprise. As she approaches him she sees his face is white – almost translucent. And – could it be his eyes were wet? She can't tell because he keeps averting her gaze.

"Rich, help me out here before the other guys arrive. Give me something... Gary wants this for first edition."

"Oh! First edition! Well, why didn't you *say* so?" the chief nearly shouts in a voice dripping with sarcasm. Meg's jaw drops. Rich has always been such a gentleman to her.

What the hell?

"You need a story?" the chief fairly bellows. "Here's your story, Meg. Right here... just walk between the tape and take a gander at what the monster did to that little girl."

Meg ignores Rich's sarcasm in favor of taking him up on his offer to view the crime scene. Just a few feet away lay something that looks like a rag doll. But it is no doll. This is the body of a girl – she looks to be no more than five or six years old. She lay on her back, just at the edge of Luna Lake. The cedar water of the lake is inching ominously close to the tiny body. The little girl is dressed in a pink skirt and purple top. The pink skirt is pulled up to her neck, and the pink tights she had been wearing are discarded nearby. Her tiny lace panties lay in tatters nearby. They are nearly torn in half. Meg immediately knows what that means: Probable sexual assault. Meg's eyes take in the limp body from her tiny shoeless feet, up her torso... and stops.

The tiny body is contorted in such a way that her face – her skin the color of sweet chocolate milk, her dark hair in a ponytail with a lavender wool bow – is clearly visible. Meg can see the scarlet stain that permeates her purple top. There is so much blood it is almost impossible at first to discern its origin. And then Meg sees it – like finding a toothbrush in a tree in one of those children's "Highlights" magazines. There is a gaping wound – a huge gash that literally travels from tiny ear to tiny ear. It could have resembled a macabre smile – if it were on her face, not her throat. Ah, her face, the sweet, round face of innocence. Someone has bashed the side of her head in so hard, it is almost concave. Still, her pretty hazel eyes are open wide, the only part of her face not covered in blood. Even from this distance, Meg can make out the thick, curly lashes that frame those lovely, lifeless eyes.

Meg has been to so many crimes scenes – some explosively, projectile-bloody – that one story blends in with another. This scene, though… this scene cut through her bland attitude toward crime stories and, without warning, imprinted its grisly image on her brain: Innocence stolen; life stolen; family destroyed.

"Got what ya need, Meg?" Rich says, his tone still derisive, from behind her.

"Chief, Rich. I'm sorry... I...," for once Meg is speechless.

"No, I'm sorry," the chief says, shaking his head. His voice is contrite. "I didn't mean to take it out on you. I just never had one this young. And now I have to tell her parents. God help me."

Meg touches his arm.

"You have a chaplain to do that, Rich."

But he waves her away.

"The chaplain will be with me, but no, this is *my* job. I'm not looking forward to it, though."

Meg does her job, collecting information for a story that no doubt will be on the front page. The little girl's name is Tammy Brenner. Meg interviews police and neighbors and the little girl's first-grade teacher Mrs. Barnet, who is so overemotional, to the point of being dangerously-near the stage of hysteria. Meg is barely able to squeak out two quotes from Mrs. Barnet. Meg even makes the obligatory attempt to interview Tammy's parents, but they are too distraught to speak to the media. Meg loathes this part of the job. But it is a necessity. The family has assigned Tammy's Uncle Bill as the family spokesman. He relays – in-between sobs – to Meg and the other reporters who have arrived how much Tammy enjoyed double-dutch jump rope competitions and playing with her cousins. He says even at her young age, she showed promise of being a writer. She loved to read and write poetry, and even won a composition contest hosted by the town library last summer.

Returning to her car, Meg turns the radio off and drives in stoic silence back to the newsroom. She walks trance-like straight to her desk, filtering out the cacophony of the hectic activity around her. The next week passes in a blur. Meg does her follow-up stories, the usual top-notch caliber of reporting for which she is known. She dutifully covers the funeral, listening to Tammy's preacher eulogize a life cut so short – what else is there to say? Not much.

Tammy was a good girl, a church-going girl who loved reading and writing and SpongeBob SquarePants and oddly, for someone so young, gardening. She loved to help her mother tend to the roses in their garden.

Meg files the last of her stories on Tammy Brenner's murder close to the midnight deadline one night. She has just finished checking with the chief to see if there was any movement on the case.

Sounding dejected and frustrated, Rich says there are no suspects yet and no promising leads. The newsroom is abnormally quiet and Meg sits at her desk, so deep in reflection she doesn't hear Gary Elliott come up behind her.

"Great job, Meg. Good work on the murder." Gary waits for Meg to respond.

A "thanks" would be nice, he thinks.

But Meg has her chin in her hand and is staring off into the distance.

"Tammy Brenner," Meg says softly without looking at him. "The little girl who was murdered – her name was Tammy Brenner."

Gary nods his head knowingly. He knows all too well that some stories – particularly those involving children – can get under your skin. He instantly realizes this is one of those stories for Meg.

"Of course," he says.

"I want off major crimes," Meg announces abruptly. "I don't want to see any more of this shit. Do what you have to do, Gary. Find me a spot somewhere else – anywhere else – and I promise I won't let you down. I'll do the best wherever you put me. But if you have to fire me, I understand."

"What the hell are you talking about, Meg? You're the best goddamned crime reporter I've ever worked with! You've got the gift – the *gift*, Meg. A lot of reporters can cover crimes, but they don't get *inside* the story like you do." Gary's voice is growing high and louder. "Look, take some time to think this over. You don't have to make up your mind right away. Please, Meg."

"Made up my mind, Gary," Meg says tersely as she stands up and thrusts her chair into the hole beneath her desk. "Find me a place where I can keep some kind of sanity. I'm done with the crime beat. It's up to you."

She put on her jacket, oblivious to Gary's open jaw, and strides out of the newsroom. Over her shoulder, almost as an afterthought, she yells, "Oh, look, Gary, if you have to fire me, no worries, no hard feelings."

The Strategy

Meg props an arm on Mary's desk and leans forward after she plops her body down on the rickety chair next to it.

"You ready to start, Cupcake? We're working together, you know. So let's get this shit on." Meg eyes her new story-partner while sipping a scalding-hot cup of battery-acid-strong coffee from Starbucks – she detests the "chocolate-carmel-cappuccino" that her co-workers seem to worship so much.

That stuff's nothing but a chocolate laxative, she thinks. *There oughta be a law: coffee is strong and black – period.*

Gary has already filled her in on the story that Worldwide wants. Her long-brewing cynicism is in high gear, but she's never turned down a story, and she's not about to do so now. She also isn't crazy about working with Mary. She has nothing against Mary – she just prefers to work alone. But she has her marching orders, and she's hoping to make this as painless as possible.

"How do you want to approach this thing?" Meg asks as she blows on her steaming coffee.

For someone who was more accustomed to the gritty reality of the streets, Meg has adapted unusually fast to the more ethereal realm of the Features Department. She misses the adrenaline rush of the streets from time to time, but digging her heels into a story like this – *the afterlife, for Christ's sake* – is too tempting to pass up. As Meg begins looking down the barrel of age forty, she begins to think more and more of her own mortality. She never married, has no kids – really, no living family left at all – and suddenly the *afterlife* doesn't seem as far down the road as it always had before. Nor does it seem quite as unbelievable as previously.

That spring day – the day she stared at the broken, bloodied body of Tammy Brenner – was a defining moment in her career. Meg continues to be haunted by Tammy's huge, lifeless, hazel eyes. Even though she surrendered her crime beat, knowing there were a number of other reporters salivating

81

at the idea of taking her place, she secretly follows the story religiously. The killer apparently had been wise enough to use a condom. But he wasn't quite savvy enough to be crime-scene careful. Techs at the lab had been able to pull up a number of pubic hairs from the little girl's skirt and panties. None matched any specimens in the DNA crime data base. Evidence at the crime scene was practically nil.

"I'm not real optimistic about this one," Rich had confided to Meg in a private moment of reflection. For some reason – reporter's instinct or just her female gut – Meg is quite sure the animal who ravaged Tammy would never be caught.

Meg thinks of Tammy Brenner almost constantly. She often dreams of those huge hazel eyes glinting in the springtime sunshine, of the pink frilly skirt and tiny top, the top which once was girly-purple but had morphed into a scarlet stain that all but obliterated its true color. On more than one occasion Meg awoke from a "Tammy nightmare" in a shaky sweat. Why this little girl's death jostled her so – she had covered so much murder and mayhem, and yes, even children's deaths – she was at a loss to figure out.

She remembered two years ago covering the murder of a local teenager named Leslie Ann Stanton. Leslie, the high school homecoming queen, had been raped and sodomized. The image of the blond beauty-queen's body, her peachy complexion, the silky blond hair and designer top and jeans that covered her curvaceous body was at odds against the frantic, bloody chaos of the murder scene.

From all she had been able to find out, Leslie Ann was no "Queen Bee." Meg couldn't find a single schoolmate or teacher who had anything remotely negative to say about her. As she wrote the story, Meg recalled thinking what a shame that such a promising life was cut short. But she slept well that night, knowing she had done her job well and submitted one hell of a story that landed as the lead on the front page.

What makes Tammy's story different from Leslie Ann's? The age difference, perhaps – or maybe their race? Meg was guessing that Tammy was biracial. She didn't ask because it wasn't germane to the story. Or could it be the economic status? Tammy's family lives in subsidized housing, while Leslie Ann was decidedly upper middle-class. No. The only tangible difference in the two cases is that Leslie Ann's killer was nabbed. Jesse Hypes, a jealous ex-boyfriend, is safely behind bars for the rest of his natural life.

Maybe that's it, Meg often thinks. Maybe, just maybe, if they had found Tammy's murderer, the creature who snuffed the light out of her, those hazel eyes would shine with justice – instead of the accusatory phrase, "*Why me?*"

Meg had another of those so-called "Tammy nightmares" last night, and didn't get much sleep after awakening in a clammy sweat at four o'clock this morning. She has consumed enough coffee to sober herself into a reporting mood. Sitting at Mary's desk now, it suddenly hits her that this is her third cup already.

"Uh, yeah, I'm ready when you are," Mary replies, a hint of anxiety edging out the excitement in her voice.

Mary had been a reporter on her high school paper, but never worked professionally in that capacity. She is very much aware that Gary selected her, a copy editor, not only for the reasons he outlined to her, but because cost cuts have taken a large bite out of *The Beacon*'s editorial budget.

Gary could not justify assigning another full-time reporter to work on this story with Meg. In his eyes, it would be the best of both worlds: Saving money using a lower-paid fact checker, who, in turn, could possibly add some spiritual perspective to the story. Gary knows about Mary, her accident and her long journey back to normalcy – knows that she has a spiritual sense about her.

Meg, on the other hand, is a great, practical, cynical reporter. The editor is not about to have a novice reporter being hoodwinked by a sweet lady who claims she saw the proverbial white light at the end of the tunnel before returning to her body. He has heard what he calls "spook tales" repeatedly over the years, and they are almost always told most convincingly by sincere, honest and earnest people. The stories are always the same. The person sees a tunnel and a white light; then a meeting takes place, usually with various dead relatives.

This story, as Gary envisions it, needs more than the familiar near-death-experience tales. He especially wants Meg on this story. She is a strong and confident woman who can smell an exaggerated or dramatized story when she hears one. He doesn't forget the way Meg up and quit her beat after covering the Tammy Brenner story. To make that change in her life and career took major chops.

Gary also knows that Meg – as pragmatic as they get – had been so rattled by the death of the little girl at Luna Park, she is softened just enough not to snub her nose at any "paranormal" nugget that she might encounter.

"What's first?" Mary asks, trying to contain her excitement as much as possible. Meg props her crossed legs up on Mary's desk and is still sipping from her steaming cup. She is wearing her signature True Religion jeans and a suede jacket. She long ago forfeited her impractical Christian Louboutin heels for more practical – but still Louboutin – boots.

"First I say we get to know each other a bit before we take to the open road," Meg says without looking up. "Shit, I have no idea where to begin. Let's do an early lunch and spitball ideas. You know, just throw out ideas and see if anything sticks to the wall."

"Sounds like a plan to me," Mary says, still trying to hide her over-enthusiasm.

Mary and Meg walk down the road to the Wicked Pigeon, a 24/7 diner that isn't exactly a four-star restaurant. But the Wicked P is clean and comfortable with good food and prices that fit well into *The Beacon*'s budget for business luncheons. The reporters take a booth in the back to avoid distractions. For the next seven hours the two women exchange their life stories, discuss the state of grammar in today's society, how technology is wonderful but dangerous in the wrong hands. The glint of the beginning of the sunset in the diner's front window is like an alarm clock to the pair. They are surprised at the time – the sun is about to exchange places with the moon.

"Fuck me!" Meg exclaims, looking at her Mickey Mouse watch. "Do you have to go home? I don't believe we've been sitting here yapping the day away. We really should at least talk a little bit about the story. Don't ya think?" Meg is laughing. It was the first time she had laughed in a long time. She is beginning to like this Mary-person, who seems refined but not shocked at Meg's colorful language.

"Oh my God, you're right!" Mary says. "Let me call David and tell him I won't be home for dinner. Thank God he's off today. He can feed the girls."

Mary makes a hurried call on her cell phone.

David doesn't sound thrilled, but he grudgingly agrees that Mary should continue discussing the story since he knows how important this assignment is to her.

"Love ya, David," Mary says and snaps her phone shut.

"How 'bout you, Mary? Meg asks bluntly, without waiting for Mary to put her cell phone away, "you ever have any experience with the afterlife?

"What, oh, me?" Mary stutters in surprise.

"Ever see any ghosts or goblins? Ever see your dead relatives wandering through your house? It seems like everyone I talk to has a story of some kind or another. I'm wondering what yours is."

"No, I'm sorry, I've got nothing. Only ghosts I ever saw were on Halloween."

"Well, that makes two of us then," Meg says in frustration, putting down her coffee cup. "We are officially starting at the bottom of the barrel."

"You know," Mary starts... "Oh, never mind."

Apparently through some office gossip anomaly, Meg is one of the few *Beacon* staffers who doesn't know of Mary's accident/coma/near-death experience. Gary made it a point not to tell Meg this story.

"Nevermind my ass!" Meg lurches forward. "If you got something, spill! I don't especially relish the thought of interviewing gypsy fortune tellers or police mediums who are usually dead wrong anyway. What'cha got? C'mon Mary, for Christ's sake, talk!"

"Well, I don't have anything really. It's just something that's been bothering me a long time."

"Yes?" Meg says with an urgent sigh that signals to Mary to get on quickly with her story.

"Well you know I was in a bad accident some years back -- actually got hit by a bus. A bus... I kid you not! Thus, the charming limp you see before you today."

"Geeze, I'm sorry, I didn't know," Meg says. "I always wondered about the limp. Damn, hit by a bus. But what the fuck does that have to do with anything?"

Mary interrupts her.

"The surgeon said I was clinically dead for two minutes. *Two minutes.* Now, before you get excited, there was no tunnel, there was no white light, I didn't see my dead grandma. Truth be told, I don't remember a damn thing. It's like it never happened."

"Get outta town!" Meg nearly shouts. The couple in the next booth look up but Meg doesn't notice. "And don't you think this is something you might have brought up before?" she adds sarcastically.

"Well, it's just that it doesn't *mean* anything to me. How could it? I all but forgot about it. It's like it never happened."

"What you're saying is your *conscious* mind doesn't remember it," Meg says authoritatively. "Who's to say what your *subconscious* mind remembers? Don't you get it, sweetie? We're sitting on fucking gold right here!"

Mary brushes her off with a wave of her hand.

"No, no, you've got it all wrong. Meg, remember what I said – there was no tunnel, no white light, no dead relatives, no pearly gates. I barely remember half of the time I spent in that hospital bed. And I sure as hell would remember a near-death experience."

Meg rolls her eyes in exasperation. She tosses back her long blond hair and leans forward, almost inches from Mary's face. "Right... right... that's your *conscious* mind that didn't see any of those things. We've got to find a way to get to your *subconscious*. And I'm not talking about psychoanalysis that's going to take years – we're on a deadline, hon.

I know this great psychiatrist in the city – I did a story on him once. And when I say "city," I don't mean Philadelphia.

86

We're talking Manhattan here, Mary. *Manhattan.* He's not just a licensed hypnotherapist – he's considered the best in his field."

Manhattan, to Meg, was the center of the universe. She had lived there when she was in college, and fell in love with the constant thump, thump, thumping of the city's heartbeat. It truly never slept. Any other town seemed tame – almost boring – compared to Manhattan.

"Hypnosis," Mary says, her body language clearly communicating her disdain for the idea. Mary can't help recalling that smug quack Dr. Regan – who was wildly unsuccessful in trying to hypnotize her into believing that all the furniture in the room would disappear when she reopened her eyes.

"I don't think so Meg. I don't think I can be hypnotized. And to be honest with you, I really don't think anyone really can. I think it's a bunch of baloney."

"Wrong!" Meg nearly jumps up in her chair. She has a huge grin on her pretty face.

"Believe me, this guy is the real deal. He doesn't make people cluck like chickens or any of that parlor game shit. This guy uses hypnosis strictly for medical purposes. His name is Dr. Lee. I did a piece on him awhile back. Believe me, there's nothing phony about him. I can spot a phony a mile away. This Doc is on the up and up. Hey, what have we got to lose?

He comes at a hefty cost, but what the hell, we can expense it. Gary practically gave us carte blanche on resources. C'mon, Mary, what do we have to lose? At the very least, we get to go into the city, do some shopping while we're there, and Dr. Lee will help you with a little, uh… relaxation session."

When Meg puts it in those terms, it is hard for Mary to resist. A day away from family woes and work, and all she has to do is sit and relax for an hour or two while some shrink works his alleged magic on her? He just might get to the root of her panic attacks, although she neglected to tell Meg about the panic attacks. So what if it doesn't work? At least she can say she tried.

"Oh, what the hell," Mary says. "Set it up and let's do it,"

Meg claps her hands together in joy.

"Great! I'm on it. Probably going to take a while to set it up, but I got to know him pretty well. We hit it off. I think he'll make room on his calendar for us."

Nine

October In Manhattan

It is one of those October days that screams "Halloween!" The front window of Norton's Candy Store is spilling over with candy corn and other orange and black licorice treats. Because the neighborhood caters to many Latino immigrants, there also is lots of sugar candy shaped like skulls or skeletons.

It's like killing two birds with one stone for Norton's. Skulls and skeletons for November first, or for some, the second; the Mexicans' *Día de los Muertos* (Day of the Dead); and, of course, Halloween. The century-old candy store, which stands sentinel on Church Street in Manhattan, has been handed down from father to son for more than a century, and the generations are savvy enough to know how to keep their sweet merchandise changing with the demographics of their market. That's how they keep their little shop from being gobbled up by entrepreneurs who tingle at the idea of owning a storefront that can be transformed into a law office or insurance office, devoid of any personality and out-of-character for the mom-and-pop neighborhood.

The autumnal wind huffs and heaves its way down the street, tugging at Mary's long tweed coat. It makes Meg's stylish wool cape that she picked up last week at Nordstrom's flap like bird's wings. Brown oak leaves dance a gusty pirouette near their feet. The sky is overcast, a distinct warning of calamitous weather approaching.

"Boy, something wicked this way cometh," Meg shouts with a laugh to Mary, holding her cape about her and trying to be heard over the blustery voice of the wind. "Seriously, Mary, you're going to like this guy. He's a real sweetheart – very unpretentious. And believe me, he's not going to make you do anything you don't want to do."

89

Mary nods, but it is only a half nod. She still isn't thrilled to see yet another psychiatrist whose specialty happens to be "hypnotherapy," which, to her is just a waste of money.

Oh screw it, she thinks. *I'm not paying for it. What the hell.*

Mary follows Meg as she turns into an alleyway – a neat little spot that seems to be a relic preserved out of the 1800s. The other alleys in Manhattan stink of urine and vomit and deeds better left to the imagination. But this alley – it is like taking an unexpected turn down the Yellow Brick Road. There is a sweet aroma of incense and orange peel drifting from the brownstones which have been transformed into cozy-looking shops and tiny offices. It is like entering a different city and a different century. Flickering gas lamps hug the space between the ancient front doors.

"They call this alley 'The Tunnel,'" Meg says. "I have no idea why."

The skyscrapers, and litter and pretzel vendors and homeless people that are the mainstays of Manhattan magically disappear. Two cars could not pass through "The Tunnel" simultaneously, and it is very doubtful any motorists had tried to do so recently. It is so peculiar to see this cobblestoned alley/street in the heart of Manhattan. It is lined on each side with vintage brownstones, and – unlike the other alleys in the city, is spotless, save for the oak leaves and their endless dance. There is not so much as a discarded candy wrapper.

The two steps leading up to the shop doors are made of white marble. Black veins running willy-nilly through the white stones give them a decidedly posh look. The slim townhouses appear as if they were the width only of one room and the rest of the abode –   kitchen and dining area and bedroom – are akin to the New Orleans "shotgun cottage" styles. The rooms are in a straight row.

The term "shotgun cottage" refers to the Louisiana myth that one could stand at the end of the house and have a clear path to the front door to shoot the taxman, dare he show his face. Mary wonders if that was the same purpose here.

Probably not, she smiles.

Near the massive 18th century front doors are pots of yellow and gold chrysanthemums and plump orange pumpkins, those wonderful harbingers of autumn.

Mary and Meg walk more than halfway down the tunnel, until Meg stops abruptly.

"Ah, hah! Here it is." she cries in success. Mary looks at the wooden placard hanging horizontally out from above the front door. It is swinging in the gusty wind. It has weathered its fair share of snowstorms, hurricanes and other rants of Mother Nature. But it is still legible.

Dr. Harold Lee

The exterior of the office is quaint, and, in Mary's opinion, exudes an almost simplistic eloquence. She had expected a neon sign touting Dr. Harold Lee as the "Premiere Hypnotherapist of our Age." But the sign mentions nothing of hypnosis. Truth-be-told, if one doesn't know where to look, there is a good chance that they would walk right past this unpretentious little office, nestled between two twin townhouses.

"C'mon," Meg says, elbowing Mary while she is still studying the sign. "He's expecting us... it's eleven sharp. He doesn't like tardiness."

Meg opens the massive oak door without knocking and Mary follows her into the red-and-gold carpeted hallway, the wind still slapping their backs. A wooden coat rack that seems a century old, extends its arms just waiting to embrace whatever outer garments might need babysitting while their owners conduct their business with Dr. Lee.

"Hello?" Meg shouts.

"What? No receptionist?" Mary asks in awe.

"Shhhhhh. He doesn't take patients anymore," Meg fairly whispers.

"Then what the hell am I doing here?" Mary asks, a bit of sarcasm tinting her voice.

"Honey," Meg replied, "you're not a *patient.* You're a *client.* Big difference. Dr. Lee only takes cases that pique his interest."

"Don't tell me!" a thunderous voice bellows from another room. "Gotta be my favorite Irish reporter in the whole world!" Mary cranes her neck to see the source of the voice which makes the walls shake.

Before she has a chance to turn the corner completely, Dr. Lee appears. He is holding a huge book open as if his reading has been interrupted. If he is annoyed, he doesn't show it. Quite the contrary, with his sizeable girth, and flowing silver hair and beard, he resembles the Santa Claus of the 1950s Coca Cola ads.

If he starts howling 'Ho, ho, ho,' I'm so outta here, Mary thinks.

But even with his booming voice, he clearly is no Santa. Despite his size, he wears what Mary immediately recognizes as L.L. Bean clothes; a plaid shirt, nondescript trousers and a gray sweater vest.

"How are you Dr. Lee? Keeping a low profile these days, aren't ya?" Meg says, first shaking his hand vigorously and then giving him a hug that is capable of only covering half of his ample trunk.

Mary puts him at well past retirement age. She is instantaneously drawn to him, which is very unusual for her. Meg is right. No pretension here. This fellow bears no resemblance to the pompous Dr. Regan of years ago.

"And this, this must be Mary," Dr. Lee says, holding out his hand and robustly pumping hers. "Meg has told me quite a bit about you. Fascinating, just fascinating. I can't wait to get to know you better, dear. Come on in, please sit down."

Meg and Mary follow Dr. Lee into the small parlor – it once had served as his office when he was still seeing patients, but he had unofficially "retired" some years back. The massive mahogany "office desk" is the only telltale-hint that this had once been a working office. The room is adorned in Victorian-era furniture: An antique baroque sofa with matching chairs, and some sort of dark-wooded fixtures. But the one small stained glass window that hugs the alleyway provides some light – and there are low-lit crystal lamps scattered throughout the room. It smells slightly of pipe smoke – one of Dr. Lee's vices that he is loath to surrender.

When Mary walks into the room, she can feel the tension and apprehension of this visit drain steadily from her body. Whether it's Dr. Lee's cheery voice or the homey atmosphere that engulfs the room, she cannot say. But it doesn't seem to matter.

"Where are my manners? Let me take your coats," Dr. Lee says, helping both women off with their outerwear and hanging

93

them carefully on the old coat rack. "Sit, sit. I just made some tea. It seems I've become quite an expert on tea in my old age. Today I'm serving white tea. Do you realize white tea is the least popular in the West, although in China it is considered to be a delicacy? I like it because, quite frankly, it's healthier for you," Dr. Lee explains excitedly. "It's a little more expensive because of the hand-processing, but believe me, it's worth it. Would you girls like some?"

"No, thank you," Mary and Meg respond, in unison.

"Thanks for taking time out for us, Doc," Meg says as she and Mary sit gingerly on the antique sofa.

"Oh, please, you're kidding," Dr. Lee says. "I'm staring down the barrel of eighty; I gave up my regular practice ages ago; and the only speaking engagements I do are at universities that don't realize I'm past my prime. Would you believe I don't even take payment for them anymore? I'd feel too much like I'm cheating them."

Meg chuckles at his self-derogatory attitude. She knows this man is revered by his colleagues. When she did a piece on him years ago, she was awestruck with his knack of weaving a gregarious down-to-earth nature with the brilliance of his mind. His "specialty" – a term he refused to use – was hypnosis.

"There's no hocus-pocus about hypnosis," the doctor's favorite saying, amused her then and still brings a smile to her face when she thinks about it. The words appear to sum up his dismissive attitude toward wannabe stage magicians and poorly-trained practitioners. In fact, he does not really like the term "hypnosis," preferring to use "hypnotherapy" instead.

"Meg has told me about your unfortunate experience with hypnosis," Dr. Lee says to Mary. "I don't like to cast aspersions on my colleagues, but…" He doesn't finish the sentence. Instead he just shakes his head as if to say, *"that doctor must have been some nutjob."*

"Let's talk about hypnosis," the doctor suggests. The office, in which the three of them are sitting, is snug but cozy. A small blaze is crackling in the fireplace. "There is nothing magical about it," Dr. Lee tells Mary, looking into her eyes. "I'm no magician. I simply help the patient relax through a

94

series of suggestions or images. Relaxation allows the subconscious mind to 'take over' the driver's wheel, so to speak. When you're under hypnosis, you usually feel relaxed and very calm. At that point, your subconscious can better focus on a singular thought or event, without the outside distractions of the conscious mind. Under hypnosis, you're more open than usual to suggestions. This can, in turn, be used to modify your perceptions, behavior, sensations and emotions."

Dr. Lee carefully explains how the mind works under hypnosis to Mary without a hint of pomposity. He relates that Meg explained the stunning revelation of when Mary's doctors had informed her she had been clinically dead for two minutes.

"We just want to see if your subconscious mind picked up any 'signal' while you were, well, *dead*," Dr. Lee says. "Believe me, my dear, if it doesn't work, you won't come out any worse for the wear. I can't *break* your mind, you know!"

He chuckles and Mary finds herself laughing with him. All her apprehensions of "going under" seem to dissipate more and more as Dr. Lee speaks.

"Let me explain how I do it, my dear," Dr. Lee says, touching one of Mary's hands lightly. "I use 'color hypnotherapy.' It's extremely simple. I am going to ask you to lie down on this sofa; I'll get you a pillow so it's more comfy. I'm going to ask you to close your eyes and just relax – quietly – with no interference from me. I'll ask you to take deep, deep breaths… the kind that comes from deep inside you. So many people are so tense these days, they spend all their waking hours amidst shallow breathing, not even realizing it. That's why there's so much anxiety and stress in the world. That, and all that damn faster-than-the-speed-of-sound technology."

Dr. Lee realizes he is starting to wander, and snaps back to the task at hand.

"Anyway, Meg, I'm going to ask you to sit very quietly in that chair in the back of the room. Don't make a sound. Breathe quietly. Cough once and you're out. I'm sorry, but that's the way it's got to work. There can be no distractions. You want to record this? Fine. I just don't want to hear any clicks or noises from any taping device."

He turns to Mary.

"From now on Mary, it is just you and me. Do you trust me?"

"Yes," Mary replies without hesitation.

"Good. Because that's the only way this is going to work. You must trust every word I say to you. Can you do that?"

"Yes," Mary again replies without missing a beat. Perhaps it is because Dr. Lee's demeanor is so drastically different from that pompous Dr. Regan that she trusts him so readily.

"Fine. Then let's get this show on the road," Dr. Lee exclaims with a smile. The doctor helps Mary recline on the sofa, giving her a pillow on which to prop her head.

"Just close your eyes and relax," he says.

She feels her tensions and apprehensions circle the drain and disappear until they are soon gone. Mary must have been much more exhausted than she realized, because after only a few silent seconds float by, her breathing begins to decelerate slightly.

Mary knows that Dr. Lee and Meg are in the room but the only sound is the rhythmic ticking of the antique grandfather clock in the corner. The silence continues for several minutes. Her breathing deepens as her thoughts begin to wander into strange corridors.

Why have I come here? Did I make that appointment with the dentist for the girls last month? Did I pick up milk yesterday? We need milk. And Cheerios, too.

"Mary, can you hear me?" a voice calls out. "This is Doctor Lee. We met a little while ago and we spoke about relaxing you so you could remember things. Do you recall that?" His voice is deep and soothing.

Mary nods.

"Good, now I'm going to relax you even more – more than you've ever been relaxed in your entire life – so relaxed that your body will feel as if it is sleeping, but your mind will be listening and hearing and absorbing everything I say."

Again, Mary nods.

"I want you to think of the color red –a bright red shiny apple. You turn it this way and that way and you can see the sun shine on the bright red color. And now I want to you think of lipstick – the reddest, most luscious lipstick you ever saw. It's in a gold tube and you just swizzle it out. Look how red it is – deep, deep, scarlet red – a shimmering, glistening red. Can you see it Mary?"

Again, a nod.

"Now I want you to think of the first crop of red roses that come out in summer. Can you see them, Mary? Can you see the scarlet ones and the deep red ones? You can pick them up and examine them because they have no thorns. Look closely at them Mary. Let the color seep into the corners of your mind. You've never seen such a blood-red hue before. Can you see that, Mary?"

Again, she nods.

"We're going to move on now, Mary. I've just handed you an orange. I want you to look at it closely – this orange is plump and juicy. I want you to feel as if you could dive into the lush orange color. And now it's Halloween. You're in a giant field of pumpkins. The field you are in is awash in bright oranges. The pumpkins are vividly bright orange. Can you see that, Mary?"

"Yes," Mary whispers. Dr. Lee's voice seems to be coming from the sky.

"That's fine. We're moving on to the color yellow. Can you see the bright yellow lemon in front of you, Mary? Pick it up. Look carefully at the color. Squeeze it. Smell its pungency. Now look at the bunch of bananas, also in front of you. See their yellow skins? Touch them. Look carefully at them … they're ripe, not green. They're completely yellow. Next to them is bunch of sunflowers that someone picked just for you. They're bursting with yellow – bright, screaming yellow. Can you see that Mary?"

Again, she nods.

"We're moving into green now, Mary. It's a warm summer day but it doesn't matter because you're cool and

97

comfortable lying on your back on the velvety green grass. You can smell the grass. When you rub your hand across it, it feels like velvet. The green is so vivid it's almost melting like a green candy in your hand. It's a lovely spring day out – sunny and pleasant, but when you look up you can't see the sun. All you can see is the canopy of green elm trees swaying to and fro. They are doing a ballet in the soft wind above you – it's mesmerizing. Green is all around you. Deep green. A green so deep that if you touched it, your hand would come away with a green stain. Can you see that Mary?"

Again, a nod. Mary's breathing now is decidedly deep and slow and pleasant.

"Mary, we're going down the color ladder now. We're stepping into blue. You're walking across a bridge over blue waters. The water is moving slowly over rocks and branches. It is the bluest water you've ever seen in your life. And when you look up – the sky – oh my gosh, the sky – it is the bluest sky you've ever seen! There isn't a cloud in it. It is as if someone laid a blue satin cloth over the entire Earth. Can you see the shiny blue sky above you Mary? It's changing colors from ocean blue to azure to pale blue. But it's always a soothing shade of blue. Touch it, Mary. Touch the blue sky above you."

Mary doesn't realize she has just reached her hand out into the air.

Meg, who is sitting quietly across the room, puts her hand over her mouth to quell her surprised gasp.

"Mary, we're at the lowest level now. Everything around us is lavender. Soothing, relaxing lavender, drifting all around you now. Everywhere you look there is lavender. There are stunning lilac bushes over there. Walk over to them and hold the flowers in your hand. Smell the sweet aroma of lilac. Can you do that Mary?"

Again, a nod.

"Look down – at your feet. The ground is covered in lavender-colored crocuses – thousands and thousands of them, as far as your eye can see. You're standing in the middle of a field of crocuses – all of them are pale lavender. There's no harsh purple crocuses here – only lavender, sweet, sweet lavender. And now everywhere you look you see lilac bushes in full bloom. Their aroma is filling the honeyed air all around you. You feel as if you're in heaven, for surely only heaven could be this wonderful. Do you feel it, Mary?"

A slight smile accompanies Mary's nod this time.

"I'm going to speak to you now, Mary. I'm going to ask you some questions and you are free to answer them if you wish. No one – I repeat – no one can hurt you. There are no consequences to your answers. There are no "wrong" answers. There is only one rule here, Mary. You must tell me the absolute truth. It might be embarrassing, but that's okay, because it's just you and me. And I am your doctor – I cannot repeat anything you say here. Do you understand me, Mary? The only thing I'm trying to do is to help you. You must trust me one hundred percent. I'm going to help you remember things you may have forgotten. Are you comfortable with this rule? You can answer me now, Mary."

"Yes, Dr. Lee," Mary replies in a soft voice, her eyes still closed.

"Good, good," the doctor says, his hands on his knees, his shirt sleeves rolled up as if he is about to get down to serious business.

"Mary, do you remember a long time ago you were in a bad accident? You were hit by a bus. You were in a coma for a time. Do you remember anything from when you were in that coma – anything at all. Don't be afraid that you might sound ridiculous. We all have strange dreams. When the subconscious takes over we really have no control over our rational thoughts – the thoughts we have during our everyday lives. You know, Mary, the doctors said you were clinically dead for two minutes. Where did you go? Do you remember anything – anything at all while you were in that coma? Or when you died?"

The slight smile lighting up Mary's face slowly slides away, and she furrows her eyebrows, trying to think.

A full minute passes before Mary utters her one-word answer.

"No."

If Dr. Lee is disappointed, he doesn't show it. He simply nods in agreement.

"Okay, then. Let's take another tack. You came out of the coma, that much we know for certain. What was the first thing you remember when you came out of the coma?"

"I'm looking down at my hand," Mary says softly. "I can see that body temperature plastic thingy on my finger. The room is an ugly green color, and there's hardly any furniture in it. It stinks of bleach and Comet." Mary speaks deliberately, but in a strange kind of cadence.

Meg, meanwhile, is stretching forward, trying desperately not to miss a syllable while not making a sound. The room is tomb-quiet.

"Did you hear anyone when you came out of your coma? Was your family there, around your bed, Mary?" Dr. Lee asks matter-of-factly.

"No," Mary replies without hesitation. "It's early in the morning, I think. No one is around. So quiet ... so ... so ... quiet. But I can hear footsteps coming down the hall."

Meg is hanging on every word. She is surprised that Mary's voice sounds so "normal."

"Go on," Dr. Lee urges Mary after several seconds of silence. "What else do you see? A person? A nurse? A doctor?"

"No, I see my wrist glowing."

Clearly baffled, Dr. Lee repeats her words back to her. "You see your wrist *glowing*? How is it glowing, Mary?"

"It's like a rope around my wrist, like a bracelet... and connected to it are several different lines of glowing rope. They go from my wrist to underneath my hospital door."

"Tell me more about these ropes, Mary," Dr. Lee prods. "Can you touch them? Can you feel them?"

"No. They're just... *there*. I can see them clearly. I have a bracelet-type of thing around my wrist – it's glowing – and there are about a dozen of them connected to it and they're all going out underneath my hospital room door."

"I'm taking her deeper." Dr. Lee whispers, looking at Meg. "Let's find out what this is all about. I think she is suppressing some pretty important stuff. I've got to dig deeper."

Dr. Lee leans forward, close to Mary's face. "You have these beautiful glowing bracelets, or ropes. Surely someone must have given you something so rare, so lovely. Do you remember who gave it to you, Mary?"

Mary can hear Dr. Lee's question, but feels no urgency to answer him. She leaves Meg and Dr. Lee behind. For a brief second, she thinks she is flying, but quickly relegates that thought to the ridiculous. She knows that physically, at least, she is back in Dr. Lee's living room with the good doctor and Meg – but spiritually she might have well been in Xanadu.

Seamlessly, she transitions from "flying" to strolling happily down a path lined with flowers of every kind – crocuses, tulips, hyacinths, roses, lilacs along with some species she cannot name. The perennial pain in her hip is gone. She finds herself practically skipping down the path. Orange blossoms bloom next to thick evergreens and palm trees. None of it makes any sense, since each species of flowers and trees blooms at different times of the year and in vastly different climates. Mary cares not a whit in the absurdity around her, taking in the spectrum of colors and dizzying array of aromas – sweet and luscious. She feels a bit like Alice in Wonderland or Dorothy arriving in Oz.

"Mary, I'm going to take you deeper now," Dr. Lee says.

Mary hears his voice – it sounds reassuring and far away, yet very close. She finds it easy to trust *The Voice*, and is willing to do anything it commands.

Ten

The Woman

As Mary walks down the great garden path she sees it divide into three distinct directions. Somehow she knows that no matter which path she takes, it will be the *right* one. She strolls down the first narrow pathway, the tall gladioli tickling her hair and the hum of bumblebees settling on sunflowers and bleeding hearts and daisies. Butterflies of every hue perform a ballet in front of her and dragonflies dart here and there, their iridescent wings sparkling in the sunshine.

It is only then that Mary realizes her feet do not touch the ground. She is walking, but her feet are at least two inches off the ground. Looking down in amazement, she can barely remember the sensation of the perpetual pain in her hip – where her body connected with the bus. She feels energized and curious and happy.

"Lose something, dear?" An unfamiliar voice emanates from around the corner. Mary sees an elderly woman, her skin the color of dark coffee. Her snow-white hair is pulled back in a bun. The woman is wearing a faded house dress, covered by an apron with faded blue flowers. She is sitting on the front porch of an old farmhouse. She sways back and forth on a wooden rocking chair that has seen many better days. The woman is surrounded by a frosty pink mist that obscures almost everything around her.

Mary can barely make out the outline of the woman, who is grasping something luminescent in her ancient, wrinkled hands. Mary can't make out what it is, the glow in her weathered fingers is so blinding. But as her eyes adjust to the light, she sees the *glow* travel down the length of the woman's legs and out in every conceivable direction – off to places well beyond the horizon. As her eyes become more focused, Mary is able to discern that the beaming, pulsating glow in the woman's hands isn't solid at all. It is a huge ball of light. Mary looks closer. The *ball* consists of many individual silver strands. She stares at them in wonder, slowly realizing that each strand also owns a secondary color underneath the silver. Every silver strand has its own "identity" – its own secondary shade, each one more brilliant than the one before it. Mary can see now that the woman has knitting needles in her hands, and she is busily weaving the strands from the luminescent ball in her lap.

Mary focuses on one strand that hangs individually down the woman's dress. It drifts over the green hills, past the prismatic, vividly-colored garden and into the distance. It disappears over the horizon, leaving just a hint of a glow in its wake, like a sunset melting beyond the skyline of green hills and valleys.

The woman speaks without taking her eyes off her needlework.

"Ye must have lost something, my dear, otherwise ye wouldn't be here." She throws her head back, wisps of white hair escaping the bun, and cackles in laughter.

It is not the scary-fairy-tale-witch kind of cackle – it is a sound that conflates the tenderness of a grandparent's laugh with the music of a thousand violins. It is soothing and reassuring. Even though wrinkles cover her face, it is blessed with Shirley Temple-like dimples. Her brown eyes are wide and bright. Mary is close enough now to see what the woman's nimble hands are creating from that single ball of light. It is all so confusing. She feels just like Alice after falling down the rabbit hole.

"Where am I?" Mary finally spits out. "Who are you? What's going on here?"

The woman doesn't stop knitting or even look up as she answers Mary.

"You're here – and *here* is a place like no other. Yer going to see things that will make yer heart rejoice in rejuvenation and things that will repulse and devastate you. But ye see this?"

103

On closer inspection, the woman's face is soft and friendly, despite the deep furrows that make it look like a completed jigsaw puzzle. The woman holds up the glowing mass in her crinkled-skin hands so Mary can see it better.

"Looks like a little bonfire, right?"

Mary wrinkles her nose and sniffs to see if she could smell anything burning.

"Go ahead, touch it," the woman urges, a look of sly impishness flowing over her face. "It won't burn ye and it won't bite ye."

A soft snow begins to fall, and Mary feels as if she is standing in the middle of a giant snow-globe. She takes a cautious step forward and looks closely at the glowing neon object the woman holds. As her eyes grow accustomed to the throbbing glow in the woman's hand, she now can clearly see the individual strands in the luminescent object. The pulsating light makes the snow sparkle and dance, like the sunshine the day after a snow storm – the kind of sparkle that puts to shame the diamonds in an upscale jewelry-store window.

The old woman smiles as she watches Mary.

"Go ahead, child. It ain't gonna bite ye." She is still rocking to and fro ever so slightly on her chair, but stops long enough for Mary to examine the glowing globe. "Go 'head, now. Touch it. Ye've earned the right, and there's not too many people who can lay claim to that."

Mary raises her hand cautiously, and places her index finger on the incandescent ball the woman is now cradling in her arms. Mary brings her face nose-close to the glowing silver mass. It is only then that she can see the ball is actually a jumble of hundreds – thousands? – millions? – of individual silver strands.

"Rope?" Mary exclaims, a twinge of disappointment in her voice. "That's all it is – shiny rope?"

The woman leans her head back and lets loose that cackle/sweet violin laugh which emanates from deep in her soul.

"No, dearie. We don't call it *rope*. They are *strands*. *Silver Strands* if you must know. Now look closer at them, Mary. They ain't just rope."

How does she know my name? Mary thinks, bewildered. She blinks several times at the glowing bundle in the woman's lap, the old lady's crooked hands clasping it tightly now.

"Don't be afraid, child, it can't hurt ye. Touch it."

Mary hedges.

"Uh, I'll just watch, if you don't mind. And what the hell is it – or them – or – whatever the *hell* that is?"

"I have been blessed," the woman says in a solemn voice. "I have been chosen to deliver the Silver Strands of Life – your life, my life, the blessed and the wicked."

Mary's head is spinning, trying to make some sense of what this old woman is talking about. That's when she first notices the individuality of the ropes – or the *strands*, as the woman insists on calling them.

"Why, there must be thousands of those.... uh, strands in your hands." Mary exclaims. She realizes she doesn't know the woman's name and abruptly says, in a tone tinged with embarrassment, "Oh, I'm so sorry. My name is Mary. I didn't mean..."

But the woman knows that already, doesn't she?

"I know who ye are, child. I've been waiting for ye. Call me *Momma* or *Mother*. My Spanish dolls call me *Mamacita*, or *Madre*. My Jewish children, they call me *Maven*. Lord, everyone around here calls me something different. Names – labels. What difference does it make? You call me whatever you're comfortable with."

Again, the cackle/violin laughter pierces the air. The sun – or at least Mary guesses it is the sun – is kneeling at the horizon. The silver strands are positively glorious now, against the dimming, yawning light of the fading day.

"Sit here, child," the woman says softly, patting the wooden front porch near her rocking chair. The porch doesn't look sturdy. Its paint is peeling off, and one wooden front step had all but surrendered to the termites and the weather.

Mary carefully makes her way through the brambles, brushes the minion of pine needles off a section of the porch and sits on another old rocking chair next to the woman. The air smells of sweet freshly-cut grass. A soft warm breeze hugs Mary periodically. Mary is still trying to reconcile the warm wind with the falling snow, when the woman speaks again.

"I think ye... ye should call me *Momma*. That seems to fit you."

Mary nods, but says nothing.

"What questions do ye have for me, Mary? I know ye got the questions," the woman asks, staring at her fingers' work. She doesn't look at Mary and continues to knit the silver strands. "Ye came here once before but ye didn't stay. I was sad to see ye leave, but it wasn't yer time. Ye know what I'm talking about, Mary?"

"Yes ... yes," Mary replies without missing a beat, "the time the doctors said I was dead. I came here, didn't I? I know that now. But how come I never remembered any of this before?"

"Ye weren't meant to, Mary," the old woman says. "It is just one of... what do you call them? That wonderful lady wrote about it in her children's book *A Wrinkle in Time*. Thankfully, ye didn't remember any of it."

"Thankfully? Why *thankfully?*" Mary asks sarcastically. "I would have *loved* to remember this!"

"Ye think so now, dear, but ye don't know what I know. And some of the things I know would break your sweet heart." The woman is looking solemnly at Mary, her face a mask of concern and dismay.

Mary looks deep into the old lady's eyes and nearly gasps at the sudden desolation and despair in them.

The woman stops momentarily, heaving a deep, mournful sigh.

"Occasionally, m'dear, these strands, they get tangled up with each other. Could be a good thing, or, maybe not." She looks at the confused expression on Mary's face.

"Child, ye were sent here before your time. And believe me – no matter how much ye think ye've been cheated, ye've

106

been blessed. It's a random scale, ye know – good and evil, darkness and light, hopeless and hopeful. I guess the good Lord decided He didn't want ye to see all the darkness – at least not yet. But somehow or another, ye slipped through the veil and ye got yeself a peek. No sense lying to ye now."

Mary remains silent, waiting for the woman to continue.

"Mary? Mary can you hear me?" It's that distant voice again," faint and even farther away now.

Mary looks at the woman to see if she hears it too.

"Don't care for doctors much myself," the woman says without looking up. "I could always tell when I got sick. Didn't ever need no medicine man to tell me. I knew I had the cancer before any of them high-priced white coats did. Aw, well," the woman says jovially, waving her hand dismissively. "Water under the bridge now. Don't have to worry 'bout that no more. Like I said, ye got a good doctor out there. Most people – ye pull that hypno-tease thing on them and they never get this far. He's good, that one is."

"You're talking about Dr. Lee, right, Momma?" Mary asks in disbelief. She is shocked at how easily she utters the name "Momma" to someone she had never met. But it feels perfectly natural – as if she is speaking to her own mother.

How could this imaginary woman know about a real-live person? Is this a "lucid dream?"

Mary had heard of the phenomenon but thought it was a myth. A lucid dream supposedly is a state in which one is aware that he or she is dreaming.

"I suppose I am, child," Momma answers Mary, "if Dr. Lee is his name. Chinese? No, I'm gettin' that ain't his real name. His real name is Leefeld. His parents must've had it shortened when they came here. It was a different time, ye know – not a good time to be Jewish." Momma is starting to ramble now. "I don't get a lot of people like ye – ye know, that make it past the Silver Gateway with the help of those head doctors. That's why I'm sayin' he must be good."

Momma notices Mary's gaze slip down to her creased, age-spotted hands and smiles.

"Ye want to know about the Silver Strands, right? Well, make sure ye do, because if it's just curiosity that's running ye, ye're making a big mistake, child. These here strands – they look simple, but they hold onto lives. Or, maybe I should say, *lives hang onto them*. Oh bananas! They are what they are!

I'll ask ye once more time. Ye want to know about my Silver Strands?' Lord, listen to me – *my* Silver Strands! I guess I've been holding them so darn long I feel like they're mine. Well, they ain't. I'm just the caretaker. Ye know, the guardian. That's my job, to hold on to the strands and to keep makin' new ones. Babies get born all the time ye know, no stoppin' that!"

Momma takes a breath and releases a chuckle punctuated by a bout of dry coughing.

"Here, child, pick a strand – a string if you're more comfortable with that word." Momma holds the giant bouquet of shining, glowing strands out to Mary. The woman says it with such nonchalance; she could have been a two-bit magician, saying *"Pick a card... any card."*

Mary hesitates. She doesn't know why but for some reason, she feels a cloak of apprehension and fear tossed over her.

Momma sees Mary's expression and rolls her eyes in exasperation.

"Here, child, I'll make it easy for ye. I'm putting *yer* strands on top. That way ye won't be so shocked at what ye see. It may not be all peaches and cream, but at least ye won't bug out. I had an old man here the other day..." Momma realizes she is prattling on again and stops in mid-story. "Well, never mind 'bout that," she says, waving her hands. "Ye ain't gonna have no problem. I can tell ye that. Ye's a tough cookie, ye are. I could tell that the first time I saw ye all those years back."

"Wait... wait... wait... please," Mary says, holding her hand to her forehead. "This is all too much. Can't we start out with the basics? I mean the immediate basics, because I'm sure there's going to be several more layers of 'basics' before we're through here. What the hell are these ropes – or strands – whatever you want to call them?" Mary asks, a pinch of worry coloring her voice.

"It's very simple, child. The day ye were born – the very second ye were born – ye had a Silver Strand wrapped around yer tiny little wrist. Oh Lord. I remember that day... ye came out kicking and screaming like ye couldn't wait for yer life to begin!"

"You were *there* when I was born?" Mary fairly shouts in disbelief.

"Child, I was there for the birthing of every one of these here people," Momma says, briefly holding up the shiny mass of strands. "The good and the bad. I am the connection, the wire, the center. Ye understand?"

"Uh, *no*," Mary exclaims in frustration.

"The strands – the ropes – the wires – whatever you want to call them, they exist for a reason, child. The Good Shepherd does nothing without a purpose. From the moment ye – and they *(holding up the strands in her hand)* are created, yer given the gift of bonding. For every life ye touch, a silver strand attaches itself to that other person. Ye may mean a mother/daughter thing, or husband/wife thing or even that janitor Tom ye always rush by when ye leave the office. Ye all have strands connected to each other, even that Tom fella. Ye are – and always will be – a part of each other's lives. Even beyond death. Lord, look at *me*."

Momma again crows that scratchy laughter. She clears her throat and becomes serious again. Her knitting needles are performing a repetitive, glowing gymnastic act on her lap. She doesn't look at them. She is looking straight at Mary, but even as she speaks, she never stops her work.

"Ye may have a five-minute chat with a stranger at the grocery store, and ye are connected to that person once and ever again. Yer part of their lives and they are part of yers. We touch each person's life for a reason. Of course they don't know it – just like ye didn't know it, child. Ye were snatched from the maws of death all them years ago because ye still have things to do in that, that *space of yer existence.*"

Mary's head is spinning.

"So the whole human race is connected with these silver strands? Is that what's behind all this?" Mary says loudly, incredulously and sarcastically. *This is the secret to life?* She is shocked at the simplicity of the notion.

"Well, someday, in the future, a long, long time from now – everyone will be connected. Let's just say I'm one of a handful of keepers of the strands. Someday there'll only be one keeper – because there'll only be one strand. And oh, what a joyous day!" Momma lifts her eyes upward and Mary can see the glint of a tear in one.

Momma looks at Mary like a teacher who has to teach a lesson to a reluctant student.

"Now do like I told ye, child. Pick a strand."

Mary is shaking slightly as she picks up the glowing strand that lay on top of all the others. She picks the strand – the only one she can see clearly because the light blinds her eyes so. To her surprise, it doesn't even feel like rope – or anything else for that matter. It has the weight of feather. Mary has to look closely to see if she really is holding it.

As she grasps the weightless strand, she feels a slight electric-type of shock making its way through her body so quickly and gently it is nearly imperceptible. Mary examines the strand for several seconds, watching its throbbing illumination like a firefly on a summer evening.

"I'm sorry..." Mary starts to say as she turned to Momma, but the woman is no longer there. Instead, there is a perfect tableau of David and the girls at the dinner table.

"I don't want pizza tonight." Marlee pouts, her arms crossed defiantly. "I want a hot dog!"

"You don't like hot dogs." Cecee scolds her. "You wouldn't even eat the one Daddy bought you at the ball park. Now come on, Marlee, eat your pizza. It's got the pepperoni on it that you like so much."

"Yeah, that's right," Kandee chimes in. *"You just want what you know you can't have."*

Cecee immediately throws water on the growing verbal fire. *"Kandee, mind your own business – and your own pizza."*

Mary watches the scene play out before her eyes, but realizes, inexplicably, that she is merely a spectator – not a participant in her family's mini-drama. Her family cannot see her. That much she knows.

"All right, girls, enough." David is holding down the fort today, not one of his favorite tasks. *"Let's just eat in peace and quiet, okay?"* David says in an annoyed voice.

"Marlee, you love pizza. And besides there's chocolate chip ice cream afterwards, okay?" Cecee goads her.

Mary is amazed watching her girls. She hadn't noticed how *mature* Cecee is becoming, almost overnight. "My girls," is all she can mutter before Momma returns and gently takes the strand away from her.

"There's much more for ye to see, child – when yer ready. Ye don't have to look now. Some people need time to absorb these things."

"No, no. Please. Please, I want to see," Mary begs. "This is amazing. It's like I'm seeing my girls for the first time. Cecee has grown so much. How could I have missed this?"

"We all miss the things that are right in front of our noses," Momma tells her softly. She is leaning in closely to Mary and whispering in her ear now. "That doesn't mean the world don't go on – just 'cause we don't notice it."

"More, please, Momma, let me see more. I had no idea that I am missing so much."

"Well, child, remember, not all yer goin' to see is goin' to be pleasant – that much I gotta warn ye. Some of it will haunt ye all the days of yer existence. There are things that ye might not want to see. Really ugly things. *Evil* things."

111

"I don't care," Mary says, now thoroughly entranced by the power and insight of the Silver Strands. "Please, Momma, please let me see more. I *need* to see more."

"Pick a strand, dearie. Pick this one and then see if you want to go on. Ye seen the good. Ye should see the bad too. It's yer destiny child. It's yer Silver Strand. Ain't no one got one just like yours. All these – the woman held out the weightless load of crocheted strands on her lap – they're all different. Every one of them. Ye will see."

Eleven

Shy and Gentle

Mary picks up the next glowing strand that Momma silently offers her. Its incandescent light flares up unexpectedly like a furnace in February getting its second wind, but it isn't hot. As she looks around, Mary sees that Momma is gone. The porch is gone. Mary is standing in woods so deep, so cavernous, that the leafy canopy above her blots out any remnant of sunshine. Mourning doves chirp in periodic rhythm, piercing the silence. A cool breeze, carrying a hint of lilacs, drifts through her hair.

"Shut the fuck up you little bitch!" a voice bellows in back of her.

Mary is startled not only by the intensity of the scream, but by the viciousness and vulgarity of it. It is followed by the sickening sound of several blunt thumps:

Whack! Whack! Whack!

Faint whimpering follows. Mary can hear – barely – what sounds like the cries of a child. Her first instinct is to cry out, *"Stop that!"* but she wisely says nothing. Instead, she creeps cautiously closer to the commotion.

Nearing the origin of the sounds, she realizes once again that her footsteps make no noise. It is as if she glides inches above the dried oak leaves and skeletal branches that have been shaken off the trees by the endless parade of storms over the years. The forest breeze morphs into a hefty wind, separating the trees' leafy quilt above her. Daylight has faded and now it is dusk. A huge full moon shines down like a spotlight on the ground below. The familiar surroundings are easily recognizable. It is Luna Park.

As Mary inches closer, she can make out the back of a young man standing over a small pink-and-purple lump of clothes. He appears tall and wiry, but muscular, with thick blond hair that is weighted down by sweat and the humidity of the night. Skin on the back of his neck is red and throbbing, while his voice brims with rage, the likes of which Mary has never encountered. He is wielding a huge baseball bat and repeatedly whacks the pink and purple lump.

"Bitch! Bitch! Bitch!" he yells with venom each time he swings the bat.

Mary watches in horror as tiny arms and hands wail in futile defense. The lump of clothes is a child, a little girl, attempting to scream, but the man has stuffed a dirty cloth in her tiny mouth. He squeezes the small round neck with such force, Mary actually thinks she can hear it snap. The child stops fighting, but the man isn't done yet. He resumes his assault with the bat.

Every time the man lifts the bat upwards to attack the tiny body, straight, thick blobs of blond hair vibrate like so many wild and loose violin strings. Mary winces as he brings the bat down again and again; but she can't speak, can't move. She exists as if a ghost, silently haunting this entire volcanic, violent episode.

The little girl is silent and motionless. The man yanks up her pink skirt, pulls off her pink tights and rips off her lacy white panties, tossing them aside. He unbuckled and unzips his pants in a frenzied manner and climbs on top of the little body. He is in control now and he knows it – he deliberately, swiftly rips open the condom package and puts it on.

"He's raping her!" Mary screams – only no words come out. In reflex, she attempts to scurry over to the violent scene, but her legs won't move. Her motions frozen, she looks down at her hand and realizes in horror that there is a Silver Strand of light wrapped around her wrist. It travels over to the man's hand. Mary feels nauseous; she somehow feels connected to this violent madman. She claws at the Silver Strand on her wrist, trying to remove it, but to no avail. It is not made of substance; only the essence of silver neon light.

Mary sees that the Silver Strand on the man's hand has looped around the little girl's tiny wrist. The moonlight shifts and Mary can make out a lavender woolen bow in the little girl's hair. The light shifts again, and Mary recognizes the sweet, pretty face of Tammy Brenner, the little girl who had been murdered in Luna Park – the little girl about whom Meg had written so much. It is the story that had so touched the normally stoic heart of Meg, the hard-nosed reporter. The little girl's large hazel eyes scream out silently in fear.

Why did you do this to me? Why me? Why me?

Violently, ferociously and without mercy, the blond man, his pants down to his knees now, thrusts himself into Tammy's tiny body, pumping her diminutive frame with such force that Mary feels certain the little girl's body will be torn in half. His body spent, he heaves in relief on the little girl.

Miraculously, Tammy is still alive. She is mustering what little strength she has left, trying to cry for help as best she can. It amounts to nothing more than the yelps of a wounded animal. Her cries earn her several savage slaps to her small face, still bloodied and bruised from the previous baseball bat assault.

"Shut up. Shut up. Shut up you little stinking bitch! Why the fuck won't you just fuckin' die already."

The young man with the blond hair is nearly apoplectic that his prey is not dead yet, something he intends to rectify immediately. He pulls his pants up, zippers and buckles them. He then draws a serrated knife out of a leather holster wrapped around his left ankle.

All the while, the Silver Strands are connecting Mary to the young man, and the young man to Tammy. Mary is still trying, vainly, to claw them off of her. They are the consistency of a silvery mist.

Mary is frozen in horror and heartbreak as she gazes at Tammy's beautiful eyes framed by those long lashes, staring lifeless before her now. The little girl's photo had been in the newspaper so many times that she instantly recognized her; she had even met the child on the playground one time, when she went to pick up her own girls.

When Mary first "arrived" in the woods at Luna Park – surely it must have been just an hour or so ago, the sun was just

115

starting to sink below the horizon. But it is dark out now – darker than any other night she can remember, which is odd, since a full luminescent moon is frowning down on them. The night smells of death. Mary can do nothing but watch while feeling helpless and guilty – and very, very afraid of what the young man plans to do next. The man slid the knife out of his ankle holster with a graceful swipe. He held it up to the moonlight for a mille-second, watching as it glints as bright as the silver strand around his wrist. Tammy had long stopped squirming. She is barely alive, of that, Mary is sure. But apparently the young man isn't about to take any chances. In one swift motion, he slices her throat, literally from ear to ear.

Her tiny heart is still pumping blood, creating a scarlet fountain.

The man backs away slightly.

Even though Mary is looking at him from the rear, for some inexplicable reason she is sure he is surveying his handiwork with wonder and pride. The glowing strand that connects Mary and the man and Tammy never breaks – never even stretches through the fury of the attack. Feeling the connection, Mary feels queasy again.

After several horrifying minutes, the blood life drains fully out of Tammy's tiny frame. The man turns around and pulls out a duffel bag. The full moon clearly illuminates his facial features. His clothes are covered in Tammy's blood.

Mary gasps. Underneath the blood and dirt and dead oak leaves that cling to his hair and clothes, Mary recognizes the man. It is her cheery young postman, Robbie – shy, gentle, Robbie Renwood.

Behind the Mask

"I told ye that you wouldn't like everything you see," Momma says. Mary turns around. She is back at the ancient front porch, the elderly woman swaying to and fro again on her rocking chair, still knitting rhythmically.

"That monster! Oh my sweet Jesus. Momma. It was Robbie who killed that little girl? *Robbie?*" Mary exclaims in disbelief. "I talk to him every morning. Dear Lord, I even gave him a Christmas bonus last year!"

"People, they wear masks sometimes, child. We all wear masks sometimes. Thank the sweet Lord Himself that we don't all have that kind of evil to hide. Some people have affairs that their wives or husband never find out about. Some people walk around with a smile on their face and a dark heart of depression or hate all the time. But know this Mary," and the woman stops knitting just long enough to look her in the eye, "Ye'd be surprised at how much we all have to hide. And ye'd be even more surprised at the way we're all connected in one way or another without ever even knowing it. Ye'd best get used to those two things. If ye still want to see what I have to show ye that is. Yer choice. Stay or go. If ye listen hard, you can hear Dr. Lee's voice. He's giving you that choice right now. Do ye want to stay – to see the underbelly of your friends, families, enemies and strangers? Or would ye rather walk around in ignorant bliss? The good Lord, he chose ye for a reason all those years ago... ye died for two minutes... he rewarded you with a gift that ye may never have unwrapped if not for Dr. Lee. And he's asking ye now, 'Continue your journey or awaken?'"

Mary listens. *The Voice* emanates faintly from far in the distance.

"Mary, can you hear me? Are you OK?" Again, defying time and space, Mary knows she is assuring Dr. Lee that she is fine.

"I need to stay, Momma," Mary says, instinctively. "I need to see more."

"It ain't all bad, child," the woman says softly and reassuringly. "There are some mighty fine people out there who live their lives without ever getting any praise – or even acknowledgment for it, whatsoever. Them folks, though, they're getting harder and harder to find. You want to go on? Tell the good doctor. He's waiting for your answer."

Although Mary cannot not hear Dr. Lee she is sure, in that other plane in his cozy Manhattan office, she told Dr. Lee she wanted to continue her hypnotic pilgrimage, no matter the destination.

Twelve

On the Dunes

Mary feels the gritty sand between her toes. The sun is being a coward on this particular day, darting in and out between threatening clouds. Suddenly she feels a cold, wet blanket of blue-gray and white sweep across her feet. The tide is coming in.

She is on a beach with no idea of which one –the Atlantic Ocean, Pacific Ocean – or perhaps the Caribbean? Floating through the air is a distinctive odor of salt water and beach flotsam. Sounds are muted except for the ebb and flow of the ocean, playing a game of tag with the shoreline and the wind, punctuated with the screeching laughter of sea gulls.

"Mary, for goodness sakes will you finally come in now, you've been out there forever!" A familiar voice in back of her rings out like music.

Mary looks down and follows the Silver Strand of light she knows will be wound around her wrist. As she turns, , her hair is gently lifted by the sea breeze and blows in front of her face, completely obscuring her view. It doesn't matter – she readily identifies her father's voice in the distance. He and his wife Kathy are sitting in Adirondack chairs up in the sand dunes; their none-too-sturdy chairs with once-white paint peeling off the ancient wood have seen better days. They wobble from the increasing intensity of undulating gusts of wind.

"Come sit up here with us, Doll," Sam, calls out. Mary watches the silver strands traveling from her wrist to her father and mother – and beyond the dunes. She gasps at the sight of her dead father, who looks tan and strapping and healthy again.

Dad... you're dead, she thinks, words she wants to scream out, but best kept inside; they might be too rude.

119

Mary's head is reeling. She feels a deep shame marching through the wet sand. Her last words with her father were a promise she never intended to keep.

But if her father holds any resentment toward her, he refrains from showing it. He looks happier and more vigorous than ever. When he died, the cancer had whittled him down to a skeletal version of his former self – but looking at him now, that memory seems like just another bad dream.

"Daddy! Mom. Esther." Mary squeals in delight and confusion.

Kathy, her mother, is still very much alive. So how could she be sitting next to her beloved husband, Sam, whom she had buried several years ago? And what about Esther – lovely, loud, exuberant Esther, whom Mary had grown to love as a second mother – and whose funeral Mary had attended? In some strange way, it doesn't matter who is *dead* or *alive* when she looks down at the Silver Strands that connect them all. She is so filled with joy at the sight of her loved ones, the questions and confusion melt away.

Yet, she cannot shake off the blanket of shame over her broken promise to her father that she will have her marriage annulled.

"Daddy, I'm so sorry," Mary says, unable to erase the guilt from her voice, as she marches up the dunes, feeling more grounded with the texture of sand and stubble under her bare feet.

"Daddy, I'm truly sorry. I just couldn't do it." She sits on the sandy mound next to her father and grabs his hand.

"Do what, Doll Face?" her father asks, a bewildered smile sweeping across his tanned face.

Mary looks at him in disbelief. Surely he hasn't forgotten this life-altering request he had made of his daughter on his deathbed.

"Daddy, I love David," Mary says simply, staring into her father's blue eyes.

Wait – blue eyes? Her father has *brown* eyes. Mary is barely done contemplating the contradiction of eye color before her father speaks again.

120

"Yes, I know you do, dearest. When you find a love like that, you treasure it. It's a rare gift. Just like your mother and me." He gently takes Kathy's hand, stretching the Silver Strands that connect all three of them.

Kathy has been nearly schizophrenic about her hair color over the years. Mary was never sure of her natural hair color. One unforgettable time, she dyed her hair red for Christmas then wore a green dress. Mary couldn't help but think that her mother looked like a pimento olive. But today everything about Kathy seemed natural – healthy and natural. Her smiling face framed by short dark hair, and her sun-browned skin making her brown eyes radiant, gleamed at Mary in the sunlight.

Kathy smiles at her daughter with love, and her sparkling white teeth match the glow of her eyes.

Wait –my mother wore dentures – and not good ones at that, Mary recalls, chuckling. With some difficulty, she tries to refocus away from her mother's face and back to the subject at hand.

"Mom? What are you doing *here*? *With Daddy*?" Again, she doesn't want to point out the obvious – that her mother is alive while her father is dead – because it just seems disrespectful and rude.

"Well, where *else* would I be?" Kathy replies, in amazement. "I never stop thinking of your father. He's always with me. You know, as many years as we were married, I never – ever – was attracted to another man other than your father. I'm still not. I find that amazing."

You find that amazing? Mary thinks, but doesn't say it aloud.

Kathy gently squeezes her husband's hand, and they look at each other like two love-sick adolescents. The Silver Strands on their wrists cross and glow so much that Mary puts her hand up to block the glimmer from her eyes.

Mary's guilt-ridden mind still can't let go of her father's deathbed request.

"Daddy, you do know I'm still married to David. Right? I know I promised you I'd get an annulment, but we have a

121

family – the girls – and I love him. I could never leave him. I'm sorry, Daddy."

"Oh that!" Sam exclaims, waving his hand in the air. "Don't give it a second thought, honey. That was when I was – when I was – uh ... let's say.... *uneducated.*" I can see now that David is a good man. And you're lucky to have him."

"But Daddy, you said you couldn't abide having a divorced, Jewish man as a son-in-law," Mary prods in disbelief. "You made me promise…"

"I told you, honey," Sam interrupts, looking down a bit sheepishly at the Silver Strand around his wrist. "That was before I was *educated,* before I realized every door leads to this one room. All our differences… they shouldn't separate us. They should *join* us. We're all going to end up here anyway." He kisses Kathy's hand.

"Well!" Sam slaps his hands on the creaky old wooden arms of his Adirondack chair and stands up and stretches.

Again, Mary is astonished by his sturdy, tanned body which bears no resemblance to the skeletal cancer-ravaged remains his family had buried.

"Of course, I'm biased about you, doll, but I think David's lucky to have you too." And with that, Sam throws his head back and bellows in laughter. He hugs his daughter tight – a big bear hug, his strong arms enveloping her.

Mary doesn't want this moment to end.

"Thanks Sam. Appreciate it," booms a familiar voice from over the dune.

Mary's senses heighten as she becomes aware of the glowing strand traveling up and over the hillside. Her heart skips a beat when she sees David and the girls in the distance playing in the sand.

"Hi Hon!" David shouts to Mary.

Okay, now this is getting too weird, Mary thinks. *The living and the dead exchanging niceties.*

Marlee, Kandee and Cecee, clad in matching pink bathing suits, are pouring ocean water from a pail onto the sand in the desperate hope of constructing a sand castle – or at least something that bears a resemblance to one.

"Mommy!" the girls yell in unison. The glowing strands around their tiny wrists are a jumble of luminescent lights that flicker this way and that as they play.

Mary starts up the dune to talk to David and the girls. She looks down once to get her footing in the shifting sand, and when she lifts her head, they are no longer there.

Poof.

She turns to ask her parents something, but they too are gone. The Adirondack chairs are the only hint that her parents had really been there at all.

"Mary. Mary!"

She didn't need to follow the glowing strand around her wrist to find out who owned that unique voice. It could only belong to Esther, David's mother.

"Mary, my darling, how are you, sweetie?"

She is clothed in a one-piece bathing suit of the most regal shade of purple ever created, and atop her head sits a huge floppy straw-and-lace hat. Enormous, Elizabeth-Taylor-type rhinestone-studded sunglasses left only her nose and mouth uncovered. But it is definitely Esther.

"Sweetie, wait up, you're going to give me a stroke." Esther shouts, flailing her arms, the Silver Strand around her wrist thrashing about in the ocean breeze. Ordinarily, a purple bathing suit on a beach would appear garish, but Esther looks … well, almost *perky*. Not bad for a woman who was past eighty when she died. But now she looks younger, more vigorous; not model territory, but what magazines call *a handsome woman* when they don't want to say *she looks great for her age.* Even her huge rhinestone sunglasses do not seem out of place on this beach.

"Good Lord, honey, don't *do* that to me." Esther shouts in her New York-accent. "You're making me schlep all the way to you? C'mon over here and give me a kiss." As she walks through the slippery sand, her huge straw hat bounces on her head like a giant Yo-yo.

123

Mary had missed the opportunity to say goodbye to her deceased dad – he and her mother had disappeared before her confused mind could wrap itself around seeing the man she had buried years ago. She isn't about to make the same mistake twice.

"Esther. Esther!" Mary nearly crushes Esther as their bodies collide.

"Oh my God, Esther, I missed you so much."

The cumulative effect of seeing her dead father, still-living mother, and now long-deceased mother-in-law finally takes its toll. She hugs Esther long and hard.

This is no illusion, Mary thinks... She can feel Esther's flesh and bones and hair. She can even smell the vanilla note of Esther's "Shalimar" perfume. Mary bursts into tears.

"Oh sweetie, don't cry, I didn't mean to make you cry," Esther says with a mix of amusement and endearment in her voice.

Eventually, Mary surrenders her grasp on Esther. She wants to see her – *to really* see her. Mary takes off Esther's sunglasses to look in her eyes. They no longer are the cataract-cloudy eyes of the old woman who died years ago. Esther's eyes are bright blue, and even on this cloudy beach day, they sparkle with the intensity of tropical waters untouched by the sloppy hand of mankind.

"My lovely." Esther exclaims. When she strokes Mary's face, the glowing strand around her wrist bobs this way and that. "My lovely Mary!" Esther's face is a mix of bemusement and adoration. "I didn't expect to see you, my lovely. This is the best surprise – ever!"

Finally, Mary thinks, *someone who is as confused as I am.*

"Where am I, Esther? Why do these people dart in and out? My father – *my dad* – was just here and now he's gone. I didn't even have a chance to tell him how much I love him and miss him. You've always been straight with me Esther. What's going on here? And I don't even know where *here* is. And these strands of light… they're everywhere. They connect from person to person. What's this all mean?"

"Slow down, dearie," Esther says, putting her sunglasses back on. She takes time to adjust them at *just* the right angle before guiding Mary over to the Adirondack chairs on the dunes.

"Sit. I don't know how long we have. I want to talk to you. You're here now, but you won't be for long. And I don't know how much of this you'll remember when you... well, when you're not here anymore."

Mary sits next to Esther and listens in stunned silence. She grabs her hand and holds it tight. She dares not interrupt with a question for fear that she might topple whatever plane of the universe she might be on now.

"Mary, dear... from the day we're born – maybe even before, I don't know, we are connected to every person we come in contact with. And I do mean *everyone,* dear. I can't emphasize that enough. We're talking about husbands and wives and daughters and sons, but also so much more. Your boss...your gardener...the cashier at the supermarket. Anyone who ever touches our lives – physically or spiritually – we have a connection.

"These," she says, pointing to the glowing strings, "well, you're right. I call them the *Silver Strands.* There's no big secret about it, and yet... the strands are the most important thing we should all know. Every time someone enters your world – in any way, whether it's your new cousin or the garbage guys hauling away your trash, you are connected to them with a Silver Strand. And one day – a long time from now, but some day – all the strands will be connected. And the world will be... oh, how do I say this? *Complete.*"

Mary listens intently, not daring to interrupt.

"You see that's the whole point, my lovely...to finally be connected with everyone else. Do you understand what I'm saying?"

Hesitating, Mary at last breaks her silence.

"I think so, Esther. We're all the same. Right? We're equals. Is that right?"

"Yes," Esther says, bobbing her head cautiously, "but it's so much more than that. You know how your father was so dead-set against you marrying my son – because he's Jewish… and divorced?" Mary is surprised to hear Esther talk about something so personal, so private, in a matter-of-fact tone. She certainly never told Esther about her father's misgivings for fear of hurting her feelings. That left only David… how else would Esther know?

Mary looks down, embarrassed, but Esther is quick to pull her back to the subject at hand.

"My lovely, what I'm saying is. Those things… the things we used to view as '*differences* aren't differences at all. They're connections. It's really very simple. We're all like pieces of a puzzle. We're all different – shape, color, size, you name it – but we're all part of the bigger picture. And one day that puzzle will be solved."

"And you mean heaven, right?" Mary asks bluntly.

"Whoa, wait a minute, my lovely, I never said that. I don't know what heaven is. I'm just telling you everything I know. And I don't know anything about heaven – or hell. Or what you Catholics call Limber."

"Limbo," Mary corrects her, chuckling. "Or purgatory. Same thing."

"Okay, *Limbo*," Esther says, rolling her eyes, and with an impatient smile on her face. "I'm telling you everything I know. And that's all I know, my lovely. But I can tell you this, Mary: You see these two strands here on my wrist? My parents are here – you know the very *Jewish* ones? And guess what? We're closer now than we *ever* were. And not only that, Mary, but guess what? They have a Christmas tree! They say they never realized how pretty and calming all those colored lights are. Can you beat that one?"

Mary puts her hand over her mouth to stifle her laughter – the hand with the strand connected to Esther – and she giggles, closing her eyes for a second. When she opens them, Esther is gone, leaving only the sweet scent of Shalimar in her wake.

Nelson Bitterman

Mary hears the strangest sound – something that seems so out of place on a beach. It sounds like a man weeping. *Oh no... this can't be,* Mary thinks in disbelief. *Now what?* Things she has seen and heard, or felt, in the last few hours – or was it days or weeks – have predicted that nothing is out of bounds. The Silver Strand around her wrist trails off in the direction of the dunes, out of sight.

Mary cranes her neck to get a better idea from where the sound is emanating. She looks up at the highest peak of beach dunes and sees a middle-aged man – dressed improbably in a black Armani suit and exquisite leather shoes – Italian designer shoes she guessed. After all, what else would you wear with Armani? He is sitting on a dune, his face in his hands. Yes, Mary thinks, that definitely is a *weeper*. She can hear him sobbing clearly now.

The dunes are barren, save for patches of dune grass and, inexplicably, a small rose bush which had insinuated itself in the sand. Three blood-red roses are in the first blush of blooming. If he notices the oddity near him, he simply doesn't care. He holds his hands over his face – a handsome face from what she could see – sobbing, deep heaving waves that seem to flow out of his soul. Several times he wipes his eyes, but they are only temporary fixes. The salty tears spring unabated and roll down his rugged, middle-aged cheeks. His thick tuft of salt-and-pepper hair dances in the beach breeze, but he is oblivious to it. He is oblivious to everything except his own spiritual and emotional angst.

As Mary walks laboriously through the slippery sand toward the man, she realizes she is wearing an exquisite, hand-crocheted bohemian lace skirt and matching top with long, billowing sleeves trimmed in baby blue silk ribbon. Underneath is a demure flesh-colored bodysuit that hugs her slight frame. The salty air balloons the lace all around her. She feels as if she is in one of those glamorous perfume or feminine hygiene ads.

127

She shakily makes her way over to the man, her bare feet slipping and sliding in the sand. Even as she gets closer, she realizes he doesn't notice her. She finally gets a clear sight of the man's face. Somehow – she knows not how – she becomes aware that it is Nelson Bitterman, the manager at the sand plant that is making her family's life hell.

Mary feels a rush of indignation come over her.

So this is the jerkoff I've been hating all these months! This is the bastard that's been stealing my husband's time with our family?

He is entirely different from what she had envisioned, this corporate head-slicer whose only goal is lowering the bottom line, and fuck the poor schmucks who slaved there all their lives. When he finally notices Mary, he immediately stands up and wipes his eyes. The oddity of an elegant Armani-suited man sitting in the sand dunes seems to escape him.

"Oh, I'm so sorry, Miss," I didn't see you there," he says, still wiping his eyes and brushing the sand from his expensive trousers. "I came here because I didn't want anyone to see me like this."

Mary eyes him warily. She doesn't know whether to feel sorry for him or slap him.

She cannot not bring herself to say that, *"Yes, I already know who you are, and boy, do I have a thing or two to lay on you."*

He reeks of whiskey, and it is then that Mary finally notices the near-empty bottle of Jim Beam near his feet. She feels the anger draining from her being.

"Uh, are you okay, sir?" Mary asks softly.

"No."

Mary isn't prepared for the monosyllabic answer.

"Is there anything you'd like to talk about?"

He says nothing.

Dressed as they are, an unsuspecting observer might mistake them for indiscreet lovers.

"May I ask you your name?" Mary queries, though she already knows the answer, but believes the question to be a good ice-breaker.

"Nelson Bitterman, Ma'am."

Ma'am? Mary chafes at the matronly title. *How old does he think I am?*

"May I ask your name?" he asks.

"Absolutely," she replies, shocked that there is not a hint of dislike or annoyance in her voice. "My name is Mary. Mary Miller."

"Well, Mary Miller, I think it's safe to say you've seen me at my worst. Would you like to sit down?"

Nelson reaches in back of him and pulls out a baby blue beach blanket; and with a crisp snap, he lays it on the undulating sand dunes.

"Believe me I don't bite," he says, a half-grin working its way across his handsome face. You can call me Nelson or Nel, whatever you like."

Mary doesn't hesitate. The minute she sees the Silver Strand connect her wrist to that of Nelson's, she knows the natural order of things to follow. She and Nelson are connected in some way and curiosity gets the better of her.

"So do you care to share? You're working through some pretty deep problems I'm guessing," she says, eyeing the bottle of Jim Beam. "I have tight lips and open ears. What have you got to lose?"

Mary has utterly forgotten her annoyance at Nelson's interference in her personal life. At this moment, she is more interested in his life. Nelson turns to look directly into Mary's face, only inches away from his now. Their eyes meet and both feel an electrical-like current flow through their bodies, as if someone has plugged an electric cord into a socket – voila, a connection is made.

"I guess I'm just feeling sorry for myself," Nelson says, swiping his thick hair back. "I lost my family two years ago. We were living in New England – ideal spot. Paradise, really," Nelson says without a hint of emotion in his voice. "My wife and two sons were killed by a drunken driver. One day I had the world on a string – the next day I had nothing.

"In the blink of an eye some punk-ass kid who blew too many shots of tequila and ingested too much weed was traveling down the freeway. Head-on. Wanna know the bitch of it? He hardly suffered a scratch. His daddy had bought him a Hummer. My wife was driving a Hyundai. She and the boys didn't stand a chance. It was like a giant – I dunno, like a huge spider squashing three ladybugs. The cops wouldn't even let me see their bodies. Said there wasn't too much left of them to see." Nelson is speaking in a monotone, but Mary hears the undercurrent of devastation and rage bubbling just under the surface.

"Oh, Nelson, I'm so sorry." Mary starts to console him, but he waves her away.

"Appreciate the condolences, but…" his voice trails off. "So my company – I work for South Jersey Sands – it's a sand-mining operation. I don't suppose you know this, but South Jersey has some of the finest, purest sand in the world.

They want to buy up more land down there, but their budget, well, let's just say it's like sands shifting through their fingers, no pun intended. They think I don't know what goes on, but I do. Thousands of dollars a year on hookers, trips to Barbados, a private jet. So what's their answer? Get rid of the hookers? Noooooooooo… they make the guys down here work overtime until blood comes out of their eyeballs. So the guys who can *deliver* stay, while the guys who can't keep up throw in the towel, even at the cost of their pensions.

That's just what they want. They get rid of the higher-salaried people, and hire new ones at minimum wage. Now, I'm talking guys that have been here twenty… thirty years. Pretty shitty way to run a company – I mean, assuming you have scruples, ya know." Nelson is slurring his words, but only slightly.

Mary assumes his love affair with the bottle has been going on steadily for some time.

"Poor guys," he moans. Management doesn't even think of them as *people.* "

Mary doesn't reveal to Nelson that her husband is one of those "poor guys" under the gun.

If Nelson notices the Silver Strand connecting him to her, he is either too blitzed or too self-absorbed to say anything about it.

"I hate what that fucking company is doing to me," Nelson says, a sob interrupting him in mid-sentence. "They're making me into one of their corporate zombies. Oh sweet Jesus, that ain't me! I wanna leave that fucking company, but at fifty-six where do I go? I can't change companies. I don't have a family anymore, but I still got bills." Mary is stumped. There truly was nothing she could say to provide a balm to his desperation.

She gives it her best shot.

"I know, Nelson. I hear your dilemma. Your wife would want you to be happy, I have no doubt of that... and your boys. I didn't know them, but I know a loving family man when I hear one. And you sound like you were blessed – at least for a while. Cherish it."

But Nelson is on a roll now; he doesn't seem to hear Mary.

"You know what those horny greedy bastards told me down at corporate? 'Slice the payroll as close to half as you can.' Do you believe that? What about safety? Don't they give a shit about safety? I know you never saw those big cranes they use, (*Actually, David drives one and she feels a distinct chill run up her back*) but those things – not handled properly, they can kill someone. I'm terrified of cutting back so badly something terrible happens. I couldn't live with that, Mary. I know what it's like to lose the people you love."

Mary isn't sure whether it is emotion or the booze or both, but Nelson puts his hands back over his face and begins to weep again.

She sits close to him, her strand-entwined hand covering his. The two strands touch each briefly.

"Nelson, I don't know you that well – or at all, really, other than our conversation on this beach. I just know you are a good man. Please remember that. You have to do what you have to do to survive. It may not be your choice, but like it or

131

not, you're caught in the middle. You have no blood on your hands, Nelson."

As she looks down she sees the strand on her wrist is thoroughly entangled with the strand on Nelson's. If he sees it at all, he says not a word.

"Thank you Mary. You don't know how much our little talk has meant to me. I try to hold it in – Lord – I can't let the guys at the plant see me like this – it's a sign of weakness. And they jump right on that. You came into my life just like... like an angel."

Me? An angel? Nelson, if you only knew that hours ago I wanted to scratch your eyes out for disrupting my happy home, she thinks, but instead says once again, "You're a good man, Nelson Bitterman. Don't you ever forget that. Your wife and kids know that. Don't ask me why, but I know."

Nelson leans over and gives her a hug – not one of lust, but of affection.

"Wherever you are, wherever you go, you remember you were an angel to a weepy middle-aged man with the beginning of a paunch and a receding hairline. You are lovely – inside and out. God bless you, Mary." As he turns to leave, Mary realizes that the three red roses have opened their petals wide to the shining sun, suddenly blooming with such rich exuberance she can inhale their perfume even though she is several feet away.

Mollie

Mary sits alone on the dunes, her long skirt billowing in the wind.

Nelson had long ago disappeared into one of the many pastel-painted beach cottages that dot the shoreline.

The clouds overhead seem to be planning a rainy coup – complete with thunder and possibly some very nasty hail. Mary has spent enough time at the Jersey shore to know when it is, reluctantly, time to leave the beach and go indoors. This is one of those times. The wind kicks the dry sand in her eyes and the crack of lightening seems to scream, *Better get a move on, lady, we're in no mood to wait for a daydreaming broad.*

She runs as fast as she can in the shifting sands toward the petite, pastel-colored, cookie-cutter cottages. For sure, the pretty, well-kept tiny bungalows had weathered their share of sunny family beach days, as well as a hundred atrocious storms and hurricanes. Their sweet colors – pink, lavender, baby-blue, yellow, sea-green – make the beachside look like a collection of antique dollhouses.

Following her Silver Strand, Mary heads straight for the pink cottage. The glowing strand slithers under the closed gingerbread-adorned door. Though unable to understand *why,* it becomes clear to her that home is her destination. She makes it to the front steps just as the clouds part, surrendering a torrent of rain and hail the size of Ping Pong balls. She thrusts open the front door without knocking, realizing there is no need to announce her arrival.

Her eyes take several seconds to adjust to the changing light. The faded wallpaper was once white with lavender wildflowers wending their way throughout. A plump, yet charming and comfortable, chintz-covered sofa sports frilly decorative pillows embellished with faded pink cabbage roses. The sofa faces a popping and crackling fireplace with a low flame, producing little heat, which seems more cosmetic than utilitarian. A delicate, flowered china tea set is on the coffee

133

table in front of the sofa. Silverware glistens next to crisply-folded white linen napkins. A small lavender-scented votive candle flickers nearby. Taken in simultaneously, it makes for a delightful, cozy invitation.

"I've been waiting for you, Mary. I'm glad you didn't get caught in that storm."

The woman's voice startles her; Mary turns to see a middle-aged, motherly-type woman wiping her hands on a full-length apron. The house smells like homemade sugar cookies.

"Come, sit," says the lady with red hair pulled back in a large braid. Her cherubic, be-freckled face has bright blue eyes.

Where have I seen those eyes before? They look so familiar.

The woman smiles and sits on the sofa. She pats the seat next to her, a silent invitation for Mary to join her.

"I had heard you were coming. We have some things we should talk about."

Muted, Mary stares at her for several seconds.

"I don't bite, honey," the woman says, chuckling. Sure enough, the Silver Strand attached to Mary's wrist that traveled under the cottage door is connected to the woman's wrist, glowing brightly. Mary sits in silence on the well-worn sofa next to the woman. "And you're wondering who in tarnation I am. Right? Well, my name is Mollie."

Mary's expression remains stoic as no recognition registers on her face.

"My last name is Booth."

Mollie Booth. Mollie Booth. Mollie Booth. Mary feels she should know the name, but can't place it.

"I'm Mr. Booth's daughter… you probably know him better as 'Mr. B,' " the woman finally says. "We never met. But I think he mentioned me to you once or twice."

"Oh, yes, yes," Mary says, shaking her head in instant recognition. "I do recall him talking about you. It's a real pleasure to meet you," she says, reaching out her hand to shake the woman's hand – the separate Silver Strands around their two wrists jiggle in the process.

"You know there's a reason you never met me. There's a reason he didn't talk about me very much. I live in England now. In Southwold. That's where we are now."

"What? *Really?*" Mary asks in shock, her mind reeling.

"Yes, I felt the need a long time ago to get as far away from my father as possible. I know you don't want to hear that, Mary, because you're very fond of him. I hear he had become quite the town fixture in New Jersey. I'm glad for him. I have no bitterness toward him. You carry around that bitterness and it eats you alive."

What on Earth is she talking about? Mary wonders.

"I'm sorry, Mollie. I'm not sure I know what you mean. I don't think we're talking about the same man. I'm talking about that sweet old guy who has the produce stand in southern New Jersey. He's a very sweet old guy. I don't think we're talking about the same person."

Mollie smiles demurely, knowingly, as if she could have predicted the answer she receives from Mary.

"Yes, *sweet.*" There is a hint of sarcasm in the last word. "Mary, you have to be aware that people aren't who they seem – or aren't who they *used* to be...." Her voice trails off. "I was only 12 when my mother died."

"Maureen was her name. Right?" Mary asks, suddenly realizing they are, in fact, talking about Mr. B.

"Yes, Maureen was her Christian name, but she was *Mother* to me. My beautiful Mother. Pancreatic cancer – it took her fast and it took her painfully. When she died, my father went half crazy. It was as if he was split in half. Took to drinking – that hard stuff – whiskey. Moonshine if he had to. I just remember him bringing the liquor bottle into his bedroom and locking the door for weeks on end. I tried to get him to eat, to go back to work – just to get out of the darn house – but no. Nothing worked.

"And then one night I was just drifting off to sleep, I remember that real clear... he came in my room and he... lay down on the bed next to me. He stank of the whisky and not washing in a long time. I thought he was going to talk to me about Mother and start crying again. But he didn't. He turned

135

me over, and said – *and I'll never forget this* – "I can't love another woman than your mother. You're the closest thing to her that I have left."

Mary unsuccessfully tries to stifle a gasp before it escapes.

Mr. B? No, I must be hearing this wrong, she thinks, not daring to interrupt Mollie's story.

Mollie is holding onto an old handkerchief, twisting it angrily, and appears enraged as she continues her story.

"He turned me over that night and he touched me. I tried to push him away, but it was my *Daddy*. He was all I had left. He said he loved me, and now that Mother was gone, he could never love another woman. But he still had... needs... and so he figured I could take Mother's place. He said when he looked at me he saw her. That went on for years. When I saw the glow of the light under my bedroom door I knew we were going to 'love Mother.' I never told anyone – and I wouldn't be telling you this now except that Daddy has died. His secret – *our secret* – is out now."

Mollie takes a deep breath.

I left when I was sixteen. Didn't know where I was going or what I was going to do. I just had to get away from him. It's wrong, you know. It's in the Bible. It's a sin."

Mary says nothing. She tries to conceal her shock and disappointment by staring at the Silver Strand that now joins the two women. It is throbbing with luminescence as if the words being spoken out loud are a scab being torn off a deep emotional wound.

"I headed out to California," Mollie says, rolling her eyes. "California – L.A. What a cliché. But at sixteen you don't know your tail from your ponytail. So there I was... did all the things you read about in a bad novel – got hooked on heroin, started whoring around to support my habit. It was a bad time for me."

Mollie turns her back to Mary and stares at her handkerchief for several seconds before continuing. Suddenly she turns around and looks up.

"That man is trying to talk to you," she says. "Can you hear him?"

No sooner had the words left Mollie's lips, than Mary heard a man's voice – faint but instantly recognizable. Dr. Lee. Again.

"Mary? Mary can you hear me?"

The Voice seems to be faint and far away. Mary knows the routine by now. She knows that back in that cozy office, she is reassuring Dr. Lee that she can hear him and wants to continue her journey.

"Go on," Mary urges Mollie. "You've had a rough time, haven't you?

"Well," Mollie says, picking up her story. "I went on like that for a couple of years – drugs and then hooking just to get enough money to pay for a fix. Then L.A. had that serial killer – you know, the one they called the "Our Father" killer because he carved a cross across the victim's forehead. That was the one thing that finally got to me. I was scared.

Got myself into a dirt-poor rehab. Didn't give it much hope though – I loved the 'horse' too much. But I stayed, knowing if I walked out of that place, no matter how bad it was, there was a darn good chance I'd end up slaughtered with a cross carved across my face.

Never caught the bastard – excuse me, the *perpetrator*. I wouldn't be surprised if he's still out there. I finally gave in and phoned my Aunt Barb – that's my daddy's sister – called her from L.A. and told her everything. I thought Daddy would try and find me. Thought by now he'd realized that what he did to me was wrong. But he never came – never even asked about me. He just swept me under the rug like a dirty secret. Never did talk to him again. Now that he's dead and buried, I thought I'd feel – something – but I don't. He was my daddy and I loved him, but he did me wrong.

"I had to move halfway around the world to escape his shadow," Mollie says softly, her voice cracking. "Maybe I should not have forgiven him, you know. The people in rehab said 'no' – they said 'take your power back, confront him.' I

137

know what he did was wrong – but he did it out of a perverted love for my mother. He couldn't take another woman to bed – and in his head I was the closest thing to her."

"Mollie, I'm so sorry," Mary says after several seconds of awkward silence. "I didn't know. He was always so sweet. The people of the town loved him."

Mollie nods her head, knowingly.

"Yes, I heard that. After a while, I stopped hoping he would reach out to me. He had made a new life for himself. And I made a new life for myself. I got married to a wonderful man and raised two good girls. I gave up on my father a long time ago. He just didn't know how to deal with Mother's death. Turns out he dealt with it in the worst way possible. But I've forgiven him."

Mr. B's death – and secret past life – makes Mary question everything she has thought about people and their sense of morality. She and Mollie enjoy the tea-and-chat ritual, mostly focusing on their mutual love of the beach.

"You've had a long day, dearie," Mollie says after a while. "Put your head back and close your eyes."

Mary doesn't protest at all. She is surprised at how incredibly weary she suddenly feels, as if she has been swimming all day. She drinks the last of her tea, puts her head back on the sofa, listens to the crackling of the fireplace and almost immediately nods off.

Thirteen

Carol and Bob

Mary rouses from her sleep, opening her eyes cautiously and trying to absorb everything around her. The luminescent Silver Strand, as usual, is the first thing to catch her eye. The strand is loosely draped around her petite wrist, almost in danger of slipping off – if it had been made of substance, that is. No longer is she in Mollie's parlor but in a large, well-appointed house. Her surroundings, the furniture and décor, all look vaguely familiar, as if she has been here before.

"I told you to shut the fuck up!" a deep meaty voice bellows from the other room. The voice drips with disdain and malice.

She hears the distinct sound of *whack!* – skin-meeting-skin – in a most violent fashion. The Silver Strand of light around her wrist yanks a bit, but didn't move her arm.

Where I am? Mary wonders. *I know this house. Of course!* She nearly shouts. It is Bob and Carol Warren's home.

In front of the unlit fireplace, is a rich leather sofa with velvet-and-brocade armchairs. The mantle above the fireplace bears a cavalcade of photographs, all elegantly framed in porcelain and silver. Each photo features the polished, gleaming-white-teeth-smiles of Carol, her husband Bob and two stunningly beautiful, teenage girls: pretty fair-haired Kelli, wearing her cheerleader uniform and caught by the camera in mid-jump; and Tiffani, dazzling in a midnight-blue sequined prom gown. The rest of the photos showcase the girls' other talents: tennis, soccer, and an award for some charity event.

Mary had first met Bob and the girls a couple of years ago, when she had to drop the work papers off at Carol's home. Bob had sat, sullen in the living room, in front of the television, watching a baseball game, gripping a Heineken bottle in his

139

hand. He barely eked out a grin and a forced "hey," when Carol introduced them. The girls, on the other hand, were poised and confident, like their mother. They had grabbed Mary's hand with a healthy vigorous shake, clearly inheriting their sterling social skills from their mother. Mary only stayed a minute, and really didn't have a chance to drink in all the features of the lovely three-tiered house.

As Mary slowly scans the room now, she begins to absorb the sleek lines of Carol's gorgeous home. She is sitting on the leather couch, her bottom dipping deeply into the padding of the plump cushion. Suddenly feeling like an intruder rather than a guest, Mary feels embarrassed – like a voyeur or eavesdropper, or worse yet – a burglar. She can hear voices emanating from what she guesses is Bob's den.

"I've had it with you, you lazy bastard!"

Mary recognizes the voice as Carol's, although she had never heard her use those words or that tone. She is used to Carol's efficient, soft-spoken and articulate voice.

"I'm tired of carrying the load around here while you fuck around with silly gadgets and tell everyone you're an entrepreneur – an inventor. Bullshit. You're like a kid playing with video games. Get a real job or get the fuck out! Even the girls are embarrassed by you."

"You know what your problem is, you bitch?" comes the reply, in a slurred, masculine voice. "You think small. You can't understand the mind of a genius. How do you think the light bulb was invented – the phone? That top-of-the-line car you're so fond of driving? You think they just *appeared* one day? Hell no! It takes deep thinkers like me – people who don't give up after each little setback. You could never get that, you dumb bitch! You sit at your little nine-to-five secretarial job and think that place can't survive without you. Well I got news for you, doll, you're very replaceable. You go and they'll replace you with a high-school kid before the day is over. You're anything but *unique*. You people are a dime a dozen. And guess what? The same goes for around here." It is unmistakably Bob's voice, and it is beginning to ascend to an ominous tone of rage.

140

Carol walks into the living room. Mary sees a nasty bruise forming under her left eye. The Silver Strands between the two women – also connected to Bob – are the only things that remind Mary that she shouldn't be there, eavesdropping on a very private moment between a husband and wife. Then she realizes they cannot see her.

Well, this is a new one, Mary thinks.

Carol and Bob continue their verbal fisticuffs.

"I'm done. I can't do this anymore. I want you out of here – *now*! I know it will break the girls' hearts, but I'm *through*!" Carol screams, wiping away tears from her puffy eyes. The sight of the petite Carol standing up to the bear-of-a-man, Bob, borders on the ridiculous.

"Oh, listen to her," Bob says in a voice dripping with sarcasm like honey that had gone bad. "You'd think she doesn't have anything... well, look around, doll. You have everything you ever wanted. And don't fool yourself, doll, you need *me*. I'm one of the most important props in your world. Remember? You have your two beautiful girls and you're *'happily married.'*" Isn't that what you tell everyone? Isn't that the picture you paint for your snotty friends?"

"*Enough!*" Carol shouts back.

Bob looks at her with a face that resembles a thermometer on a broiling August afternoon; the red flush of fresh rage rises from his neck to his forehead.

For a flicker of a second, Mary is certain he is going to strike Carol. In horror, she knows that since she isn't really in the room, there isn't a damn thing she could do to protect Carol if it came down to that.

Carol had tried to keep the tattered remnants of her marriage together, not only for the sake of the girls, but to preserve the image she had carefully crafted for the rest of the world. As she plops on the sofa now, she realizes with renewed clarity that she has been trading in her dignity and happiness – indeed her very sense of safety and peace – to maintain this pretense to the outside world. Carol sits stone-faced on the sofa. Bob is continuing his nasty, drunken tirade, slurring his words and occasionally spitting in Carol's face.

Oh tell him to fuck off! Mary says silently, which is all she can do right now. *He's just dragging you and the girls down.*

Carol may not have been able to hear Mary's words of encouragement, but she follows them just the same.

"We're over. Done!" she shouts at Bob, who clenches his fists and does an about-face.

"Fine. Go. Get the fuck outta here. I'm not leaving. I'm staying right here. Let's see how long you last by yourself. Go. Now!"

Bob's face is glowing with rage, but Mary is looking at the Silver Strand connecting her wrist to Bob's in disgust.

"My sister Laure will be happy to take me and the girls in for tonight. Truth be told, she always knew there was something violent about you, Bob. She downright asked me one time if you ever hit me, and I lied. But no more. And *I'm* not leaving Bob – *you* are. Just try and get a judge to award you custody of the girls and give you this house. We all know about your – oh, what should we call them? – *enterprises*? How many people did you suck dry, Bob? Oh, no, I won't have any shortage of character witnesses willing to testify about your shady business tactics!"

Mercifully, the girls are spending the night at a friend's house. Mary is unaware of how she knows this, but she does.

"Good! Three bitches. You bitches are all the same. The three of you. You turned those girls against me with all your poisonous talk." With that, Bob grabs his keys and slams the door so hard the walls shake in his wake.

Carol collapses in a heap on the sofa, mourning the death of a marriage she had tried too hard and for too long to pretend was ideal, but in reality was a paper moon.

Mary yearned to tell her: *Don't worry, Carol... you're doing the right thing. Don't tell me the girls haven't noticed how he treats you. You'll all be better off without this.*

Carol lay on the sofa for nearly twenty minutes, until her weeping finally dissipates. Mary thinks of that old saying "all cried out." She wants desperately to put her arms around her friend and hold her close, telling her everything will be all right. But all she can do is watch in dismay.

Grandpa

How many minutes – or hours – have passed before Mary realizes she no longer is in Carol's house? She looks around, and the elegant house that belongs to Carol and Bob is gone. Instead, she is standing in horse manure and hay. She looks around her and realizes she is in an ancient barn. The roof is held together with so many wood planks nailed down like rough hued Band Aids, the glaring sunshine easily pierces its way through the ceiling slats to where Mary stands below. The barn smells pungent – sickening, with an abundance of horse manure on the ground and floating feathers of hay dancing cartwheels in the filtered sunbeams. She sees the Silver Strand on her hand, but before her eyes can locate its destination, she hears a farm vehicle spewing gravel coming from behind her.

"Don't smell so sweet now, does it, pumpkin? I mean it's not the way you remember it, is it? Memories have a way of changing over time."

Mary turns around.

"Grandpa Joe! Grandpa Joe! "Mary bursts into tears at the sight of her long-deceased paternal grandfather. He had been the patriarch of the family until the day he died – and even then his legacy lived on. He owned a huge farm in rural Pennsylvania, and Mary and her cousins would often spend long lazy summer weekends dashing through the cornfields or riding behind their grandfather on his huge John Deere tractor.

Joe Mariucci had one of those rare faces that always seemed to have a secret smile lurking in the background, ready to burst through. His huge brown eyes were a show-stopper for females, but it was that perpetually sly hint of a smile that was the real enticement. His body was chiseled with the undulating muscles that are the result of laborious farms chores. But – and Mary was quite sure of this – he would never be unfaithful to his Abigail. Abigail was his soul mate in every sense of the word. When she died, he was only fifty-two. His Marlboro-Man good looks were an easy magnet for older women –

143

widows mostly. But he never remarried because he knew no woman could replace her. Theirs was a true love story.

"Grandpa Joe!" Mary yelps again in joy.

Joe's smile beams at the sight of his beloved granddaughter.

She latches onto him, feeling the brass buttons from his overalls digging into her flesh and she, not caring a whit.

"Grandpa... I missed you so much. It wasn't even a family after you left... we just all went our separate ways."

"Well, my pumpkin, that's what, happens. Families – even close families – have a tendency to scatter to the wind like milkweeds. But they take up root and build their own garden. Just like you did, pumpkin."

Mary is in heaven – figuratively speaking. She had often dreamed of her Grandfather Joe holding her once again – his warm, protective arms keeping the dragons and witches and the hobgoblins away.

"We all missed you so much, Grandpa." Mary is trying to keep the conversation flowing so that this image of her cherished grandfather dare not turn out to be a dream or hallucination. So overcome is she at the sight of her grandfather, Mary does not even wonder why he can see her when Carol and Bob could not.

Mary was fourteen when Grandpa Joe died. Even now, decades later, she can recall the day vividly. She had come home from school and saw a slew of automobiles lining both sides of the street near her house. Her stomach sank. She instinctively knew, even at her young age, that something dreadful had happened. Something that was about to change her life forever.

When she walked through the front door, she could hear both loud sobbing and muffled whispering. Relatives and strange people filled her house. Mary's mother Kathy sat demurely on the sofa, wearing a brand-new terrycloth housecoat and satin slippers. Her sister Alice had her arms around her, and she was doing her fair share of shedding tears. Kathy was crying quietly into a hand-embroidered handkerchief. Looking up, she saw her daughter through red-swollen eyes.

"Mary," she whispered. "Mary, come here."

Alice scooted over to make way for her niece.

"Mary, Grandpa Joe is dead. He died of a massive heart attack while he was out in the fields today."

Mary burst into tears, while her mother held her gently. "He's with the Lord, baby. He's gone home. He's at peace."

That's not what Mary wanted to hear. She didn't want him to "go home." She wanted him right here, sitting at the head of the Sunday table as he did every week, overseeing both the consumption of food *("Mary, eat your salad!")* and political conversation *("I don't give a hoot what those damn liberal Democrats say – you can't trust a one!")* Mary was devastated that she did not have the chance to kiss her beloved grandfather goodbye.

Sam, who along with his older brothers, Sal and Frank, worshipped their father, was distraught. This was the first time Mary had ever seen her father cry. It was a shocking scene to her. Sam sat alone in a huge armchair, a plate of untouched food perched on his lap. Though he kept his eyes lowered, Mary could still see the tears drip down onto his potato salad. It wasn't long before he was joined by his brothers. Mary decided not to bother him just then; she knew this was a special time just for Joe's sons.

Mary thought often of her Grandpa Joe over the years; he symbolized to her all that was good and decent about a family man. She admired his moral compass and missed him terribly.

But here she is – holding on to her precious grandfather once again.

"Dear God, please don't make him disappear," Mary prays silently as she hugs the elderly man hard. Grandpa Joe takes Mary by the hand and guides her over to the neatly-stacked bales of hay. They sit down.

"Let me look at you," he says, holding her at arm's length. "So beautiful – my beautiful Mary."

Mary blushes at the compliment. She wonders if her grandfather is seeing her at age fourteen or as a woman.

"You know there's a reason you're here to see me," Grandpa Joe says slowly. "In your mind, you idolized me all these years as if I were the perfect man. I wasn't. I'm not," he says, softly, dipping his head down to look deep into her eyes.

"Grandpa, stop it. You were what every man should be. Lord, the world would be a happier place if more were like you. You always put family first. You loved your wife and were faithful to her all those years. Oh my Lord, the way you stayed by her side at the end, it was magical to see."

"Mary," Grandpa Joe stands up now, his well-worn overalls showing a patch here and a hole there. "That's the thing, Mary. You must realize your worship of me isn't real. The truth is, pumpkin, no one can live up to the kind of man you've built up in your mind. He doesn't exist. See, we're human. And humans, by nature, are flawed." He glances at Mary to make sure she is still listening to him.

"I'm not the perfect man you think I am," he repeats, scratching his forehead, causing the Silver Strand connecting him and Mary to quiver. "My Abigail... My Abby... my sweet Abby..." His voice begins to crack. "I betrayed her. I lay with another woman, Mary. I did your grandmother great harm and heartbreak. Why she stayed with me, I'll never know. I just thank the Lord that she did."

Mary listens in silent astonishment – trying to picture her straight-laced, God-fearing family-man of a grandfather carrying out an extramarital affair. His words now are like bullets, each one piercing the saintly image of him which she has retained for so many years.

"It's best you know, Mary," Joe says. "No one is perfect. I was forty-five or forty-six. Now don't get me wrong. I wasn't looking for anything. I was so in love with your grandmother. She was the world to me. And you kids... well, you were just kids. You had your own life, going on 4-H meetings, Girl Scouts. All that stuff. Abby, she was busy with her Women's Club and Gardening Club. Well, after a while, it started to get – well, *boring*. I mean it was just the same old routine day in and day out. Work the fields, come home, eat dinner, watch TV and then bed.

146

"That's when I met her – her name was Betsy and she worked as a cashier for the local feed store." Grandpa Joe stops to collect himself and to make sure Mary is absorbing the words. "We met one day when I had to buy some feed and seed. We liked talking to each other. We never ran out of things to say to each other. I knew I didn't love her – not the way I loved my Abby," Joe adds quickly. "But I had a definite affection for Betsy. I guess I was young enough back then to call it 'chemistry.' I'd tell your grandmother I was going to the Grange meetings, but each week I'd meet Betsy down at the Pink Cloud Motel. Sometimes right here in this barn."

Mary feels a cold chill travel up her back.

"It lasted a year and then some before your grandma found out. I should have known I couldn't keep it a secret forever, the way women talk and all. I think some old crow told her in the beauty parlor. Your grandmother, well, she just held her head up high and didn't utter a word. She came home and cornered me with the rumor.

"Is it true?" she asked me. "She just blurted out those words… nothing more. I knew exactly what she was talking about, and I loved her too much to lie to her anymore. I just said, 'yes.' Worst day of my life. I broke her heart. I was terrified she was going to leave me. And I wouldn't have blamed her one bit if she did. I guess it was that old cliché – a midlife crisis. "Your grandmother just asked me one other question: 'Do you love her?'"

"Well that was easy enough to answer. 'No, absolutely not,' I said. 'It's over – on my life. I'm so sorry I hurt you, my love and the only thing I can promise is never, never again. Please don't leave me. I'll die without you.'

"I begged her. I knew I would die without her. I really would have. It's amazing when you're young… the precious things you have that you take for granted. Your grandmother, God bless her soul, forgave me, and we never spoke of it again."

Mary listens in disbelief for several seconds. Finally she asks with a voice tinged in anger, "Why are you telling me this *now*, Grandpa? Why is it so damn important that I know this *now*? I could have gone my entire life without knowing that." She didn't realize her voice was heavy with disgust.

"Because you have to stop worshipping at the altar of perfection, pumpkin," her grandfather replies. "It's time you realize that human beings – by their very essence –are flawed entities. You don't stop loving someone because they're flawed. You just *love* them – flaws and all. That, my dear, is true love – not the flowers, not the candy, not the dinners out. It's the willingness to forgive that makes true love. If you can love someone enough to forgive a hurt like that... well, that's the real deal. And then let it go. You can't bring it out like a weapon each time you fight. That's true love, pumpkin. Your grandmother, God bless her soul, she knew that."

Fourteen

Aqua Girl and Pink Girl

Mary feels like ginger ale is bubbling in her head. For a second she is downright dizzy. She finds herself sitting astride a carousel horse – a wooden equine frozen in mid-gallop. It is swaying up and down in rhythm to sing-song calliope music. The horse with its purple paint is impossibly gaudy but yet bewitching to children, adorned with huge faux rubies, sapphires and other glass gems which are supposed to pass as diamonds. Its mouth is open in an oddly realistic shape, as if trying to get his breath, as he marches along the English moors. The bridle surrounding the horse's head is also studded with jewels of every shape and color – all fake, of course, but that doesn't dampen the glitter and glow of the tableau.

How on Earth did I get here? Mary thinks. She had so been enjoying her visit with Grandpa Joe.

No one else is on the ride, as far as Mary can see, but she has learned to look down at her wrist when she comes out of her *trance* so she will know her destination. The glowing Silver Strands never fail to tell her where she is and who she is about to meet.

The shrill music continues, but at a soothing pace. She climbs off the wooden horse and walks between the other wooden equines. They all are painted magnificent, if not implausible, colors – azure, sunflower yellow, cherry red, cotton-candy pink. All are aglitter with the same fake gems that sparkle on her purple horse. They are caught in mid-gallop, the frozen legs, "marching" in an endless circle.

Mary follows the glowing strand around her wrist as it snakes around the frozen, garish menagerie. She wends her way through the carnival setting to the other side then steps cautiously off the metal rim of the ride's base, which continues

149

its slow, rhythmic rotation. She can easily see that she had indeed, been on a child's merry-go-round.

Seemingly out of nowhere, a little girl about seven or eight-years-old appears. She is wearing an aqua rain slicker covered with white polka dots and holding a matching umbrella, hat and boots. The outfit really stumps Mary, since it is a brilliantly sunny day.

"Hello," the little girl says softly and shyly, but without a hint of fear.

She was expecting me, Mary thinks, but merely replies, "Well hello there. Who are *you*?"

The child's silky hair is lemon-bright and very straight, although with her rain hat on, Mary can only see the thick bangs that frame a most incredible set of round, unwavering blue eyes.

Aqua Girl gazes intently at Mary for several seconds before she finally utters a few words in a barely-audible voice that sounds like the soft breeze that sweeps a summer beach.

"I wanted to say thank you. They told me you would be here. And so I wanted to come and say thank you."

Perplexed but amused at the serious tone of this little girl's voice, Mary is about to ask her who *they* are when another little girl – also dressed for rain and holding an umbrella, appears. Similar to her companion, she also has blond hair and huge blue eyes, but appears to be a tad younger. She wears a bright Pepto Bismol-pink rain slicker, with matching hat, boots and umbrella. No polka dots, though; her outfit is sprinkled with pictures of Dora the Explorer. The Silver Strands connect the girls and Mary.

"They told me, too," Pink Girl says. "I want to tell you 'thank you' too."

Mary stares at the two pretty girls in astonishment and bewilderment for several seconds. She immediately notices she is connected to the girls by the Silver Strands.

"Where are your mommies?" Mary finally spits out.

The two girls exchange cryptic glances. Pink Girl at last decides to enlighten her.

"We have the same mommy. We're sisters. Mommy's home baking cookies with our big sister."

Now that they are standing side-by-side, Mary sees the resemblance between the two girls – both blond, both blue-eyed.

Okay, Mary thinks: *Can there be any more of a ridiculous answer? All right, I'll play along.*

"And why do you feel the need to tell me 'thank you?' " she asks the girls.

Again, the girls exchanged curious glances.

"You saved us," Pink Girl says stoically. "We're alive because of you."

If the girls' appearance perplexes Mary, their answer stuns her.

"I *saved* you?" she repeated. "And tell me – how did I *save* you?"

Aqua Girl says, "We were at the county fair. You were there with your little girl. We were all waiting to ride the merry-go-round. We were in line." Aqua Girl waits for some recognition to her words.

But Mary is as confused as ever. She remains silent.

"The merry-go-round had already started," Pink Girl adds in her child-voice. "They had started up the ride to show us how pretty it was. That's why we all wanted to ride it." The girls exchanged glances and giggles. It is the laugh of the innocent.

Mary, meanwhile, is still drawing a blank.

"I'm sorry, girls, I don't know what you're talking about." She is bemused by the childlike expression of exasperation that had by now washed over their baby-doll faces. Aqua Girl sighs, a bit impatiently, and continues her story.

"You were here with your little girl – her name is Cecee. I remember that name because I never heard it before. It's pretty."

The girls have Mary's full attention now.

"We were waiting in line," Aqua Girl says, "when that big thunderstorm touched down. Later on they called it a (and here she deliberately slows down to try and pronounce the word correctly) "de-rech-o."

Duh! Of course. The derecho – that odd weather phenomenon of damaging storms, rain and wind that appeared out of nowhere one broiling summer and slammed into the southern New Jersey area.

When Cecee was a toddler Mary took her to the County Fair. The glitter and shine of the children's merry-go-round had caught Cecee's eye and she was determined to ride it, no matter how long the line was.

Marlee and Kandee hadn't arrived on the scene yet, so this was a special mom-and-daughter outing for Mary and Cecee.

It was a Saturday afternoon, in early summer – the blast of heat and humidity had already set in making everyone uncomfortable. When Mary and Cecee left the house the weatherman had called for a "chance of showers," but the sun was blaring down through occasional clouds. Mary decided to chance it. Besides the idea of being cooped up in their small apartment with a cranky toddler all day didn't appeal to her a bit.

Glancing upward to the graying sky as they stood in the merry-go-round line, Mary thought, *Oh no, I hope those showers hold out.* But it was too late.

An eardrum-shattering clap of thunder pierced the cries of happy children and the merry-go-round's calliope cheery music. The summer breeze had morphed into a full-blown storm with a sudden fury that sounded nothing short of demonic. Rain poured down like water flowing from the Hoover Dam. People scattered everywhere. Panicky adults grabbed their children's sticky-fingered, cotton-candy-covered hands and ran to whatever shelter they could find. Cecee burst into frightened tears. The whirlwind – the weathermen later called it the rare *derecho* – headed straight for the fairgrounds.

Mary grabbed Cecee and sat her down under the only canopy at the fairgrounds. Everyone was scrunched under the canopy in a desperate effort to stay at least slightly dry. That was when Mary noticed the two little girls standing on the merry-go-round – only now did she remember their sweet

152

faces. They were Aqua Girl and Pink Girl, although then they sported only pastel sundresses. They looked terrified and confused, crying and desperately trying to find their parents through the blinding downpour. The merry-go-round had stopped, but was shaking from the force of the tornado-like winds.

The claps of thunder continued to pound the fairgrounds with frightening regularity – almost in cadence. The two girls huddled together on the merry-go-round, terrified of making a move. Mary could see one end of the merry-go-round actually being lifted off the ground, the thunderous wind like a demonic hand, pulling it up. Without thinking, Mary turned to Cecee and shouted, "Stay right here!"

A kindly female stranger grabbed Cecee's hand and tried to comfort her. Mary ran out in the downpour, slipping and sliding in the mud, and grabbed both girls with one swoop. She ran back to the canopy and dropped the girls off where strangers comforted them.

An earth-shattering clap of thunder reverberated through the canopy and beyond mere seconds before a deadly sliver of lightening impaled the ground where the girls had been standing only minutes before, leaving a large black scorched stain. One side of the merry-go-round was scattered in pieces like Lincoln Logs.

The next hour was filled with desperate screams and chaos as parents tried to find their children. Mary did not see the two girls again. She assumed they had been claimed by their parents. In any case, they were safe, so she didn't give them a second thought, turning her attention back to Cecee. Fortunately, there were no serious causalities that day.

And now here the two girls she had rescued stood before her. Mary was sure they were the same children.

"What are your names?" Mary asks, bending over to match their height.

"That doesn't really matter," Aqua Girl answers solemnly. "You didn't know our names back then either."

"Well, perhaps I can ask why you're all dressed up for rain. There's not a cloud in the sky," Mary says as she places her palm out and looks up at the Earth's blue ceiling.

"Well," says Pink Girl, "you can never be too sure, can you? Remember they said it wasn't going to rain that day either."

Mary tries to hide the smile on her face, trying desperately to treat these two little imps like adults so as not to offend them.

"Well, you're certainly right there, sweetie. You can never be too sure."

The two girls simultaneously put their umbrellas down – almost as if it had been a planned synchronized move – and hug Mary with their tiny arms.

"Thank you," they utter in unison. "We waited a long time for this," Pink Girl says with all the sophistication of a lady. And with that, the girls march away, leaving Mary with a feeling of awe, delight and confusion.

Mary follows the girls with her eyes as they skip, hand-in-hand, out of sight.

Time is a blur. She can hear *The Voice*, once again checking on her.

Are you okay, Mary?

Mary knows that back in Dr. Lee's office she is nodding her head.

Fifteen

Father Neeley

St. Lucy's, an old gothic Roman Catholic Church, is a gorgeous edifice constructed by her ancestors from the Old County. Its builders were true Italian masons who didn't just *build* a church; their rare craft displays a solemn and magnificent monument of gratitude to God for bringing them safely to this new land of opportunity. Mary is sitting in a back pew at this neighborhood church.

The church is nearly empty save for one man in the front row. Red votive candles flicker throughout the front of the church. The glorious stained glass windows depict Jesus and the Virgin Mary along with various saints and angels – true old-world artistry throughout. The sunlight outside splits the stained glass light into brilliant floating prisms that dance on the walls. Visitors and parishioners alike are cloaked in that distinct *church smell* of incense and burning wax. The air seems thick with the reverent silence and holiness that one can only find in these old cathedral churches.

Mary isn't sure if she should kneel, the usual gesture of Catholics for being in the *"House of God,"* as the nuns call it. She hasn't been to church in years. Before she can move one way or another, Mary hears a soft muffled sound in the distance. She cranes her neck to find the source. A Silver Strand winds its way around her wrist and up to the front of the church, out of Mary's view.

Several seconds pass before she realizes the noise is coming from a young man in the front row. She hadn't been able to get a good look at him when she first arrived at church; the massive marble pillars standing sentinel in the church building had blocked her view. She begins to realize her Silver Strand must be connected to this man.

155

She walks quietly, stealthily as her Catholic upbringing forbade her from making any sound in church, up to the pew behind where the man is kneeling.

She pauses a moment, studying him from the side. He is wearing a pale blue Polo shirt and, from what she can see from her angle, Dockers trousers. His watch looks suspiciously like a Rolex.

Dockers and a Rolex? What an odd combination.

She can only see him from a side angle, so his thick crop of raven-black hair is his only outstanding feature – that and his extraordinarily broad shoulders. He is holding his face in his hands – and Mary realizes it is the sound of his soft sobbing that had caught her attention. She feels trapped – what to do? Did he see her? Should she quietly slip away and allow this poor soul to have his privacy? Should she approach him and ask if he is all right?

Too late!

Lifting his head to wipe away the tears, he spots Mary in his peripheral vision. Taking in the handsome young face literally causes Mary to gasp. His black hair is a wonderful, clashing contrast to his tear-filled, but still striking turquoise-blue eyes. He looks to be about twenty years old. A student from the nearby community college, Mary guesses.

Oh, the angst one feels at twenty years old when you get a bad grade or worse, get a girl pregnant.

Either way, Mary averts her eyes quickly; it really is none of her business – although the Silver Strand that connects them contradicts her.

"Mary? Mary Miller?" The man looks surprised when he turns around and sees her.

She looks at the man's handsome face, covered in tears. Slowly the recognition seeps into her consciousness. He is using her maiden name.

"Oh Christ! Father Neeley." The words escape her before she had the good sense to censor herself. A glimmer of a smile erupts on Father Neeley's face; he couldn't avoid being amused at Mary's reaction.

156

"Father Neeley. Oh... I... didn't...." Mary stutters. "You're so young!" Mary flinches at the words that fly out of her mouth before she can stifle them.

"You can call me 'Butch' here, Mary."

She never knew Father Neeley's Christian name.

It is Brian, he explains, but no one has called him that since he was a boy. He took on the nickname *Butch* after a particularly grueling touch football game when he was fourteen. The nick name stayed with him in high school and seemed tailored-made for the preppy crowd at Princeton, his alma mater.

"Father Neeley... Butch," Mary almost chokes on the name, it feels so disrespectful. For a minute she forgets her own odd predicament. She was used to the silver-haired, distinguished Father Neeley – not this young strapping fellow. The older Father Neeley – the priest with whom she grew up – was confident and commanded respect without uttering a word. Father Neeley had always been a handsome man as long as Mary knew him. But now – now he appeared to be a GQ model, his chiseled good looks and magnificent physic making Mary blush at the thoughts they create. Gone is the confidence, the calm reassurance that Father Neely is normally able to dispense to his flock. In an instant their roles are reversed. The man with whom she often vented throughout her life now needs some ministering himself.

"You're so upset. May I ask – what the problem is? Why are you crying? Are you all right?" Mary finally spits out.

Father Neeley – Butch – heaves a deep sigh and a sarcastic smile swipes across his mouth for a second.

"No, Mary. To be honest with you, when I'm here, I'm not 'all right.' I'm 'all right' when I'm with my people – when I'm doing my job. I guess that's the closest I come to being 'okay.' "

Mary is entranced by this comely young man whom she had known in another life. She always considered Father Neeley handsome, in a venerable, dignified sort of way, but this young man was knock-your-socks off, smokin' hot. A part of her feels sadness that she already knows his veneer of youth

157

will wear off in time and she can't help but compare the youthful man in front of her, *Butch,* with the silver-haired, dignified *Father Neeley* he later will become.

"I'm sorry. I didn't mean to interrupt you."

"No need for apologies, Mary. If you're here, chances are there is a reason I must tell you my story. And before I begin, let me apologize for any misconceptions you may have had about me."

Mary is confused, but also curious. She gingerly steps into the pew and sits down, next to Father Neeley.

"I'm guessing from the tears it's not a happy story," Mary says, trying her best to avoid his piercing gaze.

"Well, yes… you could say that," Father Neeley/Butch says with a slight snicker.

"Oh it can't be all that bad," Mary says, very conscious of being so close to such a handsome man – and connected to each other by the Silver Strands. It seems her intimate, affectionate – *Okay, lustful* – feelings are very inappropriate.

This is her parish priest for God's sake! Still she can't help quelling her growing curiosity and prodding *Butch* into telling his story.

Father Neeley/Butch takes a freshly-folded white linen handkerchief out of his Dockers' pocket, wipes his eyes and blows his nose hard, emitting a noise like a clogged-up vacuum.

"Sorry you had to see me like this," Butch says, folding his handkerchief and putting it back in his pocket. "Here," he says, sliding over in the pew to give Mary space.

Like the obedient Catholic school girl she once was, Mary dutifully sits a respectful distance from him.

"I know you, Mary. You're way too polite to ask about my display of emotion so I'll just tell you. If you're here, then you were meant to hear it. And then there's this," Butch says, nodding toward the strand of light that connects them. "We're certainly in touch, both figuratively and literally," he adds with a slight smile.

"Father… I mean, Butch… I don't want to upset you anymore than you already are, but I have to ask you again,

'What's the matter?' " After uttering the words, she feels regret – maybe they aren't the right words – but what would the *right* words be?

"Mary, my dear, you knew me after I lived most of my life. You don't know my previous life. I'll tell you my story, dear, and if you feel the need to judge me, so be it. I really can't say I blame you.

"The date was October 31, 1973, *Halloween*. It was a Wednesday – full moon, huge moon. I think it might even have been a harvest moon. It looked too big for the sky. This was my first semester at Princeton, majoring in medicine"

He looks up, and seeing the shocked look on Mary's face, chuckles.

"Yep, you got it. *Me, pre-med.* What a disaster that would have been. But my family – they're great people, don't get me wrong – but they had certain *expectations* from the Neeley offspring. My family is very wealthy. Did you know that Mary?" he asks.

"No, I had no idea," Mary replies, genuinely shocked.

"Yep. You know the chain of Save-A-Lot-Mart stores? That's my folks. My dad, second generation Irishman, started it with a little shop in Manhattan – worked his fingers to the bone. Funny, I look back now and I can hardly remember him. Hardly ever saw him, since he was always at the store. Well he and my momma, they vowed their kids were never going to have to work like that. Me and my two sisters – I'm the baby. We all were going to have the best education their money could buy.

"Thing of it was, I was never into academics, if you get my drift. I was willing to just work as a cashier in one of the local Save-A-Lots. But, hey, I was a force on the football field! Would you believe it? Won a partial scholarship to Princeton, and you don't turn down Princeton, right? My parents happily paid the rest. Nothing but the best for their kids. Aileen, my oldest sister, graduated Yale with honors and went on to practice law at some Manhattan firm. They only have millionaires as clients. Kathleen, the second youngest, blew off college to join the Peace Corps. We had some very interesting

159

Thanksgivings in our house," Butch says, sarcastically, but with a chuckle.

Mary listens intently. This was a part of his life she had never imagined, and she is raptly soaking up each detail.

"I wasn't the best student in the world, but I wasn't the worst," he continues. "I kinda straddled the academic line. Honestly, I viewed college as a big party with the obligatory hangovers in class the next morning. I belonged to a great fraternity – great bunch of guys. Really. Damn, those were the days."

Mary can tell Father Neeley/Butch is enjoying his vacation down Memory Lane immensely, savoring each thought that pops into his mind.

"First semester, right?" Butch turns and looks at Mary for acknowledgement.

She nods, her face aglow in the dancing candlelight.

"September was great – man, I'm talking endless parties and oh Lord, the girls." He stops, embarrassed when he remembers that he is talking to one of his parishioners. "Well, let's just say there was plenty of action back then. No shortage of alcohol or drugs either. Man, could we ever party! Two months this goes on – partying and then dragging myself to class in the morning – if I wasn't throwing up, that is. Two great months – and then we had a *real* reason to party. October 31st. – Halloween – biggest party day of the year, next to New Year's Eve and the Super Bowl, right? Oh man, we were so psyched. Like I said, it was October 31, 1973, a Wednesday. I've got that day tattooed in my brain somewhere. That's the day..." Butch's voice trails off and when he stops, he rubs his eyes.

Mary says nothing, waiting for him to compose himself and continue.

"We were heading off to a fellow frat party. We're talking a blow-out, neighbors-calling-the-cops, hang-your-underwear-from-the-trees, total-blackout party. Awesome. And the costumes! Oh man, Mary you should see some of the costumes we kids had. Nothing homemade. All this stuff was from top-notch costume designers. It's what money does to you Mary.

"Remember all the fun you had as a kid with your home-made fairy costume or hobo outfit? But we were nineteen and twenty, and we all felt it was beneath us to make our own costumes. There was a Richard Nixon and the standard Marilyn Monroe, but there also were some really innovative things. Four girls dressed up as different colored crayons, standing together all night in a "Crayola" crayon box. What a hoot! My best friend Rob went as Popeye and his date, Betsy Cuff, was Olive Oyle. She was so skinny, she was perfect for the costume.

"Anyway, I lost count of how many kegs we had but man, the booze was flowing that night. And on the coffee table, next to the punch bowl, was the most exquisite Waterford-cut crystal bowl. Believe me, after you've imbibed enough booze, inhaled enough drugs and popped enough pills, you notice these things. Well this sparkling crystal bowl held the largest quantity of white powder I'd ever seen in one place. There was enough coke to keep us all happy – all night. I remember my roommate and his band playing "Monster Mash" the whole damn night. To this day, I get queasy when I hear that song. It was almost dawn before anyone even thought of calling it quits. No one wanted that night to end. But Halloween can't last forever, right? So we packed things up, and my buddies and I and decided to hit the Queen Diner for breakfast. None of us were feeling any pain, I'll tell ya that," Butch, says with a hearty laugh.

"We were on route Route 41 in my new BMW and we were all packed in like sardines. I was driving and Joey Butler was shouting something from the back seat. I couldn't make it out – he was under a pile of girls. I turned around just for a moment – just a moment." Butch stops and puts his head down. He is silent for several seconds. "Just a moment," he repeats softly.

"I remember the headlights coming right at us. I didn't have a chance to swerve back into my lane. The noise, oh Sweet Jesus, the noise – the most God-awful noise – the screeching sound of metal colliding with metal, that awful sound of shattered glass. But it was the screams I remember the

161

most – screams of unfiltered terror and death. I heard it, Mary. I swear to God I could hear people dying. I knew they were dying. There was the most awful hum of death in their voice.

"You're lucky, you know. You came out of your accident not remembering anything. Oh Sweet Jesus how I wish I was as lucky as you. But, no; I remember everything – the smell of steaming hot metal; the gasoline and the fire; and the odor of burning flesh. I was able to climb out the driver's side window. That was the only part of the car that was left in one piece. Hardly a scratch on me; I remember Marjorie Bennett – she was costumed as a nurse. Those poor people still stuck in the car – the ones who hadn't been ejected from the car like human missiles – were begging her to help them. They were so out of it they didn't realize Marjorie was no real nurse. She sat next to them in English Lit class. And poor Marjorie – I don't know if it was the costume or just her sweet nature – but she felt she had to help these people.

"Don't touch them!" I screamed to her.

"It was the only nugget of information I retained from med classes. I remember limping, covered in blood and knocking on doors, pleading for help. Most of the people were asleep, though. We didn't have cell phones back then. Christ, it seemed like hours, but I'm sure it was just minutes before I heard the sirens."

Mary is shocked to hear Butch swear. But as she looks at the tortured young man in front of her, his words are very appropriate. In fact, Mary thought, they are quite refrained considering the hellish nightmare he is retelling.

"By the time the EMTs got there..." Butch stops to catch his breath, "I could hear one old veteran guy say, "Jesus Christ!" I guess when you hear that from a guy who's seen some pretty gnarly stuff, you gotta figure it's pretty bad."

"Here's the kicker. You know what I was dressed as that night? The Grim Reaper – can you believe that? Black silk robe, complete with hood and professional skull makeup on my face. The only thing missing was the fake scythe that I had carried all night as a prop."

162

Mary barely moves. She is mesmerized by the story Father Neeley is telling her. She is just getting over the shock of seeing her elderly parish priest peel back the years to his younger days and reveal a personal hell. Father Neeley/Butch suddenly seems to recall that he has an audience as he is telling his story, and looks at Mary.

"I'm sorry... if you rather not hear..."

"Oh no," Mary says. "Please. Please continue." The cavernous church is serenely, reverently silent, as if it knows Father Neeley is giving Mary *his* confession instead of the other way around.

"Mary, there are pictures from that night I can't get out of my head. Jimmy Reed – he was dressed as a cheerleader – don't ask me why I remember these stupid details – he was walking around looking for his arm. It had been sheared off in the crash. I remember the look on his face – shock and desperation – he had one mission right then, and that was to find his arm. The firemen and the EMTs – they tried the Jaws of Life to get the others out, but the smell of gas was overwhelming, and they were afraid of an explosion.

"My Beamer was a jumble of metal that no longer bore any resemblance to a car, I'll tell you that. But it was the other car: A 1999 Hyundai that took the brunt of the crash. We collided straight on.... I told you that, right?" Butch asks, looking at Mary.

"No, Father Neeley... I mean, Butch," I don't believe you did. It must have been truthfully awful."

The aging Father looks at Mary's sweet, genuinely-concerned face, and softly smiles.

"Yes, Mary. It was truly awful. I wouldn't wish that on my worst enemy."

"So there these firefighters and EMTs are, trying to get my friends out of what's left of my Beamer. It was surreal. There was Denise McElroy, wearing a bright pink wig – only half of it now was colored red. Her head had been bashed in half, but believe it or not, that silly pink wig stayed on her head.

163

"Don't ask me why I suddenly needed to know about the people in the other car. I just did. They had sheets up around the crash site to deter any gawkers but I walked around the sheets. Oh Mary..." Again, his voice trails off for several seconds.

"A young husband and wife – dead. And their two-year-old strapped in the back seat. When I asked one of the firemen if they would be all right he looked me up and down. Don't ask me how, but I'm sure he knew I was the coked-up kid who caused the accident.

"They're dead, buddy," was all he said.

"He was pissed off. Hey, it was a righteous anger. The official trauma count that night showed that I killed a young couple, leaving their baby an orphan, plus, the two dead in my car. Jimmy Reed uses a prosthetic arm now – they never found his arm to even try to reattach it. Last I heard he dropped out of school and tried to commit suicide about a half dozen times. Denise McElroy? She's got about one-third of her brain left. She's in a wheelchair now – can't feed or dress herself. Her dream to work at a pretentious Wall Street firm as a broker – well it's truly just a dream now that she herself doesn't even remember.

"I crushed so many lives back that night, Mary. When all was said and done I spent little more than a year in prison – I'm sure my family's connections had something to do with that – should've been at least twenty years. The civil suits nearly bankrupted my parents. Their money kept me out of prison, which just added to my guilt. They lost their franchise; lost everything – all because I had to play College Joe, Big Man on Campus. That changed my life, Mary. I'm not going to say I was 'born again' because that's a crock of shit. I simply saw more clearly than ever before that there are paths to be taken in life. And we have to choose our own. And I made an incredibly shitty choice.

"I quit Princeton and joined the seminary. They sent me to this little Catholic/Cajun church way down in a small New Orleans parish. It didn't even have an official name. It was just called *The church on the bayou.* Talk about feeling like a fish

164

out of water!" Father Neeley/Butch manages a slight chuckle. "But they were kind folk. They took me in and asked no questions, although the church board certainly knew my background. They changed my life. See?" He held up his wrist to show the dozens upon dozens of strands attached to his wrist that faded off in the distance. They're always with me. They never judged me. They accepted me for who I am. And for once in my life I felt as if I was truly repenting for my awful past.

"It was an old parish – both the building and the people who filled it. The oldest parishioner Minerva Devereaux, God love her, was 102, and never missed a Sunday service. Well, they died off until there was just a handful left.

"The diocese shut down that little church. Ancient clapwood, it doesn't last forever. I envisioned termites holding hands as the only thing holding it upright. That, and years of repeated coats of white paint, I think were the only thing holding it together. It wasn't worth the upkeep. In fact, it was downright dangerous. I knew it was just a matter of time before the doors closed my little church – *the church on the bayou* – for good.

"There was another church, actually a cathedral, down the road from my little *church on the bayou*. Different kind of people, they were, and let me tell you, that's an understatement. It was a well-connected parish – lots of politicians.

"They drove to Mass in their Beamers and Lincolns and designer clothes. They didn't go to church to worship. They went for show. They dressed impeccably, a far cry from the tattered clothes that my previous congregation wore. But that cathedral, that's where the money was, so the Catholic diocese didn't see much sense in rebuilding our little *church on the bayou*. I tried to visit the handful of parishioners left to me, to give them Holy Communion in their homes. But that didn't last long. The diocese needed me here. I was heartbroken. And... well, here I am. In New Jersey."

"You sound disappointed," Mary states. "Are we that bad?" she adds jokingly.

165

"No, no, dear," Father Neeley says as he grabs her hand. "It's hard to explain.

"Those folk down in the bayou – church was their *life*. I'm sure my parishioners here, their faith is every bit as strong as my little flock. But my *church on the bayou*, their lives *revolved* around the church. There are no golf courses or fancy restaurants or movie theaters in that section of New Orleans. The heart of their community was that little church with no name. I loved that little church..." Father Neeley says, his eyes straight ahead, and his mind lost in a time and place far away from this huge glittering edifice in New Jersey.

"Don't get me wrong, Mary, I love my parishioners here, but I'd give anything to be able to be that young priest, fresh out of seminary, bringing the word of God to people who are really thirsty to hear it.

"Here," Father Neeley says, his hand still on Mary's, "here it's different. Those people, they *got* it. They just *got* it. I was able to give sermons about everyday life. You know, the stuff we all get mired down in – and how Jesus would handle it. They not only listened, they practiced their faith. God forgive me, I felt like I was performing *magic*. And in a way, I was – *God's* magic. I miss that.

"Over the years I lost that feeling. When I try to give an honest service, I look at those blank faces looking back at me in the pews, and I just know that the words are bouncing off the walls. So I fall back on the Catholic regiment. The *RULES*. You know, the holy days of obligation, mortal sins and venial sins, Sunday is a day of rest. Sometimes, Mary, I just feel like it's a bunch of bullshit.

I'm sorry," Father Neeley/Butch says, rubbing his eyes. "But sometimes I feel as if I'm just repeating military commands from rote and my parishioners are my soldiers. How awful is *that*?"

He puts his hands over his face and begins to weep again.

"Every time I get up at that pulpit – every time I give religious advice, I feel like a charlatan. I've lost my faith, Mary. And what's worse – I'm beginning to wonder if I ever really had it."

166

Sixteen

Meg at Work

The smell of pine wafts through the woods like a ghostly evergreen specter gliding swiftly through the spaces of the trees. Mary breathes in deeply the sweet and spicy aroma. She is standing on a blanket of pine needles, layers and layers that must have accumulated over the decades. She recognizes her surroundings as Luna Park, near the lake. Mary soaks in the momentary silence and wondrous smell before she hears a familiar woman's voice cry out.

"Chief, can you give me any idea what we have here? I'm told we have a body wash."

The voice belongs to Meg.

Part of Mary's brain is telling her that no, it can't be true.

Meg is in that room with me and Dr. Lee.

The other part of her brain is following the glowing strand that travels from her wrist to Meg's.

Mary watches Meg talking with Police Chief Rick Shaw, and she can't help but notice the luminescent strand that connects Meg to the chief. She can barely make out what they are saying, but Mary easily deduces it is a crime scene. The chief sounds angry. There is that ominous yellow police tape draped over bushes and looped over tree trunks.

"That's me," a tiny voice says from behind Mary.

Mary turns to see an impossibly beautiful black girl, about five or six-years-old, she guesses. The girl is smiling and looking at her intently with a bit of curiosity, as if she isn't sure Mary can really hear or see her. She has the most disarming dimples Mary has ever seen.

"What's your name, sweetie?" Mary asks, trying not to spook the child.

167

"Tammy. Tammy Brenner. That's me that they're looking at – your reporter friend and the police chief." She is holding her hands clasped behind her back, almost in an *at ease* position designed for soldiers.

When Mary looks back at Meg and the police chief, she finally sees what has captured their interest so intently. It is the body of a little girl wearing a pink skirt and purple top. The pink skirt is pulled up above her waist; pink tights have been discarded nearby; and her lacy, once-white panties are in tatters and tossed aside. The child's curly dark hair is pulled up with a lavender wool bow – exactly what this little girl, who calls herself "Tammy" is wearing, only much dirtier and torn.

"I guess you'll need this now, too," the little girl says, wrapping a Silver Strand around Mary's hand. The other end of the strand is on the little girl's fragile sparrow-like wrist. She looks at Mary with huge hazel eyes, framed with the curliest eyelashes imaginable. "You weren't supposed to have this yet – pointing to the strand of light – but honestly, we weren't expecting you."

About this time, Meg and the police chief part enough to form a clearing for Mary to finally glimpse what had kept them in rapt attention. It takes Mary mere seconds to confirm that the purple-and-pink clump they were studying so intently is, indeed, Tammy's tiny body.

"Oh sweet Jesus!" Mary exclaims as the flood of recognition comes over her. This little dimpled doll of a girl standing next to her is dead – the victim of a violent attack by a monster. The chilling slicing of Tammy's neck is both macabre and inhuman. Mary isn't sure what to say or do.

The little girl standing next to her, still has her hands clasped in back, but shows little emotion.

Mary bends down to match Tammy's height, and takes the tiny face in both her hands, looking directly into her huge hazel eyes.

"I'm so sorry, my baby," she says. "I'm so sorry some sick person did this to you. But you're with me now, and I won't let anything happen to you. I promise."

168

Tammy says nothing but hugs Mary hard. When she finally unlatches her grip on Mary, she is smiling, her adorable dimples in full force now.

"Thank you, Mary. I'm okay at the moment. I'm not scared. He can't hurt me anymore. I'm safe, but, my parents – my mommy isn't doing very well. And Daddy... well, he just sits in his big chair and cries. Can you help them? You're going back; I'm not. I can't. And you have my strand now too, just like Mommy and Daddy have."

Mary is surprised at the adult, matter-of-fact tone that Tammy's voice has. It finally dawns on her that age is irrelevant here. Tammy knows much more about what is going on than she does.

"People are going to call you *psychic*, Mary, but really, you've just seen things that most other people don't ever see. When you go back, I really hope you see *these...*" she says, pointing to the strands of silver light that encircle her wrists and wander out into the distance, until the only thing visible on the horizon is the sun, which is melting fast.

"If Mommy and Daddy know about these, I don't think they'll be so unhappy. If they know we're connected, forever and ever... I'm not with them now, but I will be some day. Daddy was signing me up for soccer. I wanted to play soccer so bad. But that bad man..." her voice trails off and she stares at the ground.

"Who?" Mary prods Tammy. "Do you know who took you away from your Mommy and Daddy?" Mary wants to know if Tammy knows it was Robbie Renwood.

"That's not important *here*," Tammy replies solemnly and firmly. "It's important somewhere else – that they catch the bad man, because he does bad things to little girls, and he is going to keep doing them until they catch him. But here – *where we are now* – that's not important."

Tammy's eyes suddenly blink, and her attention becomes focused elsewhere.

"Look," she says, pointing her tiny finger behind Mary.

Mary turns around and sees a man and woman sobbing and desperately hugging each other in a darkened parlor room.

169

The drapes had been drawn and a single votive candle is lit in front of a photograph of a beaming Tammy, encased in a sterling silver frame. Mary barely makes out the rest of the room. In this strange dimension, her eyes still have to adjust themselves from the bright sunshine to the dimly-lit room.

The man and woman, both middle-aged, sob the cry of the doomed – those persons who no longer can see any reason to live.

Mary winces at the sounds of the parents' pain. The whines of despair start deep in the pits of their bodies and screech out in an agony so intense it is almost an entity unto itself. The man heaves and moans just as much as his companion, even though Mary can tell he is obviously trying to muster the strength to comfort her.

These must be Tammy's parents. Mary thinks, feeling embarrassed at witnessing such a private moment. Her stomach is churning, and she begins to turn away in distress.

But Tammy is standing in front of her right now, her huge hazel eyes saying everything:

Don't look away. I need you to see and hear this.

Reluctantly, Mary turns back to the somber scene.

"I can't do it!" the woman cries, suddenly standing up and pulling her hair out in tiny clumps. "I can't do this! I don't want to live without Tammy, Carl. There is nothing left for me here."

The man called "Carl" desperately tries to calm the woman, tries to hold her by putting his arms about her, but she will have none of it.

"I want to die, Carl. Oh Jesus, why don't you take me now? Oh Jesus. Sweet Jesus."

She is banging her head hard against the wall near the fireplace mantle.

The neatly-appointed mantle is covered in a lace cloth and displays nearly two dozen photos of Tammy in various stages of growth: *Tammy as a newborn; Tammy as a toddler on a tricycle; Tammy in a ballerina frou-frou outfit; and Tammy dressed as a kitten for Halloween.* From the display it is

170

obvious that Tammy is the familial nucleus of life in this home. There are no photos of any other children.

Carl, himself a picture of despair and desolation, is finally able to get his arms around his wife and hold her tight.

"Louise, we have to accept that Tammy's gone. But we'll be with her someday – we will. I promise. The Lord will hold us all in his loving arms."

Mary notices that as he holds his wife, he is also trying to dial a number on his cell phone.

Louise is inconsolable.

"Fuck Jesus. Fuck you. I want Tammy here with us *now*! Not sometime in the future. *Now! Now! Now!*"

Each time she screeches the word, she punctuates it by trying to bang her head on the wall. Carl pulls his hysterical wife back by her hair and hugs her close to him.

Mary cringes in shock at the intensity of the woman's grief – something she has never encountered before. Mary wants to intervene in some way, but she doesn't know how; she does know that it won't be possible to help because she isn't physically there in the room.

The sound of sirens drawing near is a big relief to Mary. Carl evidently realized he could no longer assuage his wife's distress by himself and had dialed 911 before allowing something more drastic to occur.

The EMTs arrive, their flashing red lights the only thing announcing their entrance. The three emergency techs open the door without an invitation and are efficiently trying to assess the situation.

Louise is enraged, and looks at her husband with pure hated at what she perceives as his betrayal.

"What did you do? Who did you call?" she snarls at him through gritted teeth.

"Louise, baby, I'm worried about you... you're going to hurt yourself," Carl says gently. "Let these nice people help you."

"*Help* me? *Help* me? How are they going to *help* me? Are they going to bring my baby back to me? Because if they can do that, that would be just swell, Carl. If they can't do that, tell them to get the fuck out of my house!"

Carl steps back for a second to whisper something in the ear of one EMT.

Louise sees him, and smells a conspiracy. Her face again fills with fury, as she watches the EMTs briefly confer, whispering among themselves for a few seconds. She continues to eye them suspiciously, ready to pounce lest they make a move toward her.

"Mrs. Brenner, I'm so sorry for your loss," one young EMT says. "Believe me, I have a little girl. If anything ever happened to her I don't know what I'd do. But we both know if Tammy was here she wouldn't want to see her mommy like this. You'd be scaring her, now wouldn't you?"

Something in his words reaches the motherly instinct in Louise. She collapses against the wall, sinking down to the floor in a heap.

Automatically, the man's professional training kicks in; using a *slight-of-hand magic trick*, he pounces on the grieving woman, injecting her with a sedative. Louise's body becomes a mass of ticks and sobs as the sedative begins to take effect.

Standing nearby, Carl looks on, his hand over his mouth and tears streaming steadily down his face.

"We're going to have to take her to Bright Psychiatric Hospital, Mr. Brenner. Do you know where that is, sir?"

Carl nods silently, unable to speak.

The young medical technician puts his hand on Carl's shoulder in sympathy.

"They'll take good care of her there. Trust me."

Sad and still incoherent, Carl watches in disgust as the EMTs carefully place Louise on a gurney, and then put restraints on her wrists and ankles.

"It's for her own good as well as ours," the EMT explains.

The scene unfolds before Mary as she watches with all the heartbreak that only another mother can understand. She realizes she has been crying when she tastes the salty drops forming in her mouth. Not wanting to see any more, she turns away to see Tammy still standing there.

172

"I didn't mean to make you feel bad, Mrs. Miller "but you have to help my mommy. She's going to need you. That's why I gave you the Silver Strand. You have to give it to her. She has to know it came from me. She must know I'm still here and I love her. If you don't make her believe that, she's going to do something bad to herself."

Mary is perplexed by her mission, but even as she is pondering a scheme to meet with Mrs. Brenner, she feels her thoughts melting into a foreign place.

Will Wheaton

Mary is standing at Main and Poplar, the scene of the fatal pedestrian hit-and-run accident Gary had assigned reporter Will Wheaton to cover. She can see that the truly gruesome remnants of the accident have been cleared away. Firefighters are hosing down the huge scarlet stain, a grim-colored scar left on the road. Clearly, this encounter involved copious amounts of blood. The smell of gas and oil and tragedy hang heavy in the air. Mary isn't surprised when she sees the Silver Strand that connects her to the reporter.

Will sidles smoothly over to one of the uniforms guarding the scene. Before he can get a word out, the officer puts up his hand.

"Nothing to say. Ask the chief." Almost as an afterthought, the officer whispers to Will, "Just some homeless guy. Drunk driver ran him over."

Will is getting more angry and frustrated by the minute. He detests bureaucratic red tape, particularly when it involves something so minor.

Probably a five-inch blurb that will end up on Page 7, he thinks sourly.

Although he has made friends with many of the cops on the local force, there are still some who regard reporters as the enemy. Chief Rich Shaw has dictated that all information to the media would come only from him. Will has made off-duty camaraderie with many of the cops, however, and they discretely slip him information; this officer was not one of them.

Mary laughs out loud, knowing full well that Will can't hear her. She doesn't care for him really, anyway. One of those young guys who have visions of breaking another Watergate, when in fact, they're just cutting their teeth in a small-town paper. Mary watched in glee as Will wearily heads back to his car. He has to trek to the station to talk to the chief.

"Fuck this," he mutters under his breath as he gets behind the wheel of his Volkswagen Bug. Will is practically seething

174

as he drives the short route to the cop shop to get the official information from Chief Shaw.

Mary isn't surprised to see a gaggle of Silver Strands wend their way from Will Wheaton's wrist out toward the direction of the Police Station.

Just how many police officers had Will thrown back a couple of beers with over the years? Mary wonders.

By the time Will gets to the station, it is time for a shift change, so nobody stops him when he deftly slides through the mass of uniforms and makes his way to the chief's office without being stopped. The door is half open, and he can see Chief Shaw engrossed in paperwork. He knocks lightly.

"Howya doin,' chief?"

Rich Shaw works hard to not show his frustration at being bothered by a reporter. *Not today. First a little girl is murdered, and then a fatal hit-and-run.*

Will feels no guilt – not one bit. The chief had made the edict himself, that information regarding violent crime and fatal accidents would come directly from him. So – hey, Will figures, the chief had made his bed; now he can lie in it.

"Close the door behind you," the chief says with a sigh of resignation.

Will doesn't wait for an invitation. He shuts the door and plops down on the chair across from the chief.

"OK, chief, wanna give me the goods so I can go back and do some real work?" Will says sarcastically. The two men have a strained relationship; in other words, they can barely stand each other.

All the time the reporter and the chief speak, Mary is near them, unseen and listening intently. She is enjoying this secret power of invisibility, hearing and seeing everything first-hand, with no one being the wiser. There is a price to pay, of course. By being that proverbial fly on the wall, she now finds a Silver Strand connecting her, Will and the chief. Their lives already had intersected.

"It was Big Red," the chief says solemnly.

Will stares at the chief for several seconds before finally shouting, in disbelief.

"No!"

Big Red was the unofficial leader of homeless people in town. He did not speak at all – ever. He had been around as long as anyone could remember, wearing an old tattered raincoat, even when the summer heat inched toward the 100-degree mark. He had been tall once – topping well over 6'6" and also once had flaming red hair; thus, the nickname that some silly, thoughtless young scalawag had dubbed him. The nickname stuck, even though Big Red had shrunk over the years and his hair had turned silver. He was harmless – never begged for food. If someone saw him sitting on a street corner – his appearance was the epitome of a vagrant – they would try to give him money, but he would just silently shake his head in polite refusal.

Chief Shaw would see him diving for food and necessities in the Dumpster behind the stores. Big Red would sleep in the woods that hugged the Save-A-Lot-Mart parking lot. The chief worried about him, especially in the bitterly cold winter months. He often would leave a McDonald's meal out for him near his Save-A-Lot spot, but Big Red refused to touch it.

It took a while for the chief to catch on, but the light bulb eventually went off. He would crumple up the McDonald meal so it looked as if it had been picked over, and then wait until the Dumpster was full, laying the food carefully on top. Thinking it was a cast-off Big Mac, Big Red would scoop it out of the trash and gobble it down. Occasionally, the chief would toss an old blanket or some used clothes ("extra tall" from the Salvation Army) into the Dumpster. The chief was pretty sure that Big Red was hip to his game, but played along – to a degree.

Rich knew that Big Red enjoyed puffing on Swisher Sweets, those small pungent ubiquitous cigars sold in area bodegas. How and where he got them always baffled the chief. One time the chief bought a box of the Swisher Sweets, unopened, and laid them next to the disheveled McDonald's wrapper in the Dumpster. Big Red took the cold Big Mac, but left the cigars. From then on, the chief knew better. He would open the small cigar box, take one out, and then put the open box in the Dumpster, as if someone had tried one and disliked it so much they chucked the box. That's when the Swisher Sweets started disappearing along with the cold McDonald's meals. The chief would have loved to have left something other than fast food, but he knew that Big Red would snub anything that remotely resembled charity.

Big Red was a fixture on the main streets of the town, his long stretch of a figure gliding smoothly through the throngs of shoppers, his head always bent down, carefully averting strangers' eyes.

No one knew anything about "Big Red," although there were countless local legends and myths that surrounded him: He was a Vietnam War dodger who fled to Canada and then returned; he was a Vietnam War hero; he had done time for robbery; he was a wealthy businessman who lost his mind. The truth of the matter is that nobody knew the real story, and for the most part, no one really cared. He might just as well have been a statue in the park. Everyone saw him, but paid him no mind.

Even as Will is still absorbing the news that "Big Red" is gone, he is assessing whether this raises the story to a higher news level; cold, but true. It is a hazard of the reporting profession – distancing yourself from the subject of your story. Will keeps his real thoughts to himself.

"Wow, it's hard to believe he's not going to be around anymore," Will said. "I mean...*wow*. It is as if a landmark in the community has been demolished."

"Now, what the fuck," the chief mutters under his breath upon hearing a soft knock on his door.

"Enter." he says.

The chief's secretary, Rose, pops her head in.

"Chief, Mrs. O'Quinn is here to see you."

The chief looks at her, confused.

"Big Red's mother," she whispers. "She wants to talk to you."

"Oh shit! Oh, my God, show her in," the chief says, glancing at Will with a look that clearly conveys, *Not a word, or you're outta here.*

177

Will nods, instinctively knowing the rules.

Kelly O'Quinn is the quintessential Irish motherly type. Her silver hair, streaked with some die-hard red strands that refuse to give up their pigment, is pulled back in a loose braided ponytail that lies over one shoulder. Some renegade strands of red-tinged silver sway to and fro on her head. Her blues eyes are still clear and bright. She is wearing a well-worn tweed coat that matches the wrinkles on her face.

"Mrs. O'Quinn, please come in," the chief says. "I'm so sorry for your loss. You know your son was quite the fixture in our little town. He will be missed. I'm truly sorry." There is an awkward pause of several seconds as the chief realizes he has nothing to add to his condolence, since he had never spoken to the man and doesn't even know Big Red's Christian name.

Mary watches this scenario intently. Funny, she had never thought of Big Red having a mother – still living that is.

"Thank you for seeing me, Chief Shaw," Mrs. O'Quinn says in a thick Irish brogue. She looks to be a hundred years old. The chief is just about to ask Will to leave when he notices the pleading look in Will's eyes. Will obviously smells a good story here. The chief relents and introduces Mrs. O'Quinn to Will, but merely as a *journalist*.

Mary – invisible to those in room – sees the Silver Strands that had connected her to Will and the chief now include a sliver of light, which, predictably by now, wraps around Mrs. O'Quinn's wrist.

Mrs. O'Quinn shakes hands with Will and Chief Shaw. Mrs. O'Quinn's blue eyes are red and puffy and she periodically dabs an old lace handkerchief to them.

"Please, please... sit down. Where are my manners," the chief says quickly, sliding a chair over to Mrs. O'Quinn. The chief doesn't feel right about deceiving Mrs. O'Quinn about Will. He fesses up.

"Mr. Wheaton here is a reporter for the local newspaper, *The Beacon*. Would you rather he leave?"

Will bites his lower lip, pathetically eager to be included in the meeting.

178

Mrs. O'Quinn seated now, studies Will up and down with her dim blue eyes. She must approve, or at least trusts him enough to allow him to stay.

"No. Maybe it's better this be in the paper, she says firmly, after a couple of seconds. Maybe it's better the people around here know my son – my Aiden. I'll betcha not many people knew his name

Both Will and the chief, looking embarrassed, avert her eyes on this comment.

"His name – his *Christian* name – is "Aiden," she repeats for emphasis. "You make sure you put that in your story, young man," the old woman says pointedly to Will.

"What can I do for you Mrs. O'Quinn?" Chief Shaw is taking back charge of the conversation. He pulls his chair up to hers.

"Well for one thing, did you catch the brute who ran over my son? They told me he was the victim of a hit and run. I don't understand. Aiden didn't walk in the streets, he walked on the sidewalks – always. There's something more going on here."

"We don't have anything concrete yet, Mrs. O'Quinn, not yet," the chief says. "But I promise you – *I promise you –* we're going to do everything we can to catch the person or persons responsible. We pursue these hit-and-run accidents with everything we've got."

Mrs. O'Quinn shoots him a skeptical look as if to say, *"Even my son, the town's homeless joke, the one the children make fun of because he talks to himself and smells bad?"*

"Believe me," the chief says, as if he is reading her mind, "we will find whoever did this to your boy, Mrs. O'Quinn. You have my word on this. My detectives tell me we have some trace evidence left at the scene, valuable evidence. Trust me," he says earnestly, putting his hand over the old woman's.

The chief feels terrible lying to this poor woman. Truthfully, there are no leads whatsoever. But Chief Shaw can't think of any other way to comfort her.

She looks up at him, tears still streaming down her face.

179

"I have to plan his funeral, I do," she says in her thick accent. "I have to plan the funeral of my child. I don't care if your child is six or sixty, it's not natural to bury your baby. It goes against everything that's natural." Mrs. O'Quinn wipes her eyes again and looks straight at the chief. "You know, I used to tell him an old Irish saying when he was just a wee lad – and even as he sprouted in manhood. My mum told me and her mum told her... just a thought of good luck: '*May you get all your wishes but one – so you always have something to strive for.*' "

"That's lovely, Mrs. O'Quinn," the chief says sincerely.

"Yes," she says, "it's about a simple as you can get, but if it's given from the heart, it's worth all the fancy words of Yeats put together."

"Well," Mrs. O'Quinn says as she stands up shakily, the chief holding her arm in physical and emotional support, "I have to plan his funeral, I do. I have to plan the funeral of my child. I don't care if your child is six or sixty, it's not natural to bury your baby. It goes against everything that's natural," Mrs. O'Quinn repeats, wiping her eyes again.

Will walks over to Mrs. O'Quinn, his demeanor uncharacteristically and seemingly sincere.

"You know, Mrs. O'Quinn," he says politely," your son – in his own way – was an important part of this town. Even though not many people knew him personally, everyone *knew* him. I'd love to be able to do a *legacy* piece on him for *The Beacon*. He was a part of the fabric of this town, and now he's gone."

Mrs. O'Quinn nearly had forgotten Will is there. *And who in great Moses is this fellow again?* her eyes seem to ask. Will picked up the signal of confusion immediately.

"I'm the reporter from *The Beacon*. I'd love to write something about your son – so many people would be interested in his background."

Mary waits intently to hear the woman's response. It could go either way. Will is on his best, gentlemanly behavior.

Mrs. O'Quinn waits several seconds before she says in a voice drenched with scorn, "Oh, yes, people would *love* to read

180

about the strange man who walked up and down the streets babbling to himself – the fellow who ate from the garbage. I doubt that's a good idea, Mister whatever-your-name-is. The answer is 'no.' They had their humor at my boy's expense long enough. My Aiden is going to be buried right and proper, in a Catholic funeral in a Catholic cemetery. He never hurt no one. You know he kept some of the food that he found so he could feed the stray dogs and cats? Did you know that? No. Of course you didn't. No one did. Because that's the way he wanted it. Good deeds – truly good deeds – are the ones no one knows about except you and God. That was my boy, Mr. Newspaperman. Find yourself another story to entertain your readers."

Will is not about to be dismissed so easily.

Mary watches him with amusement, knowing full well he can easily turn on the charm with the ladies – even the elderly ones.

"Mrs. O'Quinn, please, just hear me out. Please, it won't be anything like that. And I'll go one step further: The only person I'll interview is you – no one else. So basically, you'll have carte blanche as to what would go into this piece. I'll even let you see it before we run it so you can take out things you don't like

Mary knows this is a clear breach of *The Beacon* and all mainstream news groups' policy. She wonders if Will is low enough to lie to a grieving mother to get a story, or if he intends to keep his word.

"*Carte what?*" Mrs. O'Quinn repeats, staring at Will as if he is some kind of strange bug.

"It means you have final say of what goes into the paper – and that includes the online version," Will says, trying to suppress the tone of desperation in his voice.

Mrs. O'Quinn stares at Will for several seconds.

"Oh, what the hades…" she finally says, "but I do want to see everything you write before it goes in that paper."

Will pounces on her ambivalence.

"You know, the celebrities around town aren't just the politicians – the mayor or the city councilmen. They're the everyday people, like your boy. Those bigwigs die, their stories end up on the front page. Don't you think your son deserves the same thing? Hey, he was a legend in this town."

Mary desperately wants to tell Will not to sound so eagerly pathetic.

Mrs. O'Quinn again eyes Will up and down, mulling over his words.

"But I don't trust that internet stuff. So if I find out you hoodwinked me into putting something else on that internet of yours...."

Will grabs her wrinkled hand, dotted with age spots, and says, "No worries, Mrs. O'Quinn. I'll even show you the online version. You'll see everything, I promise."

Hmm.... Mary thinks, he's either one helluva liar or he really does have a heart where I always thought there was a stone."

"Well... okay," Mrs. O'Quinn says warily. "But not now. Not until I bury my boy in sacred ground. You know, I'm afraid those teenagers – the mean ones – will do something to his grave. I don't want anyone to know where my son is buried. I'll call you. Don't you go bothering me and mine at a time like this. You have respect for the dead, and their loved ones, you hear, young man?"

Will nods agreeably.

As Mrs. O'Quinn gets up to leave, Chief Shaw shoots Will a look that clearly says, *"You do that woman wrong and I'm coming after you personally."*

The elderly woman hobbles toward the door, the chief scooting ahead quickly to open it for her. He notices that the clothes that he can see under her coat are a well-worn, pastel housedress, spotlessly clean and starched. She smells of fresh lilacs.

Mary watches as the Silver Strand now connecting her to Mrs. O'Quinn follows the woman out the door.

Just before she leaves, Mrs. O'Quinn turns toward the chief and Will.

"You know the last time I saw Aiden?" she asks through tears. "Five years ago. We all tried to help him. But after that damn war, he wasn't right in the head. Now… take me to him. I want to see my boy."

Will looks at the chief – clearly relieved he didn't have to hang around for this, and promptly excuses himself.

"Uh, Mrs. O'Quinn, your son isn't really in any shape… that is, you wouldn't want to remember him this way," the chief stammers.

"He's my boy. I brought him into this world, and now I'll see him out. Don't you worry 'bout me, Mr. Police Chief," Mrs. O'Quinn says with a resolution that seems to declare, "This conversation is over."

Chief Shaw clears his throat.

"I'll have one of my men escort you to the funeral home. We didn't realize he had relatives."

The chief stops briefly in embarrassment.

"Well, I mean, we didn't have a contact person, so we took him down to Ambrosia's Funeral Home."

"What!" Mrs. O'Quinn fairly screams in disgust. "That *Italian* place? No. No! I want him taken to Delaney's. That's where our family goes to bury our dead. Good Irish stock who go back to the old country. They know our ways."

"Of course," the chief says, accommodatingly. He shouts out to a peach-faced rookie police officer who has the bad luck to be standing nearest to the chief's door.

"Officer Dooley, would you please escort Mrs. O'Quinn to Delaney's Funeral Home? Her son was the victim in that hit-and-run. Mrs. O'Quinn would like to see her boy. I'll call Delaney's and let them know you're coming."

Dooley is barely able to hide the feeling of panic washing over him, but he is composed enough to take Mrs. O'Quinn's hand and say, "I'm so sorry, ma'am, for your loss. I certainly will." Mrs. O'Quinn seems pleased to hear the Irish name, "Dooley."

A small comfort, Mary thinks as she watched Officer Dooley take Mrs. O'Quinn's arm to lead her to his patrol car. Mary is no longer surprised to see the Silver Strand appear and connect the two – and then wind its way to Mary, deftly wrapping around her slim wrist.

Officer Dooley treats Mrs. O'Quinn the way he would treat his grandmother; with the utmost respect and dignity – plus a dose of solemn compassion for a mother who has just lost her son. He opens the front door of the squad car for her and makes sure the hem of her dress is inside the door before he closes it. They drive in near-silence the twenty minutes it takes to reach Delaney's. Small talk seems awkward and somehow disrespectful.

Mary finds herself in the back seat, watching Officer Dooley and Mrs. O'Quinn.

The funeral home seems ancient. It's built of faded, cracked bricks with a single gargoyle atop the slate roof that straddles the top of the front door. Officer Dooley pulls his cruiser around to the back of the funeral home, where the bodies are transferred in preparation for funerals.

Mrs. O'Quinn is determined to see her son – her Aiden – whose mental illness made him shun the people who loved him the most. She doesn't know what to expect... would she recognize him after such a terrible accident? It doesn't matter to her though. It is her maternal responsibility that lasts from cradle to grave. Of course, she had always thought that saying applied to *her* grave, not her son's.

The young officer parks his cruiser and dashes around the back of the car to open the door for Mrs. O'Quinn. He helps her out carefully, compassionately, but she doesn't seem to notice. Her mind is somewhere else. Dooley offers Mrs. O'Quinn his hand.

Mary watches in a kind of sad bemusement as their two Silver Strands jumble together.

"What's your first name, son?" Mrs. O'Quinn says, speaking for the first time since they climbed in the car. She gratefully takes the officer's hand.

"Patrick," Mrs. O'Quinn. Please feel free to call me Pat."

For the slightest second Mary sees an expression of satisfaction flit across Mrs. O'Quinn's face. The name "Patrick" hails from good Irish heritage.

The front of Delaney's Funeral Home is warm and welcoming, but the back entrance is all business. There is a dark Hunter green painted door, with an intercom system on the side wall. This is the part of the funeral business families of the deceased rarely glimpse.

But Mrs. O'Quinn doesn't notice. She is determined to see her boy – her Aiden – one last time before they bury his body in the ground. It has been five long years since she had laid eyes on her son. He was an intense toddler, that one was. Out of her five offspring, Aiden had been the scrappy one. At any time you could find the other four with their noses buried in books, but not Aiden. Aiden was the daredevil, and it drove his mother wild. They had lived in the *Blarney Section* of town, so-called because that's where all the Irish immigrants congregated.

Mass every morning at 6 a.m. sharp, before getting her children off to school – she would then take in laundry, and wash, iron and starch clothes until the children returned. Mr. O'Quinn worked the night shift at the local bottling factory, so he often wouldn't come home until her mothering duties were completed. And then he would sleep the day away, often with a whisky in one hand and a cigarette in the other. If he was aware that he had a wife and five children, he never showed it. And that was fine by Mrs. O'Quinn, as long as he handed over his paycheck each week. She would dole out enough money to him to keep him liquored up all week. It wasn't the best arrangement, but it worked.

Mrs. O'Quinn was thankful for her Irish-immersed community, because each mother in the neighborhood was a mother not only to her own child, but for all the young ones who dare dabble in mischief. And the children knew better than to disobey any maternal figure, even if it wasn't their own flesh-and-blood. Yes, there in *Blarney*, Mrs. O'Quinn felt quite comfortable.

As her kids aged, however, they wanted to break free of the traditional Irish/Catholic conformities. They all had twelve years of Catholic schooling. The O'Quinns weren't rich, but by gosh, Mrs. O'Quinn would consider it a personal defeat as a mother if she did not send her children to Catholic school. There were two major differences between Catholic and public schools: Catholic schools required prayers before and after each class, as well as a major subject aptly titled *Religion*; plus, of course the annual tuition. Mrs. O'Quinn sometimes took extra house-cleaning jobs to make ends meet.

There was no prayer in the free public schools. Mrs. O'Quinn was horrified at that. She had seen those public school kids smoking cigarettes outside of school and using foul language.

Heathens, she thought. *Pure heathens. That's what happens when you take prayer out of schools.*

Her youngest, Kathleen, no longer attended Sunday Mass. If she had told her mother she considered herself an agnostic now – well, let's just say the sight wouldn't have been pretty. And so Kathleen avoided the topic of religion at all costs. When Kathleen divorced her husband, her mother snubbed her for two years. It didn't matter that her husband smacked his wife about whenever he felt stressed. Catholic law dictates that marriage is for *life* – period.

Mrs. O'Quinn and Officer Dooley are met at the door of Delaney's Funeral Home by the proprietor, Sean Delaney. He is wearing an impeccable dark navy suit with a blue silk tie and seems to be very young for such a serious job. He has dark – almost jet-black hair – and blue eyes. He had inherited the funeral business from his father, who had inherited it from his father. Their Irish roots run deep in the community. The Delaney Funeral Home was a mainstay in the Irish community. When it was time to bury their kin, anyone who had a fraction of Irish blood in them went to Delaney's.

"I've been expecting you, Mrs. O'Quinn," Sean Delaney says, holding her hand. "I'm so very sorry for your loss."

"Thank you boy," Mrs. O'Quinn says, and then declares: "I want to see my son now."

Sean Delaney is taken aback for a minute, but composes himself quickly enough.

"You understand," he says, "Your son was in a bad accident. "Are you sure you want to see him this way?" Mrs. O'Quinn is getting tired of these warnings. "Yes, sonny, I want to see my boy. *Now*. Please."

186

Officer Dooley gently holds onto Mrs. O'Quinn's shoulder as they prepare to enter the back hallway. They walk cautiously from the bright sunshine into the fluorescent lighting of the hallway, down the long sterile corridor. White walls, white floors, white furniture, as if everything had to be scrubbed clean every day with bleach. Whatever warmth and comfort the funeral home provided in the front of its building stops abruptly when one reaches the inner recesses of the edifice. Here, it is all hospital-sterile white, sparkling silver autopsy tools and sinks – about as cold as one can get. They pass several sterile rooms with gurneys and sinks and other equipment.

Officer Dooley wonders if Mrs. O'Quinn knows this is where the morticians prepare the dead, while Mary follows, now very comfortable in the knowledge that she cannot be seen or heard. They stop at one room at the end of the hall and enter slowly.

"Mrs. O'Quinn," I'm so sorry for your loss," the white-cloaked morgue attendant says, showing the appropriate amount of compassion and confidence. As he takes her hand, the Silver Strands that Mrs. O'Quinn and Officer Dooley share loop effortlessly, snakelike, around the wrist of the nameless attendant. Mary notices this and now she anticipates it.

She remembers The Woman's words, *"The strands – the ropes – the wires – whatever ye want to call them. They exist for a reason, child. The good Lord does nothing without purpose. From the moment ye – and they (pointing to the strands in her hand) were created, ye were given the gift of bonding. For every life ye touch, a silver strand attached itself to that other person. Ye may mean a mother/daughter thing, or husband/wife thing or even that janitor Harry you always say hello to when ye leave your office. Ye all have strands connected to each other. Ye are – and always will be – a part of each other's lives."* The magic of the strands does not fade for Mary.

Mr. Delaney escorts Officer Dooley and Mrs. O'Quinn into a small room on the left. Mary knows she is not visible to these people; still she respectfully keeps her distance as a mother says a final farewell to her son.

Aiden O'Quinn's body lay on a stainless steel gurney, a sheet covering his body almost to his chin. But Mrs. O'Quinn could still see the top of the ugly "Y" that has been carved in his body for the autopsy. Officer Dooley hovers close to the elderly woman, bracing himself in case she feels faint. But she walks deliberately and with purpose up to her son. She lovingly brushes his bearded, aged cheek. It is deeply scarred from the accident and years of unhealthy living.

"Your red hair is gone," the woman says softly, sadly, like a mother scolding her child for going outside without a coat. It is true – the color of his hair, the color which gave him his nickname "Big Red" is only a memory. He sports a silver beard and long silver hair. His face also has suffered the ravages of time – deep crevices and pock marks.

"Aiden, my child. May you dance with the angels now. No more suffering. No more pain," Mrs. O'Quinn whispers to her son.

Her voice is colored by the agony of a mother losing a child, but Officer Dooley is certain he detects a slight twinge of relief in her voice.

"Godspeed, my child." She then recites an old Irish prayer that Officer Dooley vaguely recognizes from his grandfather's funeral. Mrs. O'Quinn closes her eyes and whispers in her Irish brogue, without stopping for a pause:

"God looked around His garden. And found an empty place. He then looked down upon the earth. And saw your tired face. He put his arms around you and lifted you to rest. God's garden must be beautiful. He always takes the best. He saw the road was getting rough. And the hills were hard to climb, So, He closed your weary eyelids and whispered 'Peace be thine'."

Mary stares at the Silver Strands on "Big Red." They loop around every person in the room.

Will is waiting outside the room. It is one of the more unpleasant, but necessary facets of the newspaper job; talking to the victim's family so soon after the tragedy to get the best quotes. It can be a cold business, but Will assuages his guilt by reminding himself that's what readers want.

When Officer Dooley rounds the corner and sees Will, he shoots him a look as if to say, *"Go away, vulture!"*

Will ignores him. In his most charming voice, Will introduces himself once again to Mrs. O'Quinn, hoping she remembers him and his request – he doesn't relish asking her again.

"You're the reporter," Mrs. O'Quinn says stoically. "You want to talk to me about Aiden. Well now's as good a time as any. We can use your car to go to my house.

"My daughter Kathleen is taking over the arrangements, so I need something to occupy my mind or I'll go loony, I will. I'll put a pot of tea on and we can talk. I have some fresh-made biscuits too."

She turns to the police officer and says, "Officer Dooley, thank you so much, my dear lad. You've been a perfect gentleman. God bless you."

"My pleasure, Mrs. O'Quinn. I'm just so sorry we had to meet under these circumstances." As Officer Dooley walks away Mary watches the Silver Strand attached to his wrist dance and bounce as he walks back to his cruiser.

"Here, let me help you in," Will says, a genuine empathy in his voice as he cleans out the front seat of his rusted 1998 Honda Civic of the copious amounts of note papers and fast-food wrappers. He is treating Mrs. O'Quinn with careful respect. He helps her as she slowly climbs into the front seat.

Mary, who often saw the crude and rude side of Will at the newsroom, can't help but smile. This elderly, adorable woman reduced the machismo, bull-dog reporter to mush. The Silver Strand had already wrapped itself around Will's and Mrs. O'Quinn's wrists. Their paths had crossed – under incredibly tragic circumstances, but that was irrelevant. They would be connected eternally.

Will pulls his wreck of a car up to Mrs. O'Quinn's house. It is an old wooden farmhouse that has weathered more than a century of sun and storms. Will follows Mrs. O'Quinn as she slowly wedges the key into the lock of the huge wooden door and wiggles it several times before it surrenders. Will follows her into the front foyer and puts his coat on an antique hat stand just inside the door.

"Let me put the kettle on and I'll get those biscuits," Mrs. O'Quinn says matter-of-factly. She leaves the room, and Will takes full advantage of the time alone by studying his surroundings. A plethora of crucifixes – one more elaborate than the other – adorn each fading papered wall of the small living room. He sits on a plump couch, but he soon realizes it is the heaping amount of needlepoint pillows that give the couch its softness. Many of the pillows sport Gaelic symbols; there was the obligatory shamrock pillow and the claddagh heart. The green color of the wool Mrs. O'Quinn used to knit the pillows' designs had just begun to fade with time. There are doilies on every table in the room. Cape Cod curtains, pulled back, let in the afternoon sun.

Will examines the mantle over the well-used fireplace. Black soot from many a winter blaze has stained the brick. The air smells of an odd mixture of lilacs and the smoky remnants of faded embers. He can't help but notice that a Purple Heart framed under glass is displayed proudly in the center of the mantle. To its left is a Silver Star, also framed and under glass.

Mary watches him trying to read the inscription when Mrs. O'Quinn speaks, halfway between the kitchen and parlor.

"Don't mind the clutter, dear," Mrs. O'Quinn says as she returns to the parlor. The *Lady of the House* has become much more personable now as she plays hostess. Will guesses she rarely entertains company. When she enters the room, she is carrying a tray holding a delicate porcelain teapot decorated with tiny violets and shamrocks, and two teacups and saucers. The matching creamer and sugar jar complete the set. There also is a small plate of sugar cookies. Will is amused; he can find no discernible "clutter." His own mother had the same habit; the house was always neat and tidy, but she always offered a, "Forgive-the-clutter," to anyone who came by, lest a pillow be out of place or a photo askew.

190

"I'm sorry to have to intrude on you at a time like this," Will says, sincerely, for once in his reporting career. It is clear that this frail, elderly, stoic woman truly amazes him.

"I've done my crying over Aiden, Lord knows," Mrs. O'Quinn says. "He's my son and I loved him – I still love him – but there reaches a point when you realize sometimes you just can't help the people you care about the most. I've been thinking; my Aiden – you're right – people should know about him. The children, they made fun of him. The fancy businessmen in town looked down their noses at him because he had no home. But they didn't know the real Aiden – I knew him. All those people who gossiped whenever he walked by. They only knew the Aiden who came home from the war."

As Will listens, he notices the framed Purple Heart and Silver Star on the mantle, obviously belonging to Aiden. He had heard that Aiden was a Vietnam veteran, but that was so long ago, he had forgotten. Instinctively, he takes out his pad and pencil and a tiny recorder; he points to the latter and asks Mrs. O'Quinn, "Is this okay? I mean me recording our talk?"

Mrs. O'Quinn doesn't answer, but waves her hand, as if to say, *"Sure, what harm can it do?"*

Mary is watching her *Beacon* colleague at work. This polite, respectful side of Will is something unfamiliar to her. She is delighted, and more than a little surprised. Mary is as curious as Will now to hear the story of "Old Red."

Will is pleased that he seems to have connected well with Mrs. O'Quinn on some level. It will make the interview so much smoother.

"I guess I don't act much like a mother who lost her son," Mrs. O'Quinn says in her soft Irish accent. "I will always love Aiden – always. Please put that in your story, Mr. Reporter. That is important. It's just that I didn't lose my Aiden when he was hit by that car. I lost him a long time ago, when he came home from the war. I lived through a couple. of wars, that is. They're always bad. But Viet Nam... ugly thing, that war was.

Viet Nam." Mrs. O'Quinn says the name with a distinct tone of bitterness. "Never heard of that place before. It was just a jungle to me. As the mother of a son who fights in a war, she looks at war like no one else. Aiden... oh dear Lord ... he was just eighteen when he joined the Marines. He went in the Marines... said if he was going to do something right, he was going to be the best. That's the way Aiden was. Oh Lord, you should have seen him in high school. Straight A's, star of the basketball team and handsome as the day is long, yes he was.

"When he was just a wee lad the other children used to tease him about his height and his hair. Red, like the setting sun it was, beautiful thick red hair. But of course, children don't appreciate that. They make fun of anything that makes you stand out – didn't bother him, though. When he got into high school – oh, my, how the girls flocked to him. His red hair turned the color of the last of the burning embers of an October bonfire. Handsome, oh so handsome and tall, too, and I'm not just saying that because I am his mother," Mrs. O'Quinn says, staring deeply into Will's eyes.

They both are oblivious to Mary's presence, as Mrs. O'Quinn starts her tea ritual. She pours the heady brew first into Will's cup and then hers.

Mary moves closer to hear the conversation.

"Would you care for something more 'potent,' in your tea?" Mrs. O'Quinn whispers with a half-smile. "I've got some Bailey's Irish Liqueur."

Mary can't help but giggle.

Will stammers at the question but declines it, saying he has a long evening of work ahead of him. Just then, Paddy, her Jack Russell Terrier, comes jumping into the room and makes himself at home on Will's lap.

"Paddy, get down! Where are your manners?" Mrs. O'Quinn says, only half-scolding.

Mary watches in surprise as another Silver Strand slithers deliberately around Paddy's collar and attaches itself to Will's wrist as he accepts his tea.

"Thank you, ma'am," he says.

Animals too? Mary smiles as Paddy's Silver Strand slowly wraps around her own wrist. The Silver Strands, no longer a mystery to her, are accepted as the price a child might have to

192

pay for an amusement ride – and she is more than willing to offer her due.

"Talk to anyone who knew him back then," Mrs. O'Quinn says, finishing her thought. They'll say exactly what I'm saying. Truth is, he lost so many of his classmates to the war or drugs, there aren't so many around anymore. That's why he came home to..." Her voice trails off for a second.

"There's an old Irish proverb: *'A man loves his sweetheart the most, his wife the best, but his mother the longest.'*

I loved my kids but it wasn't any secret that Aiden, my boy, was special to me. Even more sensitive than his sister Kathleen, he was. "He left for Viet Nam in June 1967 – didn't even have a steady girl when he left. He was in the infantry. They called them 'grunts.' They're the troops on the ground – didn't have the armor of a tank or a plane between him and the Viet Cong. Just his flak jacket, his rifle and his two hands. He wrote to me when he could, but I could tell just from the tone of his letters..." Again, her voice begins to trail off. Mrs. O'Quinn is silent for several seconds, and Will doesn't utter a sound.

"The letters – the *tone* of them – they just started getting... I don't know... darker and darker. A mother can tell when there's something bothering her boy – even if it's just written words and a world away. I could tell he was getting more and more... I don't know, different. *Darker. Depressed.* Funny thing about that – you don't hear a person's voice, you just read their words, but you can tell. A mother can *always* tell.

"Fourteen months he was there. Fourteen months in hell. When the letters stopped coming I knew there was something wrong. I mean *really* wrong. I wrote to the Marines, I wrote to the Red Cross... trying to find out what was going on with my son. Nothing. So I waited. Day after day I would sit on the outside stoop waiting for Mr. Harper, the mailman. I would always say a prayer before he got here, that he would have a letter from Aiden."

Mrs. O'Quinn, who has been lost in a kind of stupor as she tells her story, suddenly looks up at the reporter.

Will is staring at Mrs. O'Quinn in rapt attention. In any other story, he would be taking copious notes, but here he just jots a word or two down every so often. He is more enthralled with Mrs. O'Quinn's story than he ever thought he would be. He's going to let the tape recorder do the work.

"I knew there was something that summer day as I waited for Mr. Harper," Mrs. O'Quinn says, speaking almost in a trance. "I knew there was something wrong. It was so hot... the sun, it was the Devil himself. When Mr. Harper handed me my mail, he didn't look me in the eye.

The letter from the War Department just said that Aiden was 'missing in action.' But the whole mess came out later. It was about 1968. They called it the "Tat Offensive." I still don't know what that means. I just guess that's when we began to lose the war. I don't know the politics of it. I don't understand politics. I just know it was chaos, which is redundant when you're talking about war, eh?" Again, Mrs. O'Quinn looks up at Will to see if she still has his full attention.

"Of course," he says, nodding.

That satisfies her. She picks up where she left off.

"The Viet Cong made an all-out attack. Our boys didn't stand a chance. They put up as good a fight as they could, but the Viet Cong had those – what do you call them? 'Guerrilla fighters,' I think. The Marines said that my boy had been seriously wounded for" – and here Mrs. O'Quinn looks up at the ceiling, trying to memorize the words exactly: 'Gallantry in action against an armed enemy of the United States.' He was being shipped home. They said I should be very proud of him. I couldn't care less as long as my Aiden came home to me alive. Whatever wounds he suffered – if he was paralyzed or blind or whatever – I prayed to the Lord, just bring him home alive.

"The Marines also awarded him the Purple Heart – you know, the medal they give the boys who are wounded?

Will nods his head in recognition.

"It was only when he came home they told me what really happened over there. Aiden put his own life in danger saving five of his fellow Marines that were pinned under enemy fire. He made five trips – all in the path of enemy fire – to help

194

carry each of those wounded boys to safety. It was the fifth trip – the last trip – that his luck ran out. The Viet Cong got a clean shot – right to the abdomen. He saved those boys but he almost bled out himself in the helicopter ride back. The government awarded him nine medals in all. Did you know that, Mr. Wheaton?" Mrs. O'Quinn says in loud voice, mixed with defiance and pride. *Nine medals.*

"The only ones I display are the Silver Star and the Purple Heart. I want people to know how brave my Aiden was and that he took a bullet in the head for his country. Of course if it was up to Aiden, I wouldn't be displaying any of them. I found them by accident. He had packed them under his dress blues, beneath his underwear, almost as if he didn't care."

Both Mary and Will are enthralled by the story that Mrs. O'Quinn is telling about the man they knew only as "Big Red." It is hard to believe that the shuffling, homeless man, perpetually hunched over and clad in the dirty raincoat, the filthy figure who talked to himself, who roamed the town streets like a dark specter, was a war hero. Will finally realizes he had been so intent on the story, that he hadn't taken any notes. Thank God for the tape recorder.

"Well, his body came home, but not his mind," Mrs. O'Quinn says as she sips her tea and stares straight ahead. "I knew the minute I laid eyes on my boy that he wasn't right. I knew there was something wrong. Oh, the body wounds, they heal up just fine. Left him with some aches and pains, but nothing serious. Still has some shrapnel in his leg. When that feckin' war was over, (Will had to restrain himself from chuckling at this prim lady's use of a profanity, even if she did mispronounce it) you know what the Marines told him? They 'suggested' he not wear his uniform home. That way all those snot-nosed hippies wouldn't target him as a 'baby killer.' My Aiden didn't give a rat's ass. He wore his Marine uniform home. I know he got spat at several times. But my Aiden was never one to shy away from something he knew to be right.

"When he came home the local VFW wanted to give him a big to-do – a barbecue and parade to welcome him back. He didn't want it. I had to beg him to go. I should have known there was something wrong right then," Mrs. O'Quinn says, shaking her head. "They had a big ceremony, but some of our so-called 'neighbors' never even shook his hand. Never even said, 'Welcome back.' Just came for the barbecue and then left. Just as well. The mayor and the city councilmen gave speeches, talked about what a hero my son was. Aiden sat there like he didn't hear a word. Those medals he won might have been made of tin for all they were worth to him.

"When the big barbecue was over, some of those damn hippies stayed behind as the ladies of the VFW cleaned up. I know just who they were – fancied themselves 'war protestors' and the like. I think they were just plain mean. After everyone left, those snot-nose kids shouted terrible things at Aiden. Held up photos of Vietnamese children all burned up... terrible, horrible pictures, just awful. And they kept telling him, 'Look at this...this is what you've done!' "

Mrs. O'Quinn takes a deep breath.

"I think that was the final straw for my Aiden. He got home that night and burned his Marine dress blues and every other hint that he was ever in the military – a really big bonfire in our backyard. Went up like twenty feet. I got scared it was going to spread to the house. I had to call the Fire Department. It was like he couldn't exorcise his demons from the war fast enough.

"I wanted him to live with me until he got on his feet. He was in a terrible way."

Mrs. O'Quinn utters an almost indiscernible, sarcastic giggle.

"I had no way of knowing then that was never going to happen. I thought he could put the war behind him, go on with his life, maybe meet a nice girl and settle down, you know."

Mrs. O'Quinn looks at Will again, for confirmation.

He nods, knowingly.

"The firemen, they took pity on Aiden. Some of them came back from the war themselves. Anyhow, they never reported it to the police.

196

"But later that week it just got worse. Lord, I should have known right then and there the night of the fire that Aiden wasn't right in the head no more."

Normally-stoic, Mrs. O'Quinn dabs at her eyes with an old lace handkerchief.

"He would no sooner get to sleep than the screaming started. Oh Lord, he scared me half to death – screaming the most awful things – terrible, filthy words. My Aiden never used words like that before. I tell you, that night I knew I had lost my boy forever. *I knew it.* People said 'give him time. He needs time to adjust.' But I knew I lost my boy forever. It sounds terrible, but sometimes I think it might have been better if he had died in that war. Lord knows he never had any kind of life after he came home.

"I took him to the 'mind' doctors at the veteran's clinic, and they talked with him. They diagnosed him with Post Traumatic Stress Disorder and gave him pills. They didn't do any good. They wanted to see him once a week, but Aiden refused.

"The doctors don't understand," he said.

Every night it was same – the screaming. Oh dear Lord, the screaming, like old Scratch himself was after him, snapping at his heels. Or he'd be screaming for forgiveness, for what, I never knew. He must have felt he had done something awful. He kept begging God for forgiveness, over and over and over."

Mary choked back tears. *What if I do cry?* she thinks, absurdly. *Well, at least they can't see me.*

"Do you have children, Mr. Wheaton?" Mrs. O'Quinn asks Will.

He is flustered by the question, chokes a bit on his tea, but composes himself quickly.

"No ma'am, I don't."

Mary thinks Will has many more questions, but he probably feels it is best to let Mrs. O'Quinn tell her story first.

"Well right, there, dearie, we might have a problem. You don't know how far a parent will go for their child. Their child – like my Aiden or my Kathleen – they become a part of you. They hurt, you hurt. They succeed, you succeed. They fall ill,

197

you share the pain. A strange relationship the good Lord gave us – parent and child – it's like no other. So when I tell you this story, you keep that in mind, you hear?"

Will nods silently.

"The screaming fits – the night terrors – oh my sweet Jesus, the night terrors. I went in his room one time when he was screaming. He latched his hands onto my neck and squeezed and squeezed. I thought for sure I was going to die. I felt things go black. But just as quick as he jumped on me, he let go. And then he rolled over and went back to sleep, sound as a baby.

"One night I heard my cat Binky making the most horrible noises – they were ungodly – I never heard an animal scream for help, but I swear I did that night," Mrs. O'Quinn says, a hint of horror in her voice. "I followed the sound straight to Aiden's room. He had shaved Binky and he was strangling her just the way he was doing to me the other night. I tried to save Binky, but Aiden was too strong. He knocked me down and killed that poor animal. And I finally, finally, realized that I didn't only lose my son, but that there was another soul who took his place – someone I didn't know –someone who no longer could feel love.

"My Aiden was never cruel – never. Couldn't even bring himself to kill a bat that got in our house once. He spent two hours trying to trap it before he released it outside. That was my Aiden – my Aiden with the red hair. And now he's gone."

Mrs. O'Quinn looks down at her tea, lost in her thoughts for a second, her face blank. She sips her tea and resumes her grim story.

"I was still working back then. I would get phone calls from the police in the middle of the day. The neighbors were complaining that Aiden was naked, on our front lawn, screaming and crying:

"Forgive me! Forgive me. Forgive me."

"I hired caretaker after caretaker to stay with him while I worked... but no one could handle him. He was a big man. Those caretakers couldn't handle him. One by one, they left. I held no grudge, mind you. I was surprised they took the job at

all. My Aiden – my boy – he was gone and someone left a
zombie in his place. Didn't ever talk, just went through the
motions of living. Truth is, I saw it in his eyes. He gave up on
life. Once, only once, did he ever give me a hint of what was
wrong. He said, 'Mum, I'm going to Hell. Jesus can't forgive
me for what I've done.' And that was the last time anyone
heard him utter a word."

Mary listens intently, carefully watching the exchange
between Mrs. O'Quinn and Will.

The Voice beckons her again, but she pays it no mind. She
knows it is Dr. Lee back in his office and that she is nodding
her head that yes, she is okay. Mary is a bit annoyed at the
interference. She wants to hear the rest of Mrs. O'Quinn's
story.

"And then *that* phone call came – dead of winter, it was –
snow on the ground two feet high. I remember it was
Valentine's Day. The police called me and wouldn't explain
why over the phone. Just said, 'Mrs. O'Quinn, I think you
should come down here quick.' They were at my house, but
they wouldn't tell me anything more. Oh Lord, how fast I
drove from work to home. The police cars were the first thing I
noticed when I pulled up to the house. There must have been
ten of them, their red and blue lights a-flashing like a Ferris
wheel. There were so many police officers. They were looking
at each other – looked like they couldn't figure out what the
heck to do.

"Well, it seems Aiden – he was butt-naked – had removed
all the furniture in my house and put it on the front lawn. He set
up the furniture in the exact same spots I had them in my
house. In two feet of snow, mind you. He kept saying, 'Now
they're free. Now they're free.' That was the day he stopped
talking. They took him away to the veterans' hospital, but he
kept escaping. And they finally gave up. 'He's an adult, Mrs.
O'Quinn,' they told me. 'He's not a danger to himself or
others, and we have no legal right to keep him here.' "

"He took to the woods; made himself a tent and gathered the necessities. His Social Security Disability came through for his PTSD, and I went to his campsite; I knew where it was because he went there often as a boy. I tried to give him his checks, but he wouldn't – or couldn't – look at me. Wouldn't talk to me, no matter how hard I pleaded. So I left, figuring I'd come back the next day. Only the next day he wasn't there. He found a discarded camp site and liked it, so he started sleeping here and there. The bushes in back of the Save-A-Lot store, or the bench all the way in the back of Luna Park, behind the evergreens.

"It was like he was trying to disappear – trying to turn into nothing. He found a raincoat, a filthy thing, but he began wearing it all the time. He would come in town early in the morning to hit the dumpsters for food. I know for a fact that people tried to give him food but he wouldn't take it. All he would eat were the leftovers from the bakery and the restaurant – half-eaten bear claws and half-filled cups of coffee – and lots of French fries. Would you believe some kind soul even left him some of those small cigars he was so fond of? Well, I guess people can't be all bad, thank the Lord. I figure he was happy in his world, so who am I to judge?"

As the images of Aiden and Mrs. O'Quinn and Will melt away, Mary finds herself back in the Warrens' home.

Seventeen

Back At The Warrens

Carol and Bob are in the downstairs bathroom. The room is spit-polish clean and smells refreshingly like Pine-Sol and an expensive French soap. The fixtures glisten. Carol and Bob, as usual, are screaming at each other. The argument is about money. It is almost always about money. Carol has been trying desperately to keep up her fashionable suburban supermom-image, but with one income – her's – it is become increasingly difficult. Their arguments increase with direct correlation to the increasing stack of bills and charges on their credit cards.

Their teen-age girls, Kelli, and Tiffani, know exactly what financial predicament their family is in; and, it isn't pretty. They try their best to support their mother – the real breadwinner and also the only stable emotional influence in the family. The girls' afternoon jobs at McDonald's don't make much of a dent in their debt.

Bob's gambling debts are much worse than Carol had imagined; she inadvertently saw the credit card statements before Bob had a chance to retrieve the mail. Now she is kicking herself for believing Bob's silly, incredible lies that he was winning at the casinos and that their finances are just fine.

"What now, Bob?" Carol asks, walking into the master bedroom, anticipating the worst.

"The girls' college funds are gone," Bob says. Following her, he adds, "I guess it's community college for them. It won't kill them." He sits down on the huge double bed, hanging his head.

"Won't kill them? *Won't kill them?*" Carol's voice is reaching a fever pitch.

"Remember, we *planned* their futures – all that money for tuition to attend one of the better schools in the country? And

201

who's going to break that to the girls? It sure isn't going to be *me*."

Unlike previous times, Bob has lost his bravado and confidence. He mutters unconvincingly, "I'll figure something out." He is fooling no one, and he knows it.

Mary is still confused as to why she would be back at the Warrens' house, and in their *upstairs* bathroom, now.

Suddenly Kelli rushes in, making a bee-line to the toilet. She bends over the oval porcelain, puts her middle finger down her throat, and gags several times before vomiting the sparse salad – sans dressing – that she had for dinner that night, trying not to make too much noise. Kelli's long brown hair hides her face.

As usual, a Silver Strand now connects Mary to Kelli. Mary follows Kelli into her room.

The room is teen-aged girly, and punctuated with pink accents. Its ivory walls feature a top border stenciled with pink roses encircling the entire area. A magnificent handmade quilt covers the huge double-bed. Stuffed animals are arranged neatly at the head of the bed, propped up against the frilly pillow shams. Dainty white lace curtains dance in the breeze from the open windows. Kelli can clearly hear her parents arguing downstairs. She knows exactly what is going on and has known for some time. She had always been "Daddy's Little Girl," but not for the normal reasons. She has an uncanny insight into her father's flaws.

Others may have believed that gambling was his major vice, but in truth he suffers from a myriad of other problems including depression and anxiety as well as stress. The struggle to present a successful image to the world is a constant bolder dangling over his head. There can be no nine-to-five job for Bob. It has to be bigger, grander than anyone in their gated community. He feels an unfounded hunger to show everyone that, yes, indeed, he is a success.

Kelli understands these things – a wise girl for her young age. She, in turn, feels the pressure of walking a tightrope every day. She wants to please her parents just as Bob wants to please his peers. Success – for Bob and his girls – is the only option.

Mary continues to watch Kelli in bewilderment.

Kelli cleans herself up; then she rearranges small plastic garbage bags stored in her closet which contain some kind of a liquid that stinks of something rancid. She covers them up with her precious, small collection of Christian Louboutin knock-off shoes. The plastic bags are completely camouflaged with the fashionable footwear.

Mary knows – she doesn't know how – that Kelli will sneak out later that night and throw the week's worth of vomit into a larger garbage bag, and then in the family garbage pail at the curb. Come Wednesday, the garbage men will haul away the evidence. It is a routine that has continued undetected for nearly two years.

Mary puts her hand over her mouth, herself now gagging. She barely has time to recover from this awful sight when she finds herself in Tiffani's room just as girly, but not as large.

Tiffani's eye makeup is smeared from tears, her hair a mess and resembles nothing of the sleek hairstyles she sports in the framed photos downstairs. Tiffani spreads a terry-cloth bath towel on her bed then rifles through a dresser draw until she finds what she's been looking for – a razor-sharp X-acto knife. Mary watches in horror as Tiffani sits calmly on the large bed and places her arm – connected to Mary's by a Silver Strand – over the towel, and uses the knife to slice a small cut in her skin – just enough for blood to seep out and drip on the towel. Tiffani's face registers a strange kind of peace and relief.

Watching the pain unfold in this family is almost more than Mary can bear. Lord knows, she always felt there was an undertow of dysfunction in this family – she simply had no idea it ran this deep.

Does either girl know they each are suffering their own individual version of hell? Mary wonders.

The Cherry Festival

Mary inhales the delectable aroma of strong coffee. It is wonderful, but there is a distinct underlying smell lying just beneath the java. She sniffs and sniffs again, trying to recognize the smell.

Cherry pie. Definitely, cherry pie. She looks about and sees huge signs everywhere.

Emmett Cherry Festival

Emblazoned on each white sign are huge painted red cherries and green leaves. There are tables set up everywhere, weighted down with everything cherry – cherry pie, cherry cobbler, cherry preserves.

Mary soaks in the sight. Everywhere she looks, the town is draped in red and white stripes, with a dash of blue. Mary feels, amusingly, that she is ensconced in the pocket of a giant clown's costume. All the charming white clapboard cottages sport American flags flapping in the warm breeze. Women and men alike are dressed in red, white and blue. Three little girls, none older than six, giggle next to her. They are clad in different outfits – all different patterns of the American flag.

Mary is bewildered, an emotion that is becoming all too familiar to her.

One elderly woman is dressed in a blue denim jumper and a snappy straw hat. She wears a full apron adorned with dots of cherries and green leaves stenciled on it. She carries a bowl of juicy red cherries, as if to emphasize the Americana colors of her outfit.

Without thinking, Mary taps the lady on the shoulder.

"Excuse me, Ma'am," she asks. "I think I took a wrong turn somewhere. Can you tell me where I am?"

"You can see me then?" the woman asks in surprise.

"Wow, yeah, I guess I can," Mary answers, equally surprised. For a single moment there, Mary had forgotten that she was an unearthly visitor on the road to... who knows where?

The woman waves her hand in dismissal. She sports a coiffure of neat brown hair, cut bluntly to her chin, and has brilliant blue eyes.

"It happens now and then. Don't know how or when. One of those freak things, I guess. I was born and raised here, so I visit here often. We don't get many of your kind here. This isn't your destination. By the way, I'm Bernice. You can call me Bernie."

Mary grasps Bernie's outstretched hand, and says, "I'm Mary."

Neither one is confused or even surprised when the Silver Strands appear and connect their hands weightlessly. The woman looks at Mary, slightly confused, but smiles as she answers her unasked question.

"Why dear, you're in Emmett."

"Emmett?" Mary repeats in confusion.

"Yes dear," the woman replies, a look of concern starting to form on her face.

"Emmett, Idaho."

Idaho? *Idaho?*

Mary composes herself enough to continue talking, quick to ask questions.

"I'm just wondering what all this is," she says, looking around at all the cherry-themed decorations, including a display of gorgeous handmade cherry-themed quilts. Some are dotted with blazing red cherry appliqués, while others are made with nearly fifty different types of cherry-printed cloths. The quilts hang on a clothesline stretching the length of half a football field. The effect is breathtaking.

Mary can see a child's parade beginning to get under way – with a "cherry theme," of course. The children already are adorning their bicycles with red, white and blue crepe paper streamers. A huge folding table groans under the weight of paper foam cups full of cherries (a quarter each, thank you) and Ball jars holdings a cavalcade of cherry delights: Cherry-orange relish; rustic cherry shortcake and – if sweets aren't your thing – "Cherry Tuscan Salad" a delicacy made with cherries, various peppers, capers and grated Parmesan cheese. And, of course there are the inevitable souvenirs. A potter had set up shop to create one-of-kind mugs to commemorate the day. The Silver Strands are in full force, connecting Mary to every person at the festival. Mary stopped marveling at them long ago. They are becoming routine and she is becoming quite used to them.

Bernie smiles as she sees Mary look around in wonder.

"This is our Cherry Festival." the elderly woman says in an understanding tone. "We hold this every year. It's our one claim to fame, and we make the most out of it! The entire weekend is dedicated to cherries – all kinds of cherries. Don't ask me why Emmett soil is so perfect for the fruit, but it is. I was born and bred here. That's why I still keep coming back for the festival. It's part of my life, and eventually, my death – always will be."

Mary doesn't know that Emmett is only about thirty miles from Boise, the country's potato capital. Just thirty miles away from the famed potato-land monument is a river that wends its way over hills and valleys, eventually finding its way to Cherrystone Orchard, a huge plantation whose trees explode in breath-taking pinks and whites every spring. From afar, the landscape looks like someone had sprinkled pink and white cotton candy on all the trees. It is a magical setting.

The trees' fruit transforms its candy-for-the-eye into candy-for-the-mouth. Mary knows she must have come at the peak of cherry-harvest time. The ubiquitous fruit in the charming town is hanging ripe and heavy from the trees, a bounty just waiting to be plucked. It seems that every child – even those not yet weaned from diapers – wave an American flag.

My God, talk about Smalltown, USA! Mary thinks in delight. *"This is what they mean when they say 'The Heart of America.'"*

Mary looks around in profound pleasure, taking in the sights and smells of the hometown harmony, when she notices a man. He looks deceptively familiar: Square jaw, blue eyes, brown hair. He holds a small pad and pen as he rough-houses with a toddler, a little boy who seems to be about one or two, on the lush green grass route waiting for the parade to start.

The woman with him is strikingly alluring. She has flowing auburn hair, green eyes and is dressed in the patriotic colors of the day, just like everyone else. Her denim skirt swirls in the breeze and her white peasant blouse flaps pleasantly, like ripples of water. A giant red straw hat shades her face from the sun. When she laughs, it sounds like a sweet sonata.

The man wears a red Polo shirt and blue jeans. No doubt about it. This June day isn't just to celebrate the cherry harvest. It is clear the Cherry Festival pre-empts the July 4th holiday in this town in more ways than one. It is a day to celebrate family and kin and friends. Optimism wafts in on the early summer breeze.

Mary can't stop staring at the man who is totally absorbed in his little son. Only when the man turns completely around does she recognize him: A much, much younger version of Gary Elliott, her city editor. Mary gasps, smiling, at the happy tableaux for several minutes. She guesses by the paper and pen in his hand that he is the cub reporter who has been assigned to cover the parade for the local hometown paper – a small daily with circulation, she guessed, at about 13,000. Mary delights seeing Gary as a young reporter, starting out his career with child and wife in tow. While Gary plays with his son, his wife is buying him the coffee mug with the cherries on it, the one that says *Number 1 Dad!* She is going to surprise him with it. It is the same mug from which he drinks his morning coffee every day now at *The Beacon*. It doesn't have any chips, however, and the red and green cherry on it is newly painted. My Lord, Mary thinks, he must have kept that mug all these decades.

"Sad," a voice next to her whispers.

Mary jumps.

"Oh, I'm sorry dear, didn't mean to do that." It is Bernie.

"What do you mean 'sad'?" Mary asks Bernie. She could see nothing "sad" in this picture of a happy family.

"They lost him – the little one. Virus attacked his little heart. He never got to see this third birthday."

Mary doesn't ask Bernie how she can see into the future. There no longer seems to be any point.

"Oh no," Mary says in a genuine tug of sympathy. She suddenly understands the rarely-seen dark streak that simmers just beneath the surface of Gary Elliott's enthusiasm and frivolity.

"Yep," Bernice says, as she eats a piece of celebration cake. "Damn-near killed the parents. They didn't last more than a year after they buried their boy. Truth be told, I don't think they could stand the sight of each other. Wait – *that didn't come out right*. I mean, when they looked at each other, all they saw was a reminder of their boy. It works out that way sometimes. Couples who lose a child, they either get closer or they separate. Gary and Gwen eventually went their separate ways. Gary took some big newspaper job out of state. Truth of the matter," Bernice says, still munching on her cake, "I don't think he could get far enough away from this town. It hurt too much. I hear he went on to win some big newspaper awards. But you know, all the awards in the world won't fill that hole in your heart when you lose a child."

The Camp

Mary's skin shivers against the biting cold. It takes her several seconds to realize she is wearing just a dirty, tattered cotton dress. She is barefoot and when she can see her breath, she knows it is the bitter heart of winter. A soldier – at least she guesses that's what he is by his military uniform – is screaming into her face, repeating the same word over and over again. She winces each time he yells it at her, his spittle dotting her face. She did not have a clue as to what he wants her to do.

A merciful woman grabs her by her thread-worn dress – she can see now it is only rags, and pulls her back into line with the rest of the women similarly dressed in vertically striped *dresses*. The Silver Strand immediately appears as the woman touches her.

"Get in line, quickly," the woman whispers urgently to Mary.

"What is he saying?" Mary asks. "Where am I?"

The woman purses her lips and puts her finger up to her mouth.

"Not now. Later," she whispers. Mary looks around her. The barren barracks contain bunk upon bunk of starving, sickly, dirty people nearly stacked one upon the other. Mary is struck dumb with fear as she realizes she is in a Nazi concentration camp, but which one? Auschwitz? Dachau? It doesn't seem to matter. The soldier barks another order, and Mary and the rest of the women – some of them, skeletal-looking – shuffle obediently into the tent. There is a woman in military uniform there too, but if Mary expects any empathy from her, she is sorely mistaken. An elderly woman slips and nearly falls. The uniformed woman, using a riding crop, snaps it across the old woman's back swiftly, three times. Mary sees a scarlet stain begin to form on the back of the old woman's ragged dress. The woman in uniform screams something at the old woman, who cowers in fear, not daring to raise her eyes.

Once the women form a single line in the freezer-like barracks, the man in uniform bellows something else that Mary cannot understand. She merely follows what the rest of the women are doing. Mary is terrified.

"Lie down here, next to me," the woman who had grabbed her arm earlier, says. "I'll tell you what you need to know."

Mary can't help but feel relieved when she sees she is connected to the woman by a Silver Strand.

Mary does as she is told. Once the barracks goes dark, the woman whispers to her:

"I don't know who you are, but I've been told to expect you. I know you're not going to stay. But while you're here you should know… *things*."

Mary is certain that everyone is speaking in a foreign language, but the only person she can understand is this woman.

"I am Beatrice Miller. Everyone calls me Bea."

Mary is trying to place the woman's face; she is certain she has seen it before. She stares at the sunken eyes, the deep lines engraved in this woman's face and tries to imagine how she would look in good health. After a minute, the realization washes over her like a wave: This woman is David's paternal grandmother.

Mary had seen photos of David's grandparents, Beatrice and Arthur, the ones who perished in the Nazi concentration camps... Bea's face is gaunt and her dark eyes have sunken into their sockets and her white brittle hair is falling out in clumps. There are patches of baldness on her head. Nonetheless, Mary recognizes her as the woman in the old, grainy photograph Mark kept on his fireplace mantle and David always keeps in his wallet. Mary looks closely at Bea and can see a glimmer of the once-elegant woman she was – the lady in the photograph.

"What's your name, dear?" Bea asks Mary.

"My name… is… Mary," she replies slowly as she surveys the horror around her.

The woman looks deep into her eyes. "I had a dream last night – the first night I actually slept in this toilet. But it wasn't really a dream – it was more like a premonition. A woman's

210

voice told me to help the woman who looked 'lost.' And, my dear, you look about as lost as a person can get. I knew the moment I laid eyes on you – you are the one I'm supposed to help."

Mary stares in horror at the crowd of women all wearing the striped, ragged clothes, a yellow star sewn crudely on the front of each one. Many of them have shaved heads. The star has "Jude" written on it. Mary looks down and sees that she is similarly garbed. Her head feels cold. She touches it and realizes in panic that her hair, too, has been shaved off. Many of the women look ill, some look exhausted and some look like this is going to be their last night on Earth. A woman in the corner keeps coughing, coughing, coughing, until finally a pocket of blood trickles down her mouth and onto the tattered cloth that barely covers her breasts.

"Listen and do exactly what I tell you to do when you're here. You can't understand German and that's okay. We'll make do. Do you know where you are, Mary?" Mary shakes her head no.

"You're in Ravensbrück." The name means nothing to Mary.

"That beast, Heinrich Himmler, just opened this camp this year," Bea whispers.

"What year is this?" Mary whispers back.

"It's 1938," Bea answers. "This camp is only for women. I suppose we should be grateful for *that*," Bea says sarcastically. Mary is still marveling at how she could be talking to David's grandmother – a woman David has never met and a woman who had died long before David and Mary were even born. But one thought actually makes her happy: The Silver Strand she now shares with Bea, she hoped to be sharing with David one day. He has always longed to know more about his paternal grandparents. He had only heard stories about his grandparents from his parents.

The female guard enters the barracks and barks something several times.

"We have to go to sleep now," Bea whispers to Mary. The dim lights are extinguished and the women crawl quickly and obediently into their assigned bunks. Some kind of odd tiny insects scurry between the sheets.

Sleep is impossible. The stark shelter stinks of urine and feces and vomit. Some women are trying to vomit – but mostly it is just dry heaves. Few of the women have enough food in their stomachs with which to vomit. Mary herself is gagging. She will find out soon enough that food is a rarity in this place.

"Food" consists of an oatmeal-like substance that provides a luke-warm home for maggots. What is in plentiful supply is death by starvation, beatings, torture, hangings and shootings – there is no shortage of those. Mary is certain Bea is speaking German, a language she doesn't understand – and yet in this dimension, communication is evolved beyond mere words.

Mary has a bottom bunk, with Bea only inches above her on her own tattered *mattress*.

After the lights go out, Bea – obviously no newcomer to Ravensbrück – whispers the rules of survival to Mary. "Keep your head down – never make eye contact with the guards. You have to be strong. They want you to work. The women who are too weak to work are transferred to the Uckermark "Youth Camp" near Auschwitz. We never hear or see them again. So it's important you be strong and a hard worker. They make us work day and night. Do you understand me, Mary?"

"Yes," Mary whispers back, terrified. She had read in history books why these people were never seen or heard from again: They have been gassed to death. She doesn't share that historical nugget with Bea, which she rightly assumes Bea already knows. The gas chambers prove to be very efficient as an eradication tool of *useless* human beings.

"If they think you're sick, they let the doctors have you. And the doctors aren't there to help heal you," Bea whispers. Mary knows all too well from her history books that these "doctors" perform unspeakable medical experiments on the sick. "Every two weeks or so the SS commandant and his doctors pick out the ill or old women here," Bea continues. "They have to lift their skirts up over their hips and run in front of the guards. Women who are ill, or have swollen feet or are just too weak to run are sent for a "recovery" period. I don't think it's a *recovery* period at all.

"They took my children from me," Bea continues, breaking down in tears.

"You don't have children, do you?" The past is getting tangled up with the future, Mary thinks in alarm. Under the circumstances, Mary decides it was best to lie.

"No, I don't."

"Yes, yes, that's good," Bea says.

"They took my children and I hear the most horrible stories – drowning of newborns, beatings, killings..." Bea's voice trails off as she thinks of her own children. Mary can hear Bea sobbing softly. "I pray my children are strong enough to work. If they can work, they're valuable. They won't kill them. And my husband, Arthur – they separated us from the start. I don't know where he is. I don't know why, but I believe he's lost to me. Bea melts into sobs again. "All I have to pray for now is my children."

Mary looks down at the Silver Strand that connects her to Bea. "I think your children will be fine. I truly do."

"Thank you, Mary," Bea says, still sobbing quietly. "I wish I could be certain of that." Mary has no way to prove to David's grandmother that her children would not only survive the camps, but they will thrive and have children of their own. So she simply stares down at the throbbing string of light that connects her to Bea. Someday, Mary thought, with renewed conviction, I will make sure that Silver Strand reaches David.

Guilty

Mary finds herself wearing a conservative pants suit, sitting on a hard wooden pew, surrounded – almost elbow-to-elbow – with other people. It takes her a second to realize she is in a courtroom. The judge – who resembles a curmudgeonly Wilford Brimley – sits on a huge pedestal-desk in the front of the room, his spectacles propped on tip of his nose. His face is a mask of intensity as he peruses the document in front of him.

"The clerk will please publish the verdict," the judge says in a gravelly voice, solemnly handing the papers in front of him to the bailiff.

Mary sees the back of a young, blond-haired man sitting at the defense table on the left side of the room. She guesses the well-dressed man next to him is his attorney. On the right side of the room sits the county prosecutor and his second lead. It is clear this is a trial, but Mary has no clue as to which one. It must be a pretty important one, she surmises by the crowded courtroom. She hears muffled sobs behind her, and turns around.

She recognizes Carl and Louise Brenner, the parents of the murdered little girl, Tammy. Carl's arms encase Louise in a loving embrace, but Mary can easily tell that Louise is on the precipice of emotional disintegration. The air in the courtroom crackles with anticipation. The only sound is stifled, muzzled sobbing on both sides of the room. In the split second it takes Mary to look at Tammy's parents to the time the polished, uniformed bailiff clears his throat to read the verdict, Mary realizes this must be the murder trial of Tammy Brenner. Police must have had enough evidence to peg Robbie Renwood for the crime.

Thank God, Mary thinks, as she stares at the back of his blond head.

"That monster will finally get what he deserves."

The bailiff's voice is loud and unwavering. "In the case of The State of New Jersey vs. Gary Garson, indictment No.

214

NJA06652, we, duly empanelled in the case, find the defendant, Gary Gilbert Garson, guilty of the charge of first-degree murder."

Mary, fully expecting to hear the name "Robert Renwood," thinks for a moment that she must have misheard. But when the blond man turns around to be cuffed by sheriff's officers, Mary sees a face similar that doesn't belong to Robbie at all. The young man looks eerily like Robbie, but it is definitely *not* him.

The defense attorney stands and addresses the judge: "Your honor, my client asks that if he is found guilty that he be sentenced immediately." The Wilford-Brimley-judge leans back in and asks if the State has any objections to the request.

"No, your honor," the prosecutor answers succinctly.

The judge asks the young man if he wishes to speak before his sentence is imposed.

"Just this, your honor," he answers in a loud, grim and bitter voice. "I am innocent. And I believe with my whole heart and soul that I will be exonerated one of these days. And I expect an apology from the prosecutor, the police and this court."

The judge clearly is not pleased with this answer.

"Fine, young man, you've had your say. Now this court will have its. What you did – snuffing out the precious life of a young girl – promising in so many ways – and then to steal her innocence in such heinous and inhumane manner... I want you to reflect on the pain you caused this family, this community. I hereby sentence you to the New Jersey Department of Corrections for a term of life in prison without the possibility of parole."

With that, sheriff's officers lead Gary Garson away through the courtroom doors, toward the hallway that leads to the county jail cells – but not before Mary notices the Silver Strand that now connects him to the Brenners. Gary – and his wrongful conviction – have become part of them now. Mary is surprised to see a second strand of glowing light emanating from Gary Garson's wrist to the back of the room. Her eyes follow the linear glow and find at its end a slightly grinning

Robbie Renwood. He apparently has been attending the trial to make sure the wrong person would be convicted of murder and he would be off the hook. He blends in with the crowd, many of them neighbors and friends of the Brenners who attended the trial in support. Mary wants to cry out that justice has not been done, but her words are silent exclamations. She isn't really there, after all.

Faintly, Mary can hear *The Voice* in the back of her head. It is saying what it always does:

"Mary, are you Okay? Do you want to continue?"

And, as always, Mary knows she is really back in Dr. Lee's office with Meg, and is assuring the good doctor that she wants to continue her journey.

Ralph McGee

The leather seats in the immaculately-clean backseat of the luxury car, are baby-bottom soft and emit a sweet smell of leather. Mary isn't good at identifying cars, so she assumes it must be a Cadillac or perhaps even a Mercedes Benz, for all she knows.

The driver is singing along with a CD of "Madame Butterfly." The man's voice is loud, and he sings with such gusto, and enthusiasm that Mary finds herself chuckling in the backseat. She has to wait through the nighttime shadows for a streetlight to see the face of the driver. To her surprise, and delight, Mary recognizes Ralph McGee, Kate's blustering, boastful, egotistical husband. She stifles a loud giggle, even though she knows he can neither hear nor see her. The only light within the car gleams from the dashboard instrument panel –and, of course, the familiar luminescence of the Silver Strand connecting her to Ralph.

Ralph is singing with wild abandon – and wildly out of tune – but obviously enjoying himself. In a flash, Ralph's operatic attempt transforms into a wild, terrifying scream. The car veers so swiftly Mary fears they might tumble out of the car and spill into the nearby ravine. A small car has slammed head-first into a utility pole on the other side of the street, snapping it in two like mere tree twigs. The crash downs the pole's electrical wires, which now dance willy-nilly on the road, leaping here and there, leaving sparks in their wake. The compact car has all but wrapped itself about the bottom of the pole. The top half of the pole, with its jumping wires, lay perilously close to the passenger's side of the car.

Gasoline leaking from the car is creating a small puddle in a pothole located precariously close to the scene of the accident. The sparking wires are snapping to and fro, missing the gas pool by inches.

Ralph dials 911 on his cell phone and calls in the accident but knows he can't wait for help to arrive. The puddle of gas is too close to take that chance.

Without hesitation, he rushes out of his car and tries desperately to release the young woman behind the wheel. But her seat belt has been pulled snugly and won't give an inch, as Ralph tugs and pulls, trying to loosen the straps enough to pull her from the smoking debris.

Even in the murky chaos, the Silver Strands appear, connecting Ralph and the woman.

All the time Ralph keeps a close eye on the electric wires, which are doing wild jumping jacks and getting much closer to the gasoline puddle. The airbag has gone off and the hundreds of shards of glass scattered about, make Ralph's job even harder.

Realizing his efforts are for naught, he remembers the pocketknife he always keeps in his back pocket. He swiftly unsheathes the small, but sharp blade, from its beat-up leather holster.

Periodically peeking at the wires, still performing their dangerous ballet above the gasoline pool, Ralph tugs with all the strength he can muster to cut the belt across the young lady's lap. It surrenders with a sudden snap. Then he repeats the same action with the strap across her chest.

The young woman drifts in and out of consciousness, muttering "*Help me.*"

A spot on the victim's forehead, just above her right eye, is spewing blood. Ralph has no medical training, but he had read somewhere that you should never let someone with serious head injuries fall asleep or lose consciousness.

"I'm Ralph!" he shouts into the young woman's bloody face. "What's your name, dearie?"

"Victoria," she whispers. "I'm Victo..." She rallies just long enough to mutter her name,

"Victoria! Stay with me." Ralph shouts with all his might: "Victoria! Stay with me. I'm Ralph. I'm going to try and help you out of this car, okay?"

218

It is difficult to keep Victoria conscious. Her legs appear to still be trapped under the rubble of what once was the front of the car, and Ralph is doing some serious multi-tasking: Keeping an eye on the electric wires, trying to keep her alert, and most difficult of all, trying to pull her out of the car, which now distinctly is a fire/explosion hazard.

"Sweet Jesus, please sweet Jesus, help me!" Ralph prays as he musters all the strength in his middle-aged body. Suddenly, he yanks Victoria free, out of the crumpled mass of metal that once was her car. She pops backward out of the car, landing on Ralph. She is a petite thing, but the force of the impact makes them land on the ground with a loud thud.

Ralph's suit has soaked up some of the gasoline on the road. Broken shards of glass pierce the back of his hands. The smell of gasoline and smoke is so thick in the air they both are gagging. He drags her across the street and props her against his car, thinking all the while, *Where the hell are the ambulance and cops?*

He continues shouting Victoria's name, trying to keep her from slipping into unconsciousness. It seems like an hour, but in fact only minutes have passed since Ralph made the 911 call. The police and firefighters, their blue-and-red lights lighting up the desolate night sky, close off the road, taking charge of the dangerous situation. An ambulance arrives shortly thereafter, carefully placing Victoria on a gurney and then loading her into the ambulance.

"Ralph," she screams out of her fog of pain, please stay with me!"

The EMT asks Ralph if he is "family."

When Ralph says no, he is told only family can ride with the patient. The EMTs slam the doors of the ambulance and head full-speed down the lonely road, with its sirens blaring and the red-and-blue lights flashing in the darkness.

"Sir, step over here, please," a state trooper says authoritatively. The trooper asks Ralph several questions, and takes down his name and phone number. Since Ralph arrived after the crash, the trooper has no further use for him. He thanks him politely and heads back to his cruiser. It's a busy night, and this is just one of several accidents the trooper is investigating.

Ralph leans against his car, his adrenaline level slowly leveling off, but his knees still shaking. With jittery hands, he sneaks a cigarette, knowing full well it's not good for a politician to be seen smoking, and tries to calm his frayed nerves. He stays there for more than half an hour – just smoking and thinking.

Mary watches in surprise. This man, whom she can barely tolerate, is nothing less than a hero tonight. The trooper had jotted down his name and phone number, but said nothing more, despite the life-saving feat he has just accomplished. Mary watches with a slight smile as the Silver Strand continues its journey from Ralph's wrist off into the distance – the path taken by the ambulance.

Ralph watches somberly as the red and blue lights disappear over the horizon. Ironically, being a hero to a fellow driver would make great political headlines. His campaign workers would love to leap on the chance to play up their candidate, he knows. Ralph, however, who is still shaking and sweating, feels that whatever transpired just now is not meant for others to know or to use as political fodder. His campaign workers would love to exploit it:

"Local official saves woman's life in auto accident." Ralph can envision the headlines now. But for some inexplicable reason, he realizes that it is only meant to be between him and God – and Victoria, if, indeed, she remembers anything at all. He is not even going to tell Kate. Ralph glances at the wreckage that once was Victoria's car. Two tow truck workers have just arrived to haul the mess away. Alone now, he slowly opens the door to his car and climbs behind the wheel, sitting there quietly for several minutes.

Eighteen

The Eversons

Mary is standing in the middle of a suburban street. Well-kept lawns and tidy little ranchers are adhering to a kind of neighborhood uniform. Subtle colors on the house, decorative shutters on the windows, lacy curtains covering the windows just enough to provide privacy to the owner, as well as sunshine, if available, on that particular day. Sunset is nearing now as evidenced by the chill in the hazy, smoky air. It's that magical time when the heavens are pulling up their covers, yawning and ready for the dreamy night ahead.

Dried leaves swirl around Mary's feet, teasing her, inviting her to partake of the autumn dance with them. It takes her a second or two to get her bearings, before she realizes she is standing in the heart of her very own childhood neighborhood, decades earlier. There is Larry and Sue Harper's modest house; there is Karen and Bob Rose's rancher; and the Loper house, now occupied by only one parent. Patty Loper had gone through a rather acrimonious divorce with her husband Peter. Patty came out on top – sole physical custody of their kids, Peter Jr., ten, and Lauren, seven. She also walks away with the house and everything in it and the family car, a brand new Lincoln Navigator.

Boy, that was one nasty divorce, Mary thinks, even though she hadn't really realized it as a child. Whenever one of Mary's girls wanted to have Lauren over for a sleepover, it was a major legal battle between Peter and Patty. Mary now is sure the constant bickering and name-calling between the couple must have created some psychological scars on the children, but it isn't anyone else's business, and Mary's mother still tried her best to include the Loper children in the festivities, be it a pool party or birthday party.

221

Yelps and screams behind Mary shock her out of her reverie about the Lopers' divorce. They are hoots of laughter and delight – the kind of sound that only deliriously happy children make. Mary sees a small *ghost* nearly trip over his bed-sheet costume, a pirate, complete with plastic sword; a noticeably-homemade costume of a witch; a pink be-sequined princess; and the inevitable Superman. It is Halloween – Trick or Treat night.

Mary is delighted to find herself also garbed in costume: A white silk gown complete with gossamer wings. And, although she cannot see it herself, she knows she is wearing a gaudy, feathered and glittered ivory satin mask that can rival that of any Mardi Gras reveler.

She watches in joy as children – from toddlers to tweens – gallop from house to house squawking in delight at the coveted prize of a *full-size* Snickers bar or Reese's peanut butter cup. The entire scenario is a monument to Mary's favorite holiday. The neighborhood of yesterday magically transforms into the neighborhood of today. This is a day set aside purely for the enjoyment of children.

From where Mary stands, she can see Silver Strands emanating from her wrist to the many children she knows from the neighborhood. Three strands are obviously different, glowing decidedly brighter than the rest. Mary has no doubt they lead her to her three girls: ten-year-old Cecee, will be the leader, with her younger sisters Kandee and Marlee, rounding out the pack.

In an instant borne out of motherly instinct, Mary scampers in the direction of the three special Silver Strands. When she reaches her destination, she sees it is the Eversons' home. She sees Cecee dressed as Amy Winehouse, beehive poof and all; Kandee as a yellow-and-black bumble bee, complete with a giggly antennae headband; and Marlee – no surprise since she watches the animated movie obsessively – is costumed as Cinderella. Mary throws her head back and laughs with gusto. Little Marlee has the soul of a hopeless romantic, she thinks.

222

The Eversons, a young couple, have gone all out this Halloween. John and Bella Everson are only married a couple of years, but are settled comfortably in the neighborhood. Even though they have no children of their own, they usually put up a dramatic Halloween display every year. This year, however, they manage to outdo even themselves.

Their huge, newly-built gothic Victorian house seems tailored-made for this autumnal festival. Strobe lights cast an eerie glow on their ample wrap-around front porch with its ornate gingerbread trim. Elaborately carved pumpkins and others left natural, are everywhere. There must be a hundred of them. Some are lit and glow with battery-operated flames.

Trick or Treaters, in order to reach the house, have to pass through a fake spider-web-covered arbor, its rose tendrils long past their prime, cut back to mere vines and thorns. There is even a fake spider or two on the vines to install a bit of atmosphere. Visitors at the front porch are greeted with the recorded sounds of creaking doors, witches' squeals, and other unearthly sounds. The older kids love it. And the little one love it too – as long as they are holding onto their parents' hands.

Mary finds it amusing that all the children in the neighborhood always found the Everson's' house a *must-visit* for Trick or Treat – besides, the Eversons gave out *full* candy bars, not the bite-sized pieces.

Nope, the couple never skimps on anything when it comes to Halloween. And they *never* run out of candy as they relish hearing the squeals from the neighborhood children. Appearing to be in their mid-thirties, they are in full Halloween regalia when they answer the door – John Everson in a pirate's swashbuckling outfit and his wife Bella as Little Miss Bo Peep, complete with a pink taffeta gown, bonnet and staff. Mary is sure their costumes are rented – they are elegantly made of the finest silk and there is not a hint of plastic or fake metal to be found. Besides, the couple dresses up differently every year. Mary finds herself a bit envious – buying her girls' costumes at the local Save-A-Lot or making them by hand.

Still, she really likes the Eversons, who never seem to put on airs, despite their obvious wealth. John – a "hottie," as Kate

McGee would crassly say, is "a woman's wet dream" with his blue eyes and cornflower yellow hair. He holds down a prestigious job as a top officer at the local savings and loan and also is a successful day trader in his spare time. He has done quite well for himself, that much was certain. Pretty Bella seems fragile and shy, but exceedingly sweet. She doesn't dare start a conversation, but once pulled in, she can easily hold her own. Even though they are good neighbors, the women in the area often offer each other theories as to why the Eversons are childless. The general consensus is that they are content alone with their wealth and do not want to be encumbered by little ones. Mary, however, doesn't buy that.

As the night marches on, the number of Trick or Treaters trickles off until finally, the stream of children has ended. The lot of them are finally satisfied with their cavity-inducing booty.

Mary is now standing in the Eversons' elegant living room and adjacent parlor. The house is immaculate.

So this is how houses look when there's no kids, Mary thinks. *No stuffed animals draped over the banisters, no Barbies lining the stairway like landmines just waiting for an errant step.*

She feels guilty, noticing a twinge of jealousy. Her house is in a state of constant chaos, no matter how many times she lectures the girls to pick up their toys or their clothes. Not that her house is filthy or dirty – it just has that "lived-in" look. Let's just say when one walks into the Miller house they certainly know this house belongs to a family with little ones, complete with sticky fingerprints and an affinity for using the kitchen sink for Barbie's swimming pool.

Mary walks around the living room, eyeing each perfectly-placed artifact or photograph in sterling silver frames placed carefully on the fireplace mantle and atop the elegant Steinway piano. Mary longs for a house that was like the Eversons' – again, the "Architectural Digest," style. The large rooms – chambers, really – look as if their owners had just given the maids the night off so they could give out the treats for the little ones themselves. If there is a speck of dirt on any table, Mary can't find it.

Confident now that she can neither be seen nor heard, Mary climbs the ornate staircase to the second floor. She can't resist seeing the rest of this magnificent house. She had always wondered if the top floor of the house is as elegant as the downstairs.

As she climbs the thickly-carpeted stairs, she is accompanied on her way up by family portraits hanging on the stairway wall. The family photographs range from antique tin-types through the decades, ending with a stunning portrait of John and Bella on their wedding day. The portrait is, in itself, a work of art. It has been painted in oils, obviously copied from a photograph. It is huge: Mary guesses it to be at least three feet high and a foot-and-a-half wide. Mary is mesmerized by the image, aglow in an overhead light. Bella is breath-taking in a designer gown, Vera Wang, perhaps. The bodice of the flowing white satin gown, complete with a wisp of lace and pearls lay flawless atop Bella's milk-white neck. Her bridal veil – although lifted well atop her blond hair, is still visible. It reminds Mary of an understated dollop of whipped cream atop a five-star dessert. John is dashing in his Armani tuxedo, a pale blue robin's-egg-blue vest the only color breaking the monochromatic black landscape of the tux.

But it isn't what they are wearing in the wedding photo that makes Mary literally gasp for breath. It is the complete and utter honest effect of happiness – no, make that bliss – that emanates from the bride and groom's faces. In their smiles, Mary feels she can read their minds:

We have found each other. We have fulfilled each other's dreams. Nothing can stop us now. Together, we can accomplish anything. Look out world!

Mary is lost in the painting when she first hears the soft sound of what sounds like sobbing coming from a room down the hall. Mary stays very still for a moment, trying to make out the source of the sounds. She feels guilty eavesdropping on what surely must be a personal conversation. But surveying the trappings of the Eversons downstairs had made her curiosity unquenchable. She wants to know more about this perfect family. Slowly, she tiptoes, from force of habit, down the hallway. There are regal-looking bedrooms on either side of her, but Mary can tell the sounds are coming from the room straight in front of her. She assumes it is the master chamber.

Mary's consciousness moves to Bella and John's room. She flinches a bit in guilt. This is clearly an extremely private conversation between two people. Nonetheless, she is riveted with curiosity to the scene before her.

Bella has stripped off her Bo Peep outfit and is wearing a simple satin teddy. Her arms are wrapped around John, himself in just in his underwear now. The French doors to the bedroom are wide open and the cool October breeze tickles the floor-length lace curtains.

It reminds Mary of the tragic death scene in the movie "Wuthering Heights" with Merle Oberson and Laurence Olivier.

Bella is softly crying and John is trying to comfort her.

"There's no reason to give up now," John says, stroking Bella's shiny hair. "We will have a child. I promise you. We will have a child – one rosy-cheeked, sticky-fingered terror that will drive us crazy and longing for the days when our house was quiet and clean." His brave attempts at humor are not successful. Bella feels defeated and desolate – and barren.

From the next exchange of words, Mary learns that Bella has suffered another miscarriage – her fifth. She had been five months along. This time, it was a girl.

Their initial exuberance at being pregnant and all their plans to become a real family were dashed in one fell swoop. The emotional plunge from joy to mourning is cruel, at best, Mary thinks.

As soon as the sonogram had detected a girl the Eversons already had named her: Alexandria – Alexandria Everson. They thought it had an elegant yet unpretentious air to it. How Mary knows this now, she has no idea. After the miscarriage, neither Bella nor John ever says the name out loud. And yet Mary is as certain of this as if she had seen the birth certificate.

"We've tried everything John. We're at the end of the line here. Even Dr. Berma is preparing us for the worst. You heard him," Bella says through her tears.

"What I heard was Dr. Berma saying that we shouldn't give up all hope. There are new discoveries every day. Scientists are making remarkable strides in fertility treatments. So why don't we listen to the good doctor? That's what we're paying him for, sweetheart."

Bella buries her face in her hands, plops on the huge velvet-covered bed and continues to cry.

"All those years, I was told to be a 'good girl,' that I should worry about pregnancy out of marriage. Ha! Who knew?" she asks rhetorically. "Who knew I'd be as barren as a sand trap on a golf course? We'll never have a baby. Never!" And the tears, tinged with a profound despair, flow unrelenting. John props her up to him by her shoulders and looks deeply in her eyes.

"Bella... I know this wasn't your first choice but please reconsider adoption. With my connections we can be on a short waiting list. Won't you please reconsider it?"

Bella is not to be mollified so easily, however.

"I want a child of our own!" she shouts. "I want to know what it's like to give birth. To our child!"

John puts his arms around Bella and holds her tight. The two Silver Strands that connect them are a jumble of throbbing lights now.

Funny, Mary thinks, if I didn't know better, *I'd swear those lights are crying tears as well.*

Bella sobs quietly and John holds her close.

Mary thinks of all the youngsters that run wild in the city – two and three o'clock in the morning. You know they are up to no good. Drugs, partying, and Lord knows what else.

Where were their parents? The answer, of course, is simple: The parents themselves are out, looking for their next fix, leaving their young brood home to fend for themselves. And here are two loving people who would have devoted their lives to their children. Sometimes, God, you're just not fair, are you? Mary thinks, looking up to the heavens.

227

Still feeling like an interloper of the worst kind, Mary concentrates, closes her eyes and wills herself not to be there. It works, but not before she notices that the Silver Strands have stretched their way from the Eversons' wrists to hers.

Nineteen

The Secret Garden

Years ago, Mary and David went on a tour of gardens nestled in the English countryside. It was their one and only vacation, and the best part – at least to Mary – was that they did it on a whim. David was not one given to spontaneity. Perhaps both she and David could feel the daily grind of work, school, soccer and cheerleading pulling them apart. When David – who never really cared for traveling, made the suggestion, Mary at first thought he was joking. When reality sunk in, she threw her arms around him in delight.

David knew Mary always admired the English countryside for both its natural and manmade beauty. He had done some shopping around travel sites before he mentioned to Mary to make sure they had enough money to pull it off. It was a tight squeeze, but it was do-able. *The Secret Garden Tour* is one of the highlights of Mary's life. It was everything she had hoped it would be, and then some. From time-to-time she still dreams of it.

The highlight of the tour is a garden built around a desacralized Gothic church, deep in the village of Chalford in Gloucestershire. The kindly young couple who owned it welcomed them to their home enthusiastically.

Mary found herself revisiting that magical place time and time again in her dreams. They only had a short tour, and Mary longed to know more about the fairy-tale-like place. If indeed there is a heaven, she recalled thinking to herself, surely it must resemble this. She no sooner completes the thought than she finds herself back in The Secret Garden.

The ancient desacralized gray-stone church hugs a deep hill, so there was no room for a graveyard when it was built many decades ago. But there are other oddities that the two

229

young owners, Jonathan and Christa – professional artists both – had to overcome. For instance, the entrance to the front door is gained only through a breath-taking mountain-steep flight of granite steps. The *backyard* was a steep rise of ground filled with rocks and weeds, when they first arrived. The young couple didn't see obstacles, however; they saw opportunities. Jonathan and Christa aren't just artists of the oil canvas. No, they also specialize in gardening and landscaping and the land also is their canvas.

The result is a castle-like structure that could have hailed straight from a Cinderella storybook. Jonathan, and some of his friends, spent long hours doing electrical and plumbing work to make the church more utilitarian for a home. Bella handled the cosmetic part, sewing the massive draperies herself, but being careful not to cover the magnificent stained-glass windows. She picked out every stick of furniture, every pillow, every *object d'art*.

The *backyard*, of the old church, however, presented a special challenge for the young couple. It consisted of centuries-old tree stumps and boulders – not exactly the kind of terrain that lends itself to gardening. But Jonathan was undaunted. He once again enlisted the help of his good friends; together they laboriously yanked out the aging stumps, lugged the boulders away, and chiseled steps out of the deep granite-and-stone hill.

Jonathan and Christa both had taken horticulture classes at the local university, but they never anticipated facing such a grand undertaking. It took nearly a decade of back-breaking work, along with some very enthusiastic, dedicated friends, to transform the scarred landscape into this paradise. Now, Mary is standing in the completed project – a breath-taking monument to the power of love and determination.

Jonathan and Christa, older now, are walking through the garden when they notice Mary, who is once again wearing her flowing outfit from the beach session with Nelson Bitterman.

"Well, hello there." Jonathan says in a hearty voice. "Your name is Mary, right? You and your husband were here many years ago. How are you? And your husband... his name is David, right?"

Mary is shocked that they remember her and David. At least a decade had passed since Mary and David had taken their short tour of *The Secret Garden*.

"I just love your place," Mary says awkwardly. "I mean... it's just lovely."

Christa smiles, and a slight blush washes over her pretty face. You and your husband took the *short* tour, right? Would you like to take the *long* tour now?"

"Oh yes, please." Mary exclaims, and they all laugh at her enthusiasm.

Jonathan lags behind Mary and Christa, also wearing a long flowing sundress, as they make their way through the garden. Jonathan knows that his wife will be the better tour guide here. Women like to talk about home decorating and flower gardens, not like the men, who prefer to talk about the grunt work and the crafting of the land.

Mary and Christa chat about the varied flowers. They are like tiny musicians in an enchanting garden orchestra. One note alone is beautiful, but taken together, all at once – they are awe-inspiring. The combined scents delight Mary's spirit. But rather than overwhelm her, the many scents, combined, are soothing and peaceful.

Christa stops along the way to admire a simple pink daffodil.

"See these?" Christa points to the flowers. "You don't see a pink daffodil every day. I call it 'Mrs. Mead's Daffodils' because she gave me the bulbs once when I was admiring them in her garden. I love all my flowers – heck I even love my weeds," she exclaims in an exuberant yelp, laughing.

"Look at this." Christa points to a patch of land covered in primroses, bluebells, celandines, lords and ladies – and even some more daffodils, only these are the traditional yellow. She picks up an odd-looking flower. "Do you realize that these flowers were once plentiful here – and all over the country? Do you realize that it's against the law to pick them unless you're the landowner?"

231

"Wow, I didn't know that." Mary exclaims in sincere surprise.

"Sure enough, true," Jonathon says.

Mary had forgotten that he was walking behind them.

"I built this garden special, for my lovely wife," he says, looking at her with adoration. "Christa always wanted a garden that depicted the stages of life from infancy through middle-age and then on to mortality. So I decided to give her wish to her."

"The ground," Jonathan explains, "was too hard for the congregants of the church to have their graveyard here." He then explained that he and his friends dynamited deep into the hard-stone earth to make way for a garden.

"But I knew we could still put something spiritual – flowers – here," Christa says, looking around. "This land has a soul."

"We started the garden at the bottom – infancy," Jonathan clarifies. At the bottom of the church, near a small chapel building, Christa planted borders of sweet pastel floral – tiny lilies of the valley and pink tulips meant to represent the beginning of life. Then Jonathan had carved out a pathway for Christa to complete her floral/life mural.

Next up the hill is the part of the garden symbolizing life's adulthood. Occasionally, along the path, there is a statue of a stone angel, Christa's favorite symbol. The pathway forks; the left branch leads a wanderer to an orchard – a symbol of fertility. The right branch of the path leads to a small pond, complete with koi, a small fountain, a tiny grotto and a stone-sitting garden where one can take time to not only admire the colors, but inhale their bewitching fragrances – some spicy, some fruity, some vanilla-like, and others like a summer evening. The sun is still high in the sky, but is tempered by the leafy canopy shade of the massive, ancient oak trees.

"Do you garden?" Christa asks Mary in her exquisite English accent.

Mary blushes, thinking of her repeated failure at the task.

"No, it's not my forte," she finally says. "I guess I don't have a green thumb. And I certainly couldn't do anything as grand as *this*."

"Nonsense, my sweet," Christa says softly. "Everyone has a green thumb. They just don't know it. You really have to get into the swing of things. Every day, after work, Jonathan and I still come out here and do weeding. Now, that may sound like a terrible task, but we often listen to Gregorian chants while we work. It makes everything so pleasant. You simply must give it a try. Wait here. I'm going to make us some tea." Christa and Jonathan disappear into their home.

Mary is enchanted by her surroundings, and closing her eyes, imagines this must be what Heaven is like.

Christa comes back bearing a dainty tea set and cookies. Mary chats with the couple about gardening and flowers.

Refreshed, Christa urges Mary to continue *The Secret Garden Tour.* Both paths – the one by the orchard and the one with the pond – reunite several hundred feet later, turning the landscape into a kaleidoscope of nature, with the exuberant purple mourning color of summer irises mixing and melting with spring lilacs and purple sweet peas. Whenever an errant flower insinuates its way into the garden, Christa says she just "lets it be."

"I don't want the garden to feel regimented," she says. "Remember, this garden represents the stages of life – and as we all know, life throws us a curve ball every now and then." Throughout the massive garden, Christa has planted roses of every hue to represent the unexpected delights of life.

Mary thinks of David, whose idea of gardening is mowing the lawn, and thinks he would enjoy this tour as much as she.

It is nearly impossible not to be swept up in the beauty and spirituality of such a landscape. The fact that the main building was once a church and a nearby chapel only enhances the feeling of being closer to any deity. And, if perchance you are atheist or agnostic, this piece of paradise might just be the ticket to make you rethink your beliefs.

The last leg of the journey – the part of the garden that symbolizes death – is filled with purple blossoms of every hue. The bounty of flowers hugs the cliff until there is no more room. The garden has ended.

Why am I here? Mary asks herself. She can come up with no good reason, but is enjoying herself immensely just the same.

It was a magical, mystical, almost dream-like experience and revisiting it now she can clearly see the Silver Strands that had connected the four of them, halfway around the world. Mary feels especially ebullient – and, yes, blessed – that the Silver Strands are connecting her to this particular piece of Heaven. It is the most serene, tranquil peace of mind she has ever felt. For a few unique seconds – a blur as quickly as a brush stroke of paint on canvas – she feels closer to God than ever.

"Is this what people mean when they say that art can be a religious experience?" she thinks out loud.

"That's exactly right," Christa replies suddenly and unexpectedly. "Sometimes you have to dig hard and deep to find the treasure. Nothing worthwhile having is easy. But in the end, we all make our own paradise."

Tom

Mary is able to refocus her eyes and she does not like what appears. Tom – that filthy, sneaky-looking handyman at the paper. Why he repulsed her so was a mystery to her. It wasn't the stale smell of cigarette smoke and rubbish; that she could take.

She had worked in a homeless shelter for God's sake; and she'd seen just about everything. The homeless people would go sometimes months without showering. Mary just trained her olfactory sense to overcome her gag reflex. No, whatever so repulsed her about Tom was not through the physical senses.

And she was no stranger to the tattered clothes of the homeless. Oftentimes they had gone through twenty or more owners, each leaving their distinct *scent* on the clothing before being washed. Mary could take that.

No, Mary's repulsion was born out of something deeper – could one put a scent on the term *child molester*? Because that's the vibe Mary picked up each time she was within sight of Tom. She couldn't bear to be less than twenty feet away from him. She had always felt badly, because she liked to think of herself as a caring, nonjudgmental person. But the sights, smells and faint hint of refrained sexuality which Tom emanated never failed to make her queasy.

Tom stands with his back to Mary, staring deeply into her eyes and making her extremely uncomfortable. He is standing next to his mother in her hospital bed. He doesn't move – not a blink of an eyelash, not even the heaving of his chest as he breathed.

For a second Mary thinks she might actually be looking at a statue of Tom. She is frozen, afraid to speak or move. The visual show-down lasts several seconds before Tom finally turns to Mary and speaks.

"You don't like me much, do you?" he asks without the least bit of recrimination in his voice. "That's okay. I like it that way. I keep my distance from people – better for all concerned. I know why you're here. I know what you're

235

thinkin'… Nah, I ain't dead. It's my momma. We been so close all these years… I guess I'm close enough to my dying momma to see you."

Mary is taken aback at how matter-of-fact Tom is speaking, as if seeing her image is the most natural thing in the world.

Tom continues his tirade, born partly out of grief and partly out of rage.

"Twenty-two years of cleaning up after her, making her meals, feeding her, changing her soiled diapers. Soon it will be over. And what will I be left with? No family, no wife, no nothing. She done that to me.

"I love my momma. Don't get me wrong. But I swear she took ill so I would never leave her. How *could* I leave her? I'm her son. And now she's gone. And I ain't got nothin' – nothin' to show for all those years of working at that crummy job at the newspaper, then coming home to her. She wouldn't let no one else touch her. The county, they offered a certified nurse's aide to come in daily. But no, 'I got my *son*,' she'd say. 'He loves me. He'll take care of me.'

And I did, Mary. I did, for all those years."

Mary is still shocked that Tom not only can see her, but is talking to her. It is the first time Mary has heard Tom speak her Christian name, and it takes her by surprise, although she tries to conceal it – but not very well.

Tom picks up on her discomfort immediately.

"What? You think you're too good for me to use your first name? Look 'round, Mary, we're all the same here. No one's better than anyone else. There's no class system here – all these people in the hospital beds. They're all just sick animals, like an ailing cow or sick dog." Tom can barely hide the indignation in his voice.

"I know you walk just a little bit faster when you pass me in the hall, shinin' the floor," Tom fairly snarls. "Can't wait to get past me, like I carry the plague or somethin.'" With that, Tom sits down in the chair next to his mother's hospital bed.

Tom's mother – she believed her name was Nancy – was somewhat of an enigma around town. She was barely seen, partly due to the fact that she was an invalid and partly due to the fact that she was a near-recluse. It was a rare sight indeed to spot Nancy sitting on her front porch on a summer evening. The school kids called her "Invisible Nancy," and she had become a legend in town. After a while, the adults also adopted the moniker. They may not have done it to be cruel, but Mary can see now that's exactly what it was – cruel.

She knows very little about Nancy other than the myths about her later years. She had heard she was a schoolteacher when she was younger, but then she also heard she owned a pig farm at the edge of town. Some townsfolk swear she buried three husbands, at least two under suspicious circumstances. It is hard to thrash through all the rumors and put a real history to Nancy's past.

Of course, Mary, like many of the other adults and parents in town, had conjured up visions of what she looked like. Is she a skeletal figure with spider-web white hair? Or perhaps an old lady who had refused to acknowledge her age, smearing makeup on her face punctuated by flamboyant blush and blood red fingernails – applied, of course, by her own son, beloved, Tom. Visions of Bette Davis in that movie "Whatever Happened to Baby Jane?" were bandied about by the townsfolk. There also was talk of witchcraft, voodoo, and any other oddities that rumors left to the imagination, tend to conjure up.

Mary walks over to Nancy's bedside, and realizes that the woman she sees lying before her, who appears to have just died, is none of these. She is a woman well past her prime, her white cloud-like hair tousled and unkempt. Her skin is porcelain, even through the tiny wrinkles. She must have been a great beauty in her prime. Her pale blue eyes are still open – and clear; Mary guesses they were once dancing sapphires, which probably attracted a flock of hopeful suitors.

Mary touches her hand, which she had expected to be cold to the touch; but it isn't. Apparently, she hadn't died that long ago. In truth, she had been dead for more than an hour, and Tom cannot bear the thought of some nurse or doctor in silly-designed scrubs declaring his beloved mother's *time of death*.

237

Mary holds her hand – it just seems the most natural thing to do. It is only then that she notices the Silver Strand that loops their hands together, and then continued on to Tom's hand. Tom stands several feet away to give the women their privacy. Mary literally jumps when Nancy suddenly speaks.

"I know why you're here," she says, softly and deliberately.

Mary gasps.

This dead woman is talking to me... she's dead and yet she's talking to me.

"You have to listen. We don't have much time," Nancy says. Her vacant eyes once again dancing with a beautiful blue shade, pierce into Mary's. She holds Mary's hand tight, and Mary feels the warmth of motherly love pass from Nancy's hand to hers.

"Tom has been my whole life. He's taken care of me. He's been my savior for so many years. He's still a young man, as young men go. But he's taken a bitter bite out of the apple. He thinks people look down on him, and yes, I know they do. I know *you* do. But do you understand that every spare moment he had, he gave to me? He would work nights because he knew I slept well at night. I needed help during the daytime. So he waits until the building is almost empty to start his 'workday.' He's never had a chance to develop social skills. I've been selfish. I should have looked out for him more. I knew I didn't have long. I guess I was just so terrified of dying alone.

"Please, Mary, I don't know the full reason of why you're here, or what it means. I just know I have this small pocket of time to find someone to help my son. Please, please, help Tom. He's my only son."

Nancy's hands are starting to turn cold again, her bright blue eyes are fading, one of them covered up with a filmy glaucoma haze. Letting go of Mary's hand, Nancy lay her head back down on the pillow, looking exactly as she did when Mary first saw her.

Did this just really happen? Mary wonders.

Mary turns to look at Tom, who is standing several feet away. His arms are crossed and his face is buried deep into his

238

chest. She isn't sure whether or not she had heard his mother's last words, but Mary makes a mental note:

We (The Beacon newspaper staff) will work tirelessly to bring Tom out of his shell. Nothing too flamboyant – that would merely embarrass him – but a gentle strategy of addressing him as a person when we meet him and his mop in the hallway. We'll treat him as a person, with a soul and with a personality, even if it means a simple, "Hey Tom!" as we walk past.)

Nancy's revelation shatters Mary's preconceived notions of Tom as the resident child-molester. He is anything but. He has devoted his life to caring for his mother. It is clear that the mother-son bond is as tightly intertwined as two strands of canvas rope. Mary feels horrible that she had so misjudged this man. Yes, Tom had lashed out in anger earlier, but now Mary realizes it wasn't anger at all – it was grief – the most profound grief of losing a parent.

She peers over her shoulder for one last look at Tom and his mother. She knows it will be a bittersweet sight, but she feels compelled to do it. Tom is kneeling at his mother's bedside, holding her hand and weeping, as gently as the beginning of a spring shower.

Out of nowhere, Mary hears *The Voice*, again.

"Mary? Can you hear me, Mary?"

Mary knows she is in two places: In this sterile hospital room as well as back in Dr. Lee's office, where she is assuring him that all is well.

Twenty

Aunt Suzanne

It is cold and wet. Mary finds herself gasping for air as her mouth hits the surface of the water. Her arms flail about as she tries to get her bearings. She isn't the best swimmer in the world, but she can hold her own. She spits and sputters, gasping for sweet air. Once she hits surface level, all she can think is, *"Where the hell am I?"*

Her head swivels above the water line, trying to take in the surroundings. In the luxurious in-ground swimming pool, she hears the soothing sounds of a waterfall and feels the undulating flow of the warm water and a slight breeze as it strikes her face.

Mary barely has time to swim over to the shallow end of the pool when she hears the splash. The thundering *whoosh* reverberates throughout the pool, creating large waves and ripples. She rushes to catch her breath again then wipes the chlorinated water from her eyes so she is able to focus on the source of the sound.

She turns to see her Aunt Suzanne standing at the other end of the pool. A mask of shock and relief washes over Mary's face. Truthfully, "Aunt Suzanne" is not an aunt to Mary at all. She is one of Kathy's closest friends, and the "aunt" moniker just blossomed over time. By now, Mary is not a bit surprised to see a thin Silver Strand wending its way across the length of the pool, connecting her wrist to Aunt Suzanne's. But Mary is bewildered at the strand that travels from Suzanne's wrist and into the water.

Mary has learned not to fret wondering why some people can see her and others cannot. There doesn't seem to be any rhyme or reason to it; it seems willy–nilly, and she merely accepts it. Right now, Mary can tell that Suzanne does not see her.

It has been decades since she last saw Suzanne, who has gotten on in years, that's for sure. Her jet-black hair has more salt than pepper in it now, and the Jacqueline-Susann-looks that once turned mens' heads is creased and furrowed. But her eyes – those deep-set, ebony eyes that seem to have a secret key to eternity – still sparkle. She somehow has retained her model-slim figure, and even though she is wearing slacks, Mary guesses her legs are still as shapely as when she was younger.

Mary remembers her Aunt Suzanne from the many visits with her mother, Kathy. The two women would sit at the kitchen table for hours, smoking cigarettes and drinking black coffee. They were an unlikely pair as friends. Kathy was a homebody, rarely attending social events other than her women's weekly bridge game. She dressed in the conservative manner of the day, an unadorned housedress, buttoned up to her neck, and flat, nondescript pumps. Her only jewelry was her watch, which her husband had given to her several birthdays ago, and, of course, her gold wedding band.

Suzanne was everything Kathy was not. Kathy was an introvert, uncomfortable in large social settings, while Suzanne clamored for the limelight. Her clothes were *unconventional*, to say the least. She was always at the front door of fashion, and preferred loud, gaudy colors to anything bland. She abhorred pastels. Her necklines often plunged just enough to force men to make a concerted effort to maintain eye contact when speaking with her. Her attire often started local women's tongues wagging, most likely out of jealousy. Her raven hair was long and straight and shiny. She felt the admiration and jealousy as she tossed her mane about in the summer sun, and enjoyed both immensely.

Unlike Kathy, Suzanne's jewelry glinted in the light – a shimmering gold chain, diamond stud earrings, her wrists clinking with the noise of a gaggle of gold bangle bracelets. But it was her engagement and wedding rings that signaled the true measure of her wealth. The whopping six-carat flawless diamond on her engagement ring was hugged on each side with a row of smaller — but no less brilliant – baguettes. Her wedding band was less ostentatious, with only a small row of diamonds. As a child, Kathy often would take Mary with her to Suzanne's plush plantation-style mansion set back from the world by a mile-long driveway, magnificent pine trees lining each side. Mary would frolic in the shallow end of the huge built-in pool. Through the crystal clear water, one could see a luxurious Greek design inscribed on the bottom of the pool.

There, the two women kept a close eye on Mary, while they sipped their coffee or iced tea on an ornate white wrought iron dinette set, under the canopy of a huge yellow beach umbrella. It would be years before Mary discovered what the two women, so different, talked about for hours. Suzanne had married Warren Blaze, a business tycoon several decades her senior. It was the general consensus around town that Suzanne had married Warren strictly for his money. In reality, nothing could be further from the truth.

They had met one Saturday morning at a local charity promoting local artists. Warren may have been wealthy, but he also was unpretentious. He went to this party as a personal favor for a friend. He disdained large parties and affairs, preferring the smaller gatherings in his small hometown. He could afford Armani, but disliked shopping for clothes, and when he did, he could often be found in the men's department at Wal-Mart.

He was free with his checkbook, but not his time. He was a pragmatist, a bear of a man who grew up in the Pennsylvania coal mine areas, where his father worked – and ultimately died of black lung when Warren was only 14. His mother, a barely functioning alcoholic, had died the following year. Warren was an orphan.

Determined not to suffer his father's fate, living and dying much too young in the coal mines, Warren left home before he graduated high school. He found he had a natural affinity for mechanics. He loved the smell and feel of grease on his hands as he worked on the fancy sports cars that came into the auto shop where he was employed. It took him years, but eventually he scraped up enough money to open his own mechanics shop on Main Street. Warren's affable, cheery nature and reasonable prices resulted in most of the town's people gravitating to his shop for their car repairs.

His first year in business, Warren was successful enough to hire two mechanics. By his fifth year in business, he had added two more shops in nearby towns. A decade later, he found himself with a franchise of shops that catapulted him into the millionaire's club. Despite his wealth, however, romance escaped him. He was a *catch*, that's for sure. Handsome and wealthy, there was no shortage of women who would throw themselves at him. He dated sporadically, but true love escaped him – until that Saturday morning when he met Suzanne.

She was a beauty – there was no denying that – but Warren was more impressed with her down-home charm. She was quite a sight – an unabashed red, figure-hugging dress that she must have picked up on sale. Warren correctly guessed that the baubles that adorned her ears, neck and fingers, were costume jewelry. Yet somehow she was able to pull it off without looking trashy. Her easy air of declaring a painting by a beloved local artist "a piece of junk" made him chuckle.

Suzanne easily spoke her mind without thinking of the consequences. Warren found her unpretentiousness refreshing, and surprised even himself when he nervously asked her out for a date just an hour after meeting her. The fact that she didn't answer quickly pleased him greatly. This was no fortune-hunter. This was a naïve little girl who was oblivious to the moneyed caste system of upper society.

Her warm charm made her all the more appealing to him. The more she spoke – rattling on about the "artsy fartsy" world of high-end art – the more he fell for her, as when she once said that a Jackson Pollack painting "looks like the vanilla drizzle of the chocolate doughnut I had this morning." Warren stifled his laugh, as Suzanne continued her venomous criticism of the abstract expressionist movement. But he found it difficult to pull her away from the lusty colors and fanciful designs of Vincent Van Gough. It was quickly apparent to Warren that Suzanne did, indeed have taste – she just had her own unique brand of taste, and was not about to kowtow to the propensity of the snobby art critics to say she liked a painting or artist if she didn't.

Despite the difference in their ages – nearly 30 years – Warren was enchanted with Suzanne. He was delighted that she enjoyed a good baseball game and a hot dog and beer or an unplanned walk in the woods as much as he. Warren courted Suzanne for more than a year asking for her hand in marriage seven times before she finally relented. Of course, that was when the town gossip, which up until now had only been under-the-breath whispers, turned into full-blown rumors. If one was to believe some of the rumors, Suzanne was a gold-digger; a pill freak; a nouveau riche social climber. In reality, she was none of these.

Suzanne and Kathy met when they joined a yoga club at the local YMCA. Kathy found Suzanne friendly and down-to-earth and enjoyed talking to her. They became fast – and very close – friends. Suzanne had no children of her own, and doted on Mary. The snotty women in the community were quick to point out that despite her wealth, her money could not buy the one thing she wanted – a baby. Suzanne had suffered several miscarriages. As the years marched on, Suzanne and Warren Blaze had to accept the fact that they would never be parents – at least not biological ones. It was a sore point that Suzanne rarely talked about. When she did confide in Kathy, her face would take on a far-away, dreamy "what-might-have-been" melancholia mood.

Kathy was careful never to bring up the subject first. If Suzanne wanted to broach it, fine. But Kathy always left it up to her. Besides, Suzanne and Warren seemed content with just themselves. As opposite as they were, they fit each other like a puzzle piece.

Over the years, Suzanne traded her off-the-rack wardrobe for designer clothes, and her jewels were now the real deal. But Kathy knew that it was Warren that wanted the best for Suzanne; his wife would have been perfectly happy with the Sears clothes collection. Suzanne couldn't tell the difference between Jeffrey Bean and L.L. Bean, and was quite sure no one else could tell the difference either. But Warren wouldn't have his beloved Suzanne shop anywhere but the best – despite her disdain of "hoity" fashion labels. Rather than get into a row over it, Suzanne surrendered to Warren's pleas.

The result was that the sales clerks at Nordstrom's and Bergdorf Goodman had their hands full searching for designer clothes in the outlandish color and styles that Suzanne relished. The commission they received from Warren's bank account kept the grumbling to a minimum. The result was Suzanne wearing the very best, crass-colored fashion designs available. The jewels she sported were big and anything but eloquent, their huge sizes making them appear garish, but they were the real deal. The diamonds and gems with which she adorned her ears and fingers and wrists were dazzling.

Mary remembered once as a teenager, swimming in Suzanne's pools with her girls. She had come up for air, and the sun struck the huge diamond ring on Suzanne's hand, temporarily blinding her with its glint.

Suzanne was oblivious to all the nasty comments tossed about her by the denizens of old money. If she cared at all, it didn't upset her. The couple traveled – from the Eiffel Tower in Paris to the Grand Canyon. Whatever struck Suzanne's heart – all she needed to do was to point out what she wanted and it was hers. Except a child; that was the one thing Warren could not give her. The doctors said Suzanne's ovaries had been scarred by severe endometriosis, and there was little hope for a pregnancy. Their hope for a child faded over time. The couple found security, warmth and love in each other's arms.

"We love each other... I think we've been blessed with each other and that's enough for me," Warren would whisper to Suzanne whenever he thought she was beginning to dwell on the subject.

The couple spent many happy years together. Neither cared a fig that the snobby *old money* townspeople would return dinner invitations unopened or that their Christmas and New Year's parties were snubbed by the upper class. The Blazes were just as happy partying with the middle-class – their plumber George and his wife Maude, their mailman

Steve, and their gardener Jose and wife Juanita. The house was always filled to the rafters with party-goers who enjoyed a good beer over a martini.

Suzanne loved doing all the decorations herself, but as she got on in age, she was forced to have a party planner come in and transform their huge mansion into a holiday extravaganza. No one needed an invitation. The Warrens' childlike enthusiasm for the holidays was the real ticket to the party. The old money didn't like it one bit. They felt it was gauche. *The Beacon*'s Society Section also snubbed the Blaze's events. If Suzanne or Warren were insulted, they never showed it. They were just too consumed with having a happy time, with genuine friends. As Warren got on in age, they adapted. The house had a ramp built outside for his wheelchair and a built-in lift for the stairs inside.

It was a cold February day when Warren received the news. He was well into his 80s, and he had a multitude of ailments. The worst, by far, was when his doctors diagnosed him with multiple sclerosis. MS, the disorder of the central nervous system, is slow and painful, like small evil elves pounding away with tiny sharp hammers. The patient's immune system attacks the myelin in the brain and spinal cord.

By the time he received the diagnosis, MS had taken firm hold of his body and was rapidly becoming an unrelenting army. Suzanne and Warren retreated from the world. But Suzanne still remained friends with Kathy. Mary still accompanied her mother to her weekly visits to the Blazes, but she saw less and less of Warren as time progressed. He was often *indisposed*.

After a while, Warren did not venture outside, and he required around-the-clock care. Suzanne preferred to care for him herself, but allowed the caretaker to do the heavier lifting. Suzanne, after all, was not young anymore either, and arthritis had robbed her of much of her youthful *joie de vivre*. She cared for Warren as much as she could, even though the hired caretakers urged her to "take it easy" and let them do their jobs. The elaborate parties ceased. The Blaze house had become a kind of hospital/sanitarium. It wasn't long after that a hospital bed had replaced the king-sized bed in the master bedroom.

Kathy's visits to Suzanne became more and more scarce. It wasn't because Kathy didn't want to visit; she knew Warren's health was rapidly descending and – always a proud man – he wouldn't want anyone seeing him in the disintegrating stage in which he now found himself. He could not walk, dress himself or clean himself. The MS was ravaging his body, like a fully-outfitted army effortlessly claiming its victory until it planted its flag of death.

Occasionally Kathy still visited, though mostly to give Suzanne some well-deserved company and respite while the caretakers tended to Warren. When Mary, now a teenager, accompanied her mother to the house, the women spoke in whispers, but, Mary could understand what was going on. Warren was in pain – the kind of pain that laughs at painkillers and morphine and even marijuana. Mary thought the idea of conservative, no-nonsense Warren smoking a doobie would be so incongruous with the life he had always led.

Suzanne, meanwhile, knew she was losing the love of her life. She had reluctantly accepted that fact, since it played out each day in front of her. Mary would sit close to the women, pretending to sunbathe and trying to pretend not to be listening about what the two women were saying. But it was clear enough even for a child to deduce. Suzanne could no longer bear seeing her beloved Warren screaming in pain and begging for the sweet release of death.

On one particular grim visit to the Blazes' home, Kathy and Mary arrived, not at all prepared to witness the scene of grief they were about to encounter. Suzanne's hair – always so immaculate and chic, was loose and straggly, hanging down around her gaunt face like some kind of zombie. She wore no makeup, but it's doubtful any kind of cosmetic could hide the puffiness around her eyes or the dark circles that surrounded them.

"I'm at my wit's end," Kathy, Suzanne sobbed into her breakfast napkin. "I can't bear to see him like this!"

Mornings were the worst. If Warren was able to sleep through the pain, he would awaken with the full waves of excruciating agony sweeping over him, a perverse kind of morning greeting. Mild summer afternoons, when the temperatures kissed eighty-five degrees or so, provided the only semblance of relief. Suzanne would open the large gothic windows and the gentle breeze of the swaying curtains would lull Warren into a light doze. Suzanne was quite sure it was a psychological relief, but hey, *relief is relief.* She wasn't about to question the sweet respite her loving Warren was able to snatch from the claws of agony. On good days – which were becoming further and further apart – Suzanne would wheel him into the sunshine near the pool, always careful to lock the wheelchair in place.

This is where Mary is now located – in the Blazes's giant kidney-shaped pool. As Mary gasps for breathe, the reality of the present situation hits her full on; she no longer is the little girl who frolicked in the pool or the teenager who would sunbathe nearby.

She is an adult; and she is fully-clothed, standing chin-deep in the pool water. She is shivering. The chilly temperatures and gray skies confirm that this is not summer. It seems more likely that the autumn chill not only has arrived; it has settled in and is making itself at home.

Mary, from the shallow end of the pool, can hear soft whispers coming from the deep end. A hint of a commotion is beginning to brew.

Mary turns just in time to see Suzanne – *Jacqueline-Susann appearing young again* – tears streaming down her face, lean down and kiss an emaciated Warren, strapped into his wheelchair.

Kathy stands quietly by her side, tears flowing down her face.

Suzanne whispers something in Warren's ear.

Although Mary can't tell what his wife has said, she sees Warren's affirmative nod and hears him groan in pain.

Mary cannot detect any hint of the man Warren once was. A haggard, drooling ancient-looking, skid-row man has taken the place of the once-dapper jokester who always enjoyed a good cigar and a glass of Scotch before bed. She is mesmerized as she watches the scenario at the other end of the pool.

Suzanne walks backwards, solidly holding the arms of the wheelchair while Kathy gently pats her arm. Finally Suzanne almost sprinting forward, plunges Warren and his wheelchair into the deep end of the pool.

Mary yelps in shock, trembling.

The weight of the wheelchair keeps it anchored to the bottom of the pool. After several seconds, Suzanne's body crumples on the concrete surrounding the pool, sobbing as if her soul has been sucked out of her very being. Kathy wraps her arms around her agonized friend, also crying.

Mary can see the wheelchair, and Warren, both sunken to the bottom of the pool like heavy rocks. Silver Strands appear on the women's wrists and travel deep into the water of the pool.

Suzanne does not look into the pool. She lays prone on the concrete wailing like the autumn winds that refuse to surrender to winter.

Kathy tries to swaddle her in comfort but there is nothing she can do to console Suzanne. "He's at peace," is all Mary can hear her mother say to Suzanne.

Mary knows what is happening; Suzanne was not relieving herself of a burden. No, if it had been up to her she would have held on to her beloved Warren for every minute God would allow.

It was Warren who begged her to end his suffering. And Suzanne loved him enough to do it. Since Warren often took to sunning by the pool – and since he often fumbled with the controls on the wheelchair – no one would suspect that he hadn't accidentally unlocked his chair and plunged head-first into the pool. He was in such a degenerative state that no pills were necessary to sedate him. Toxicology reports would come back "normal" – there would be no overdose or renegade drugs in his system.

It all makes perfect sense, Mary thinks. If Suzanne had overdosed him on morphine, those snotty socialites would immediately cry "murder." Never mind that the Blazes had enjoyed a decades-old marriage.

Mary, her clothes now magically dry, walks over to Suzanne, who is crying and wailing. It is the first time Mary has truly seen a "broken heart."

Kathy wraps her arms around her lovely, loquacious and loyal friend. They rock to and fro for several minutes.

Suzanne composes herself for a moment as a single thought begins to replace the agony of her loss: *At least my love, you're not suffering anymore.*

Inexplicably, Mary can hear Suzanne's thoughts. She looks down to see the Silver Strand isn't only on Suzanne's wrist, and Kathy's, but on her own.

Mary's face-to-face meeting with true heartbreak left her cold and shivering and empty inside.

"Where am I?" she mumbles – or thought she mumbled as she suddenly recalls the phone conversation her mother had with Suzanne when Kathy's husband, Sam, was dying and in so much pain.

"No, Suzanne, I can't do that," she had said. "I know he's suffering... Lord knows I wish I had it in me to do it. But I can't. I'm not judging you. You did the right thing with Warren. But this is different. Sam is still coherent... I can't give up on Sam yet."

Mary realizes now that Suzanne was suggesting to her mother to end her husband, Sam's pain. The way Warren Blaze died was a secret to only two – and now three – people. Kathy, being the good Catholic that she was, could not bring herself to do the same.

Mary hears *The Voice* again. She realizes *The Voice* is becoming louder and more intense each time she hears it.

"Mary, can you hear me? Mary? Nod if you're okay."

Once again, she knows that her physical body is in Dr. Lee's Manhattan office, nodding affirmatively.

The voice swiftly fades away, not unlike a brief snow shower, the kind where you are almost certain you see the flakes, but they're gone now with nothing left to show for it.

Twenty-one

Mr. Yin's Exotic Antiques

Mary never liked John Yin. He is the proprietor of a small downtown antique shop she often passed while shopping. "Jun" Yin was his real name, but it had been Americanized to "John Yin," by some harried bureaucrat at Ellis Island, much to his chagrin, Mary suspected. She loved antiques, and would have loved to spend an afternoon browsing in Mr. Yin's shop, but she could feel his eyes burrowing in her back as she made her way around the room. It made her extremely uncomfortable and she rarely stayed as long as she would have liked. He barely nodded a greeting, and uttered nothing more than a grunt as she was leaving. *Not very personable for a business owner*, Mary thought.

"Sometimes I think he suspects I'm going to shoplift something," Mary once confided to Kate. "I don't know why he gives me the willies, but he does."

"Yin's Exotic Antiques" were pricey, but worth every penny. His small, spotless shop was crammed with delights from the East: Everything from pure jade hair barrettes, to delicate floral paintings and Japanese writings as well as bamboo oddities and wood carvings. He had magnificent cloisonné vases and Oriental *objects d'art*. Mary particularly loved the cinnabar boxes, carved so delicately they appeared to be made of wooden lace.

Mary now finds herself standing in the middle of his shop, with Mr. Yin staring ominously at her. She has no idea how she arrived here, or why Mr. Yin, as usual, seems to be giving her the "skunk eye," as Mary's kids call it. Her girls were terrified of him and refused to go into the store with her.

Mary blinks twice and is surprised to find a Silver Strand attaching her to Mr. Yin.

251

"You don't know me, do you, Mary?" he asks in a flat voice. It is the first time she has heard his voice, and is shocked that there is no discernible accent.

"You wonder about my story, but you never ask me. Tell me what you want to know," he says bluntly. "I have no secrets."

Mary is taken aback at his bluntness. She thinks for a bit, and then speaks up.

"I know you were born in Japan, but when did you come here, to the United States? I can't remember a time when your shop wasn't here. Even my parents remember it."

"I came here when I was just a boy. I was a musical prodigy – did you know that?" Mr. Yin is staring straight into Mary's eyes, looking for any reaction. He gets none. "I played the piano. I was just a boy when my parents decided to move here. They believed my 'great gift' would be wasted in my home country. Everyone told them, 'Take the boy to America. There are great opportunities there for the boy.' When I was formally accepted into the Julliard School, my parents made up their minds. We moved here.

My parents ran a small grocery store in New York – The Bronx. My parents – great people they were, worked hard in the garment industry to buy me my Steinway piano and made sure I got the best lessons they could afford. That's how I got the scholarship to Julliard. I am proud to count them among my ancestors."

"So you still play?" Mary asks, trying to glide the subject into something less confrontational.

"Not anymore. I haven't touched a keyboard in many years. And I never will again."

"Why on Earth not – if you were that good?" Mary asks innocently.

"Let's just say our world changed on Dec. 7, 1941," Mr. Yin says with a hint of sarcasm and bitterness in his voice. He sits down on an old wooden chair, obviously getting comfortable to tell his story. He points to another old rickety chair, an apparent invitation to Mary to sit.

She does, and waits silently until Mr. Yin speaks again.

252

"We came to America – my mother, father and little brother Akihiko – we called him 'Kiko.' We were proud citizens. My father flew the American flag every day. It was a point of pride for him – every morning pulling the flag up in our front yard, and every evening before dark, sliding it back down the pole. We lived in a little ranch house. When I got my scholarship to Julliard my parents were so proud. So imagine my parents' surprise when the local police arrived and gave them a half hour to pack their things because our family was 'being moved.' That's all the police said: 'You have to move.'

"My parents and Kiko, they hung their heads in shame as they were led out to the police van. 'What did we do? What did we do?' they kept asking, but they got no answers. The police just manhandled them and pushed them into the back of a big van, crowded with other Japanese Americans in the neighborhood. They were corralled into camps that were crowded and filthy. Their only crime was their heritage. In a matter of hours they turned from American citizens into 'the enemy.' They called us 'Japs' – God, I hate that word! Some of the camp guards would spit on us. My parents were proud people. They couldn't understand any of it. I was yanked out of Julliard, forced to leave my beloved Steinway behind. I wasn't sent to the same camp as my family."

Mary is eyeing the Silver Strand attaching herself to Mr. Yen. She isn't quite sure she feels all that comfortable with it. She suddenly feels very guilty but doesn't know why.

Mary had studied this shameful time in American history class, but Mr. Yin has put a face to it. He seems not to notice her regret. He continues his grim story.

"By the time the war was over, and my family was released, they were broken people. My mother died of a stroke a year after she was released. My father died two months later – he couldn't bear to live without her. And Kiko?" The bitterness drips off his tongue as he speaks.

"He turned to drugs – drugs and crime. At first a petty thief, to feed his habit. Later he started carrying a gun. He was only twenty-two when he was shot dead like a dog in the street. They never caught the bastards that did it... I don't think they really looked all that hard. Kiko was just another casualty in the drug war.

I turned my back on America that day the same way America turned its back on us. The beauty I had found in my music, I could no longer hear it. I scraped together some money and opened this shop. I educated myself in the intricacies of Japanese antiques. This shop is my revenge. I know how to barter for the best Japanese artworks and I then sell them to silly Americans at three times their worth. And you – you stupid people – will never hear my music again. You don't deserve to."

It is suddenly very clear to Mary why Mr. Yin is not very personable to her. His heart still harbors the bitterness of his new country's snub. He considers her "one of *them*." For a flicker of time, as she stands there, in the middle of "Mr. Yin's Exotic Antiques," she sees the world through Mr. Yin's angry, sharp eyes. The Silver Strands that connect Mary to Mr. Yin make a snake shape and slip out the bottom of the front door.

Alexandria

A voice in the distance reverberates with a childlike innocence: "Mary. Mary! This way." The acoustics in the wide open acreage of sunflowers surrounding here make it nearly impossible to find the source of the voice, although Mary guesses it is that of a little girl. Mary is wading in a sea of brilliant yellow blossoms. She is surrounded by sunflowers. She looks around, takes her best guess, and wends her way through the regiment of thick yellow soldiers, stretching upright, many much taller than she. She didn't know why, but she didn't want to harm the sunflowers – to inadvertently break a branch or a stem. These seem like very special flowers to her – almost like her friends, their large smiling yellow heads and leafy hands leading the way to the little girl's voice.

Mary has no sense of direction. She sees sunflowers all around her, and so she just succumbs to their gentle push. When she looks up, she sees a brilliant, almost cobalt-blue ceiling of sky, punctuated by lovely, lacy dollops of white clouds which ever-so-slowly change hands and sway, not unlike a square dance. She is staring at the sky before she realizes the flowers had guided her to a clearing. It is a perfectly circular piece of ground, devoid of sunflowers or any vegetation whatsoever. It resembled pictures Mary had seen of "crop circles" – those inexplicable designs in farmers' crops.

Mary holds her hand up to her forehead to shadow her eyes against the bright sunshine. It provides enough shade for her to make out the outline of a little girl – about six or seven, Mary guesses. Instinctively, Mary looks down at her wrist now, knowing full well the Silver Strand will guide her to her destination. She is not disappointed. There is the distinct glint of the Silver Strand that connects her to the little girl. It is practically ablaze and dazzling as it shines under the summer sun, seeming to connect the pair as they lock eyes.

"Here, Mary. Take my hand!" The little girl sounds chirpy and happy and kind. She is dressed in a faded pink gingham sundress that has seen a thousand summers if it had seen one. She is barefoot and sports a pink wildflower of some kind in her corn-silk-colored hair which skims her shoulders.

"When I heard you were coming, I was so happy," the girl continues to squeal. She suddenly realizes she is being – if not rude, certainly confusing – and puts her hand over her mouth. Oh dear, I'm doing it again... babbling. I do that when I'm happy."

"You have to understand it was just a rumor that you'd be visiting us. I'm just so happy you're here. Take my hand, Mary. C'mon"

Mary is hesitant to say anything. She doesn't have the slightest clue as to what she should say.

The little girl leads Mary by the hand over to an old wooden bench at the end of the sunflower grove.

"Please, sit," the little girl says as she guides Mary to the bench with her hand. "Sit right here, next to me, so we can talk. There's so much to say and we don't know how much time we have together."

"My name is Alexandria," the little girl says, and for the first time Mary notices the slight lisp in her voice – she is missing a front tooth. Her skin is flawless, the naturally rosy cheeks that rightfully belong only to children, her eyes mimicking the cobalt blue of the sky. Long curly lashes frame her eyes. She isn't beautiful in the classical sense – there is something askew about the symmetry of her face, but that dissipates each time she opens her month to speak. No, not beautiful, perhaps, but she is definitely striking and her personality is sure to leave an impression with whomever she came into contact.

"Well, hello, Alexandria. I guess you know my name, so there's no need for introductions on this part." Mary shook Alexandria's tiny hand, gleefully.

The Voice begins again.

"Mary? Mary can you hear me?"

Mary turns her head in the direction of the raspy voice.

"Oh, don't listen to that," Alexandria says, grabbing her hands. That's just some people having a party down the road. They always have Sunday picnics after church."

"So it's Sunday?" Mary asks, sincerely curious.

"Ah, yes, it's Sunday," Alexandria stammers. "Don't pay them no mind."

There is an awkward moment as the two females size up each other. The Silver Strands no longer are a surprise. Alexandria seems quite pleased with the Silver Strand that connects them. She looks at it in delight, as if it is a precious bangle bracelet. She moves her hand this way and that, daring the sunlight to glint off a certain spot.

"Alexandria," Mary gently tries to nab her attention again. "Alexandria? How do you know me?"

Alexandria looks at Mary, confused, for several seconds, before she answers.

"Your mommy knew my mommy. My mommy's name is Bella Everson."

Mary is just about to correct Alexandria – Bella had no children. This is a mistake. But before she can say anything, Alexandria continues to chirp away. "And you know everything – about my family anyway. You know my family. I won't ever grow up, but that's okay. I'm happy the way I am."

"Your mother is Bella Everson?" Mary asks, more confused than ever.

"My mommy, you mean," Alexandria answers, matter-of-factly. "Mommy dreams about me a lot. Sometimes I think she tries to make it a point not to dream about me. Do you think that's possible, Mary?" Alexandria is looking at her unblinkingly, her blue eyes searching for any hint Mary might recognize. Mary sighs a deep breath, the realization dawning on her that this was the little girl Bella had miscarried at five months.

"I have a feeling you know exactly how your parents felt about you Alexandria. You know their hearts were broken when they lost you." Bella had several miscarriages, and if Alexandria is here, it was for certain her other *siblings* also are around here someplace, Mary assumes.

"You know why I'm this old? Why I look this way?" Alexandria asks Mary without a hint of self-consciousness.

"Because this is the way my mother pictured me. If she pictured me having black hair, then, I would have black hair. I know that right now is a very hard time for my mommy," Alexandria continues, a deep furrow stretching across her forehead. "My daddy died today. I'm hoping I get to see him too, but you never know with these things.

"Right now I'm more worried about my mommy – she's not doing too well.

"I wish I could tell her that myself – that we, up here – see things for what they really are. But I can't. She'll see when she passes over herself. But until then she has to deal with everything all by herself.

"You know what I wish?" Mary asks, desperately hoping to change the subject. "I wish your mommy could see you now – such a pretty little girl. You have your mommy's eyes and your daddy's hair."

"Mommy needs you now," Alexandria says solemnly. "It's important that you help her. She took care of Daddy for so long. Now someone has to take care of her. Promise me you'll help her? She needs to have someone special to talk to. That's you. You're the only one she really trusts. Please, promise me."

Mary looks down for a second.

"I promise," she says.

When she lifts her face to talk to Alexandria – the little girl is gone, a gentle, warm breeze left in her wake. Mary wonders if she should tell Bella that she spoke to her daughter – the one she never knew. She ponders the thought as she tries in vain to touch the Silver Strand on her wrist.

Twenty-two

Dolly

The pungent odor of burning leaves is hanging heavy in the night-time air. Mary literally jumps in fright, startled by the giggles and squeals of children behind her. The streetlights outline just enough of the strange silhouettes for her to realize this is Halloween night – Trick or Treat. Mary breathes in the unmistakable smell of sweet October air – the kind of fragrance that promotes an aura of mystery, an ambiance of forgotten summer days and a harbinger of the winter chill ahead. Mary loves this time of year.

She was considered an oddball by the other children when she was younger. Who on Earth wants to forfeit long summer days by the beach, or pool, in exchange for the regime of school and homework assignments? But Mary had made a deep connection with autumn. They had a kind of pact. She would reluctantly surrender her sunny freedom in exchange for the brilliant kaleidoscope of changing foliage that punctuated the country landscape. It is a season filled with the mystery and magic of Halloween. It is the one season in which Mary felt truly in touch with nature.

Sure, she admires the crocuses that pop their heads up through the winter snow, and the salmon-colored blooms of the Westerland climbing roses that wend their way around the front-yard arbor in summer. But autumn, oh so sweet autumn, it has a persona all its own. What it lacks in summer freedom, it more than makes up for in chilly-but-cozy nights, when families gather around fireplaces, reading books in silence for hours. Mary's father, Sam, would smoke a pipe – a delectable scent that encapsulated a sense of safety and security in Mary's little world. To this day, the smell of a pipe immediately transports Mary back to a time of innocence – of family and the unspoken circle of trust and love and belonging.

As Mary looks around her now, she sees the gleeful children – a witch, a bad Madonna impersonator, a hobo – all running down the sidewalks, clutching pillow-cases full of sweet loot and yelping with the delight of sugary anticipation.

"Mary, can you hear me? Mary? Mary?"

It was "The Voice" – that disembodied raspy utterance which had called her name several times now.

Instinctively Mary knows she is back in Dr. Lee's office and is telling him to leave her alone – she wants to continue this journey.

Mary rubs her eyes and looks up and down the block. She realizes she is standing in the neighborhood of her youth. The cars parked along the streets date back to the 1950s and 1960s. She is a young girl again, and she is dressed in an inexplicable costume – a blood-scarlet gown of satin, its bodice laced up the front in black satin ribbon. She is cloaked in a matching full-length cape, with a huge hood lined in black silk. Mary stares down at her costume in awe, feeling very proud. She loves dressing up for Halloween. She has always been a shy child, and Halloween was the one night of the year in which she could climb into someone else's skin.

Her mother, Kathy, made all the costumes for her own children and some of the neighborhood kids – and skimped on nothing. Mary can still remember the year she was dolled up as a fairy princess, complete with a be-sequined pink-and-blue silk gown, glittering wand and rhinestone tiara.

Her best friend is Dolly McGeehan, who lives just a few houses down and across the street from Mary. The girls are inseparable. They use the same school bus, eat at the same lunch table and play after school together. They spend their weekend invariably sleeping at each other's house. Mary's mother – who abhorred violence of any kind – would even let the girls stay up late, meaning 11 p.m. that is, to watch *Chiller*

Theater. After watching a low-budget horror movie like *The Crawling Eye*, the girls would whisper themselves to sleep.

"Did you know Danny Stone likes Pamela McMasters?"

"No! I thought he was going with Diane Miller."

"No, they broke up last week."

"No kidding. I didn't know that."

Inevitably, the chatter surrounding the school's fifth-grade social register would drift off, as did the girls themselves. The only negative thing about spending the night at Dolly's house is the persistent night-light in Dolly's room. Even though she is almost ten, Dolly refuses to sleep without it.

Mary is used to complete darkness in her own bed, and the nightlight at Dolly's, although tiny, is a nuisance. Mary never asks Dolly why she insists on the nightlight, sensing there is a personal – and probably negative – experience at the root of it.

Whatever the reason, Dolly is terrified of the dark.

Mary recalls a class trip the girls had taken to Crystal Caves in Kutztown, Pennsylvania. The tour guide, apparently thinking he would impress the students with the depth of the caves, abruptly announced he was going to turn out the lights for a minute. The result was a darkness so profound, it forever redefined the word *dark* for Mary.

Two seconds after the guide turned off the light, a hysterical screaming erupted from the crowd of children. Mary could only imagine the tour guide desperately fumbling to turn the lights back on as the screaming became louder and more urgent. Once the lights were on, Mary was shocked to see Dolly, screaming with every breath of her tiny being. She was curled up in a fetal position on the cave ground.

Horrified, the school chaperon, Mrs. Bennett, scrambled to discover which child was in distress. When she finally spotted Dolly, she dived to the ground and picked her up; then she tried her best to comfort her. The rest of the class looked on, shocked and scared. Some of the boys made snide comments about the scaredy-cat girls. It took several minutes before Mrs. Bennett was able to calm Dolly, who was wiping away tears and oblivious to the stares around her, which lead to an avalanche of teasing later.

261

Mary never spoke of the incident to Dolly. Even at her young age, she realized that some things are best kept private and aren't worth revisiting. It baffled Mary, though, since in every other area of her life, Dolly is ambitious and politely outgoing, seemingly unafraid of anyone or anything – except for the dark, of course. One would think Halloween would not be an especially fun holiday for anyone afraid of the dark, but not Dolly. Perhaps because she is surrounded by friends and the only "ghosts" she has to face are made of sheets.

There is something very unique about this Halloween – October 31, 1963. Just like every other Halloween, Mary and Dolly, both in Mrs. Bennett's 5th grade class, dash home from school, wolf down their dinners, and scurry upstairs at Dolly's house to change into their costumes.

It was a different time then, of course. There were no set hours for Trick or Treat, and no one had to have their candy tested at the X-ray machine at the local hospital. Kids as young as Mary and Dolly were allowed to travel the neighborhood streets alone, armed only with a pillowcase for their goodies and a flashlight.

But the innocence still surrounds the Halloween of 1963. Dolly is dressed as an adorable kitty cat. She is wearing a gray fur jumpsuit. But it is the elaborate headpiece Dolly's mother, Emily, has made for Dolly that is the showstopper. It is a kind of gray-fur helmet, with cat ears, of course. It glittered with a hundred pink sequins, mostly in the ears, but also gray sequins throughout the entire headpiece. The end result is something that rivals any store-bought costume. Emily carefully applies the elaborate cat makeup to Dolly's face before she allows her to put on the cat-helmet. She finishes the job by painting on the whiskers. Emily looks at her daughter's face with a satisfied grin at the job she had done – all the while thinking how lucky she is for God to have blessed her with this little charmer.

Dolly is the only child of Emily and Doug McGeehan. Her name is no accident: She *is* their own little doll. She was a late-in-life baby, the McGeehans being in their late 40s when Emily finally succeeded in giving birth after several heart-breaking miscarriages.

Since Mary lives nearly a block farther down the street than the McGeehans, Mary and Dolly naturally gravitate toward each other on Halloween night, when every second after school is precious time, which should be spent getting into their costumes and makeup. With Dolly's costume finally completed, Emily turns to Mary to see if she needs any help.

Mary had already wriggled into the *Vampira* costume her mother had made for her – the scarlet satin gown, its bodice laced up the front in black satin ribbon. She is holding her matching hooded cape.

"Wait," Emily fairly screams before Mary puts on her cape. "Let me put your makeup on before you put on the cape. We don't want to get any makeup smudges on that gorgeous thing your mother made."

Mary is antsy, wanting desperately to hit the streets – more to show off her costume than to gather up any treats – but she surrenders to Emily, who business-like, sets her down in the same chair Dolly had just vacated. The makeup mirror – lighted on each side – is a relatively new item for ladies in 1963. Up until then, middle-class women just had to make do with their dressing room mirrors and a nearby lamp. Mary plops down on the petite pink slipper chair which is frilled to the gills in satin and lace.

"OK. Let's see," Emily says, a look of determination on her face. "Let's see how we can turn this ornery little face into a pretty – I mean *scary* – vampire."

Mary looks up at her, wide-eyed, and a bit intimidated. She had never worn makeup before, and had no clue how Vampira became, well, *Vampira*. She truly believes Vampira awoke in the morning looking that way. But she is delighted at the job Emily had done on Dolly, so she willingly lets Emily work her magic.

Emily sets down her cosmetic kit, filled with a rainbow of eye shadows, lipsticks and skin foundations, next to Mary and begins to work with all the flair of Picasso taking his first strokes. Emily had taken a makeup class earlier in life – she had dreamed of becoming a beautician to the stars. That, of course, didn't pan out, but she proudly holds the title as *beautician* to the local community theater. Over the years it is a given: Mary and Dolly don their costumes at Mary's house and then head over to the McGeehans' so Emily can utilize her makeup expertise.

Mary is still quite antsy, wanting to hit the road before all the good candy is gone, but also wanting to look the part of a *creature of the night*. It is Halloween, after all. The night calls out for a bit of horror mingled with childlike fun. The rumor around town is that Timmy Cohen's dad, a prominent doctor in the community, had used his glowing medical school skeleton to transform his son into a walking, talking bag of bones by gluing the plastic pieces of the bones onto a shimmering black outfit, so all you could see was the movement of the bones. The boys at school had started spreading the rumor last week that the bones were not fake at all – they are *real* human bones. The whole Timmy Cohen-skeleton-costume-story has become a mystery that reaches well beyond Mrs. Bennett's class. It is, as they say, "the talk of the town," or, in this case, the talk of the school.

Mary can't wait to see Timmy's costume. Still, she tries her best not to squirm with excitement as Emily McGeehan starts to apply the first strokes of white foundation to Mary's tiny face. She etches her cheekbones in ominous black makeup, dark circles encasing her eye sockets. The *coup de grace*, of course, is the red/black lips, with a concoction of red-colored corn syrup substituting as blood dripping from her scarlet-covered mouth.

"There!" Emily says, with a distinct note of pride, swiveling Mary's chair around so she can she herself in the dressing table mirror.

"Oh wow." Mary exclaims, surprising even herself. "How cool. Thanks, Mrs. McGeehan. I love it."

Emily beams with pride. "Here, put your cape on, Mary. What's a vampire without a cape? Okay, off you two go – and watch out for traffic."

There usually isn't much traffic in the rural cul-de-sac area where the girls live, and if there is, drivers automatically slow to a crawl. No errant Trick-or-Treater, even one crossing in the middle of the road, had ever been hurt. This is a neighborhood where front doors and car doors are rarely locked, and often keys are left in the automobiles.

Mary and Dolly dart out of the house, their minds filled with the visions of a bounty of goodies. Their first stop was the Stellers – everyone knows they give out the best candy – FULL-SIZED Hershey bars and Baby Ruths. They greet the homeowners with an enthusiastic, *"Trick or Treat,"* their smiles wide and their joy unbridled. They politely thank the residents once they have received their treat. Mary and Dolly travel from house to house to house, repeating the Halloween ritual, allowing the grownups enough time to "ooh" and "ahh" over their costumes, before politely going their way. Mary is eager to run into Timmy Cohen; ever since she heard about his homemade skeleton costume, she has been madly intrigued.

The twilight quickly melts into darkness, a full moon providing a natural luminescent complement to their flashlights, and helping to light the way. The wind is in full gear that night, blowing brown and orange leaves in circles around the girls' feet. Mary's cape flies up more than a couple of times – as does her gown.

This is a great Halloween, Mary thinks gleefully as she and Dolly scamper from house to house to collect their booty.

The girls are just about to head to the Greens' house when Mary spots something shining in the light down the street – something moving… slowly. Only when the shimmery object falls under the direct light of the street lamp does Mary see the glowing white bones glued to the silk black fabric.

"Look, Dolly. It's Timmy's house. Look. See it? Wow, look at that skeleton!"

Mary sprints ahead of her friend. So intent is she on getting a closer look at this mystical costume that nothing else penetrates her thoughts. At last – the costume that's been the subject of all the talk at– Timmy's skeleton with real bones!

Mary doesn't wait for a response from Dolly. She runs toward Timmy, not wanting to waste a second before finally seeing this legendary costume up close. When she reaches Timmy, she is duly impressed, but also a bit disappointed. The fabric of his costume is black, and she has never seen anything like it before. It glints and glows and sprouts different colors as the streetlight bounces off it. But the *bones* are obviously fake – just heavy-duty plastic bones glued on each arm, leg and on his ribcage. He wears skeletal makeup on his face, and the overall effect – well, it is stunning after all.

"Dolly? Dolly, look at this!" Mary shouts, holding up one of Timmy's arms, swishing it to and fro. Timmy good naturedly allows it. He is basking in the glory of his much-touted costume. He had waited all summer for this night, and he is going to wallow in the fame as much as he can.

Mary is laughing and still shaking Timmy's arm as she turns to face Dolly.

"Look at how the colors change."

But Dolly isn't there.

Confused, Mary looks down the block and can see no sign of Dolly's gray-fur cat outfit. Thinking Dolly might have found a house they missed, Mary retraces her steps down the block, looking at each front door. There is a screaming group of children at each door, but no cats. Mary begins asking the children around her: "Did you see a girl in a cat costume? Did you see Dolly?"

"No."

"Nope."

"Nah."

With each additional negative answer, Mary's internal panic alarm begins to kick in more and more. She completely forgets about Timmy and his magical-skeleton costume. She forgets about her candy and Trick or Treat. Her one goal now is to find her friend.

Still, the thought that something nefarious might have happened to Dolly never enters her young mind. She merely thinks that Dolly has wandered off in a different direction. The minutes tick by slowly – or perhaps quickly – Mary isn't sure. She stands still for a minute, as a pirate, an angel and a Monster from the Black Lagoon run by her in delight. Mary continues to scour the neighborhood, continually asking fellow Trick or Treaters if they had seen a girl in a kitty cat outfit.

No one did.

The negative responses are beginning to become a foreboding mantra to Mary. Her innocent mind finally succumbs to the horrific possibility that something terrible might have happened to Dolly. Dropping her candy-filled-pillowcase, Mary runs to her home.

"Mom! Mom! I can't find Dolly." Kathy Martucci is talking on the phone with Edna Moore, whose kids had already flown the coup for the big night. Kathy takes one look at her daughter's panicked face, and says into the receiver, "Edna, let me call you back," and hangs up without waiting for a reply.

"What do you mean?" Kathy asks, kneeling down to her daughter's height. Whether it is a mother-daughter bond or maternal instinct, Kathy immediately knows this is serious – and *very* bad.

"We were walking down the street together. I ran ahead just a little bit, honest, Mom, and when I turned around she wasn't there. I've been looking and looking for her but I can't find her. And none of the other kids saw her either."

Mary is talking quickly and is beginning to shout.

"Okay," Kathy says in her most composed voice. "Now tell me exactly where you were." Mary isn't certain – after all she had been consumed by the thought of finally seeing Timmy Cohen's skeleton costume.

"I think it was in front of Mr. Green's house. She was there… and then she wasn't!"

"Wait right here," Kathy says sternly to Mary, and turns back to the phone. She calls Emily McGeehan, who must have answered right away.

"Emily? Hi. This is Kathy. Listen, I don't want you to get alarmed, but Mary just came home, and she seems to have lost track of Dolly. I'm sure it's nothing, but I'll get Sam and if you get Doug, I'm sure we can find her. We'll meet you at the corner. I'm grabbing my coat now and getting Sam." Trying to add a light spin on things, Kathy says, "I'm sure there's nothing to worry about. How many gray fur kitty-cats with glitter could be out there?" But even without hearing the other side of the conversation, Mary can tell that Emily McGeehan is near hysterics.

Kathy hangs up the phone and shouts for her husband.

"Sam! Sam! Get in here quick."

Sam is watching some type of game show in the living room. He hears the intensity of her tone.

"What?" he says, as he walks into the kitchen. "What's the matter?" Kathy explains the situation to him as best she could without wasting a second.

Sam and Kathy grab their coats and two fresh flashlights – the batteries in Mary's flashlight are starting to ebb. Kathy looks directly into Mary's eyes, unable to mask her concern.

"Don't you move from this house," she orders. "And lock all the doors behind you. And don't let anyone in, either."

Ordinarily, Mary would be miffed that her one special night of the year is ruined. But thoughts of Dolly obliterated any selfish musings. Mary sits on the sofa, lost in her thoughts. She trembles as her imagination starts to run rampant.

The game show is still on the television, but it sounds like white noise to Mary, who is lost in her worries. She is hoping that any minute now her parents will return, heaving a sigh of relief, saying, "Well, that girl certainly gave us a scare!"

But a half hour later, the game show is over and a Halloween scare-a-thon comes on the TV channel as it does every Halloween night. But this is no ordinary Halloween night.

Another hour passes. Mary starts to cry. Something has happened to Dolly, she is quite sure of it. And it has always been an unspoken pact that the two girls would look out for each other. They had been trick or treating together since they could walk, their parents tagging along, always mindful to lag behind at a respectable pace. This is only the third time the girls went out alone on Halloween.

"The Wolfman" comes on TV, the beginning of the annual Halloween movie marathon. Mary barely notices, even when Lon Chaney Jr. changes into the Wolfman. By the time "The Wolfman" movie ends and "The Boogey Man" begins, Mary has talked herself into a full-blown tizzy. "The Boogey Man" is a bit too close to home for her right now.

She had lost Dolly – she was supposed to take care of her and she failed. And now they can't find Dolly. That is as far as she will allow her young mind to take her. It is enough. It is the first time in her short life that she feels so guilty she wants to hide under the sofa.

Wiping the tears away, Mary sees the glow of red-and-blue lights flashing through the bay window at the front of her house. There are authoritative shouts and the squawking of radio transmitters. She runs to the window to see what the commotion is all about. She sees four police cars, and several police officers, looking grim and focused. It is the first time she had really seen a police officer in uniform up close, other than the Show-and-Tell Day, when Larry Constantine had brought his police officer father, Sgt. Lawrence Constantine, to school. By now, Dolly is shaking uncontrollably. She is remembering how Sgt. Constantine explained his job to the class.

"It's my job to keep you safe and make sure everybody obeys the law."

Did I disobey the law? Dolly wonders. *Why else would the police be there?*

Whatever fun that should be left of Trick or Treat for Mary and the other neighborhood children is over. The neighborhood is in a virtual lockdown. Disappointed youngsters – not aware of the severity of the situation – are sent home with a stern warning not to talk to strangers.

Mary is still wrestling with her guilt and crying when she is startled by a banging on the side door. Her mother's words: "Don't let anyone in!" leap into her mind. But the banging continues. Timidly she nudges the curtain a half-inch away from the kitchen door so she can see through the window. Her big brother Sammy, his face is covered with a scowl, peers in at her.

"C'mon! Open up! What the heck do you think you're doing?" Sammy is yelling at her through the door. Mary is grateful for the company – even if that company is angry with her – and she quickly unlatches the door.

269

"Why are you locking the door?" Sammy fairly yells at her.

Mary pays no attention and relocks the door quickly behind him.

"They're still looking for Dolly," he says, calmly this time, after looking at Mary and starting to place the pieces of the puzzle together. Realizing, perhaps for the first time, that she might be upset, he inadvertently switches into protective big-brother mode.

"Why are the police here?" Mary asks her brother.

Sammy summons up as much maturity as a pre-teen can.

"They're looking for Dolly," he answers gently. "They think she got lost."

And with that, Mary burst into wails, certain she had let down her best friend.

"Oh c'mon," Sammy says with uncharacteristic sympathy, putting his arm around his little sister. "It's not your fault. Besides, she'll be all right. She just probably took a wrong turn or something and got lost. It happens, you know, especially in the dark. They'll find her any minute now, I'm betting."

But Mary cannot be consoled.

There is a banging at the kitchen door again, and Mary jumps.

"I'll get that," Sammy says. "You stay here."

Mary can hear her parents speaking, and shouts of men, as well as the static-colored voices over police radio transmitters.

Sam and Kathy walk into the living room, looking glum and defeated. They had left their car keys behind in the rush. Three police officers follow behind them, as well as a man in a business suit. Kathy sits down next to Mary and holds her close.

Mary can hear dogs barking outside.

"It's all right, sweetie... It's all right."

But Mary, convinced she had done some terrible deed, can't stop crying.

"Listen, baby, this nice man wants to ask you some questions. There's nothing to be afraid of, okay? He's a policeman, only he doesn't wear a uniform because he's a detective. He's helping us look for Dolly. He needs to ask you some questions right now. It's very important. And it's very important that you know you did not do anything wrong. We think Dolly got lost, and we just need some help in trying to find her. You were the last one with her, so this nice man just needs to ask you some things. Okay?"

Mary looks up at the man in the business suit. He smells of Aqua Velva and his tweed suit, silk tie and neatly pressed slacks make him look very important.

"Hello, Mary," he says in a gentle voice. "My name is Detective Richards, and I'm with the police. You can call me Jack. Okay?"

"Okay," Mary says in a shaky voice, clutching her mother's hand.

Sgt. Lawrence Constantine sits down on one end of the long living room sofa. Unlike the detective, he is wearing his neatly pressed blue police uniform. His facial expression is very intense and somber, quite different from the day he had visited Mary's class.

"I'm told that you and Dolly went Trick or Treating together tonight?" Detective Richards asks, a tiny pad and a pencil in his hands. "We think Dolly may have taken a wrong turn and got lost, so we're here to try and find her. I just need to ask you a couple of questions that will help us, all right, sweetheart?" Mary nods, but continued to cling to her mother's hand.

The kitchen door had been left open, and suddenly a loud lamentation – filled with agony and distress – emanates from outside.

"My baby! My little girl! Where is my little girl?"

Mary slowly recognizes the voice as Mrs. McGeehan's, but she has never heard it filled with such despair. Mary collapses in tears, certain now that she has committed some terrible deed – that she has let Dolly down and now Dolly is either missing or worse. And it is all her fault, because the girls are supposed to look out for each other.

Detective Richards wordlessly eyes to the last police officer in the room a gesture to close the door.

271

But even through the wooden door, Emily McGeehan's screams can be heard, occasionally punctuated by loud crying.

Mary pictures Emily and Doug McGeehan – the couple who waited so long and felt so blessed to have Dolly – trying to come to grips with the fact that she isn't *here*. No one knows where she is. All Mary knows is, she isn't *here*, and *here* is where she is supposed to be. Mary blames herself. Why else would the police want to talk to her? Surely that must mean she is responsible.

Someone – Mary isn't certain whom – had gotten her a glass of water, which she sips through her tears.

"Mary, you have to listen to me, sweetie," Detective Richards says in a soothing voice. "The most important thing you have to know" – and here he touches her face with his thumb and lifts her chin so their eyes meet – "is that you did nothing wrong. *Nothing*. Do you understand me?"

Mary nods, and she feels a cautionary rush of relief wash over her. She wipes away her tears and takes another sip of water.

"Now listen, sweetie. Just tell me where you last saw Dolly. You were Trick or Treating together. Right?"

"Yes," Mary says. Her mother hands her a Kleenex and she blows her nose, hard. "We were walking down this street" – Mary is pointing to her front door – "and we went to a couple of houses. Everyone answered their doors."

"Okay," Detective Richards says calmly. "That's nice. Everyone opened their doors. But you didn't go into anyone's house, did you?"

Mary shakes her head. "No, we just got our candy and left."

"And then what happened?" Detective Richards asks. Sergeant Richards is scribbling in a tiny notepad.

"Me and Dolly went down the block. We were comparing our candies. We started to go to Mr. Green's house. He gives out the best popcorn balls. That's when I saw Timmy Cohen."

"Timmy Cohen?" Detective Richards repeats. "And who is he?"

"He was the one with magic skeleton costume. I ran ahead of Dolly. I really wanted to see it. Some of the boys in school said it was made of real bones."

"Okay, sweetie," Detective Richards says with a slight smile. "I understand." He jots down some notes on his own tiny pad. "Did Dolly see Timmy's costume too?"

Mary thinks hard.

"No. When I turned back to her she wasn't there. I wanted her to see the shiny material close up, but she wasn't there..." Mary's voice trails off as she realizes that there is something amiss. "No, wait. We were comparing our candies before we got to Mr. Green's house. Oh, no, wait, I'm not sure. No, I think we did go to Mr. Green's house. I'm confused."

Mary is about to burst into tears again, when Detective Richards strokes her arm gently. "That's okay, sweetie. You don't have to remember everything perfectly... just as best you can."

"But that was it," Mary says, clearly disappointed. "That's the last time I saw Dolly... just before I saw Timmy."

"You're sure, sweetie?" Detective Richards asks. "Think carefully. Okay?"

"I'm sure," Mary says, nodding her head. "I'm positive."

That is the night Halloween died in Mary's neighborhood. No one sleeps that night as police officers canvass the area with scent dogs, and interview everyone – adult and child – who might provide a hint to Dolly's whereabouts. Suzanne comes over to comfort Kathy and Mary, under the guise of a *girls' sleepover.*

Mary isn't so easily fooled. The two women think Mary is asleep on the sofa when they start talking about the night's events.

"I heard they had to sedate Emily and take her to the hospital," Suzanne tells Kathy. "My Lord, I can't begin to fathom what that poor woman is going through."

Mary listens to each word carefully; she is trying to pick up anything on the radar that might indicate that the grownups believe it really *is* her fault. But no one ever does. In fact, the general consensus of everything she hears is that it is a blessing

273

"that at least Mary is safe." Slowly – very slowly – the shroud of guilt that had covered Mary since Dolly's disappearance is beginning to fade away.

Even as dawn breaks and a new month debuts, it all seems surreal, like a Halloween trick gone terribly awry. Worried neighbors stand out on their front porches, trying to catch up on the latest news. The McGeehans' house is constantly surrounded by police cruisers and other cars. Family members and neighbors come bearing the proverbial casseroles and cakes, the gifts people bring when they have no idea what words to say and hope the food will do their talking for them.

Kathy keeps Mary and Sammy home from school that first day of November. Had they gone to school, they would have heard the main topic of discussion that weaves its way through the classrooms, into the cafeteria and onto the playground:

"Dolly McGeehan is missing."

It is no use keeping them home from school the next day. By that time, the story of the "Missing Trick or Treater" is headline news in all the local papers and on the five and eleven o'clock newscasts. The fact that Dolly went missing on Halloween lends a macabre aura to the story. The story cast a pall over the once-friendly neighborhood. People no longer exchange greetings as readily as they had in the past. Parents tell children to "play close to home" or "play where I can keep an eye on you."

The town council enacts a curfew, but it is almost unnecessary, since children already are instructed to "be home when the streetlights come on." The tight-knitted fabric that had bonded the community for years is beginning to unravel and shred. For the first time in the town's history, people begin to lock their doors.

The hunt for Dolly drags into days and weeks and then months. The local paper does an *anniversary* story on Dolly's disappearance the next Halloween. But after that, the disappearance of Dolly McGeehan fades from memory – except for her parents. Doug and Emily McGeehan move away two years after the loss of their daughter, unable to live in the neighborhood which had claimed their beloved Dolly. They are always careful, however, to check in with Detective Richards each month to see if there is any news.

The detective cringes when he fields the calls, knowing he has to deliver the disheartening news. He never lets the case go "cold." He keeps a small photo of Dolly on a shelf near his desk, and doggedly pursues every tip, no matter how remote or unrealistic. But, as with most cold cases, tips dry up, witnesses who might have helped, die.

Emily McGeehan dies at sixty-one, ostensibly of heart disease, but townsfolk claim it was from a broken heart. Doug McGeehan continues to call the police for updates on his daughter's case until his own death ten years later. Detective Richards retires from the force, not with the well-deserved self-satisfaction earned from all the cases he had solved, but with a distinct feeling of failure, never having given the McGeehans the peace they deserve.

As the years pass, Mary matures and accepts – truly accepts – that she did nothing wrong. Someone – or something – stole Dolly and kept her. Dolly seemed to have simply vanished that Halloween night. Hers became a cautionary tale not only for Halloween nights, but for all play nights. The legend of Dolly McGeehan faded in time, as the children became adults.

Now, as Mary stands here, not as a little girl, but as a woman, no longer in costume, the memories of that awful night come rushing back to her. She looks up and down the street; it is her childhood neighborhood. The smell of burning leaves is screaming, "October!" and Mary can see in the distance children dressed in costumes squealing with glee, running from house to house. Oh dear Lord, she thought, I'm reliving that terrible night.

Mary walks down the street, oblivious to the children running past her. She stops at what used to be Mr. Green's house, but what now is completely renovated and transformed into a more modern split-level. She stares at the door – the last door she and Dolly had gathered their goodies, from kindly Mr. Green. She could envision both herself and Dolly standing there shrieking with delight and screaming, "Thank you, Mr. Green" in unison. She walks up to the front door and stares at it. It bears no resemblance to the plain wooden portal that once graced the old-fashioned house. It has a different door with an oval window made of a beautiful beveled glass. Mary can see people moving inside. She sees them spot her, and they, thinking her a Trick or Treater, are about to open the door. She turns and runs down the front lawn to the sidewalk.

As she reaches the line where the front lawn grass meets concrete, she realizes she is back in 1963.

"What are we waiting for?" a little girl's voice pipes up.

Oh my god, it's Dolly!

Mary is overcome with emotion, but for Dolly, this is merely Halloween, 1963. Mary and Dolly are two young chums again, embarking on the revelry of the autumn holiday and the candy bounty that awaits them.

"Let's go!" Dolly fairly screams. "C'mon, Mary, before all the good stuff is gone!"

This is the moment Mary thinks to herself.

I have to watch this closely, because this is when Dolly went missing. I can do this. I can solve this mystery.

Mary turns just in time to see a hand – a big black-gloved hand – reach out from the bushes and pull Dolly to him like a rag doll. It is so quick it resembles one of those cartoons where the Road Runner's feet take off before his body. The oddity of it, the sheer absurdness of it, is that it is eerily silent. Dolly doesn't shout, doesn't yell out, and doesn't make a sound. Dolly was there one second and the next she is somewhere in the bushes.

"Oh shit," Mary whispers, as she realizes that she is, indeed, watching the abduction of Dolly, which happened so many years ago. Tenuously, she parts the bushes to see a Silver Strand wend its way from her wrist out in the distance toward the woods.

She tiptoes through the yards, trying to catch a glimpse of Dolly and her assailant. She reaches Mr. Green's backyard just in time to see a figure dressed entirely in black, with a black ski cap. He – and from his size, she was certain it was a "he" – pours some liquid from a bottle onto a cloth and then places it over Dolly's mouth. She no longer struggles. She goes limp.

The man doesn't see Mary. Mary is wondering why he already is part of the Silver Strand connecting Mary to Dolly. Even though Mary can't see his face under the mask, she is sure he is gritting his teeth. He removes his black ski cap.

Dear Lord, Mary nearly shouts in shock. *It's Robbie Renwood!*

He's much younger now – barely a teenager – but Mary clearly recognizes his facial features. This is long before he nailed the job as a postal worker.

How long has this monster been doing this? Mary wonders.

He picks Dolly up like a dead puppy and runs off through the neighborhood's back yards.

Mary tries to follow, but it is no use. Her gown catches on shrubbery, and Robbie and Dolly fade from view. Mary stands on the damp grass for a while, dumbfounded that after all these years she had been afforded a glimpse into the myth of Dolly's disappearance.

One disturbing thought, long ago packed away like antiques in an attic, suddenly surfaces: *Dolly is being taken somewhere dark,* she is sure of that. *And Dolly hates the dark.*

Mary feels the tears flow unabated for her childhood friend, the wounds from so long ago feeling fresh and biting anew.

It had been only a second after all, Mary thought, *a mere second, when she turned away from Dolly that Robbie had grabbed her. Dolly was so tiny she didn't stand a chance. She was doomed the very second Robbie put his hands on her and snatched her deep into the dark cavernous Halloween night.*

"Mary?"

It is a child's voice, a girl's voice that seemingly comes from nowhere. Startled, Mary looks about her and sees the shape of a large furry creature – *an animal that speaks?* Mary stares, her mouth open, trying to make sense of what is right in front of her.

"Mary?" the furry creature repeats. The figure is about five feet away from her. Mary can swear it looks like a talking cat.

Slowly, cautiously, Mary tiptoes toward the figure, noticing the Silver Strand connecting them. When she finally figures out what it is, she collapses on her knees and disintegrates into soul-deep sobs. It is Dolly, looking exactly as she had so many Halloweens ago.

Dolly puts her arms around Mary and tries to comfort her. She hadn't meant to upset Mary.

"Dolly! Dolly! Dolly!" is all Mary can spit out. "Dolly, oh my sweet Jesus, Dolly!" Dolly is still a nine-year-old girl dressed in her in gray-furry-kitty-cat costume from so many Halloweens ago.

"Dolly!" Mary fairly screeches as she clings to the small figure in front of her.

"Dolly! Oh my dear Lord, all these years. I'm so sorry, Dolly, I'm so sorry. I left you behind. I should have been there for you."

"Mary," Dolly says sweetly, gently, reversing the roles of an adult calming a child. "Mary, you did nothing wrong."

But Mary is unappeased, and feels the old guilt from so long ago flood over her.

"I should have been holding your hand. No one could have grabbed you if I was holding your hand."

"Dolly you could have held my hand, you could have had a leash around me," she says emphatically in the child-like voice Mary had remembered all these years. "It wouldn't have done any good." Oddly, Dolly is speaking like an adult, but with a child's voice. "Some things are meant to be, and there is nothing you could have done about it," Dolly says, smiling and looking down at the Silver Strand that connects their wrists.

"Who was it?" Mary asks, knowing full-well it was Robbie Renwood. "Who was the bastard who took you?"

"You know what?" Dolly replies in a matter-of-fact voice. "It doesn't matter. I never saw him before. I don't remember a lot after he put that cloth over my mouth. And I'm glad. I don't want to know anything more. What's the sense of it? I wish I could've comforted my parents somehow though. They needed to know – I didn't. The only thing I remember after he put that cloth on my mouth is looking at a lump of ground. He was patting it down with a shovel. I know that it was *me* under the ground. I just knew. And you know what, Mary? I didn't care in the least. I just resigned myself that was going to be my grave. I knew my body was never going to be found. Like I said, my only regret is that my parents weren't able to bury me properly, with a Mass and Last Rites. But it really wasn't necessary."

"And we know that *now*," come voices from behind Mary.

She turns to see Doug and Emily McGeehan. The family is together again. Mary sees the Silver Strands that seem to connect all four of them like the beginning of a bird's nest. Emily and Doug McGeehan – who had died several years before – look just as Mary remembered them in their prime. Their facial expressions oozed happiness and serenity. They are once again reunited with their beloved Dolly, who sits, crossed-legged, at her parents' feet, presenting an almost nativity-like setting.

"So you don't care who the monster was that took Dolly?" Mary asks incredulously.

"Well of course we *care*," Emily responds with a hint of exasperation in her voice. "We always figured Dolly probably wasn't his first victim and certainly wouldn't be his last. We don't ever want any other parent to know the hell we went through. But we no longer obsess over it or feel the need for revenge or even justice. Look at Dolly's other wrist."

Mary does as she is told, and sees a rusty, dirty strand of iron wrapped around her delicate wrist and creep its way out over the hills, disappearing into the distance.

"We don't like knowing that creature is connected to our Dolly, but he is. We could follow that strand to see where it leads, but it no longer holds the same importance to us," Emily says. "He may have been a part of our lives, and thus the strand. But that doesn't mean we have to pursue it. There's nothing we can do about it now anyway. He will be – *rewarded*

– for his crimes, if he hasn't already. He no longer is our concern. We don't need him to complete our joy."

"Yes, and I can make this nasty thing disappear any time I want it to," Dolly pipes up, pointing to the rusty strand. "And believe me; I rarely see it – except when I'm talking to newcomers, like you."

"Where *am* I?" Mary finally asks the question she wanted to ask each person she had met along this journey. "Am I dead? Am I in a coma? Why can I see you and talk to you? You died years ago. Am I insane?" Dolly can sense the panic rising in Mary's voice and immediately runs over to her, engulfing her in her furry cat-costumed arms.

"No, Mary. You're in a very special place that you can visit whenever you want. You see, your life went on after I was murdered. You went to school and married and had children. That was your mission.

But my life went on too – in a different way – a very different way. Greeting people like you; this is *my* mission now. I'm very happy, no regrets whatsoever. I was never meant to have a husband or children. You feel sad for me, I can tell, but don't be. I'm happy, truly happy. The people who visit us here learn about the Silver Strands that bind us all together – the good, the bad, and the lost."

Mary is trying desperately to try and comprehend what Dolly is saying so solemnly in her child-like voice.

"Then this isn't heaven? I know it's not hell," Mary says as an afterthought.

Dolly and Emily and Doug smile patiently.

"No," Emily answers this time. She now is sitting on her comfortable sofa, the one that provided a gathering place for neighbors and police the Halloween night that Dolly died. Doug sits next to her, and Dolly is lying across the length of the sofa, her head on her mother's lap.

"This is a kind of way-station – a place where you get some *answers*, for lack of a better explanation. Actually, it's a way to introduce souls into a higher dimension. You know, before they go on to their actual destination," Emily says, taking a breath. "Everyone must realize that we all – rich, poor, black, white, Jewish, Catholic, Muslim – all of us are connected to each other. That can be so overwhelming for many – realizing that you are connected to every other soul. I mean we're so different from some other people. You might have been a billionaire on the plane you've known, but here, we're all the same. The Silver Strands are just there to clearly show you how you were connected to people while you lived. After you've been here for a while, you won't even notice them. You may not have had a close relationship with the person – perhaps you put a dollar in the homeless man's coffee cup – but your lives were intertwined from thereon. The Silver Strands are for the... how can I say this without being rude – the *uneducated* – for *new* people, like you, who have entered our plane for the first time. It's just a little help for you to really envision your connection to every other soul."

"And that old woman – the woman who is knitting all those Silver Strands together; what's that all about?" Mary asks, desperately hoping for a simple answer but realizing that is very unrealistic.

This time Doug answers. He takes out a pipe, fills it with sweet tobacco and lights it slowly, as if he is about to explain the mechanics of sailing or golf.

"It's her job to crochet together all the Silver Strands that connect our souls. She works day and night, nonstop, knowing full-well that her job may take what seems like eternity. She will be done only when each and every Silver Strand is woven, correctly, into the tapestry of life."

Doug casually puffs on his pipe, but is eyeing Mary closely to see if she is grasping the weight of his words.

Mary is sitting on a log, staring at the ground in front of her, trying to absorb Doug's words; they are so simplistic and yet filled with different levels of mystery, each containing their own separate catalogue of questions.

She is quiet for several seconds, and Doug can almost see her mind trying to peel back the layers of his words.

"Look," Doug says, sitting next to Mary now. "I know it's a lot to absorb all at once. It doesn't matter. You won't be here long and you may never even recall this conversation. But for the sake of argument..."

He takes a deep puff on his pipe.

"You've heard of the theory of 'six degrees of separation?' You know, the idea that everyone is, on average, about six steps away, via introduction, from any other person on Earth."

Of course, Mary had heard of that myth, which she regarded as silly and baseless.

"You mean the one about Kevin Bacon?" she asks, referring to the actor whose name had so often been the incongruous basis for the myth.

Doug smiles, and puts down his pipe.

"It's not as silly as you think," he tells Mary. By now, Emily and Dolly have joined them, sitting on the ground near Mary. "That 'Kevin Bacon' version is just a way of putting faces on the theory to, you know, *make it more palatable*. The simple truth, Mary, is that we are all connected. Every person who ever lived, or will live, is connected to each other in one way or another. You want simple? Fine. Call it 'the Human Race.' You are just as much in touch with the Australian Aborigine as you are with your husband David – or, for that matter, Kevin Bacon. We are all made of the same cloth – or 'strands' if you please.

What you're seeing now are the connections to the people most close to you – the people who have directly impacted your life so far. What you don't see – can't see – is all the myriad of other connections that weave you into the Human Race. There's just too many to see."

Dolly and Emily watch Mary's face carefully to see if David's words are finally penetrating the thick crust of the reality she has known thus far. He is, after all, asking her to reform her entire way of thinking about her soul's mission.

"Where is David – and my girls? I'm worried to death about my girls," Mary fairly shouts, unaware of the irony of her words.

"Everyone is fine. *You're* fine," Doug says soothingly. "We were quite surprised to see you, to be honest with you,

Mary. You weren't meant to enter this realm for quite a while. But something unexpected happened. You almost died – I mean, you *did* die… but not permanently. Your body was nearly destroyed. Your soul left your body for a short while and that's how you came here. But you were never meant to stay. We know that now. Everything you've seen and heard while you were on this plane – well, you may not remember any of it when you go back. And make no mistake, you *will* go back.

"I waited so long to see you again," Dolly says sadly. "And now you're going to leave us soon. But you'll be back. I promise you, you'll be back."

Emily strokes Mary's hair, the same way she did when Mary was a little girl playing with her Dolly at her house. Even though Mary is an adult now, Emily's maternal workings can sense her little-girl fears, being overwhelmed by all that she had just heard.

"Trust me, my darling, you're going to go home to David and Marlee and Kandee and Cecee. They're all waiting for you. They don't even know you're gone. As Emily strokes Mary's hair, Mary drowsily sees the glint of the Silver Strand that connects them, just as she is ready to close her eyes.

Twenty-three

The Voice

Mary hears *The Voice* again.

"Mary, can you hear me? Mary? Mary?" Unlike its previous tones, there is a sense of urgency this time.
"Mary, you really have to wake up now," *The Voice* urges.

They sit quietly for several minutes, the soft whoosh of a warm jasmine breeze punctuating the silence. Her eyelids weary, Mary can see an apple tree in full, billowing blossoms, with a gaggle of bumblebees holding a pollen convention there.
She is startled when she hears *The Voice* again; this time it is no whisper. It is clear and booming and more urgent than it had ever been. It is a man's voice.

"Mary? Mary can you hear me?"

Mary tries to ignore it – as she had successfully done before, but this time *The Voice* is insistent and authoritative – not at all soothing and gentle as it had been before.

"I'm going to count backwards from ten," *The Voice* says.

Mary is mystified.
Why is The Voice counting?

"At ten, you're going to be aware of the feeling in your toes and your feet... *ten*."

Mary's toes and feet begin to tingle. She is aware of it, but isn't sure if she is dreaming. She no longer can see Dolly or Emily or Doug.

"At the count of nine, your legs will feel rested but strong... *nine.*"

Again, Mary's physical body responds to the command of *The Voice.*

The instructions are almost repetitive, as *The Voice* counts down from ten to one. Mary feels feather-light and is certain she is flying.

"*One,*" "The Voice" finally says. "You are completely rested, relaxed and know there is nothing to fear. You are confident, and you are complete. You lack for nothing. You can open your eyes now."

Without realizing it, Mary opens her eyes. She sees Santa Claus staring down at her.

"What the fuck?" she whispers.

And then she realizes she is looking at Dr. Lee, who is staring at her with a mixture of consternation and confusion.

"Mary, are you all right? Would you like some water?"

"Huh? Uh, no, no thanks," Mary mutters softly. Mary sits up from where she had been lying on the sofa. She is shocked at how well rested she feels.

She sees Meg staring at her, her eyes as big as quarters, clutching a throw pillow and sucking on a corner of it.

"Mary? You okay?" she says in a squeaky voice.

"I'm fine," Mary replies. "I'm more than fine – except I don't remember much. How long have we been here?"

Meg finally stops staring and looks at her watch.

"Almost five hours," Meg replies with a hint of incredulousness in her voice.

"What?" Mary fairly shouted. "Five hours?" It seemed as if she just lay down for a short catnap.

"Mary, do you remember anything?" Dr. Lee – *The Voice* – asks her.

The Silver Strands

"Amazing, Dr. Lee. I saw people alive and dead, and they were all connected by these silver strings of light… no, more like Silver Strands. That's what they called them, 'Silver Strands.' And as soon as I started hearing their stories, the Silver Strands of light attached themselves to me. What the hell?"

Dr. Lee leaves the room long enough to pour Mary a large glass of water from the kitchen refrigerator.

Rather than showing shock or confusion, Dr. Lee sits next to Mary on the sofa and rubs his beard.

"You know, I've heard of something similar to this, but not quite as pronounced. I always thought it was a bit 'out there' but darling, you've given me something to think about."

He is quiet for several seconds, lost in his thoughts.

"Well? Mary impatiently shouts, "Was the tape recorder working? Did you record the session?"

Dr. Lee snaps out of his reverie. "Oh, yes, my dear, it's all on tape."

Mary instinctively looks down at her wrists. No Silver Strands. She feels disappointed.

"There were these Silver Strands… I was attached to people by Silver Strands…" Mary starts to repeat and then falls silent, wondering if perhaps she had dreamed the whole escapade.

Dr. Lee sees the confusion on Mary's face, and grabs her hand.

"This *silver cord*, or *silver strands* story you're telling has been an object of some debate for years. Many people who have had near-death-experiences claim they see their *spiritual self* connected to their *physical self* by a silver strand. Some who have experienced NDE swear they can see silver strands connecting themselves to people in their lives – both living and dead. And it doesn't matter if that person was just a passing experience, like shaking a person's hand once and never seeing them again. Of course, the more prominent school of thought in this arena is that the silver strands are more pronounced in our connection to our loved ones.

"Now, mind you," Dr. Lee says, looking sternly at both Mary and Meg, "This is just a theory. It's never been proven.

"Also," Dr. Lee takes a deep breath and sits back before continuing. "There are proponents of astral projection – you know, people who believe their spirits can leave their bodies and travel anywhere in the world. Most of these *travelers* swear they can completely leave their bodies behind and mind-journey wherever they wish. They believe that the astral body has an *aura*, the heart of all our feelings and desires. They believe this *aura* is connected between our physical selves and our spiritual selves by a very fine silver strand at the navel – in other words, your belly button. They believe this cord, or strand, is a kind of cosmic umbilical cord to your soul, if you will."

Dr. Lee barely stops for a breath before he continues. Mary realizes he has done a considerable amount of research on this phenomenon. Whether he believes it or not, she could not tell.

"Moreover," Dr. Lee continues, staring straight ahead as if in a trance, "there are some proponents of astral projection that believe if the *cord* is broken – for whatever reason – the inevitable happens. Your spirit is permanently severed from your physical body. In other words, you die."

Mary turns to look at Meg, who has been uncharacteristically silent, in disbelief. Meg's facial expression is a mixture of jubilation, shock, and yes, even fear. Her eyes are the size of quarters and she continues to absent-mindedly suck on the corner of a throw pillow she is clutching in front of her.

"Well, Mary," Meg says slowly. "Let's just say, I think we've got the beginning of our story."

Other Select Books Published by Fireside Publications

Available at: http://kadinbooks.com; Amazon.com;
or Kindle / Nook

The Crystal Angel	Olivia Claire High
Rose Cottage	Olivia Claire High
Dreams: Shadows of the Night	Olivia Claire High

Essays: On Living with Alzheimer's Disease:	
The First Twelve Months	Lois Wilmoth-Bennett
The Furax Connection	Stephen L. Kanne
The Find	James J. Valko
Above Honor: Rachel's Story	Donald Himelstein
Beyond Forever	Taylor Shaye
The Cleansing	B.F. Eller
The Long Night Moon	Elizabeth Towles
The Cost of Justice	Mike Gedgoudas
18 Days in September	Allen N.Hunt, Ph.D
Independence Day Plague	Carla Lee Suson
Odds & Ends ~Bits & Pieces	Joye O'Keefe
The Serpent Sea	Linda Lehmann Masek
Where Danger Lurks	J udith Groudine Finkel
Texas Justice	Judith Groudine Finkel
Ice Rose	Alison Neuman
Raven April	Nelson Trout

COMING SOON

Searching for Normal	**Alison Neuman**
The Wolf Deception	**Olivia Claire High**

www.ingramcontent.com/pod-product-compliance
Lightning Source LLC
Chambersburg PA
CBHW070834250626
47159CB00003B/770